PRAISE FOR GAYLE

Spring R

"*Spring Rain* weaves powerful lessons on contemporary moral issues into a wonderful story—a very powerful combination!"

BOB DAVIES, North American Director, Exodus International

"Gayle Roper's novel *Spring Rain* contains all the mystery, suspense, and romance a reader could want. As someone who has lost a dear gay friend to AIDS, I also appreciated the story's 'something extra': realism and candor. Thank you, Gayle, for speaking the truth in love!"

ANGELA ELWELL HUNT, coauthor of *Then Comes Marriage*

"Gayle Roper is in top form with *Spring Rain*. Her storytelling skills make this one a page-turning experience readers will love."

JAMES SCOTT BELL, author of *Blind Justice* and *Final Witness*

"*Spring Rain* is a heartwarming love story that doesn't shy away from tackling tough subjects like homosexuality and promiscuity. Ms. Roper handles them with grace and compassion, never compromising the hope-filled truth of God's Word while giving us a bang-up tale of romantic suspense!"

LIZ CURTIS HIGGS, author of *Bookends*

WITHDRAWN

The Decision

HOLT MEDALLION AWARD WINNER—
which honors outstanding literary talent

REVIEWERS CHOICE AWARD WINNER—
from Romantic Times *magazine*

"If you're looking for a contemporary mystery with wit and romance, Gayle Roper is the author you've been waiting for."

ROBIN JONES GUNN, bestselling author of The Glenbrooke Series

"*The Decision* packs a powerful punch as Gayle's endearing characters come to terms with love and reconciliation. Set in Lancaster County, the author's attention to detail shines in her portrayal of the Amish people. *The Decision* is one of the best novels I've reviewed to date."

ROMANTIC TIMES MAGAZINE

"*The Decision* combines gripping suspense with heartwarming romance, and a touch of humor besides. You'll grow close to Jake, Rose, and their families, share in their pain and frustrations, and exult with them in their victories from the first page to the last. A wonderful book!"

INSPIRATIONAL ROMANCE PAGE

—⁂—

Spring Rain

SEASIDE SEASONS BOOK ONE

GAYLE ROPER

Multnomah Publishers® Sisters, Oregon

SPRING RAIN
published by Multnomah Publishers, Inc.
© 2001 by Gayle G. Roper

International Standard Book Number: 1-57673-638-5

Cover image of irises by Joanna McCarthy/The Image Bank
Background cover image by Index Stock Imagery

Scripture quotations are from:
The Holy Bible, New International Version © 1973, 1984 by International Bible Society, used by permission of Zondervan Publishing House

Also quoted:
The Holy Bible, New King James Version (NKJV)
© 1984 by Thomas Nelson, Inc.
Holy Bible, New Living Translation (NLT)
© 1996. Used by permission of Tyndale House Publishers, Inc.

For information:
MULTNOMAH PUBLISHERS, INC.
POST OFFICE BOX 1720
SISTERS, OREGON 97759

01 02 03 04 05 — 10 9 8 7 6 5 4 3 2 1 0

For Lynn and Ken Roussey,
my sister-in-law and brother-in-law
with love and affection.
Who knew, Ken, when you were our best man,
that one day you'd marry Lynn
who was thirteen at the time of our wedding.
Did you rob the cradle or
did she marry a "mature" man?

Acknowledgments

Well, Chuck, we did it again. We survived the birth of another book, and I love you as deeply as ever. I greatly appreciate your prayers and all those dinners out.

Chip, my-son-the-pastor, your orthodox yet empathetic sermon addressing the issues in this book was exactly what I needed.

Lisa Herion, I thank you for taking the risk of sharing God's keeping you safe as a child in abnormal circumstances.

Bob Davies, North American Director, Exodus, Int'l, Mr. Lightning Rod, your encouragement and suggestions have been wonderful. Thank you for taking the time.

Randy King, thanks for taking the time to share your concerns and comments making *Spring Rain* stronger.

James Ley, M.D., infectious disease specialist, you not only gave me your expertise, but you read the manuscript for medical accuracy. Be assured that any errors are mine alone.

Angela Elwell Hunt, you faxed me fifteen pages of information that contained exactly what I needed! Sometimes being over-organized is a wonderful thing.

Tracie Peterson and Athol Dickson, wonderful writers with tender hearts, you shared your friends and family and your keen insights and observations. I'm so grateful.

Lisa Laube, reader extraordinaire, you gave me great advice. Hang out your shingle, girl!

Julee Schwarzburg, my delightful editor, you and all the folks at Multnomah have been wonderful in your interest and support.

Evening Writers Arena, my critique group, wonderful women all, you listened to the book as it grew and gave me your love and suggestions. I wouldn't miss our monthly gatherings for anything. Thanks especially to Bonnie who has cared and paid the price.

And last, my Prayer Board, you prayed for this project from its inception. You will never know how much your support and encouragement meant to me.

PUBLISHER'S NOTE

Few topics today are as unsettling and controversial as the issues surrounding the AIDS crisis. Debates rage over what is and isn't sin, what God has or hasn't created, and whether or not AIDS is a form of divine retribution.

There is no denying that AIDS is a frightening condition—it is contagious and deadly. As believers, however, we have a higher calling than avoiding illness and those with the potential to infect us. We are called to *love*. The broken, the penitent, and the lost need our care and compassion. We must purpose to follow the Great Physician, to offer hands of healing and hope—physical and spiritual—to those who are seeking.

In the pages that follow, Gayle Roper handles some very difficult issues with truth, grace, and love. She helps us see behind the masks that so many wear, even within the church. Read this book with a heart ready to be convicted. Read it with a spirit ready to be taught and uplifted. And when you come to Gayle's note at the end, be ready to be moved. Above all, remember: "Now abide faith, hope, and love, but the greatest of these is love."

Keep your Kleenex near and be prepared to be challenged in your own relationships because ultimately this is a book about reconciliation.

Enjoy! May God lead us all into His paths of righteousness.

For the Kingdom,

Donald C. Jacobson
President & Publisher

One

LEIGH SPENSER LOOKED at the FedEx package waiting on the doorstep of her apartment over the garage and made no move to pick it up. She felt the familiar cramp in her midsection. Johnny again. She closed her eyes and put her hand on her stomach. It was amazing how many times being his daughter felt like a bad case of the flu.

The return address read State Penitentiary, Trenton, New Jersey, her father's address for the past eleven years, right up until his death last month. She rubbed her stomach lightly as if the action would take away the nausea. It didn't work; no great surprise since it had never worked before. Even though he was dead, she was still marked now and always as Johnny Spenser's daughter.

She bit back a sigh, staring sightlessly across the yard to the sand dunes and the path through them to the beach. Beyond lay the great stone jetty and the deceptively calm expanse of water where the bay met the ocean at the northern tip of Seaside. In the far distance, Atlantic City would be dancing on the water, its towering casinos reduced to mere toys.

"Hey," said Billy, his young voice eager and excited. He poked at the package with his ratty sneaker. "It's from Pop-pop."

Leigh studied the envelope again. "It's not from

Pop-pop. It can't be. It's from the warden or somebody sending us the last of his things."

At least I hope it's the last. My nerves have taken about all they can stand.

"They already sent us a bunch of stuff. How much did he have?" Billy bent down, lifted the envelope, and shook it with enthusiasm. "I mean, he only lived in a small cell."

"Hey, careful." Leigh grabbed her son's arm. "You might break it."

Billy looked at her with that increasingly frequent Mom-think-about-what-you-just-said look, the look that made her feel every one of her advanced twenty-nine years and more.

He's only ten, she thought desperately as she released his arm. *He's still supposed to think I'm wonderful. I should have three more years before the hormones kick in.*

She shook her head as if to clear it. She was making too much of nothing. She knew that. Such looks were just a natural part of growing up. The challenge was in not taking them too seriously. The fact that she'd never have dared turn such a look on Johnny meant that she was abnormal, not Billy. All those psychology classes had taught her that, and her observations had confirmed it.

"Mom, it's not the right shape for breakable." Billy's tone dripped with condescension laced with patience. "It's an envelope, not a box. And do you really think they'd let a convict have something breakable?"

Leigh wrinkled her nose. Well, maybe, just maybe she deserved the look this time. "I guess not."

Billy nodded. "You guess right. Too dangerous. It could be made into a weapon."

"Pop-pop wasn't violent," Leigh protested, jumping to Johnny Spenser's defense as usual, though why she did was a mystery to her. He had certainly never come to hers.

"Prison policy," Billy said with all the authority of one who knew what he was talking about even when he didn't. He held the large envelope out to Leigh, and when she didn't take it, he put it down. "They couldn't make exceptions for the few nice guys like Pop-pop."

Nice? Johnny Spenser? Her stomach jumped again. Nonviolent, okay, at least most of the time, but nice? Not in her book. But if Billy thought his Pop-pop was nice, that was all to the good. And understandable. In her son's limited experience with his grandfather,

Johnny had always been on his best behavior. Of course, if one chose to be cynical, one would say that the prison guards stationed at the doors during visitation hours had helped.

Leigh reached out to ruffle her son's fine brown hair, her heart full of love for this amazing child of hers. Thankfully he didn't have to deal with scars like those she had acquired growing up with Johnny during the years when he was not so nice, the years that had made her so cynical about him, that had scarred her more than she liked to admit.

"Mom," Billy protested, ducking away from her hand.

"Afraid I'll mess your hair and scare the girls away?"

He looked at her aghast and rolled his eyes. "Girls? Puh-lease!"

Of course, Billy had his own scars to live with and his own crosses to bear. And they were all her fault, Leigh knew, every single one of them. She blinked against tears. Failure again.

She frowned as she picked up the envelope. *I must be more tired than I realized. I'm usually not so emotional.*

Billy cleared his throat and turned to Leigh with dancing eyes. She recognized the look and held her breath. She knew something outrageous was coming.

"The guys all think it's cool that my Pop-pop was in jail." He puffed his bony chest with pride.

Leigh rolled her eyes just like he had a minute earlier. "Puh-lease!"

Billy giggled.

Leigh tucked the package into her carryall filled with paperwork to be finished over the Easter break, paperwork she probably wouldn't look at until the night before school reopened. "They think it's neat because they're in fifth grade and because he wasn't their father."

If he had been theirs, she knew there'd be no cool, no pride. There'd be hurt and embarrassment and incredible loneliness.

"And there's nothing cool about getting knifed and dying in a prison shower, even if it was a case of mistaken identity." Or so they said.

Billy grinned at her again, unconvinced, his glasses so full of fingerprints it amazed her that he could see anything.

"I'm going to get something to eat," he announced. "Then I'm going over to Mike's."

He waited a split second before he moved, his way of making his statement a request for permission but without the ignominy of actually asking. Sometimes he was so clever it was frightening.

Like his father, she thought and pushed away the all too familiar combination of ache and anger, all the more painful because it was so true.

"Come home at six or when Mike's family starts dinner, whichever happens first."

With a nod he disappeared up the stairs to their apartment with enough thumping and bumping to indicate a rhino instead of an undersized boy. She refused to think about the new paint she and Julia had applied to the stairwell just last weekend.

Leigh stared morosely at the large envelope wedged in her carryall. What else could her father possibly have had? Or more accurately, what else could he possibly have had that she didn't want? She pushed the envelope down until it was no longer visible in the welter of papers.

"Out of sight, out of mind," she told the large marmalade cat who wandered over and collapsed on her feet.

The cat sighed deeply as she draped her head over Leigh's shoe, her ear twitching as it touched the ground every time she exhaled.

"My feeling exactly, Mama." She bent over and rubbed the cat's head. Mama purred in ecstasy.

Mama had adopted Leigh and Billy one frigid Wednesday in December and proceeded to make them grandparents the following Saturday morning.

Leigh had gone to bed that Friday night like every Friday with firm instructions to Billy not to waken her for anything short of blood flowing freely. Saturday was her one morning to sleep.

"Mom! Mom! You gotta come!" Billy had shrieked in her ear at 6 A.M.

Leigh leaped out of bed, blinking against the sudden blinding brightness of the bedside lamp he'd flicked on, ready to do combat, put out fires, or wrap tourniquets about Billy's skinny limbs.

"The bathroom!" And Billy's slight pajamaed figure disappeared down the hall.

"This had better be good, William Clayton Spenser," she growled as she followed, arms wrapped about her middle to combat the morning chill.

She'd never been convinced that good was the proper word for what she found, but it had taken all the venom out of her. And it certainly wasn't bad, especially considering the joy Billy received.

Lying on the floor in the linen closet, all cuddled in a pair of worn-out towels Leigh couldn't bring herself to discard, was their new marmalade cat with six tiny kittens, eyes tightly shut, nuzzling her.

"Aren't they wonderful?" Billy cried. "Aren't they the cutest things you ever saw?"

"I knew taking her in was a mistake," Leigh muttered even as she knelt smiling in the doorway. "Just because it was below freezing, and she was crying on our doorstep, and you begged—"

"Can we keep the kittens, Mom? Huh? Can we?" Billy danced around the bathroom unable to keep still, waves of delight and excitement shimmering off him.

And have seven cats? Leigh shuddered at the thought of all that cat food and litter and multiple litter boxes. Seven boxes? Did cats share? "We cannot."

Billy put on his patented pleading face. "They're so little. They won't take up much room."

"They'll grow, and the answer is still no. Absolutely no. Unequivocally no."

As Billy fondled the marmalade's ears, he said, "She's a mama now, and once a mama, always a mama. At least that's what you say." He turned and grinned impudently at Leigh. "So Mama's what we'll call her."

So Mama she had become, and Leigh stood in the early April sunshine talking to her for want of another living, breathing body in the vicinity. She pointed to the envelope buried in her carryall. "Will there ever be an end to the misery he causes me?" Her voice was weary as she remembered the media frenzy his murder had generated. Reporters at the door, at school, even interviewing students! And there were the phone calls from prison officials, the buzz of curiosity in her classroom and the teachers' room, the stares wherever she went. "He's dead and buried. It should be over. I want it over."

Mama rolled off Leigh's shoes onto her back, revealing her belly with the recent spaying scar still visible through her newly regrown fur. Leigh automatically bent and rubbed. Mama purred in delight. All her kittens were now gone, and, fickle animal, she apparently felt no maternal loss whatsoever.

Change maternal *to* paternal, *and you have Billy's father.*

No, she caught herself, trying to be scrupulously honest, always a challenge when thinking about him. As far as she knew, he didn't even know about Billy. You can't abandon what you don't know exists. She straightened and rubbed the headache beginning behind her left eye.

The back door of the main house opened, and the home health nurse walked out. Leigh waved at her, and the woman smiled back as she walked to her car parked in the drive turnaround. As the nurse drove away, Leigh looked up at the rear bedroom window of the main house, Ted's window. Sweet Teddy. It wouldn't be long now.

As always the thought of Ted's impending death wrapped Leigh in a cloak of sorrow. She couldn't imagine life without Teddy, her one true friend through the years. He would be twenty-nine next week, and twenty-nine was too young to die! She prayed constantly that God would give her the strength to stand the pain of being without the man she loved like a brother.

When had he first adopted her? She thought for a minute and decided it was the beginning of her sophomore year in high school. She had been standing by her locker, shoulders slumped as she struggled with the combination. She was wearing a second-hand top and slacks that she had thought were wonderful when she bought them at Goodwill. As soon as she walked into home-room, she knew differently.

How did the popular girls know what was cool? How did they know what shoes to buy, what slacks to wear, what hairstyle to get? It was one of the great mysteries of life. She watched TV like everyone else, but she still got it wrong. She got everything wrong! She couldn't even open her locker, for Pete's sake!

"Having trouble?" a kind male voice asked.

She spun around to see Ted Wharton looking at her. Ted Wharton! He and his identical twin, Clay, were two of the most popular boys in her class, in the whole school, and they were both handsome, handsome!

"Uh, my lock," she managed, flushing crimson.

"They can be a challenge at first, can't they?" He leveled his engaging grin on her. "Let me help."

Of course he'd opened the locker in a flash, but then he walked with her to the cafeteria, just like she was one of the real girls, not plain old Leigh Spenser. Once there he sat with Clay and their friends, but just having him walk with her made sitting alone not quite so painful. He didn't seem to care in the least that she was Johnny Spenser's drip of a daughter.

The miracle was that he'd sought her out after that, talking with her at her locker, laughing at her weak jokes, walking her to lunch most days. At first she had thought he might like her in a boy/girl way, but she understood quickly that he liked her in a better way: as a friend. She couldn't understand why, but she knew it was true. She in return loved him unconditionally. He brought light into her somber, often dark world and acceptance where she usually knew rejection.

She wasn't certain when she first realized that Ted was leading a double life—Dr. and Mrs. Will Wharton's wonderful churchgoing son on one hand and Teddy Wharton, denizen of the wild gay life, on the other. The deceit that came to characterize his life bothered her a lot, more than any moral questions.

"You're trying to be two things at once, Ted. You can't keep it up. Either you're the straight, good guy most people think you are or the gay one."

He'd just smile and ask, "Which one should I be, Leigh?"

"The honest one. No matter how open-minded I try to be, I don't like you being gay, but I can live with it if you're honest."

"I can't be honest. Too many people will get hurt."

"But, Teddy," she warned him time and again, "you're asking for trouble hanging out with those loose people."

He always waved her worries away. "I'm being careful, sweetheart. Believe me. I'll be okay."

But she had continued to worry and with reason. He hadn't been careful enough. She cried when he told her he was HIV positive. He just held her and told her he was going to beat it. He'd be okay. She should save her tears for someone who needed them.

Because she loved him, she wanted to believe he'd never get really ill. At least by now she had met Jesus, and Teddy wasn't the main rock in her life anymore, but the pain and fear she felt for him were incredibly intense.

Then came the full-blown AIDS. And now the unexpectedly

rapid deterioration. The weekend he came home "to live as stress-free a life as possible," she knew it meant he'd come home to die, however long that took. She wasn't able to stop crying. She actually made herself sick, scaring poor Billy half to death as she knelt in front of the toilet and heaved and heaved.

Now there was just overwhelming sadness whenever she thought of him.

She reached for the door to her apartment. It had been a long, long day at school. Usually her fourth grade students were fine, but a week of spring vacation began with the close of school today, and they were more than ready. So was she. All she wanted was to climb the stairs and flop in her favorite chair, a good book in one hand, a sweetened iced tea in the other.

"Oh, Leigh!"

Her hand on the doorknob, Leigh turned back to the main house. The main house. It always sounded like some great manor house in an English novel with lots of outbuildings dotting the vast estate, but there was no vast estate here, no mansion, just a large cream Victorian with dark green, crimson, and white gingerbread trim. The garage with Leigh's apartment over it sat at the back of the property and was painted the same colors as the house. Leigh and Billy had lived here for four years now, a wonder she still had trouble comprehending. There was no location in Seaside as wonderful as this property, reaching directly to the dunes, the beach, and the Atlantic Ocean.

Nor was there anyone as wonderful as Julia Wharton, resident angel. Leigh smiled at Julia as she came out the back door of the house. She didn't look like an angel, just an attractive widow in her late fifties with carefully colored blond hair and unbelievably thick brown lashes rimming her clear blue eyes, but Leigh knew from experience that she was one. She was also a crackerjack realtor, Ted's mother, Leigh's landlady, and a very good friend.

"Will you and Billy come for dinner?" Julia asked as the women met in the middle of the small backyard. Property in a shore resort like Seaside was so valuable that no one wasted much land on lawns, especially since the salt air and the summer heat made keeping a decent one nearly impossible. Julia brushed a curl behind her ear with a hand covered with flour. "I'm making a lemon meringue pie."

The mention of the lemon meringue struck a chill through Leigh, and her hand went to her heart. "Are you baking as therapy? Is Teddy worse? Did the nurse give you bad news before she left?"

In the weeks after it became obvious that Ted was dying and Julia had taken an indefinite leave from her job to be available in whatever capacity she was needed, she had baked so many pies and cakes and cookies that the rescue mission in Atlantic City took to sending a van over every day to pick up the bounty.

Julia blinked in surprise. "Ted's fine. I just felt like baking."

Leigh smiled in relief. "From scratch as usual?"

"Of course." Julia's eyes flashed. "I would never cheat with one of those store-bought crusts."

"If I baked like you, I wouldn't either," said Leigh who regularly bought her crusts premade. "We'd love to come."

Even if there weren't years of rescue and reclamation to Julia's credit, that invitation alone proved her angel status, coming as it did at the end of a long month, a long week, and a longer day. The mere thought of coming up with a nutritious dinner for Billy and herself had been draining Leigh's few remaining energy reserves.

"I'm indulging in celebratory baking," Julia said in a happy rush. She grinned, absolutely delighted with her good news. "Clay's coming home."

Leigh shivered as a dark chill raced through her. She felt turned to marble just like in the game she had played as a kid when you were flung away and had to freeze in whatever position you found yourself until whoever was *it* came to wind you up.

Only this was real.

"—this weekend."

Leigh shook her head and managed to hear the last part of Julia's continued comments. "He's coming for the weekend? That's nice." *And we can go away for the weekend, Billy and I. He will just have to miss his Little League game Saturday, and the choir will never notice my absence Sunday morning.*

"No, no." Julia patted Leigh's hand again. "He *arrives* this weekend, probably tomorrow, and he's staying until after Ted—" Julia's voice broke, and tears shimmered in her eyes.

Until after Ted dies. Words no mother wanted to speak.

Selfish, selfish! Leigh berated herself as she watched Julia blink back the tears. *Worrying about your feelings, your embarrassment in a situation like this. Are you so petty you'd deny Julia the consolation Clay could bring? After all she's done for you?*

"I'm glad for you, Julia. Having Clay here will be a wonderful comfort."

Something in Leigh's voice made Julia look at her quickly, apparently misunderstanding the restraint. "Not that you aren't a comfort," she hastened to say, reaching out and hugging Leigh. "I don't know what I would have done without you over the past three years since Will's death. And Billy. It's just that Clay's—"

"Clay's your son," Leigh finished, forcing her voice to be warm and excited. "And Ted's twin. You need him. And he should be here." Though why she hadn't realized that before, she'd never know. Something so blatantly obvious shouldn't have been a surprise. But it was, probably because he came back to Seaside so rarely and stayed so short a time. His last visit of any length had been at his father's funeral, and she had managed to keep out of sight by burying herself in the kitchen or staying in her apartment. When he came for just a weekend, she and Billy always conveniently managed to be away.

Julia rubbed her floury hand across her forehead. "Sometimes I hate what's coming so much I can hardly stand it. And I hate facing it alone."

This time Leigh wrapped her arms about Julia. When Will Wharton had died suddenly three years ago, she had been almost as lost as Julia. "I know." Leigh kissed Julia's cheek. "He was such a great guy. We all miss him."

Julia pulled back and took a deep breath. She straightened her shoulders and raised her chin. "I can do all things through Him who strengthens me," she quoted. "I can."

Leigh watched Julia walk back to the house and marveled at the woman's strength. She turned back to the garage and slowly climbed the steps to her apartment, emotions roiling.

Dear Lord, on one hand I know Julia's right. I can do all things through Your strength. But I don't know about Clay, Lord. I just don't know.

Two

CLAY WHARTON TURNED off the Garden State Parkway and onto the Ninth Street Causeway, driving across the salt marshes and bay to Seaside. He inhaled deeply, the smell of salt water, marsh, rotting vegetation, and fresh briny air filling his lungs. He realized with surprise that he had missed this distinctive aroma, the smell that meant the shore. There was simply no other smell like it.

He scanned the bayside of the barrier island he had called home for the first eighteen years of his life. Though it was located only a few miles south of Atlantic City and was as tourist intense as any shore community could be, he was pleased to see that skyscraper condos still hadn't taken over. Motels of two and three stories, private homes with docks housing boats of all sizes, marinas, and undeveloped marshes lined the bay.

He had been in grade school when the town had voted to outlaw any construction over three stories.

"High rises would block the view of almost everyone and make Seaside another Atlantic City without the casinos," his father had explained carefully. Dr. Will Wharton was a councilman at the time, and the outcome of the vote was very important to him. He saw it as life or death to Seaside as a family-oriented resort.

"Our goal is to keep the people-friendly atmosphere and to allow the sea breezes to reach everyone." Will had looked earnestly at Clay and his twin, Teddy. "Believe me, boys, sometimes 'progress' is not beneficial."

The young Clay hadn't grasped the significance of the vote. He'd been too easily impressed with the glitz and sophistication of any new idea, and rebuilding Seaside to resemble other ocean communities had seemed reasonable to him. Bigger was obviously better. Only old guys like his father missed that evident fact. Clay had thought his hometown a "quaint" community that needed a touch of modernity.

Now as he looked at the low rooflines of the houses, motels, and restaurants that lined the bay, he was thankful for men and women like his father and the building codes they'd had the foresight to put in place. Seaside was still Seaside, tourism still its primary business, but it was a comfortable, livable town.

He glanced at the passenger seat where his long-haired Jack Russell terrier sat, trying to keep his balance as he strained to see out the windows.

"Terror, you'd see better if you stood with your front paws on the edge of the window. You know. Like I showed you before we left home."

Terror looked at him, smiling happily, his tongue lolling. He didn't seem to mind that he saw mostly roofs and sky. As long as he was along for the ride, he seemed to say, it was enough.

Clay reached over and stroked the dog's head. "At least you aren't trying to sit at my feet any longer."

Clay had spent the first half hour of the trip grabbing Terror as the dog, unused to riding in a car, tried to get comfortable on the floor between the accelerator and the brake, as close as he could get to Clay, what with the bucket seats and gear console.

Terror, now convinced that the seat was preferable to the floor, licked Clay's hand, devotion shining in his brown eyes.

"Do you know why Emilie bought you?" Clay asked conversationally. "Given the fact that you're not going to be any threat to Lassie or Rin Tin Tin intellectually, I've begun to suspect that she saw the handwriting on the wall and got you for me for Christmas as a revenge gift that would keep on giving for years." Clay grinned as he scratched the dog's ears. "The laugh's on her, though.

Did you know that? I happen to like you."

In response, Terror sneezed and lost his balance.

Poor Emilie, Clay thought as he grinned at Terror. She'd never stood a chance with him, but she hadn't seemed to get the idea. Apparently she believed in the if-he-sees-me-enough-he'll-like-me school of relationship development. Accordingly she managed to be everywhere he was for over two years. It had been, to put it mildly, wearing.

Since he was very active with the high school program at church, so was she. When he decided that singing in the choir might be fun, she joined too. When he played on the church baseball and basketball teams, she came to every game and cheered him on. It wouldn't have been so bad if she'd liked high school kids, had a decent singing voice, and understood the nuances of either game.

Still, he had to admire her single-mindedness even as he dreaded her sticky-sweet, "Hi, Clay. Whatcha doing?"

It had taken a long time, but she finally seemed to grasp the idea that he was a lost cause when for Christmas she gave him Terror with a red bow about his neck, and he gave her a Point of Grace tape in a colorful little bag with no tissue stuffed in the top—the same gift he gave to everyone else on the youth group leadership team.

"Not even a CD," he'd overheard her tell one of her girlfriends. "A tape! Like everyone else!"

He'd smiled to himself, relieved, though he hadn't meant to be unkind. He'd just seen her as a friend who would never be anything more and gifted her accordingly. He hadn't been terribly surprised when the youth pastor said she was no longer working with the high school kids and the choir director noted that she'd dropped out of choir. He hadn't seen her at a basketball game since Christmas.

"Lost your cheering section?" the guys teased him. He just grinned noncommittally though he was jumping up and down inside.

But he had Terror to remember her by—Terror who had made the last few months of living in his no-pets-allowed rental house something of a challenge.

"I didn't buy him, Mr. Kelly," he'd explained to his always grouchy landlord. "He was a gift. I can't give him back."

"Gift, schmift. He's not allowed."

"He's little, Mr. Kelly. He's not hurting anything."

"*Yet*. He's not hurting anything yet. Just give him time. He has to go."

"Did a dog bite you as a boy, Mr. Kelly?" Clay kept his face as innocent and open as he could. "Because Terror will never bite you. I promise. He's completely nonviolent."

The landlord looked at the little brown-and-white dog smiling at him and almost smiled back. Clay was sure he saw the man's lips twitch before they settled into their customary scowl. "He'll ruin my yard with his—" Mr. Kelly gave a delicate clearing of his throat—"biological needs."

Clay, a career navy officer used to the earthiness of navy men, bit his tongue to keep from smiling. After all, Mr. Kelly saw him every week at church and so was trying to respect his tender Christian sensibilities. "I promise to clean up after him."

"One week," said Mr. Kelly. "You can keep him one week and one week only. I'm not a hard man. One week for you to find him a good home."

But Clay knew Terror was staying even if his landlord didn't, so he and Mr. Kelly played Keep the Dog tag until the day Clay resigned from the navy and left for Seaside, Terror beside him.

Clay hit the brakes when the car in front of him slowed suddenly. Terror went flying forward, sailing off the seat and landing in a heap beneath the dash, rear legs over his head.

"Are you okay, buddy?" Clay bent to lift the dog and place him back on the seat. "Didn't mean to upend you. It was that guy's fault." He gestured to the car with his head. "You should buckle your seat belt."

Terror looked at him and smiled.

For not being an intellectual, Terror had done an outstanding job of teaching Clay something he hadn't realized before: He no longer liked being alone. He no longer had to prove whatever it was that demanded he be independent, whatever it was he had been trying to prove to himself and the world. Coming home to the click-click-click of doggie toenails on Mr. Kelly's hardwood floors and the whuffle of a canine hello filled a need Clay hadn't even known he had. It also made him aware that he was still lacking somehow.

And all this turned his mind to the people in his life, the

people he had carefully held at arm's length for the past decade, the people who held a special place in his heart though they wouldn't know it by his actions: his mother, his brother. Sweet Leigh.

Clay smiled down at his dog as he drove off the causeway and onto Ninth Street. He was home. He smiled for a full minute before he felt the familiar clenching in his midsection. Home hurt.

Because of Leigh.

Always because of Leigh.

The problem began years ago when as a sixteen-year-old she had first attracted his eye. Not that she knew it. Not that anyone knew it. He had been good at holding his thoughts close, and he had carefully kept private all his feelings about Leigh right up until graduation night at Seaside High.

He watched her all through commencement, salutatorian of their class to his valedictorian. As such they led the procession of graduates and sat next to each other throughout the program. She barely looked at him, sitting silent and composed and unapproachable.

After the ceremony the halls were full of family groups: graduates, parents, brothers, sisters, grandparents, aunts, uncles. He was surrounded by his family, his parents bursting with pride over his and Ted's accomplishments, their gold tassels indicating they were honors graduates. His grandmother and two aunts patted him happily while the uncles stood slightly apart, waiting their turns to offer congratulations.

She was completely alone. No relatives. Not one. Her mother had been dead for years; he wasn't sure how many. And her bum of a father was in jail, awaiting trial for robbery and manslaughter for killing a man with the getaway car. If she had any grandparents or aunts and uncles, they weren't present tonight.

He watched the sway of her beautiful hair that hung halfway down her back. With every step she took, it shifted from left to right, a shining, moving curtain. He always had the urge to run his fingers through that sheet of chestnut, just to see what it felt like.

How had she turned out to be so sweet with Johnny Spenser for a father? And she was smart. He had thought there for a while that she was going to beat him out for the number one spot in the class. She was so fierce about her schoolwork, like it was the most important thing in the world. He often watched her take a test or work in the library, the tiny frown line between her eyebrows indicating her intensity. He wanted to smooth that little line away so she would feel better, so he could feel what her skin was like. He imagined it was soft, like a rose petal.

"We're so proud of you, Clay! You are such a fine boy." It was Grandmom Wharton, hugging him too hard as usual. The ardent clasps to her bosom wouldn't be so bad if she didn't insist on wearing garish pins that all seemed to have multiple lethal points that inflicted intense pain and fell mere millimeters short of running you through. Often as boys he and Ted had compared wounds after a visit with her.

He flinched at the pricks of pain somewhere in the vicinity of his ribcage as he watched Leigh over Grandmom Wharton's shoulder. Leigh pulled her cap with its gold tassel off her head and slid her gown off. She was wearing a white dress that had little pink flowers embroidered around the hem, tendrils of green reaching from one bloom to the next. All around her girls were wearing shorts or slacks, but she wore a dress. Like graduation was special, and you dressed up for it.

She lifted her hair with one hand and let it slide little by little down her back in a shimmering waterfall. Then she turned and walked out the front door of the school. No one said anything to her, busy as they were with their families.

No one except Ted.

"Leigh," he called and ran to her, thus escaping Grandmom's waiting arms and pin.

She stopped and turned, welcoming him with a warm smile.

He threw his arms around her and hugged her. She hugged him back, her smile lighting her face. She caught Clay watching her as he absently rubbed the pinpricks in his side, and their eyes locked. Her smile faded.

Clay nodded slightly, and she gave a faint quirk upward of one corner of her mouth. Then Ted stepped back, and she focused her attention on him. Clay watched his twin kiss her on the cheek and wondered why she smiled so brightly for Ted and not for him.

"Ted," his mother called. "We have to go."

Ted squeezed Leigh's shoulders once again and came back to the family cluster. Leigh continued out the door and down the steps alone.

As his family distributed itself in the various cars they had driven to the school, Clay continued to think about her. In fact, he'd thought about her quite a lot recently, and he was pretty sure God wasn't very happy with some of his thoughts. He swallowed and made an effort to curb his hormones. It was bad enough Ted had turned out to be so perverted and loose. Clay was better than that, at least most of the time. And *his* thoughts were directed toward a girl. God had to like that.

He glanced out the school door again and saw her disappear down the street. An ocean breeze blew her skirt against her legs, and her hair fanned out behind her. He sighed with pleasure at the sight.

Taken as he was with her, he still knew very little about her. He knew she never stayed after school for any activities, just hurried home. He suspected that was because of Johnny Spenser. But she'd been on in-school committees with Clay, and she was always polite, reliable, sweet. And cute as could be. But she rarely talked to him. Certainly she wasn't at ease with him like she was with Ted, though sometimes he caught her watching him. She'd always blush and look away fast.

After a few minutes the cars and drivers were sorted out, and the family all left the school. Mom and Dad went in their car, the aunts and uncles in theirs. Ted ended up driving Grandmom, and Clay was alone.

Instead of turning right toward the north end of Seaside and his home, he turned left. He drove slowly down Bay Avenue, watching the sidewalk carefully. In a couple of blocks he saw Leigh, walking alone, head down. He pulled to the curb.

"Can I—" His voice broke. He cleared his throat. "Can I drive you home? It's a pretty long walk for you."

She smiled at him, not as brightly as she smiled for Ted, but at least it was a smile. She hesitated a minute before deciding. "Thanks," she all but whispered and walked to the car.

He leaned across the seat and opened the door. She slid in and carefully fastened her seat belt. He put the car in drive and eased back into traffic. They sat in silence.

Why didn't she talk with him like she talked with Ted? And why couldn't he talk with her like he talked with all the other girls? Of course he didn't really care whether the other girls talked to him or not.

"You look very pretty tonight," he finally said, desperate for something, anything, to break the silence.

She looked at him in astonishment. "Th-thank you."

"I like the flowers around your skirt." He flushed. Talk about sounding like an idiot!

"Do you?" She spread her skirt, examining the flowers. "I wasn't certain if they were right." She grinned wryly. "I never seem to get clothes right no matter how hard I try. But I wanted to do something to the dress. It was just too plain."

"You did the flowers?" He didn't know why that surprised him so much.

She nodded. "When I realized I couldn't beat you after all, I stopped studying quite so hard and embroidered instead."

He looked at her and laughed. She grinned back until he stared too long. She flushed, turned, and studied the houses on her side of the car.

"You'd better watch the road," she said softly.

He barely heard her over the pounding of his heart.

When they pulled up to her house, he climbed out of the car and hurried around to open the door for her. He'd never been a great proponent of manners before this minute. In fact, he and his mother had had some great debates where he played devil's advocate on the topic, saying manners and etiquette made for a false and unnatural society. Besides, if women wanted to be treated as equals, then they could open their own doors like men did. She'd have dropped her teeth to see him now.

They went up the walk in the gathering dusk. When their arms brushed as they moved along the narrow and broken cement strip, Leigh shivered. She unlocked the blue door of the shabby bungalow just off the marshes that rimmed the bay and slid the key back in her purse. She reached over and placed it on the little table just inside the door.

He stared at her, a specter in her white dress, as suddenly facts clicked. "You live here alone."

She frowned, that little line appearing between her eyes. "Yes. So?"

"It just hit me." He felt like a fool. He knew her mother was dead. He knew her father was in jail. Somehow it hadn't dawned on him that the consequence of that was that she lived alone.

She looked into the dark house. "I turned eighteen two months before my father went away. Children's Services wasn't interested in someone my age. And I don't want them to be anyway." The frown was still there, fierce now.

Without thinking, he reached out and smoothed that little line. As his fingers feathered across her skin, he realized he had been right. Rose petals. His fingers trailed softly across her forehead and down her cheek to her chin. He lifted her face.

It was to be just a congratulatory kiss, like the kiss Ted gave her. And a brotherly hug, nothing more.

Or so he told himself.

But she had leaned into him so easily and slid her arms around his neck so trustingly. And she had been so warm and sweet. But it was her sigh that undid him, a sigh of delight, of pleasure. So he pushed well beyond the kiss, and she yielded.

As Clay drove into Seaside, he flinched at the memory.

"Terror, you'd think that after all these years it'd go away, wouldn't you? Or at least lose its power to cut."

Terror panted happily at Clay as he turned south on Bay instead of north toward home. Just a look, he told himself. Just a look.

Seaside was the same in so many ways. It was amazing. He knew that on the beach the old homes were being torn down, and great new homes with masses of windows and endless decks were being constructed, just waiting for a hurricane to come along and destroy them. Here in the center of town, the old summer cottages and Victorian rooming houses still stood, shingles bleached by sun and salt air. Most of them were closed up, their doors and windows shuttered for another month or two until the seasonal preparations began.

He turned a corner, and Leigh's old home came into view. Memory smote him like it was yesterday. He closed his eyes against the sharp stab of regret.

If I weren't a Christian, he thought for the thousandth time, *I'd never even remember her. She'd just be one of many.*

Instead she was his one and only.

He sighed. *Oh, Lord, I know I'm going to see her almost daily. She can't run away like she usually does because she has to stay here and go to school. You're going to have to get me through the next stretch of time.*

It will be difficult for both of us, assuming she even remembers. And of course, there's the matter of Ted.

He forced himself to unclench his teeth. He climbed out of the car, Terror on his heels.

"Don't you go near the street, boy," he instructed the dog. "Stay with me."

Terror looked at him with his happy grin and leaned against his leg. It was like he said, "Whither thou goest...."

Weeds, still winter brown, resided in the cracks of the concrete walk and in what had once been a small garden. There a few shoots of hardy daffodils moved lazily in the ever present breeze, the buds fat with nascent bloom. The lawn, never worth that name at the best of times, was a stretch of sandy dirt reaching from curb to house. An occasional clump of Bermuda grass struggled to survive in the arid soil. The only bright spot was a huge, unruly forsythia in full bloom at the southeast corner of the house.

The clapboard was so bleached that it was impossible to tell its original color, and the paint on the window frames was peeling like an old sunburn. The door was a dingy, streaked, and incredibly ugly blue. The roof was missing shingles, and the gutters and a downspout had broken loose from their moorings, leaning drunkenly across a broken aluminum chaise.

Did they fall because of a storm or just neglect? Who knew? Who cared? Certainly not neighbors, for there were none.

The Spenser property had always stood off by itself, more than a block in any direction from another house, and amazingly that hadn't changed. Pampas grass as tall as a man stretched from Leigh's house to the next house in each direction. A redwing blackbird sat on a stalk of the grass and trilled, its wing slash of crimson and yellow brilliant against its black plumage. The lots across the street were less wild in appearance though just as vacant, nothing but scrub growth able to survive in the sandy soil.

Clay always figured the Spensers lived so away from people because Johnny wanted privacy for his nefarious dealings. Unfortunately in a small town like Seaside, that seclusion isolated Leigh further from a normal life.

Behind the house was the bird reserve that adjoined the property. Back there, just the other side of the now trackless bed of the railroad that had once linked the shore communities of South

Jersey, lay the marshes with more wheat-colored pampas grass waving in the breeze. In the brackish streams that laced the marshes lived waterfowl of all kinds: blue herons with their long, snaky necks, topknotted kingfishers, straw-billed egrets, iridescent mallards, midnight black grebes with their white beaks, and a multitude of geese.

Beyond the marshes was the bay, wide and beautiful, home, at least here where development hadn't encroached, to the splendid osprey and countless less flamboyant birds. His mother had written him about the local excitement when they thought a pair of bald eagles was nesting here, but apparently the pair moved down the coast to the large preserve near Cape May.

Awash in melancholy, Clay looked at his watch. 6 P.M. He bent down and patted his dog's head. "Let's go, boy. Mom's not expecting us tonight, so I'd better stop somewhere for dinner before we show."

He pulled up to one of the few restaurants open off-season and told Terror to be a good boy and take a nap. He'd be back soon. He climbed out and held Terror in while he closed the door, sliding his hand out at the last minute. He bumped the door with his hip to get the latch to give its final click.

Suddenly, Terror remembered his lessons about standing with his paws on the window ledge. He reared up and watched Clay with sad, accusing eyes.

"I'm coming back," he assured the animal.

Terror looked skeptical. It was as if he knew how Clay had come back to Leigh.

He shook off the guilty feeling as he pulled the restaurant door open. The dog knew nothing. It was his own conscience talking, more tender than ever after the visit to the house by the bay. He took a table by himself at the back of the dining room and gave his order. He pulled out James Scott Bell's latest legal thriller and began to read.

Unfortunately he couldn't keep his mind on the well-written caper. Leigh kept popping up on the page, her brown eyes alternately warm as they'd been when he left her all those years ago or scornful as he imagined they'd be today.

"Fine Christian you turned out to be," she'd say. "Venal as any other man."

Lord, what am I going to do about her? I know she lives in the garage behind our house. I know she went out of her way to ignore me when I was here for Dad's funeral. And the other times I've been here since, she's been pointedly gone. God, I know this mess is my own fault, but could You help me anyway?

He saw her again in his mind—young, lovely, and lonely, so very lonely. And he'd taken advantage of her vulnerability. There was no other way to describe what he'd done.

Oh, not that he'd forced any intimacy on her. She'd been more than willing. She welcomed it, in fact, and for a while he allowed himself to hide behind that truth. He wasn't all that culpable because she had been eager, compliant. But he couldn't hide long from the fact that she'd been susceptible to his loving because no one had loved her in a terribly long time, if ever.

He could still see her as he prepared to leave her house that long ago night, her hair mussed, her eyes warm and full of deep emotion.

Already his conscience was screaming at him now that his body wasn't. "Leigh, I —" The "I'm sorry" stuck in his throat.

She misunderstood. "It's all right if you can't say it tonight, Clay." She raised a hand and rested her fingers gently against his lips. Her other hand lay over his heart. "I love you, too." She rose up and gave him a quick kiss. "Just hug me good night. You can say it later."

But there hadn't been a later. He'd known there wouldn't be even as he held her in his arms and kissed her again and again. He was leaving the next morning with his parents and Ted for a last family vacation, and as soon as they returned, he would leave for the Naval Academy and four years where his time wouldn't be his own.

Tell her there's no later, he ordered himself. *Tell her!*

But he hadn't. He'd been a coward, and that night had colored the rest of his life as no other single experience ever had.

He had driven past her house twice between vacation and leaving for school, but it looked unoccupied. When he'd come home at Christmas, his first break from the Academy, he'd driven past again, telling himself that if he saw her, he'd stop and apologize. Not that an apology was sufficient for the hurt he'd dealt, but it was the best he could offer. He'd been both disappointed and relieved when no one seemed to be home. Several more times during that Christmas visit and subsequent breaks he'd driven by, but the house was always dark and empty.

He knew he could ask Ted about her. Ted would know. After all, they had been tight friends. But somehow he couldn't say anything to Ted. He knew about Ted's promiscuity and had condemned it loudly like the good little pharisee he'd been. The tension between the two of them was palpable every time they were in the same room. So he'd become a hypocrite, condemning Ted and denying his own breaking of the seventh commandment.

It was during Christmas break in his sophomore year when he'd overheard a conversation that had untied many of the guilt knots constricting his soul. He'd been coming into the kitchen when he stopped to retie his Reebok.

"I found Billy the cutest birthday gift, Ted." His mother was standing at the kitchen table as she held up a little blue sweater with bears on the front and a little hood with a tassel on it.

Ted grinned at the sweater. "Leigh will love it. I'm planning on giving her a three-month's supply of disposable diapers. Not very elegant, but imminently practical."

Leigh? Baby? His heart stopped. It couldn't be! Not from one time! No!

"It's hard to believe he'll be a year old at the end of January," Julia said as she put the sweater back into its box.

January. Clay turned from the doorway and raced to his room. He counted on his fingers the whole way. He collapsed on his bed with relief when he knew January couldn't be his fault. March could have been. January, no.

But that meant—His mind balked at what it meant. Leigh, sweet Leigh, had already been pregnant when they had slept together. Sweet Leigh? Hah!

He didn't have to feel so guilty after all. Relief coursed through him. He stared at the ceiling, smiling to himself.

But if it wasn't him, then who?

Suddenly Clay was furious. Who had done this to her? What craven coward had gotten her pregnant and then left her?

His skin turned cold. Ted. It had to be Ted. He was always around her. He was giving her diapers. His mother was giving her a sweater. It had to be Ted.

But how could that be? He was gay.

Maybe she was his last gasp of hope that he could be straight?

Surely he'd rather be straight. Anyone'd rather be straight.

When he thought about it now, all these years later, it was amazing how he'd been able to deceive himself and feel the sinned against instead of the sinner. She had already been pregnant! It was like she'd cheated on him when he'd been faithful to her. There'd never been another for him, and there she was, sleeping around.

Talk about perverted thinking! Surely the heart was deceitful above all things.

He nodded to the waitress who brought him his dinner and wondered at his own stupidity and lack of honor. Could he blame it on his age? He'd only been eighteen. But he'd known right from wrong. He smiled wryly as he cut into his fried chicken. He'd known. Oh yes, he'd known.

You were guilty, Wharton. Whether she was sleeping around or not, you were still guilty. And don't you ever forget it.

Three

JULIA MADE DINNER, but her mind wasn't on the work. She kept grinning and humming the doxology. Clay was coming home!

It was amazing how the mere promise of his presence made her feel better. Of course he was her son, and she enjoyed him for that reason, but it was more than that. There was solidity to Clay, a Christian strength that communicated to her and made her feel that life wasn't so hard, so impossible after all.

She felt guilty sometimes because Ted was the son who was always there for her, but Clay was the son who gave her strength. Not that she loved one more than the other. She did not. She had vowed the day they were born that she would never be a Rebecca, favoring one son over the other. But despite the twins' similarities, which were many, they were definitely different men, and those differences were what made Clay her tower of strength now that Will was gone.

If only his visits weren't so rare. So very rare.

She blinked against tears. She knew she shouldn't take his absence personally. It was the demands of a career navy life, the distance of his assignments. She wouldn't let herself dwell on the fact that he'd been as near as Virginia for the last two years, two of the loneliest years of her life, and he'd rarely come to see her. Of course he'd called and written, and they'd e-mailed almost daily. But that wasn't the same as an in-person presence. Still the last thing she needed to do was greet him with, "Hi. I'm glad you're home. It's about time."

She had understood not seeing him during his Naval Academy years. His time wasn't his, though he did come home for the major holidays. And in the summers he had his cruises. Then he was stationed in Hawaii, and they'd been only too glad to go visit him instead of expecting him to come home.

"I'm going to get a house on the beach," he said when he first got his orders.

Sure you are, Julia had thought, amused at his naïveté.

As always he ignored everyone's skepticism and pursued his own path. He went on-line with realtors, and after his first gasp of disbelief at the astronomical prices of beachside rentals, he per-sisted. And he succeeded. He somehow found a tiny two-bedroom house with a miniature living room, a miniscule kitchen, and a wide porch that opened right onto the sand, priced within his housing allowance.

"That's Clay all the way," Will had said with a father's pride.

Ted had just rolled his eyes and made plane reservations to the fiftieth state.

Smiling at the memory, Julia sweetened the iced tea she had just brewed and put the pitcher on the table. She noticed that the saltshaker was getting low and refilled it.

How had Clay managed an indefinite leave? Not that she was complaining. Not at all. It just surprised her that the navy was being so compassionate and open-ended.

She checked the baking chicken breasts. They were almost ready. She dropped the angel-hair pasta into the boiling water and gently stirred it.

Billy burst in, disheveled and smelling like sweaty boy. It was a nostalgic smell that always took Julia back to the twins' child-hood. She wanted to grab Billy, give him a great bear hug, and kiss him loudly and with verve, but she restrained herself. Shows of affection embarrassed him these days.

"You're just in time, guy. Wash those hands, and then you can set the table."

He looked pained but said, "Sure, Grandma Jule."

Julia turned back to the stove, her heart catching, as always, on the Grandma Jule. Billy had called her that since he was a baby, and he'd called Will Grandpa Will. Courtesy titles, but precious ones.

The microwave beeped, signaling the green beans were finished. Julia dumped them in a dish, sprinkled some almonds on them, and set them on the table. She eyed the boy, almost daring him to complain about one of his least favorite vegetables, but his head was down as he laid the flatware in place.

"You've got the silver backwards, Billy. Forks on the left."

Making a face, he looked at the settings. "It's stupid to have the fork on the left. Most people are right-handed."

Grinning at his impeccable logic, Julia poured the pasta into a colander. "We'll do it the right way even if it seems stupid, okay?" She poured olive oil over the pasta and shook Parmesan cheese in a fragrant, heavy snowfall and garlic salt in a pungent spritz.

Billy shook his head at the absurdity of it all as he realigned the flatware. "We'll do it right even if right's wrong."

The last word as always, thought Julia. *Does that sound familiar or what?*

Leigh came in just as Julia set the chicken on the table. They sat and automatically bowed their heads.

"And give Clay a safe trip," Julia concluded her grace.

"Clay's coming?" Billy's eyes were bright as he reached for the pasta. "Cool."

"You hardly know him," Leigh said, frowning.

Billy shrugged. "Just because I haven't spent time with him doesn't mean I don't know him. Ted talks about him lots. So does Grandma Jule. And I've got his hat."

Clay had left a midshipman's hat at home one Christmas several years ago when the leather band inside split vertically, causing it to rub his forehead and making it very uncomfortable to wear. Billy had claimed the white hat with its black visor as his own, declaring he was going to be a midshipman too.

"Still planning to go to the Academy?" Julia asked as she poured herself some iced tea.

"Nah." Billy tried to wind the angel-hair and ended up pushing a mangled wad of pasta, numerous ends dangling, into his mouth. Julia flinched but said nothing.

"Too much work," Billy mumbled around the angel-hair. "Too many orders. Mike and I've talked about what we want to do, and we've decided." He took time to drink half his glass of milk in a gulp. He always inhaled his milk so he could have iced tea.

Just like the twins, Julia thought. *What is it about little boys that, different as they are, they're all the same?*

Billy set his glass down and eyed with suspicion the green beans his mother had served him. "Lots of the guys want to be sports stars, but Mike and I know we're too small for that. Besides, that's too much work."

"And you'd have to eat lots of vegetables," Julia said seriously.

He made a face. "And think of all that sweating. So we're going to be rock stars."

Julia couldn't help herself. She laughed out loud. "And rock stars don't sweat?"

"Oh, sure, during performances and all. Those lights are hot, you know. But they don't have to beat each other up at practice and lift weights and all that stuff. And they sure don't have officers telling them what to do or grandmoms making them eat veggies." He tried another twirl of pasta with the same unsightly results. "They just have fun."

"Uh-huh," said a bemused Julia, neatly twirling her own pasta. "I wasn't aware you or Mike played any instruments."

"We don't." It was obvious that he saw this as no impediment. "I think I'll take up the drums. *Bam! Boom! Bang!*" He punctuated his words with spoon crashes against the table.

Both he and Julia glanced at Leigh, awaiting her "Hah! Fat chance! No drums in my house." Instead, all they saw was a pre-occupied woman playing with her beans.

Billy looked at Julia with a frown. "What's wrong with her?"

Julia shrugged. "Long week, I guess."

Billy shrugged too. "If she decides to complain about the drums, I'll just come over here and practice. *Bam! Boom! Bang!*" Again the spoons crashed. "Right, Grandma Jule?"

"Hah! Fat chance." She twirled more pasta into a neat bundle. "What do you think drums would do to poor Teddy?"

He brought his last green bean to his mouth, took a deep breath, and shoved it in. He forced a swallow, then looked at his clean plate with great satisfaction. "Teddy'd love the drums."

Julia nodded her reluctant agreement. "He probably would. Why don't you run up and visit with him for a while? Tell him your plans. He was taking a nap after he ate, but I bet he's awake now and would love to see you. I'll bring up some lemon meringue pie for both of you in a few minutes."

"Lemon meringue? Your very own? Real, from scratch pie crust and not the stuff Mom uses?"

Julia cocked an eyebrow as her forkful of chicken stalled halfway to her mouth. "She cheats?"

Billy nodded solemnly. "She cheats."

Julia clicked her tongue in disappointment. "How sad."

The two of them grinned at each other, then looked at Leigh. She didn't seem to notice them, let alone their teasing.

"It's probably the package from Pop-pop," Billy explained. "We found it when we got home from school."

"Ah." Julia nodded. More of Johnny Spenser would certainly explain Leigh's distance.

"It wasn't a very big package." Billy slid out of his chair. "More like a giant envelope." He eyed Leigh. "May I be excused, Mom?"

He made a face when she gave no sign of hearing.

"Go on." Julia shooed him with her hand. "I'll bring dessert up soon."

Billy ran, calling over his shoulder, "Maybe Uncle Ted knows where we can get the dry ice to make the fog on the stage for our gigs. After all, he works in Atlantic City."

"Your gigs? And what's working in Atlantic City have to do with anything? Ted's an accountant, not a performer."

But he was gone. She shook her head at his retreating back. How he reminded her of Clay and Ted at that age. Clay had planned to be a football quarterback like Roger Staubach, and Ted wanted to be the next Steve Carlton and pitch in the major leagues. Now Clay was career navy, and Ted was going to die.

Julia closed her eyes against the sharp stab of pain. Sometimes, like now, a dagger of intense emotion pierced her, robbing her of everything but an overwhelming sense of failure. It was nothing like the agony when they had first learned their son was gay. Then Julia had been sure she'd die of the crushing pain.

"How did this happen?" she used to ask Will through her tears. "How did we raise a gay son? What did we do wrong?"

He'd pulled her close and rested his cheek on the top of her head. "I don't have any answers." He sounded tired and overwhelmed. "I just know we don't want to come between him and God."

"What do you mean?" She looked into his wise, sorrow-filled eyes.

"We don't want anything we say or do toward him to give him an excuse to ignore God and His standards by hiding behind us and our flaws."

"You mean like, 'Aren't Christians supposed to be loving and kind and just look how you act? I don't want anything to do with you or your God?'"

Will nodded. "Not that we don't tell him what we think; we do. We already have. But we're careful always to speak the truth in love."

"The old love-the-sinner-while-hating-the-sin thing."

"And it is a sin," Will said. "Regardless of what society says these days. The Bible's very clear on that in both the Old and New Testaments."

Julia felt a great weight on her shoulders. "He knows that and ignores it."

Will nodded. "But how many of us know something's wrong and do it anyway? Not that that excuses him or us or anyone, of course. Wrong is always wrong. It's just so human to act as we please and not as God asks."

There was a lot of truth in that, Julia thought. A lot.

"Julia, he will always be welcome in our home." Will's voice was adamant.

Julia was startled. "Of course he will. He's our son. We love him. But, Will, I'm dying inside." And the ever present tears dripped from her chin onto his shirt.

She knew it wasn't politically correct to feel that being gay was wrong. After all, it was the twenty-first century, and theoretically he couldn't help how he was. She was supposed to accept him and everything about him, to feel pleased and proud of him.

Well, she was proud of him in so many ways. He was warm, generous, kind. He loved to help people, and nothing was too much to ask of him. No one could have been kinder to Leigh through the years or a better friend to Billy. And when Will died, Ted was there every day for months, just to check on her. He was the one who had coaxed her to go out for her first dinner, to her first movie, on her first vacation without Will. And he'd gone to all those places with her, sometimes bringing Matt, his partner, sometimes coming alone.

But her feeling of failure never left.

"Oh, God," she had cried into her pillow more nights than she could count. "What did we do wrong? Was I too overprotective? Did Will ignore him too much? How could You let this happen? Oh, God, give me strength!"

The blackness that often filled her as she lay sweating in the dark wasn't just the cessation of light; it was the implosion of her heart. The weighty, piercing shards would lodge beneath her breastbone, making breathing difficult and sleep impossible. Through the years the pain had lessened until sometimes weeks passed between the nights of agony. Then had come the AIDS diagnosis, and the implosions began again.

She took a deep breath. Resolutely she put Ted and her failure from her mind for the moment. She thought of her pride in her other son. She didn't love Clay more, but she understood him, appreciated him, agreed with him, thanked God for him. He was so much less complicated, and he loved God with his whole heart. She felt they were on the same wavelength in spite of his lengthy absences.

For a moment failure laughed at her again. If she were a better mother, surely Clay would come home more often. Why, he'd hardly been there even when Will died. It must somehow be her, or he'd like to visit if only to see Ted and old friends.

Pushing that thought aside—after all, he was coming home now—she began cleaning the table while Leigh, coming out of her trance, rose to help her. Leigh rinsed the dishes while Julia loaded the dishwasher.

Leigh. Julia smiled as she watched the young woman scrape most of her dinner into the sink to be chewed up by the garbage disposal. It wasn't just Clay and Ted she was proud of. It was Leigh. What a wonder the girl was! Here was success, and in the best ways possible. And God had let Julia be part of it.

Eleven years ago, shortly after the boys had graduated from Seaside High, she had gone shopping at the Acme on Eighth Avenue. As she waited in the checkout line, she felt a rush of pity for the poor, young checker as she watched the woman in front of her hand over a wad of discount coupons. The girl, a pretty thing with long chestnut hair and big brown eyes, stoically punched in all the numbers, flipping the coupons one at a time. *Tap, tap, ca-ching. Tap, tap, ca-ching.*

Julia blinked as she felt a touch on her shoulder. She turned, but there was no one near. Strange. She picked up a copy of *Newsweek* and began flipping through it to pass the time. Suddenly there was a tap on her shoulder again, and again when she looked up, there was no one near her. Frowning slightly, she put the *Newsweek* back and reached for a gardening magazine. This time the tap made the back of her neck prickle.

That was when the voice spoke. Well, the voice didn't actually speak. It more or less just filled her mind. HELP HER.

Feeling like a victim of *Candid Camera,* Julia shifted her eyes cautiously, looking for the jokester. No one was paying her any attention. Certainly no one else seemed to hear a disembodied voice.

HELP HER.

A shiver went through Julia as she tried to understand what was happening.

HELP HER.

"Who?" she blurted in something akin to panic.

"What?"

Julia blinked and looked at the cashier.

"Did you say something?" the cashier asked, her brown eyes curious. Her name tag read Leigh. Julia recognized her now as Leigh Spenser who had just graduated from Seaside High with the twins. She was a good friend of Ted's. And, Julia thought with sadness, her mother was dead, and her father was in jail for a long, long time.

"Did you say something?" Leigh repeated.

"N-no," Julia said quickly with a smile. How had her groceries all been checked already? She pulled out her checkbook and wrote a check that would get her twenty dollars change. She nodded to Leigh and hurried from the store, waiting for another tap on the shoulder at any minute or another "Help her." But there was nothing. She began to relax. It had all been her imagination. Or maybe it was the beginning of menopause. Everyone said it did strange things to your mind.

That early July evening, she had a compulsion to walk the boards. She and Will rarely went near the boardwalk during the summer. They liked off-season walks when there was hardly anyone around but them, and the smells were surf and fresh air instead of grease for French fries and funnel cakes, spun sugar for cotton candy, or that distinctive popcorn aroma.

Will hadn't protested her suggestion too much. He was passing time waiting for Mrs. Redmond to go into labor.

"Then the fun will begin since the baby's breech," he told Julia as they strolled. "Again."

"How many is this?" Julia asked. "Six?"

"Seven. I just keep praying it's her last. She can't take much more."

"Let's get a soft ice cream," Julia suddenly said and pulled Will across the boardwalk and through the throng until they took their place in line.

At the first tap she turned to Will and said, "What?"

He looked at her strangely and shook his head.

The second tap made her feel creepy all over.

The third tap sent her silently screaming to God. *Lord, what's going on? Help me!*

HELP HER, came the response.

Julia stilled, struck by a new and overwhelming realization. *Lord, is this You talking to me, tapping me?*

HELP HER.

It is You! She shivered and wrapped her goose-bumped arms around herself. She'd never experienced anything comparable to this in her life. God didn't speak to her, Julia Wharton, not like this, in audible words. Or rather in audible impressions.

She loved God deeply, felt His presence, His love. She prayed regularly, daily, by the minute as needed, but this! This was incredible.

HELP HER.

"Who?" Julia said.

"What?" asked the girl behind the counter.

Julia started and stared. It was the same girl who had checked her out at the Acme. Leigh Spenser.

"Her?" Julia said.

HELP HER.

Julia stood transfixed, wondering what she was supposed to do for Leigh. "You work two jobs?" Julia asked, saying the first thing that came to mind.

Leigh looked at her and nodded. "What flavor?"

"I'm Mrs. Wharton, Ted and Clay's mother." Julia smiled. "Oh, and this is Dr. Wharton, their father." She waved a hand at Will.

"I know," Leigh said. "What flavor?"

"Vanilla for her," Will said when Julia continued to stare. "Black raspberry for me."

Leigh turned to get the cones.

A beep sounded. Will grabbed for his belt and the beeper there. He glanced at the number. "Mrs. Redmond." He grabbed the cones and threw down some money. "Keep the change," he called over his shoulder as he elbowed his way back into the mainstream pedestrian traffic. "Hurry up, Julia, if you want me to drop you at home." He handed her the vanilla cone.

Julia took the cone and licked absently. *God, I can't believe You spoke to me like that. I'll help her, but how?*

There was no voice now, but she knew, just knew, that God would show her how to help. What an adventure! What an honor! She couldn't stop smiling.

Even now, eleven years later, the memory made her smile. Watching Leigh become such a wonderful young woman had been one of the great joys of her life.

"Let's take dessert up to Ted's room," Julia suggested as she wiped off the counter.

Leigh nodded and began collecting cups and saucers, the teapot and cozy, plates and forks, sugar and cream. Julia cut generous pieces of pie, pleased at the consistency of the lemony custard. The meringue was high and light and browned just right. She smiled. Ted would love it. If he could eat it. The sores in his mouth were bothering him badly. She turned to the refrigerator and pulled out a dish of Junket. The custard would slide down easily if the pie were too much.

A car pulled into the drive.

Leigh looked at Julia. "Were you expecting David?"

Julia told herself not to blush as she shook her head.

Leigh grabbed a paper towel to dry her hands. "Maybe he decided to stop and see Ted."

"Right," said Julia with what she hoped was nonchalance. Dr. David Traynor was an infectious disease specialist, and Ted was his patient. The fact that he seemed as interested in Julia as her son made having him in the house difficult, uncomfortable, exciting, special.

I'm too old for this, Julia thought, twirling the wedding ring she still wore on her right hand. *The last thing I want is someone interested in me romantically.*

And you're too old to lie to yourself, too, Julia Wharton. You're so flattered you can hardly stand it.

Embarrassed, Julia had to acknowledge that truth. She was flattered. She just didn't know what she was supposed to do about it. Or him.

David was a good-looking man, she had to admit. His dark hair was only slightly gray at the temples, and he carried very little extra weight about the middle. And he was tall. She liked tall men. Will had been tall. Ted and Clay were tall.

Forget tall, she told herself. *Forget distinguished and delightful and humorous. Forget!*

Instead, she remembered the first time he came to the house, ostensibly to see Ted. She'd known David for years. He and his family went to Seaside Chapel just like she and Will and the boys. She'd been friends with his late wife, Leslie. She'd grieved deeply when Leslie and their seventeen-year-old son, Adam, had been killed in a tragic accident on the Garden State Parkway several years ago. When Will died, David had been terribly kind and supportive. An old friend. A good friend.

But a romantic interest? She couldn't help but grin at the absurdity of it all.

On that first visit a couple of months ago when Ted first came home, David talked briefly, very briefly, to Ted, rose, and waited for her to walk him to the door. Instead of leaving like she expected, David turned to her.

"Walk with me?" he asked. "I need to know how you're coping." He took her arm and turned her toward the narrow path through the dunes to the beach. He held her arm close to his side until they were walking along the edge of the water in the wet, packed sand left by the receding tide. Then he let go with what seemed to her reluctance.

It wasn't until he released her that Julia realized that aside from her sons' hugs, that was the first time a male had touched her in so personal a manner since Will's death. It was a disconcerting thought. Even more disconcerting was the fact that she'd liked the comfort and warmth of his touch.

Careful, woman, she cautioned herself, twirling her wedding band as they walked. *You're vulnerable.*

And more so every time he came around. The loneliness she felt somehow became more lonely. And was that special look in his eyes when he saw her just her unruly imagination, or was it real? And how could she resist his kind and understanding manner as he tended Ted's pain, or his commitment to faith that matched hers?

She sniffed. As if someone as wonderful as he would be interested in her with her hot flashes and varicose veins and sagging bosom.

She shook her head as she wiped down the kitchen table. So how come she hadn't felt this alive since Will's death?

Four

LEIGH REACHED BEHIND her for the door as she flicked her paper towel toward the trash, hoping for a three-point swish.

"Michael Jordan Spenser, basketball champeen," she murmured. She blew a raspberry when she missed.

Her hand reaching for the door missed too. She turned to see where the door had moved and bumped hard into a very solid, very warm body.

"Wha—?" She bounced like a tennis ball off a racket and felt herself begin to fall. Her arms wind-milled wildly, and she gave a garbled cry. An arm whipped around her waist, stopping her descent, and she grabbed a handful of blue shirt to steady herself.

"Thanks, David," she began as she found her foot-ing, then stared, appalled, into the face of the man she had spent more than ten years carefully avoiding. Her fist clenched more tightly in the fabric of his denim shirt.

Most times when she thought of Clay, she saw in her mind's eye the eighteen-year-old who had gradu-ated with her, undeveloped but promising, thin—no, make that skinny, very skinny and bony, with a beak nose too big for his handsome face. But he was no longer that boy in spite of the same sharp blue eyes that looked down at her. His beak of a nose finally fit his face, and his jaw was hard and lean. His shoulders were broad enough to handle any problem.

"Hello, Leigh," he said, his voice sounding strained and unnaturally husky. "Or should I say Michael Jordan Spenser?"

A flush crept from her neck to her forehead, and she glared at him.

Lord, did I have to begin this awkwardness looking like an idiot?

She needed to move from his embrace. Yes, she did, and she would, just as soon as she was able. The problem was the paralysis, hopefully temporary, that kept her ignominiously clutching the fistful of material. The struggle to gather her scattered wits was surely only a minor glitch in the unruly computer that was her brain. With something akin to panic she realized that even her involuntary systems seemed on the blink as evidenced by the trouble she was having breathing.

"Clay!" Julia's joyous cry broke the spell and released Leigh's mind. She dropped her hand and pulled back so hastily that she all but tripped over her feet. Her waist felt branded.

She turned her back, trying belatedly to hide her flushed face and still her hammering heart, as Julia flew into her son's arms. For years whenever she pictured facing Clay again, Leigh saw herself as an ice princess—cool, aloof, scorning, spurning, totally in control.

Instead, I end up hanging on him like some dithering antebellum Southern belle! Oh, dear Lord, get me out of here!

She grabbed a laden tray, ignoring the clatter as all the pie plates slid to one side under the force of the sudden motion, and headed for the door to the hall. She would deliver the dessert to Ted's room, grab Billy, and leave by the front door. Then she would go home and lock the two of them in for the rest of the week. Or two weeks. Or however long Clay was here. Anything to stay out of his way.

What a wonderful plan! What a stupid plan.

She risked a glance back as she left the room and found Clay staring at her over his mother's shoulder. The corner of his mouth lifted in a half smile. Her face flamed anew. He was laughing at her! She knew it. She turned and ran.

Halfway up the stairs she stopped, leaning against the banister. Her heart still pounded, and her mouth was dry. In contrast her hands were so moist and clammy it was all she could do to keep a grip on the black lacquered tray.

This is ridiculous! Get hold of yourself, Spenser.

But what if he figures things out about Billy?

Panic rolled through her like a hurricane surf, battering, surging, drowning her. For a moment she literally could not think. She forced herself to take several deep breaths. Inhale. Hold it. Exhale. Inhale. Hold it. Exhale.

How could he possibly figure it out? No one else had in all these years. Here she was, literally in the bosom of his family, and they'd never suspected. Why should he? Billy didn't look enough like anyone but himself to arouse suspicion. Surely she was safe; they were safe.

Oh, Lord, please, keep us safe!

She closed her eyes, willing her heart to stop crashing against her ribs before it split them. It was better this way, she tried to convince herself, bumping into him unexpectedly. She had been spared the long uncertainty of waiting, wondering when he'd come. That agony would have been terrible.

It's like a tooth extraction. It's better for me to get it done today than have to come back tomorrow and worry all that time.

Hah! That may be the theory, but in real life it still hurts just as much today as it would have tomorrow.

She looked at the tray with the plates crowded at one end, overlapping and askew. The pie wedges were dented and squished, the beautifully scalloped edge of one piece of crust broken completely off. Normally she would have felt compelled to straighten the mess. Given the current situation, she couldn't find the energy to be concerned about a few pieces of pie, even if they were from Julia's prize-winning kitchen.

They look fine. Well, they look adequate, and they'll still taste exceptionally good. Nobody's going to complain.

What Julia would think when she saw them was another thing, crunched and broken as they were. She'd just have to hand them all out before Julia saw the damage.

She sighed. Julia was downstairs reveling in Clay's return. In a couple of minutes she'd be coming upstairs to sit with her dying son. The least Leigh could do was treat her pie with respect even if she couldn't manage it for the returning prodigal.

With one hand she balanced the tray on her hip, and with the other she straightened the plates. She noted with hope that her hands weren't shaking too badly.

Inhale. Hold it. Exhale. Inhale. Hold it. Exhale.

All you have to do is act naturally, she assured herself. *That's the key to surviving the next few weeks. Act like he doesn't mean a thing to you, which, of course, he doesn't. Act like he didn't irrevocably change your life, which, in reality, he did. Act like his arm on your waist didn't feel as wonderful today as it did all those years ago, because it didn't.*

It didn't!

In other words, Spenser, act like an adult. You aren't eighteen anymore! You aren't that pathetically lonely daydreamer in love with Prince Clay Charming.

You aren't! His presence will make no difference whatsoever in your life.

Yeah, right.

Oh, Lord, help me. Please!

She lifted her chin and took a deep breath. She would show him how much she'd changed, grown. She was no longer that naïve little girl flattered by the attention of the school hero, that socially inept outcast in awe of the class's most popular boy. She wasn't that nobody in secondhand clothes thrilled by the attention from the son of one of Seaside's leading families. No, she wasn't even if she suddenly felt like it.

She was Leigh Wilson Spenser, a strong woman, God's woman. She was a college graduate with her master's just around the corner. She had survived single parenthood for ten years and had a delightful son as proof that she was doing a fine job. She had a satisfying career and a decent income. She had friends. She had Julia and Ted. And she had Jesus.

No, by the grace of God, she wasn't that girl at all.

She climbed the rest of the way to the second floor and walked to Ted's room on a spurt of confidence.

Billy was "sitting" in the comfy chair next to Teddy's bed. He was curled against the chair back, his ratty sneakers slung over one padded arm, his head resting on the other.

"You're my favorite uncle," Billy was saying.

Ted smiled. "I'm your only uncle, kid."

Billy shook his head. "You're forgetting Clay."

Ted raised an eyebrow in a typically Wharton expression.

"He's not around enough to count."

"Yeah, I guess you're right. So that makes you my favorite only uncle." He beamed at Ted who beamed back.

"Pie's here," Leigh said.

"Yes!" Billy pumped the air and ran to Leigh. He grabbed a piece and raced back to the chair, now sitting tailor fashioned. Leigh gasped as the pie plate canted far to the left as he settled himself.

"Careful, Billy. You're going to lose it!"

Billy looked at her in surprise. "Never. Too precious." Then he looked, really looked, at the pie. "But what happened to it? It looks like it got in a fight."

"I tilted the tray, and they sort of smushed together," Leigh confessed. "But they'll still taste good."

"Of course they will. Grandma Jule doesn't cheat."

"What?" Ted and Leigh said together. They studied him, ten-year-old energy crackling in the air around him.

"He makes me ache simply by comparison," Ted said, curling on his side, trying to find a comfortable position.

Leigh looked at the wasted body making barely a rise under the blanket and nodded. "I know what you mean, especially at the end of a long week."

"I wish you were mine, kid." Ted smiled at the boy and his half-empty pie plate. "I wish you and your mom were both mine."

Billy nodded enthusiastically, for once not talking with his mouth full.

Leigh smiled into Ted's sad, weary eyes and felt her own fill with tears. She never knew what mood she'd find Ted in. Tonight he was obviously melancholy and lonely. "Thanks, Teddy. That's the ultimate compliment."

She set the tray down on a stack of sheets and towels on Ted's dresser and brushed futilely at her wet cheeks. "You've got to stop being so complimentary, you know? Tears are falling as often as spring rain around here."

"That's okay. Spring rains bring life," Ted said. After a pause he added, "And death."

Life and death, she thought. Or is it death and then life? First the pain, then the joy. Did it hurt the bulbs and seeds when they burst their jackets and pushed against the soil, seeking the sun and life after months of death? It certainly hurt people to be forced by circumstances to grow in ways they didn't seek. At least it hurt her. And scared her.

"I love you, Leigh," Ted's voice was soft, barely audible, as he reached for her hand.

"And I love you, Teddy." She leaned over and kissed his pale forehead. Then she grinned cheekily. "But you're just saying that because you're too sick to marry me. Why, I'd have to carry you across the threshold."

He grinned at her and let his eyes slide shut. The afternoon sitting on the deck outside his French windows had tired him.

She sat on the arm of Billy's chair and shook her head in an attempt to fling off the sorrow, lessen the tears.

Billy's hand touched hers. "Have a piece of the pie, Mom. It'll make you feel better."

She smiled at his serious little face, a fleck of meringue caught in the corner of his mouth. How she loved him. "Good idea, sport."

She turned toward the tray to help herself and saw Clay leaning against the doorway, arms folded across his chest. Listening. Watching. Watching her. Their eyes met and held, and Leigh felt her breath go shallow and her heart expand painfully.

Act naturally.

"What is it?" asked Ted, trying to look over his shoulder.

"Shh," she whispered to him, patting him gently. "It's only Clay."

"What?"

"It's Clay. He's come for a visit." She signaled for Clay to come closer. He took the smallest of steps forward.

Ted rolled onto his back, staring in disbelief at his twin. Clay stared back impassively, but Leigh saw his hands clench into fists. It couldn't be easy for him to see his twin so ill. Ted had gone downhill dramatically in the past month, and his appearance must be terribly alarming to someone who hadn't watched the progressive deterioration. It was difficult enough for her watching the gradual, daily decline.

"It's been a long time," Ted said, his voice cool.

Clay nodded but said nothing. He cleared his throat once, twice.

"Quite a shock, aren't I?" Ted asked, all cocky and cheeky. Gone was his soft melancholy mood of a moment ago.

Clay cleared his throat a third time and held out his hand to Ted. "It's good to see you."

Ted nodded curtly as the brothers shook hands.

They stared at each other for several seconds, Clay's face scrubbed clean of all emotions, Ted's defensive. Abruptly Clay turned.

"Hello, Billy." He held out his hand to the boy who had been watching with a frown as the brothers greeted each other. "It's good to see you again."

Billy jumped from the chair and solemnly held his hand out to Clay. Leigh's heart gave a little misbeat as she watched the exchange.

A click, click, clicking noise and a whuffle sounded, getting louder as it neared the room.

"Oh no," muttered Clay, turning from Billy to the door. He was too late.

A little Jack Russell terrier raced into the room and onto the bed in one fluid motion. He stood there like a royal prince, ears at attention as he surveyed his subjects.

"Down, boy," Clay called, snapping his fingers and pointing to the floor. "You need to get down."

"Wow! Who's he?" Billy asked, eyes aglow. "Come here, guy."

The little dog ignored both commands and settled on Ted as the favored one. His hind end began to rotate under the strength of his wag. He lunged for Ted's face, tongue ready for a slurp of affection.

"Down, boy," Clay ordered again. "Down, Terror." At the same time, Billy came out of the chair and dove onto the bed, grabbing the dog.

Terror happily turned his attention to the boy, delighted to make a new friend, washing Billy's face as he laughed with abandon. Tangled together, they rolled to the edge and off, landing at Leigh's feet. The little piece of meringue at the corner of Billy's mouth was gone.

"Oh, Mom, wait until Mama sees him!"

That would be a meeting worth witnessing, Leigh thought with a brief smile. She put her hand on Billy's back.

"Come on, guy. Calm down. And don't jump on Uncle Ted's bed like that again."

Instantly, Billy was on his feet, Terror forgotten. "Did I hurt you, Uncle Ted?" His eyes were wide with concern.

Ted shook his head and put out a hand, hanging it over the bed to the dog. Terror immediately snuffled his new toy. "I'm okay. You guys didn't bump me."

Leigh and Billy both slumped in relief.

"But where did this cute little guy come from? And who is he?" Ted asked, his weariness gone for the moment.

"He's mine." Clay watched the dog happily licking Ted's fingers. "His name's Terror."

"Terror the Terrier." Ted raised an eyebrow at Clay. "I didn't know you could be that corny. Or do I mean cutesy?"

Leigh looked at Ted, surprised at the acid tone of the comment.

"He's great, Clay," said Billy as he happily collapsed next to Terror. "And I love his name. Is he?"

"Is he what?" Clay asked.

"A terror?"

Clay shook his head. "Anything but. And I didn't name him. He came named."

"A gift from one of your many admirers?" Ted asked, again with that edge of acid.

Clay didn't answer, and Leigh looked at him. He was studying the tray of pie, and he must be clenching his teeth if the muscle leaping in his jaw was any indication. A starburst of wrinkled material shone just below his left shoulder where she had grabbed him earlier.

Ted snorted. "I thought so. Always did have a way with the ladies."

Leigh reached for Ted's hand, abandoned now that Terror was chewing on Billy's crusty sneaker. She squeezed gently and shot a warning glance at him. This was not the way to welcome your brother.

He scowled at her but kept silent.

Billy stood, a wiggling Terror in his arms, refusing to lie docilely on his back like the cat did. "Easy, boy. Oh, man, Mama's going to kill you."

"Who's Mama?" Clay asked.

"Our cat that we adopted. She had kittens, but we gave them all away." He looked up at Leigh accusingly. "Mom wouldn't let me keep any even though they were so little and cute."

Clay looked at Leigh with that Wharton raised brow.

She ignored him. "They were going to grow up to look just like Mama, Billy. And you can't make me feel guilty no matter how hard you try."

He grinned at her. "It's always fun to see if I can."

She grinned back. "You're incorrigible."

"Yep," he said proudly.

"And he's going to be a famous rock musician and make millions and keep us all in the style to which we'd like to become accustomed." Julia came into the room with the tea tray. Her eyes sparkled with joy as she looked from one son to the other. "Sorry it took me so long. The water had gotten cold."

Clay took the tray from her and turned to put it down. He stopped abruptly and frowned. All available surfaces were covered with medical supplies or books or people.

"Put it on the bed," Julia said.

"Here, Grandma Jule. You sit here and relax." Billy waved toward the comfy chair. "Clay and I can pour the tea."

Clay looked a bit startled but didn't disagree.

"Thank you, Billy." Julia settled herself.

"No problem," he assured her. "The oldest always gets the best seat."

Julia barely flinched at the backhanded courtesy. "As I said before, thanks, Billy." She reached down and petted Terror who now sat at her feet, tongue lolling as he gazed at her with adoration.

"He likes you," Billy said.

"That's because I rescued him from the car where someone who shall be nameless had left him. He was crying, weren't you, baby?"

Terror responded to the loving tone of voice by climbing onto her lap.

Leigh made herself busy handing out desserts while Billy instructed Clay on the art of pouring tea.

"Uncle Ted likes a smidge of cream and two spoons of sugar. That's right." He took the mug and carefully walked to Ted's bedside table. "And Grandma Jule uses one tiny spoonful. She's trying to cut down so she doesn't get fat. Or so she says. I personally think it's because she wants to impress Dr. Traynor."

"Dr. Traynor?" Clay looked at his mother, questions written all over his face.

"Ted's doctor," Julia said blandly, meeting his look steadily. "Good man." She turned to Billy. "Did anyone ever tell you you talk too much?"

"Yeah." He grinned unrepentantly. "My mom."

"And how true that is," Leigh said as she offered a piece of pie to Ted. She wasn't surprised when Ted held up a hand and shook his head. Yesterday herpes sores had appeared on his lips and in his mouth. Dr. Traynor had started him on medication immediately, but eating was painful for the moment and would become an ordeal if the virus moved down his throat and into his esophagus.

"Junket?" she asked.

"I think I can manage that."

Julia jumped up and plumped pillows behind him. Leigh handed him the dish of custard and a spoon, then sat on the arm of Julia's chair. Clay watched, leaning against the far wall, out of the way. Somehow, Terror had weaseled his way back onto the bed. He lay beside Ted, panting, watching the Junket carefully.

"Oh, Julia." Leigh rolled a piece of pie around in her mouth. "This is delicious."

"It is," Clay agreed. "I'd forgotten what a good cook you are, Mom."

"She's the best," Billy said. "Can I have Ted's piece?"

"Please?" Leigh said as she handed it to him.

"Please." He grinned and went to stand beside Clay, leaning against the wall in imitation.

Leigh pulled her eyes from the two—it was too painful to contemplate them together, too dangerous—and looked at Ted. His hands lay in his lap, his dish of Junket sliding south, his spoon dangling from his fingers. Terror was edging forward ever so slowly.

Leigh reached for the spoon and the dish. "Here, Ted. Let me help. Open your mouth and make like a little bird."

As she fed Ted, she was aware of Clay watching them. Watching her.

Act naturally. Act naturally.

It was going to be a very long week. Or two weeks. Or month. Or whatever.

Five

HE STOOD IN THE dark, watching. He liked spying like this. It made him feel powerful, like he knew stuff no one else did.

Well, he did. He knew stuff that Leigh-Leigh didn't, that was for sure. His chest swelled with the importance of it all. Besides him, only Johnny knew, and Johnny was dead.

He sighed. He missed Johnny. The man was slime; there was no doubt about it, but he'd never had a better friend. Sure, Johnny made fun of him a lot, even called him Worm all the time.

He sighed. He could still hear Johnny chanting in that mocking voice, "Hey, Worm! Nobody likes you, everybody hates you, guess you'll go eat worms. Big, fat juicy ones; little, tiny, skinny ones—oh, how they wiggle and squirm. First you'll bite off their heads, then suck out their guts, then throw their skins away. Nobody knows how you can eat worms three times a day."

Then Johnny'd laugh and scratch his belly, and Worm would laugh with him.

People mocking him was nothing new. In fact, he couldn't remember a time in his life when he didn't get mocked. But Johnny never hit him. Never. Once Johnny even told Dooley, self-proclaimed king of their cell block, to leave Worm alone and pick on someone his own size. Dooley picked on Johnny for a few minutes, and Johnny never defended him like that again. But he still remembered that day with pride. No one had ever stood up for him before. Or since.

He smiled in the darkness. Yeah, Johnny had been his best friend. Ever. He shrugged and admitted the truth. He had been his only friend. Ever. And Johnny'd shared his secret with him, or at least part of it.

He still felt bad that Johnny got iced in the shower. To die naked must be very upsetting. At least he knew he'd be embarrassed if it happened to him.

Johnny was the reason he was here. The secret. The treasure. That was why he stood in the night and watched through windows. That was why he was going to be rich. Nobody'd make fun of him ever again.

Nobody'd ignore him ever again.

Nobody'd beat on him ever again.

He'd been watching for the past several nights, and he was finally getting a feel for schedules and routines. It made him feel professional, not like the two-bit crook he'd been before. He shook his head at how stupid he'd been. No wonder he got caught. But that was then. This was now.

Every night they all gathered in that upstairs bedroom where the guy with AIDS lived. It was like they were saying good-bye to him in case he wasn't there in the morning or something. Talk about spooky.

Personally he wouldn't have nothing to do with an AIDS guy. What if you caught it or something? Then where were you? He shuddered. Even the treasure wouldn't do you no good then.

Tonight the doctor wasn't up there, but some new guy was. The brother? Probably. Clooney said the AIDS guy had a twin. It must be weird being a twin. Like looking in the mirror all the time.

He knew lots about these Whartons because he had asked careful questions of the people he met on the beach, especially Clooney, the guy with the metal detector. Clooney liked to talk like no one he'd ever met. In the joint everyone kept to themselves most of the time, and growing up, no one talked to him either. His dad hated him and his mother thought he was just a poor joke.

And that was one of the nicest things she said.

He flinched in the cool night air as he heard her voice just like she was standing in the driveway with him.

"Get out of my sight, you little creep," she yelled. "I don't want nothing to do with you. You're so ugly you make me sick!"

Since he looked like her—everybody said he did—he was never sure why she yelled that all the time. But it always made him feel bad, so he stayed out of her way as much as he could.

He looked over his shoulder, half expecting to see her even though he knew she couldn't be here. He'd stood by her grave when she got buried. He'd smiled through the whole service. If only she'd stop living in his mind like she stopped living on the earth, he'd be very happy.

He heard some barks from that upstairs bedroom and smiled, Ma forgotten. He liked that little dog. It had come with the guy who was probably the brother. He'd almost let it out of the car himself after the guy went inside without it, but the lady came out and did it first. He hoped the dog lived in the house, not the garage. He didn't want anyone or anything protecting Leigh-Leigh.

Clooney told him she didn't have nobody but the lady and the AIDS guy and the kid, and only the kid lived with her in the garage, so he wasn't worried. What was a kid? It was good that Clooney was a blabbermouth.

Not that he really wanted to know lots of the stuff Clooney told him about the Whartons with their fancy painted house and garage, but he couldn't just ask about Johnny's kid. Too obvious. So he listened carefully to everything Clooney said because you never knew what might be important. If he had learned anything during his time in the can, it was that knowing your marks was the secret to success.

He just wished someone had told him that before.

After several days of talking with Clooney as he dug those stupid little holes in the sand and collected all kinds of worthless junk, he knew more about the whole neighborhood than he wanted to.

The stuff he'd learned sort of surprised him. He'd always thought that people who lived in pretty houses had pretty lives, unless, of course, you were Mafia. Then you killed each other all the time. But no. Rich guys were as bad off as he was. The guy in that big house a block over, the one with all the glass, beat his wife, just like his own old man used to beat Ma. At least Ma used to slug back, which is more than the rich lady did. She just drank until she passed out.

He hadn't believed Clooney at first. He did now though. He went and checked their trash last night, and it was full of booze bottles. He peered in the windows, amazed that people forgot that windows weren't just for looking out of. And there was wifey passed out on the sofa with her mouth open and a spilled glass hanging from her hand. An empty bottle sat on the carpet beside her. She had a beautiful shiner and a bruise on her arm where the guy must've grabbed her and twisted. He knew that that really hurt.

He'd sat in the swing on their deck for a long time thinking about what a waste it was to have all that money and be no better off than his pathetic family. When he got the treasure from Leigh-Leigh, he wasn't going to beat on women or drink himself into a stupor. Well, maybe once in a while for fun, but not always. No way.

He looked up at the window of the Wharton house again, and he saw them all gathered around the bed. If he was the sick guy and everybody stared at him like that, he'd get the willies.

With a shudder he turned to the garage. Johnny used to make fun of Leigh-Leigh for living in a garage. Johnny was wrong though. This place was sort of cute. He laughed a little because he used to think that she lived in a garage like where you took your car to be fixed. No matter how hard he tried, he could never figure out where the bedrooms would be.

But this place was nice, and there was plenty of room for the bedrooms even if they were little. And standing on that itsy-bitsy deck outside her bedroom, you could see all the way to Atlantic City. He liked that. When he had the treasure, he was going to become a high roller and stay in the casinos over there. He smiled at the picture of himself with gorgeous women hanging all over him as he gambled and won. Always in his pictures he won. Always the women loved him.

He reached for Leigh-Leigh's front door. It was time to begin.

Six

SHE WAS SO DOGGONE kind to Ted, Clay thought as he put the empty pie plates in the dishwasher. Feeding him. Making certain he'd taken his medicine. Putting on surgical gloves to protect herself. Smoothing cream on the sores on his mouth. Helping him rinse the sores inside his mouth. She didn't seem put off at all by his appearance, and frankly, Clay'd seen healthier skeletons last Halloween.

He watched out of the corner of his eye as she tied a red plastic bag shut and put it in a separate container on the porch. Ted's contagious waste.

She came back into the kitchen and leaned against the closed door. She sighed and drew a hand wearily across her forehead. His mother entered the room, and immediately Leigh straightened and went to her.

"I think he'll sleep through the night." Leigh put an arm around her. "He's very tired."

Mom nodded. "I don't know how many more days he'll be able to even manage sitting on the deck."

"I was wondering that myself." She grabbed a dirty pie dish and walked it to the sink. "He'll be very upset when he can't get out to hear and smell the sea anymore."

"Should we bring him downstairs? Make up the dining room as a bedroom?" Mom asked. "Would that be better for him?" She glanced from Leigh to Clay.

Clay went cold. How was he supposed to know whether they should bring him down? "What benefit is there in moving him from his room?"

Leigh looked at him and nodded, one of the few times she'd actually looked full at him. "Good question. I don't see any benefit and one major drawback. He can't see the ocean down here because the dunes are too high."

"You're right." Mom smiled wearily at them. "I felt that way myself, but I needed to hear your opinions." She closed her eyes, frowning. "He's so weak tonight."

Leigh went to Mom again. "Now don't get too worked up. You know he might be stronger tomorrow."

"And I know he might not."

Leigh looked directly at Clay for a second time in as many minutes. "It's a good thing you came home. There's probably not too much time left."

Something inside Clay shattered at the casual way Leigh spoke of his twin's death, but he looked at the two women with a blank face. "Right."

"I'll see you tomorrow, Julia." Leigh kissed the woman's soft cheek. "Try and get some sleep."

Mom just nodded.

"Good night, Clay." Leigh nodded in his direction. She turned back to the stairs. "Come on, Billy. Say good night to Ted and Terror."

Clay slid the last plate into the dishwasher slot and straightened. "Let me walk you back."

Leigh's chin went up and she shook her head. "Thanks, but that's not necessary."

"I know, but I want to."

She turned back to the stairs. "Billy!"

Clay took her arm and turned her to the back door. "He'll be along."

He could feel her reluctance in the drag against his pull, but he kept the pressure steady. He knew she had to come with him or make a scene, and he was betting she wouldn't make a scene in front of his mother.

He opened the door and held it for her. She pulled free from his grasp, ducked under his arm, and set off for the garage at a good clip.

"Slow down," he called, irritated that she wanted to get away from him so fast. "I won't hurt you."

He saw the slight hitch in her steps at that comment, but she didn't turn around. She did slow down.

When she'd bumped into him when he first arrived, he'd been as momentarily thrown as she'd been. It had taken all his concentration merely to say hello to her. He'd seen her face when she realized who had hold of her, the horror and uncertainty and—was it fear? Of him? That was a very unsettling idea. Why should she be afraid of him after all these years? Angry, maybe, if she held a long grudge. But afraid? Ridiculous. Still, she'd certainly run from the room fast enough, like she couldn't wait to get away from him.

Michael Jordan Spenser. Even now it made him smile in spite of his pique, especially the raspberry. The Leigh he remembered would have been too much a lady or too shy to make a noise like that.

"We've got to talk," he said to her stubborn, straight back as he followed her across the lawn. "Leigh, wait up. We've got to talk." He let his irritation show.

She stopped and turned to him, her chin lifted in what he recognized even in the short time he'd been around her today as a silent declaration of war. No. Not war. Nothing so overt. It was more like she had raised a wall around herself, a wall to guard herself from him. She stood there, holding herself aloof and withdrawn within its protection. A stone princess inside her castle.

He glanced out toward the ocean, miffed and strangely insulted.

She can feed Ted, tend his personal needs, tell him she loves him, yet she can barely stand to be around me.

"Leigh." He ran his hand through his hair. Where to start? "I—" He looked at her and was struck by how beautiful she was, her dark hair turned silver by the pale moonlight. She was a night sprite, an ethereal vision, a dozen times more lovely than the girl he'd known. And a dozen times more dangerous.

He opened his mouth to apologize for his past behavior, to tell her how much he regretted his reprehensible actions, to expiate a decade of guilt, but what he said was, "Now I know what you'd look like as a blonde, a beautiful platinum blonde."

"What?" She looked at him in disbelief, startled and wary, and he was glad it was too dark for her to see his flush of embarrassment. Talk about sounding like an idiot.

"The moon," he hastened to explain. "It gilds your hair."

Her scowl deepened.

"Gilds. You know, turns gold. Or in this case, silver-gold."

"I know what *gilds* means," she said, her voice clipped.

"Yeah, well…" He swallowed and wondered how he'd gotten himself in such an embarrassing quandary. He hadn't felt this tongue-tied since, well, since the night he left her eleven years ago. How did she do this to him?

She wrapped her arms about herself. "I need to go in. It's getting cold out here." She started to turn away.

"I need to apologize," he said in a rush, reaching for her arm. He couldn't let her just leave.

She froze, not looking at him but not pulling away from his touch.

He looked away from her toward the dunes and the soft shadows of the dune grasses swaying in the slight breeze. How could he tell her that the years of regret had eaten a hole in his gut? That he knew he'd hurt her? That he'd begun countless letters of apology only to rip them all up? That he'd driven by her old house time after time, looking for her, praying for her to come outside because he didn't have the courage to go to her door? How did he put the depth of his remorse into words? *I'm sorry* was so paltry!

"I'm listening," she said quietly.

He let out the breath he hadn't realized he was holding.

"But I reserve the right to rebut." Her words were cool but emphatic.

He blinked. She seemed to expect an argument or a self-serving explanation about their past. Did she think so little of him? He sighed silently. Well, why shouldn't she? He'd done nothing in the intervening years to create goodwill and understanding.

He noted her squared shoulders and hiked chin and almost smiled. She, on the other hand, had grown teeth during those same years.

"What happened between us back then—" She waved her hand vaguely, like it wasn't worth mentioning, like it wasn't important.

But it was, brutally important. It had molded him like no

other single event in his entire life. Surely it had affected her. How could it not have? How could it have devastated him and not touched her?

"It was so long ago," she said softly, looking off toward the sea. "We should just forget it. Accidents happen, right?"

Accidents happen? It chilled him to the bone to hear something of such magnitude to him called a mere accident.

"I can't forget it," he said, taking hold of her shoulders, her very stiff shoulders. "I've felt guilty for years. I was very wrong, and I want you to know that I know that."

She turned her head now and looked at him. He could read nothing in her expression, her eyes dark caves in the moon cast shadows. His face must look dark and unreadable too, but hopefully the sincerity of his voice would reach her.

Oh, Father, please let it reach her.

She twitched her shoulders slightly, saying quite clearly that she didn't want him touching her. He lowered his hands.

"I was the Christian," he said. "I was the one who knew what was acceptable and what wasn't." He reached out, palms up in supplication. "I know it's feeble, and I know it doesn't make things right, but I'm sorry. Please forgive me."

She stood quietly without saying a word, and he began to itch inside.

Say something, he thought. *Anything. Yell. Cry. Sneer. But do or say something!*

"I've struggled over what happened between us a lot." She turned back toward the water, and he had to move closer to hear her soft voice. "I resented you. A lot. I even hated you for a while. You preyed on my loneliness."

"I never meant—"

She turned steady eyes to him. "It doesn't matter what you meant. The fact remains that you did." The anger in her voice ripped his heart. "And I've had trouble coming to terms with that."

Her voice caught on the last word, and he realized suddenly that she hadn't been waving away his words because the event was unimportant but because of the pain she still felt all these years later.

She continued to stare at him. "It seemed that everywhere I turned, you were there even when you were absent. I saw your brother all the time, and it was like looking at you. Then your mother and father became my surrogate parents. They knew nothing of our history, brief though it was, and still don't. But they talked about you, the son they were so proud of, the fine example of all that was good and godly."

He closed his eyes, feeling more a heel than ever. "I'm so sorry." Hollow words.

"When I became a Christian," she said, ignoring his words, "one of the hardest fights for me was to be willing to forgive you." She gave a short laugh totally devoid of humor. "Before you showed up tonight, I thought I'd succeeded."

He found himself staring at his feet, humbled and without defense.

"But maybe I haven't after all." She sighed. "I feel very confused."

She walked toward her front door, and he followed. She stood quietly for a moment, head down. He tried to imagine what she was feeling, thinking, but knew he'd never even come close.

Then she spun and poked a finger in his chest. "And I resent immensely that you can upset me this way." She ground her nail into his breastbone with amazing strength.

"Hey!" He rubbed the crater she'd dug.

"So sorry," she said with complete insincerity.

They stared at each other for a minute, he frowning, she all wide-eyed innocence. He'd never wanted to shake anyone more in his life. Here he was, pouring out his heart, and she was mocking him.

"Shoot-out at the OK Corral," she said suddenly and lifted her index finger, the one that had dislodged a piece of his flesh. She blew across the smoking barrel. "I won."

He stared at her in disbelief.

Slowly her mouth quirked up, and in spite of himself he copied the movement. Suddenly they were both laughing.

"What's so funny?" Billy called as he ran across the yard from the house.

"Nothing special," Clay said. "We're just laughing at old times."

Leigh looked at him and rolled her eyes. "Hah!"

"Hey." Billy stopped in his tracks. "There's Mama."

Clay watched a monster cat amble around the side of the garage. "That's Mama?"

"Isn't she great?" Pride puffed Billy's bony chest.

"Marvelous." Oh, boy. Terror was going to be eaten alive.

Billy picked up the enormous animal and held her in his arms like a baby. She lay there with all the backbone of a jellyfish.

Leigh reached over, rubbing beneath the animal's chin. "What are you doing out here, baby? You're supposed to be in the house." Mama began to purr.

Billy scratched the cat's ears. "But it's more fun out here, isn't it?"

The back door to the main house opened, and Terror came rushing out, all excitement and sass.

"Uh-oh," muttered Clay. He reached for the dog who darted around him with the agility of a matador sidestepping a bull. Terror jumped happily against Billy's leg and froze, staring in surprise at the orange lump draped over Billy's arms. Then he whuffled and whined and gave one stiff bark.

Mama was slow in perceiving the threat because she'd been almost asleep in Billy's warm embrace. The bark brought her to abrupt life. She leaped to the ground and crouched, staring malevolently at the terrier dancing wildly about her. When he took one step too close, Mama reared up on her hind legs and punched him in the snout. Hissing and spitting, she socked the startled dog a second time and a third before he turned tail and ran. He fetched up on the back step, cowering, whining for Julia to open the door and rescue him.

Mama gave a mighty sniff, walked toward the door to the apartment, and disappeared.

Swallowing a laugh so he wouldn't hurt the dog's feelings any more than they were already hurt, Clay turned toward the porch. He patted the side of his leg and crooned, "Come on, Terror, boy. It's okay. The mean kitty's gone. Come on. Be a brave guy."

"Don't be afraid," Billy said, holding out a hand and clicking his fingers. "I'll take care of you, I promise."

For a few minutes the dog wouldn't move. Then he began a wary trek back across the yard, scanning the shadows continually for his enemy. Billy dropped to his knees and hugged the unhappy animal.

"It's okay, buddy. She's gone. She can't hurt you."

Terror gave a low whuffle, comforted but not convinced.

"She's just a nasty bully." Billy patted Terror on the head a few times, then looked at his mother and grinned. "You know how girls are."

"Hah!" said Leigh, eyes sparkling in the light by the door. She turned to Clay. "We girls aren't the ones who kick a person when she's down, then disappear."

"Ouch." Clay rubbed his chest as he watched Leigh move to the apartment door. "A shot directly to the heart."

She was nodding with satisfaction when he saw her freeze and heard her gasp.

"What?" he and Billy asked in unison.

"The door," she whispered. "It's not latched."

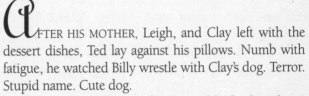

Seven

𝒜FTER HIS MOTHER, Leigh, and Clay left with the dessert dishes, Ted lay against his pillows. Numb with fatigue, he watched Billy wrestle with Clay's dog. Terror. Stupid name. Cute dog.

We should get Mom a dog, he suddenly thought. *A big one. We're kind of isolated out here next to the beach, and it'd be good protection for her. A rottweiler maybe. She'd get a kick out of its brown eyebrows. And it'd keep her from being alone in this large house after I'm gone.*

After I'm gone. He still had trouble grasping the finality of that phrase. Even with the deaths of his father and Matt, it was still difficult to wrap his mind around the idea of not being anymore, at least not being as he knew being. But soon he would be gone; there was no question, especially on days when he felt as awful as he felt today. He knew he was walking through what the psalmist had called "the valley of the shadow of death."

And death cast a large shadow as well as raising a number of questions. After he was gone, Mom would still be here, living in Seaside with Leigh and Billy. Clay would be somewhere, wherever the navy sent him. But question number one: What would happen to Ted after he was gone?

Heaven. He sighed. On days like today it sounded so good.

"Uncle Ted." Billy looked up with his arms wrapped around Terror's neck. The little dog was busily washing the right side of the boy's face.

"Um?" Ted pulled himself from his philosophizing, something he found himself doing more and more often these days.

"Don't you like Clay?" Billy's face was guileless.

Ted blinked. "Of course I like him. He's my brother." Even as he spoke, he knew he wasn't being quite truthful.

"Then did you guys have a fight or something?"

The kid saw way too much. "Why do you ask that?"

Billy shifted slightly, and Terror began on the other side of his face.

"And how can you stand that dog slobber all over you?" Ted shuddered.

Billy looked surprised. "He's just kissing me. He likes me."

"He probably does, but still. He's going to lick your skin right off."

Billy grinned. "Then I'll be a skeleton, and I won't need a Halloween costume. And did you have a fight?"

Ted grimaced. He should have known it wouldn't be that easy to sidetrack a sharpie like Billy. "I wouldn't say we had an argument exactly. We just don't agree on some basic stuff."

Billy nodded. "Like you being gay, I bet."

That was getting to the kernel of the problem, not that he was going to discuss it with a ten-year-old. "It's sort of personal, you know?"

Billy pushed Terror away from his face, and the dog began gnawing on his fist. "You mean you don't want to talk about it."

Ted looked at the boy's earnest eyes watching him through the lens of the wire frames. How many times had Leigh had to replace or repair those glasses? "You'd better put some cream on your face tonight after you wash it, or you'll have chapped cheeks from all that slobber."

"Who says I wash my face?" And Billy turned his concentration to Terror.

Ted fell back into his theological musings with relief. It was safer to think about heaven and God than to talk with the kid when he was being insightful.

What was heaven like? No harps and puffy clouds and halos.

That was the stuff of cartoons. No Saint Peter at the gates. No gigantic scales weighing his good deeds against his bad to see if he was good enough to get in, thank the Lord. He knew he'd fail if that were the way salvation worked.

God. That's what made heaven. Almighty God resided there, if God the Omnipresent could be said to reside anywhere, at least as he understood reside.

And no more suffering or pain. Not that he was enduring pain like a cancer patient did. AIDS didn't always attack a particular body part and destroy it like so many diseases did, inflicting agony upon the victims. It was a systemic immunity problem that affected the whole body, annihilating its ability to deal with germs. You ended up with problems like the herpes sores that currently plagued his mouth or virulent diarrhea or infections like the one that took the vision in his right eye. You could end up with something incredibly painful as the end neared, but basically you wasted away as your body ate itself while it tried to find a way to deal with a problem it could no longer handle. Then you got something like pneumonia, which under normal circumstances was easily dealt with, and boom! No more overwhelming fatigue or unrelenting deterioration.

While he felt God was disappointed in him, and he was mad at God much of the time for the way his life had turned out, when the boom came, he didn't doubt heaven. After all, he trusted in Jesus. He had confidence in the Bible when it said: "Believe on the Lord Jesus Christ, and you will be saved." He'd had a saving faith since he was younger than Billy. Even as he railed against God he believed. He felt like Peter when he said to Jesus, "To whom shall we go? You have the words of eternal life." He might be one of those saved "so as by fire," but he was confident of heaven.

What he wasn't confident of was the next few weeks. The process of dying was hard. He knew. He'd been through it with Matt and several of their friends. His dad had been lucky. Teed up his golf ball and keeled over. No dying. Just dead. Quick and simple. Absent from the body and present with the Lord.

He often speculated on which was easier on the survivors: the quick punch in the gut with no time to prepare or the slow, anguishing process with more than enough time to spare.

One thing was for sure. When he did get to heaven, he had a

few choice words for Adam and Eve about that apple.

Leigh's voice floated up the stairs. "Come on, Billy. Say good night to Ted and Terror."

Billy made a face. "I gotta go."

Ted nodded. "You can be my emissary and protect your mother from my brother."

"Why?" Billy's sharp eyes looked at him. "Clay's nice. Why would he hurt Mom?"

"Don't ask me, guy. Just a gut feeling."

"Billy!" Leigh's patience had obviously run out.

Billy nodded at Ted, ignoring his mother. "I was right. You and Clay do have trouble."

"It's our problem, Billy, not yours. Don't worry yourself about it."

"I have to worry. It concerns you."

Suddenly Ted couldn't swallow around the lump in his throat. If he'd ever had a kid, he'd want him to be just like Billy.

"See, I don't have any brothers or sisters." Billy sat on the edge of the bed, Terror forgotten. "I'm alone. I don't like being alone. If I had a brother as neat as Clay, if I had any brother at all, I'd want to be close to him. That's the way it's supposed to be."

Ted felt all his defensive tendencies rise to the fore. There were a lot of things in his life that weren't the way they were "supposed" to be. The last thing he needed was a lecture from Billy to remind him. "I know that's the way it's supposed to be, but sometimes things happen."

Billy sighed, suddenly looking very young. "I'm making you mad. I'm sorry. I didn't mean to."

"No, I'm not mad. It's just like I said: It's personal."

"Yeah. I know. It's none of my business."

Billy looked down at the floor, and Ted knew he was upset. Usually they could talk about anything, so Billy didn't understand Ted's reticence to discuss something he had trouble even thinking about. He looked at the bright, perceptive face none the worse for all Terror's loving bath and reached out to squeeze Billy's hand. He forced himself to say easily, "Good night, guy. Never forget. I love you."

"Night, Uncle Ted." Billy leaned over and hugged him. "I love you too."

"And I'm not mad," he called as the boy rushed from the

room. His answer was a flick of a hand.

Ted sighed deeply. He hadn't meant to hurt the kid. He didn't mean to hurt any of them, though he knew he did over and over, ad infinitum, forever and ever, amen. Apparently it was his calling in life to inflict pain. Unfortunately he did it with all the Wharton compulsion and aptitude for excellence.

He smiled without humor. If he had a few questions for Adam and Eve, they were nothing compared to the many queries he had for God.

He slumped against the pillows, wearied with thinking and conflict. Much as he loved his family, including Clay, he was relieved that they were all finally gone and he could give in to the overwhelming fatigue. He could slump without anyone rushing to plump his pillows. He could whine without anyone looking hurt or upset. He could throw things.

Didn't he wish. If he could throw just one thing, he'd feel better. He knew it. His blood would start pumping, and his mind would start clicking. But not only wasn't there anything handy to throw, he also didn't have the strength. He, former pitching ace on Seaside's state championship baseball team, could barely throw anything across the room.

Another loss. Life had been reduced to one long string of losses. First had been Dad. He still got a hitch in his heart when he thought of the phone call from his mother telling him his father had dropped over on the golf course with three other doctors for company. Not even their concerted skills had been able to revive him.

It constantly amazed him that his father, Mr. Doctrinal Correctness, Mr. Heart for the Lord, had loved him with all his godly heart in spite of who Ted had become.

"You will always be my son," he told Ted the weekend they'd confronted him about being gay. "I will never agree with what you are doing and the choices you are making, but I will always love you. This will always be your home, and you will always be welcome here."

And he had been welcome. When he finally got up the nerve to bring Matt to the house, he had been welcome too. He'd met Matt at a clinic when they both went in for HIV testing. They'd exchanged phone numbers, and Matt had called to find out Ted's test results.

"Positive," Ted said, the disbelief still strong in his voice.

"Me too. Want to go out to dinner?"

They'd rarely been apart for the next seven years.

He thought of that first visit of Matt's to his parents' house. Both of them had come in with chips on their shoulders: Matt because he viewed life as a never-ending battleground where only his personal vigilance kept the enemies, who were many, at bay; Ted because he wasn't certain how his parents would react to his finally bringing a partner home. To this point his gayness had been only in vague generalities. Matt, a tall handsome blond with a rapier wit, was very specific.

Mom and Dad hadn't been happy, and Ted suspected she cried after they left. He was just glad he and Matt lived close enough that spending the night was never an issue. He knew his parents wouldn't allow him and Matt to share a room under their roof. But they'd opened their door to Matt and fed him and loved him and even got him to lower his guard around them.

The first time Mom had sent Matt off with a kiss on the cheek just like she gave Ted, Matt had almost swooned.

"They like me. They really like me." He shook his head in wonder. "And I sound like Sally Fields giving that Oscar acceptance speech."

Ted sighed as he stared at his ceiling. He'd lost Matt too, last year. Mom had invited him to bring Matt home to die where she could help care for him, but he'd wanted that last gift of love for himself. Many, many days he was angry at God, but he was genuinely thankful that God had allowed him to stay well long enough to care for Matt.

And because of his parents, Matt had been able to trust Jesus.

"But I'm gay," he told Dad during one of their discussions. "Christians hate gays."

"Why do you say that?" Dad asked.

"I read the papers. 'God hates faggots,'" he quoted.

Dad nodded sadly. "Just don't forget that I'm a Christian, and I don't hate gays. You have to decide which one of us represents Jesus best."

It was a week after Dad's funeral, a glorious celebration of hope in Christ, when Matt had said, "I want to have the hope everyone has about your father. I feel myself slipping, and I'm getting scared. I need that hope."

"Then you need Jesus," Ted told him.

"But I'm gay."

"Yeah, I know."

"What if I can't change?"

"Matt, all I know is that Jesus said, 'I am the way, the truth, and the life. No one comes to the Father except through Me.' Salvation comes from believing that. Change comes after belief, not before."

Matt had gone for a long walk on the beach to wrestle the issue out. He'd come back with a smile. "I believe."

There had been changes, the biggest being the peace with which Matt now faced his deteriorating health and imminent death. He frequently read the Bible Mom gave him and asked questions incessantly. One of Ted's favorite memories was of Matt lying on the sofa, his Bible in one hand and a yellow highlighter in the other.

"Did Jonah and the whale really happen?" Or "What did Jesus do those three days he was dead?" Or "When the Bible says we should love our enemies, does that mean the 'God hates faggots' guy too?"

One day Matt looked at Ted and said, "We can't have sex anymore. It's wrong. The Bible says so right here at the beginning of Romans."

Dumbfounded, Ted stared first at Matt, then at the Bible resting in Matt's lap. If the Holy Spirit had punched him in the jaw, he couldn't have been thrown any more off balance.

"Well," Ted finally mumbled, "you're getting too sick anyway."

Matt shook his head. "I'm choosing. I chose to believe, and now I'm choosing to obey."

Ted made an inarticulate noise, the best he could manage in light of the fierce anger and swirling guilt that swamped him.

"It's funny, but I find myself thinking differently about things." Matt slid the cap of his highlighter on and off as he talked, the click-click rubbing at Ted's raw nerves. "I want to do what pleases God. Me, the guy who spent a lifetime scoffing at people who talked like they knew Him."

He looked at Ted, his eyes concerned. "My biggest dilemma is that if I choose to make God happy, I think I'm hurting you."

Ted flapped a hand through the air, hoping he looked unaffected by Matt's comments when in actuality he was devastated.

And the rejection as partner was the least of the pain. "Don't even worry about hurting me. I know you well enough to know you wouldn't ever be purposely unkind—at least to me."

Matt nodded acknowledgment at that reference to his often sharp tongue.

"You do what you need to." Ted slid down in his chair and reached for the TV remote. He didn't care what was on. Anything to halt this conversation. "I understand." He barely flinched as he told the lie. In truth he couldn't believe the depth of Matt's commitment to the Lord. All the man was supposed to do was get saved, get a guarantee of heaven. He wasn't supposed to become godly!

"Who'd have believed it?" Matt said, grinning, oblivious to Ted's distress. "Me, choosing to make God happy and choosing to be celibate. Almost like a priest, huh?"

Ted threw the remote down and stalked to the door. This time it was he who went for a long walk, and when he came back, he was still wrestling valiantly with God, refusing to acknowledge any wrong, any guilt. But he did understand that Matt's faith was the rock that would carry him through his final weeks, and so he carefully said nothing that would undermine the joy and hope his partner found in it.

Matt slipped into his final coma with a smile.

After that wrenching loss, Ted hadn't cared when his own health began to slip; when his vigor, for years carefully tended with diet and exercise and the latest medical treatments, diminished; when he lost weight and even lost the vision in one eye to infection before they found the right medicine.

But he did care that today he had lost his dignity. His twin, his impeccable, perfect, you'd-better-salute-me brother had seen him too weak to eat Junket. He'd watched eagle-eyed as Leigh tended his personal needs. He'd looked down that long nose so like Ted's own and barely avoided sneering.

"Judge not that you be not judged," Ted wanted to yell at him. He didn't, of course. It would have just made him look petty while Clay looked ever more the hero.

It wouldn't hurt so much if he didn't love Clay so much. They were twins! They'd been conceived at the exact same second, been born within minutes of each other, and shared everything for years.

Suddenly the little dog was on the bed again, and Ted smiled in spite of himself. He rubbed the dog's ears and enjoyed the feel of the warm body pressed against him.

"Terror." The dog smiled at him. "Stupid name for a cutie like you."

The terrier wagged his tail so hard Ted was certain he was going to wag it right off. The whole bed shook under the animal's delight. He licked Ted's hand, and to his disgust, Ted felt tears clog his throat. He jerked his hand away. "I'm not so pitiful that I need to cry when a dog likes me!" His voice was low and mean. He hated the emotional vulnerability that came with severe illness. He'd seen it in Matt when the most unexpected things would move him and make him weepy. He wasn't going to be like that. Clay'd enjoy it too much. "Go away, you mutt!"

Terror stood and cocked his head, not understanding the sudden change. He gave a little confused whuffle.

Ted felt ashamed. It wasn't the dog's fault his life was in the toilet. If he were honest, it wasn't Clay's either. Ted had made his own choices, no matter how much he'd felt forced to make them.

"I'm sorry, boy." He held his hand out to Terror. "How about another kiss?"

This time when the tears came, he just sniffed them back and kept rubbing the terrier's head.

He felt his mother's presence before he looked up at her. He willed himself to look strong. "Hey, Mom."

She crossed the room and sat on the edge of the bed. She reached out a hand to brush his hair back. "Hey, yourself." Her hand fell and began to pet the dog.

"Cute little guy, isn't he?"

"He loves you, Ted," and he knew she didn't mean Terror. "He just doesn't know how to deal with everything."

Ted knew his skepticism hurt her.

"He does," she reiterated, her eyes pleading for his understanding, his agreement. "And you love him. You've got to set things straight between you."

His back went up. "Me? He's the one who's cold and withdrawn and can't stand being near me."

She patted his hand lightly. "Pride's one of the seven deadly sins, you know." With that parting shot, she rose, kissed his cheek, and left, taking Terror downstairs to let him out.

"Thanks, Mom," he muttered to her back. "Now I'll really have a good night's sleep."

But he knew she was right. He and Clay did have to make peace. He just didn't know what to do about it, especially when pride was about all he had left.

Eight

LEIGH STARED AT her unlatched door while her heart beat double time. It was such a slight crack, a small breach, yet it signified great potential trouble.

"Billy, did you go inside and forget to close the door when you came back out?" she asked, the tension with Clay all but forgotten.

He was quick to shake his head. "No, Mom. I haven't been home since before dinner."

Leigh's hand hovered over the knob.

Clay grabbed her wrist, startling her. "Don't touch it."

"Yeah, yeah," she said, pulling her hand free and tucking it behind her back. "I know. I wasn't going to. Really."

He raised that eyebrow. "Then what were you doing? Voodooing the opening away?"

She slanted him a look. "Funny."

His quick grin slid into a frown as he studied the door. He reached out with his elbow and pushed against the door.

"What are *you* doing?" Leigh demanded, grabbing his arm.

He looked at her like that was the dumbest question he'd ever heard. "I'm going to check to see what's wrong."

"You're just going to waltz in there?"

He nodded.

"What if someone's up there?"

He shrugged. "I know how to take care of myself."

"I'll go with you," Billy said, rushing eagerly forward.

"Not on your life!" Leigh released Clay and grabbed Billy as he tried to push past her.

"You are not going in there, champ," Clay said sternly.

"Why not? It's my house. And I can take care of myself too."

Leigh made a disgusted noise. "I'm gagging on machismo here." She moved in front of her door. "No one's going inside but the police."

Clay rolled his eyes.

"I mean it." She glared at Clay for an instant, then lowered her sights to Billy. "Everyone to the main house. We'll call the police from there."

For a minute she thought Clay might move her bodily out of his way and charge in regardless. She looked at him, then at Billy, pleading that he understand her fear for her son.

Apparently he got her message because with an exasperated sigh, he turned and began walking. "Come on, Billy. We'll make your mother happy and call the cops."

Breathing a sigh of relief, Leigh hurried across the lawn to the comforting light of Julia's kitchen. She didn't realize she had Billy by the hand until he pulled free.

"I can walk from here to there by myself, Mom." He cast an embarrassed look at Clay.

"Sorry," she muttered as she slid through the door that Clay held open. She grabbed the wall phone and dialed 911. She answered all the dispatcher's questions but declined to remain on the line. She didn't need electronic hand-holding.

Julia had apparently gone up to bed, and they didn't call her or Ted. It made no sense to upset either of them and give them another reason to have trouble sleeping, especially since they didn't know yet how serious the problem was.

The three of them waited on the back steps of the main house, Billy seated in the middle. In a town the size of Seaside, a response to an emergency was never long in coming—unless you were unfortunate enough to need the one off-season night patrol after someone else beat you to it. But tonight they apparently had first dibs.

The police car, metallic blue with a huge, swirling cream logo with red and black letters reading Seaside Police and Dial 911 pulled quietly up the drive and parked in the turnaround.

Billy watched their arrival in disgust. "My one chance to have the cops rescue me with sirens and flashing lights and excitement, and look what happens. They tiptoe! You drive wilder than they do, Mom."

She bit back a smile. "This isn't TV land, you know. It's Seaside."

He snorted.

When Greg Barnes climbed out of the driver's side, Leigh breathed more easily. Given her family's long and complicated acquaintance with the local cops, she never knew what any meeting with them might bring. A couple of the older officers who had dealt for years with her father tended to treat her as his extension, something she understood but chafed at. Like father, like son—or daughter—might work many times, but she was a distinct exception, thank God. Greg Barnes knew that and treated her as a person in her own right, not Johnny Spenser's daughter.

"Hey, Leigh," Greg said. "You have a break-in?"

Leigh stood, dusting off the seat of her jeans. "It looks that way. The door I left locked is slightly opened."

"Back at your place and not at Julia's, huh?"

Leigh nodded. "Weird, isn't it?"

Greg scratched his head. "They must be after all that high tech stuff you've got up there. Or maybe it's all the family heirlooms you've got stashed under the floorboards. Every smart thief knows seemingly innocent garage apartments are really storehouses for vast wealth." He grinned at her, inviting her to enjoy his little joke.

Leigh accommodated him with a grin, and Billy actually laughed.

Greg Barnes was a nice guy and always had been. She'd met him the first day of kindergarten as she stood in the hall outside Miss Grover's room, trembling with fear. All the other girls looked so pretty in their pink and purple outfits, and they seemed to know what they were doing as they walked in giggling clumps into the room. They carried colorful book bags that were clean and new and had Mickey Mouse and Barbie on them. All she had was a little case of pencils and a pretty pink eraser. Somehow she knew that wasn't enough. And the jeans that didn't quite reach her ankles and had big scuffs for knees weren't right either.

She had thought school would be so much fun. She would learn to read and write, not just make squiggly lines that her mother made believe told stories, but write real words that she could read too. But everybody was busy, too busy to help a scared, skinny little girl who tried to disappear into the lime green wall.

Then Greg, a big third grader, had walked up, shirt pulled halfway out of his jeans and hair hanging in his eyes. He looked at her and frowned. She felt her stomach turn over and pressed even harder into the wall.

"Don't be afraid," he told her, smiling. "Miss Grover's real nice, and she likes cute little girls like you."

She stared in amazement at the big boy. He called her a cute little girl. Her daddy always told her she looked like the missing link. She didn't know what the missing link was, but she knew from the way he said it that it wasn't good.

"I'm Greg," he said. "What's your name?"

She wanted to tell him, but she couldn't open her mouth. She was afraid she'd throw up.

"Cat got your tongue?" He grinned. "That's okay, cutie. You can tell me later." He took her hand and led her into the room. "I'll take care of you."

To the best of her knowledge he'd been taking care of people ever since.

He looked up at the windows of Leigh's apartment, all dark except one.

She followed his sight line. "We always leave that one on. Living room."

He nodded, adjusting his gun on his hip.

"No one's come out since we saw the open door." Clay stood behind Leigh.

Greg nodded, then seemed to register Clay for the first time. "Clay." He put out a hand. "I'm glad you're here. Your mom sure needs you right now."

Clay reached around Leigh and shook hands with the man he hadn't seen for years. "Filled out a little, haven't you?" he asked with a smile.

Greg, who was four inches taller and fifty pounds heavier than he'd been at his high school graduation, just grinned. Greg nodded toward his young partner. "Pete and I are going to check things out. Go inside Julia's until one of us calls an all clear."

Nodding, Leigh grabbed her son's collar and pushed him inside ahead of her. She knew he'd follow the cops if he could. Clay closed the door behind the three of them.

"Get away from that window, Billy," Leigh ordered as he ran to the windows over the sink. He turned and gave her a disgusted look. "I mean it. What if there's shooting?"

"And what if I miss it?" he countered, but he moved from the window.

They sat at the kitchen table, listening intently, but they heard nothing. In a couple of minutes, Pete stuck his head in the door.

"It's safe," he announced. "Nobody's there."

"Thank goodness." Leigh slouched in relief.

Pete's young face puckered. "Don't get too relaxed too fast."

"What?" she demanded, straightening.

"There was definitely someone up there, and he wasn't very respectful."

Leigh shut her eyes. She was afraid she knew exactly what Pete meant.

"How bad is the damage?" Clay asked, obviously thinking the same thing she was.

Pete shrugged. "I've seen worse."

Now there's a statement that offers me great comfort.

"We need you to come check for missing stuff."

They were moving toward the door when Clay laid a hand on Billy's shoulder, drawing him to a halt.

"Just how serious is this?" Clay asked Pete again.

Leigh realized what he was really asking was whether Billy should be allowed to go with them. She didn't know whether to cry or get very angry at this show of concern almost eleven years too late.

"I'm not staying here," Billy said with more than a touch of defiance. "It's my house."

"You're staying here if your mom says you are." Clay's voice was crisp and commanding, his military background very clear. Even Pete looked impressed.

"How bad is it?" Leigh asked.

Pete waved a hand dismissively. "Messy but not violent. I think it's okay."

Billy started for the door, but Clay held on. "Leigh?"

She looked through the window toward the apartment. "It's okay, I think."

Clay nodded and released his grip on Billy's shoulder. The boy bolted for the door, before his mom changed her mind, and glued himself to Pete's side.

"Thank you," Leigh said as she walked across the lawn beside Clay.

He grinned at her. "Your kid, your call." He stepped back to let her precede him up the stairs.

As she climbed, she pondered how his one act of consideration and respect had undercut her previous anger. She was still very confused about how she should feel toward him, but she no longer wanted to punch him. If only she weren't so afraid of the consequences of having him around.

She bumped into Billy who had stopped abruptly at the top of the stairs. As she looked over his shoulder, she understood why and groaned along with him.

The living room was a shambles. Books littered the floor while empty bookshelves gaped. Sofa cushions were thrown about the room, and two philodendrons lay on the floor on their sides, soil leaking like blood. The desk had been emptied onto the sofa, and her school papers tumbled from the canvas carryall onto the floor.

Her eyes sought the one good thing she had, a Royal Doulton figurine that had been her mother's. Two Regency era ladies sat on a sofa gossiping, their delicate features serene and lovely. Where her mother had gotten the beautiful piece, Leigh had never known. She just knew her mother cherished it, and for that reason so did she. If it had been harmed...

But there it was, sitting on the floor beside the end table with the drawer in it. Or usually in it. The drawer itself had been pulled out, and its contents, an assortment of pens, pencils, rubber bands, a deck of cards, scraps of paper, directions for games and warranties for appliances, littered the carpet. But the china ladies in their crimson and teal dresses were fine.

Her relief brought tears to her eyes. She blinked furiously, for some reason unwilling to let all the men see how emotionally vulnerable she was feeling. It was unbelievable that someone could invade her home and in that one uncaring act rip her small secure world to shreds, or rip what was left of it after Clay's invasion.

But why her apartment? Anyone with any sense knew there was nothing worth stealing here. People with things worth taking didn't live over garages. They lived in big houses with electronic security systems and very large dogs.

God, what's going on here?

Of course there was no answer. She reached for the Royal Doulton ladies and saw that her hands shook. She set the ladies back on the end table and stuck her hands in her pockets.

Her bedroom and Billy's had suffered the same casual contempt as the living room with no real damage but lots of disturbance. In the bathroom the commode was full of toilet paper, and the sink was a masterpiece of modern art worked in toothpaste. She felt exposed as she thought about someone rummaging through her medicine cabinet and, even worse, pawing through her underwear. Some things were just too private for anyone to see!

The kitchen fared the worst. Syrup, peanut butter, and flour had been smeared together and used to coat the counter and the table. Most terrible of all, the sink had been stoppered, and the water left on to overflow. The floor was a shallow lake, the water contained by the metal strip that separated the vinyl kitchen floor from the hardwood of the living room. The little throw rug that sat before the sink floated like a low pile life raft.

"The water was on in the bathtub too," Greg said as they stood in the doorway surveying the kitchen flood, "but it hadn't gotten to the point of overflowing." He looked at the amount of water in the kitchen, then at Leigh. "He left fairly recently."

She shivered. What if she and Billy had come home while he was still here? She felt Clay's hand rest on her shoulder, doubtless offering sympathy or support. She shivered again.

"Don't let it bother you, Leigh. I'll mop up here," Clay said. "You go with Greg."

She nodded and moved from under his hand into the living room.

"Paperwork," Greg said. "Pete, get the information we need, please."

Pete sat in her rocking chair and set his clipboard on his knee. His pen was poised over a form.

"Your name?"

"Leigh Wilson Spenser." Her answer was absently given as she righted a philodendron. She tried to pick up the scattered dirt with her fingers, but it was useless. She needed the vacuum.

"S-p-e-n-c-e-r?"

"No, it's L-e-i-g-h S-p-e-n-s-e-r."

"S-p-e-n-s-e-r?" Pete looked at her with sudden interest. "As in Johnny?" It was obvious that he had just made the connection.

"As in Leigh," she said coldly.

"Right, but are you the daughter of Joh—"

Greg cut him off. "Did you know that Leigh was my daughter's teacher last year, Pete?" He smiled sweetly at Leigh. "She was Jenn's favorite teacher by far."

Leigh nodded her thanks for his turning the topic.

"Jenn's in my class," said Billy, who appeared from the bathroom with a wad of paper toweling full of mopped-up toothpaste. "For a girl she's pretty cool."

Leigh looked at him closely. Had he heard that reference to his grandfather? She wouldn't be surprised if he had and was helping Greg derail Pete's unpleasant, unprofessional prying.

"Jenn's okay for a girl, huh?" said Greg. "You have a quarrel with girls?"

Billy thought for a moment. "Not a quarrel. I just don't know what they're here for."

Greg shrugged. "They grow up to make good moms."

Billy glanced at Leigh as she tugged the vacuum out of the closet. "That's true."

"And they've got to be in fifth grade on the way to growing up, don't they?"

Leigh watched Billy frown over that thought as she flicked the vacuum on, effectively ending any conversation, good or bad. She swept long after the rug was clean, ignoring Pete and his partially filled-out form. Finally, Greg tapped her on the shoulder.

She flicked off the sweeper and looked at him.

"Just answer the questions, Leigh." Greg gave his young partner the evil eye. "He won't ask anything improper."

Pete made no more comments about Johnny, but he followed her movements with an avid and discomfiting curiosity. What did he think? That she was a criminal just like her father? That she'd done this to her own home, maybe for the insurance?

Or that she just wanted the attention?

She'd known when she let Will and Julia talk her into coming back to Seaside that people here would always connect her with Johnny. History died hard in small towns. She'd considered the stigma of being recognized as Johnny's daughter a small price to pay for the benefits of being loved by Will, Julia, and Ted and being treated as part of their family, however fragile the connection.

Over time, though, most people learned to separate her from her father. She was Leigh Spenser: teacher, friend, fellow congregant, and Billy's mother. But new people were invariably intrigued or titillated. She doubted that would ever change or that she'd ever get used to it.

When Greg finally left, dragging his partner behind him, Leigh heaved a sigh of relief. She stood at the top of the stairs until the door below shut firmly behind them. Then she sagged against the wall and rubbed the spot above her eye where a headache hammered. All she wanted was to fall in bed and sleep forever or until the problems went away. She sighed. With her luck, forever would probably come first.

Maybe if she went to the kitchen and helped Clay finish mopping up the water, she'd forget her headache. Or at least the pain wouldn't swamp her. It felt too much to ask that it go away, especially since the main cause was the man in the kitchen as opposed to the one who had broken in.

There might not be much she could do about Clay, but she could at least help him. It was, after all, her kitchen he was mopping up, and the faster it got mopped, the faster he'd leave. She turned, and for the second time that evening she bumped into the solid wall of his chest.

The dam broke.

It wasn't that she hurt herself crashing into him. It was just that the collision was the culmination of one of the worst days of her life. She sobbed and sobbed, first into her hands, then into his chest as he wrapped his arms around her. She was humiliated and comforted at the same time.

"You shouldn't sneak up on people!" she managed when she was finally able to draw a shaky breath. "It's not nice."

"Shh, Leigh," he whispered, rocking her gently. "Shh. It's going to be all right."

Fat lot you know! She clenched her fists against his chest and cried harder.

"Mom?"

Billy's scared voice put the starch back in Leigh's spine. She straightened and scrubbed at her eyes.

"I'm fine, Billy." She sniffed and wiped her nose with the back of her hand. "Don't worry."

Billy looked completely unconvinced.

"She'll probably punch me for saying this," Clay said as he offered her a clean handkerchief. "But it's a girl thing, crying like this."

Leigh punched him on cue and had to smile as he grabbed his stomach and moaned dramatically. She heard a rocky giggle from Billy.

She reached out for the boy, and he came into her hug with all the need of a kid whose world has been knocked awry. It might have been exciting while you waited for the police, but it was scary when you saw your room torn up, your models knocked on the floor, your clothes heaped into a miniature mountain on your bed, your cat's dry food soggy and floating in the kitchen lake, and your mother crying.

"It'll be okay," she said, kissing Billy's temple. "We've survived worse than this, and we'll survive this too."

He didn't even pull away. In fact, if anything, he burrowed closer.

"Come on, everyone," Clay said as he wrapped an arm about Billy's shoulders. "It's time for a group hug." His other arm pulled Leigh close. "The ultimate comfort."

The three of them huddled together in a welter of entwined arms, and Leigh felt some of her tension dissolve. It seemed the most natural thing in the world for Clay to begin to pray.

"Father, we need You right now. I ask You to be with Billy and help him feel relaxed. May he know Your peace. And I ask the same for Leigh, Lord. She's had a rough hit with this vandalism. Help her feel safe and at ease in her own home. We thank You that there is no real damage. And I thank You that we didn't meet the intruder."

Leigh listened to Clay's words and felt more tension slough away. Billy seemed to relax too. She realized that his head almost rested on her shoulder. She smiled, thinking how tall her baby was growing. He rested against her at the same spot she rested against Clay.

Against Clay.

At that thought she stiffened and lifted her head. "Thanks, Clay." She hoped her voice didn't sound too clipped.

Act naturally.

She pulled away as gently as she could and ruffled Billy's hair. "I think you need to go to bed, sweetie. We'll finish cleaning up tomorrow."

"My bed's all messed up."

She nodded. "Just push anything on it onto the floor."

He grinned impishly. "That's what I do every night."

"Tell me something I don't know," she told his retreating back.

She stepped well away from Clay and said formally, "Thank you for all your help."

He looked at her, a half smile curving his lips. "You are more than welcome."

She flushed. "I guess I'll see you tomorrow."

"It'll be hard to miss me."

Don't I know it. "Good night."

He nodded and started down the stairs, recognizing a dismissal when he heard one. He stopped halfway down and looked up at her, concern written clearly in his eyes. "Are you certain you're all right?"

"Sure," she said, reminding herself that she didn't need or want his concern. Too little too late.

The phone rang, and both of them turned toward it, startled. Leigh reached for it as it lay on the floor beside the rocker. She expected to hear Greg or Pete asking some question about the vandalism. She couldn't think of anyone else who would call at this late hour.

"Hello, Leigh-Leigh?"

The blood drained from her face.

"I know you have the treasure, and I'm afraid I want it."

"W-what treasure?" she whispered, turning frantic eyes to Clay.

"Leigh, what's wrong?" He tore up the steps and to her side.

The voice, husky and somewhat hostile, slithered through the phone and wrapped around her, squeezing the air from her lungs.

"This evening is just a warning to let you know how serious I am."

She stood frozen and dumb, unable to respond.

"The treasure, Leigh-Leigh?" he repeated.

She jerked and repeated, "What treasure?"

"Don't play games with me, girl. I mean it."

"I believe you." She gripped the phone so tightly her hand cramped. She looked at the books lying helter-skelter and saw through the door to her bedroom all the chaos there. "I believe you."

He gave a soft, very nasty chuckle. "That's a cute boy you have there."

Her legs would no longer hold her as terror bit deep, and she sank to the floor. Clay grabbed the phone as she fell.

"Who is this?" he demanded. Almost immediately he slammed the phone in the cradle. "He hung up on me!"

She nodded, not surprised. It wasn't Clay he wanted to talk to; it was Johnny Spenser's daughter.

"He called me Leigh-Leigh," she said as Clay reached for her and lifted her to her feet. She grabbed his arms to hold herself steady and stared without seeing at the third button on his shirt. "No one ever called me Leigh-Leigh but my father." *And he did it because he knew I hated it.*

She felt the shock go through Clay as it had gone through her.

"But your father's dead."

"I know." Her teeth were chattering. "It wasn't him."

"Someone he knew. From prison?"

"I don't know," she managed to whisper.

He led her to the sofa and pushed her gently down. He sat beside her and tried to pull her into his arms. She knew he was just trying to comfort her, and she craved that comfort, oh, how she craved it. But in some small area of her mind, she was enough aware of the danger he represented to stay sitting stiffly on the edge of the cushions.

"He wants the treasure." She stared at her clasped hands, then up at him.

"The treasure?" Clay frowned. "What treasure?"

She shook her head, dazed.

"You have no idea?"

"None." And she couldn't think clearly enough to formulate one.

"Could your father have hidden some money somewhere?"

She thought of her father sitting in front of the TV summer and winter in his sleeveless undershirt, beer in hand. If he had money, he might not have moved from his chair or put on a decent shirt, but he would have drunk better beer, imported beer, designer beer.

"Oh, look at them fancy beers they're advertising," he'd sneer. "So la-dee-da." And he'd look at his bottle with disgust. "Get me a new bottle, Leigh-Leigh. It'll taste just as good as those. Yeah, it will."

But it didn't, or at least he thought it didn't. And he wanted those fancy beers so much he'd have bought them if there'd been money.

She shook her head at Clay. "We never had money."

"Maybe he stole it. Before his last job, I mean. And hid it." Clay looked uncomfortable, as if he didn't want to hurt her. As if her father's reputation were a secret or something.

She shook her head again. "I don't think so. You have to be good at your work or incredibly lucky to steal any amount of money and get away with it. Believe me, Johnny was neither."

Clay was studying her carefully. She could feel his eyes on her. *Go home,* she thought. *Leave me alone. Don't be nice. I can't deal with your being nice.*

He shifted on the sofa, and she thought he was rising, preparatory to leaving. She turned to him, knowing her eyes were huge and frightened and needy.

Don't go! I'm scared!

But he was only turning to face her more directly, his concern for her evident as he placed one of his huge hands over hers. She stared at his hand, so large it overwhelmed her smaller ones. She kept her head lowered to veil the need, the panic, the relief that he wasn't leaving, and resented the comfort his touch gave her.

Of course, considering the night she'd had, it could be anyone's touch, and she'd feel better. At that thought she felt relief and let the resentment slip away. All that was left was mind-numbing fear.

"There's more, isn't there?" he finally said. "Something he said at the end when you collapsed."

She shuddered, her hands beneath his gripping each other so tightly that the knuckles were white. "He threatened Billy."

Nine

HE LAY WITHOUT moving, as invisible as could be, watching for her to come out of the main house. The dunes were a great hiding place even if the sand got kind of cold after a while. And hard. Funny when sand looked so soft and inviting that it was actually so hard.

He lay on his belly behind a clump of dune grass. The night was real dark except for that little bit of moon, and he was wearing all black. He even had some black stuff on his face like the army guys before a fight. And he wore a black knit cap pulled down over his ears.

He felt safe burrowed in the dunes, even from the ocean. The ocean gave him the creeps. It kept moving all the time. Big waves, little waves, high tide, low tide. It was too much like a living thing for him, like a scary alien or something in one of those space shows on TV. And it was gray-green, not clear and sparkly like a pool. He liked pools. No surprises. With the ocean you couldn't see what was waiting to get you. He'd seen *Jaws* lots of times and all the other deep-sea creature movies. He knew what lived in there, and he knew you never saw any of them until they grabbed you. No way was he ever going in it!

He shuddered at the very thought and scrunched more deeply into the dune. He sighed, content. He didn't have to worry about anyone sneaking up behind him here in his hiding place. There were more dunes between him and the ocean, and the grass added extra cover.

His brother used to like to sneak up behind him.

"Hey, twerp," he'd yell as he grabbed him around the neck. And squeezed.

The first time Stanley grabbed him like that he'd wet his pants. He'd been so scared! Stanley was big and strong and mean and liked to hurt people and animals. On TV brothers were nice to each other even if they had fights every so often. Stanley was never nice to him. When Stanley got killed in Vietnam, he'd been happy even though he knew from TV that he should be sad.

He bet that even the TV brothers would have been glad if Stanley had been their brother and tried to choke them all the time.

He remembered how he tried to pry Stanley's fingers off his throat, but he was too little and too weak. He struggled and struggled while his vision grew dimmer and dimmer. Stanley laughed that scary laugh of his as he squeezed, the laugh that meant he was going to hurt someone.

He had hated being that someone!

He never went to his parents for protection or help. He learned that lesson the day he and Stanley were playing carpenter with an old hammer they found. Stanley hit him in the finger with the hammer real hard. Just pounded and pounded.

"Kill it, kill it," he muttered with every blow.

It hurt real bad and got all swoll up and turned black-and-blue. He learned later that he should have put some ice on it, but he didn't know that then. He was only five. Stanley was seven.

Crying, his wounded hand cradled in his good hand, he'd gone to the old man who was sitting in his favorite chair watching wrestling.

"It's your problem. You take care of it," his father said with a sneer and a backhand across the mouth. "That's how you learn to be a man."

"But, Dad," he sniffed, a tear falling onto his mangled fingers. "It hurts."

The old man climbed out of his chair and leaned over him, both fists clenched. "Don't snivel! Do you hear me? Don't ever snivel! I can't stand crybabies." He raised his hand.

Broken fingers held to his chest, he escaped and never complained to his father about Stanley again.

Ma was usually too drunk to be of much help with anything. When she did say something, she always yelled at him even if whatever was going on wasn't his fault. And it was never his fault.

"What do you mean telling stories about Shtanley like that, you little liar?" she slurred. "He'sh a good boy, Shtanley is. You're not. He's big and strong and handsome. You're little and ugly and a liar."

So Stanley crept up on him for years.

It was a while before it dawned on him to make choking sounds before he felt like he was choking. He'd make the noises, then just go limp, and his brother would drop him. He'd end up in a heap on the ground, lying as still as he possibly could. He made believe he was dead. He even tried not to breathe. Then his brother would laugh again, a different laugh, a happy laugh, and go away. He thought he'd won.

But Stanley hadn't won. He'd won, and he loved the feeling of beating Stanley, even if Stanley didn't know it. Especially if Stanley didn't know it. It was his private secret. It made him feel smart, like a genius or something, and it gave him power.

Now he was going to beat Leigh-Leigh and get the treasure. If he could beat big, mean Stanley, he knew he could beat her. He was the one with the power. He was the one who would make her afraid. She was only a girl.

He grinned. He sort of liked Leigh-Leigh. He'd been watching her for days now, and she seemed real nice, especially to that Julia lady and the AIDS guy, though how she could be nice to someone sick like that, he didn't understand. Wasn't she afraid of catching it?

And she was pretty. Real pretty. He liked her curls. They were always flying all over her face. Maybe she was a bit skinny. Maybe? There was no maybe about it; she was skinny. He grinned. Of course he liked girls like the ones on calendars. Leigh-Leigh'd never make a calendar, never ever. Still she was pretty in her own way. And nice. He wondered why Johnny didn't like her.

Of course, Johnny was slime. His best friend, but slime.

He watched her to go up to the door, the kid and the brother trailing behind. Here came the good part. His breath came fast. All she had to do was go inside. Would she scream when she got upstairs? He hoped she'd scream loud enough for him to hear. It'd be so great to make her scream that loud.

But no! They walked back to the big house. *Not there,* he wanted to scream. *Upstairs! Upstairs!*

He moved forward into the yard and watched through the window as she used the phone. It was a quick call. Who would she talk to this late?

He almost choked when the door flew open. They were coming out! He rushed back to the dunes and dived behind the first mound of sand he came to, getting a mouthful of grit in the process. Gag! He spit and spit and spit. He rubbed his sleeve across his tongue and tried to work up some more saliva. He knew he was stuck with an ugly mouth for the rest of the night, and it was Leigh-Leigh's fault. He wouldn't forget that.

Muttering to himself, he climbed the dune and slowly raised his head to see if they'd seen him. They hadn't. They were just sitting there on the back step like they were waiting for something, her and the kid and the brother guy. But what was she waiting for?

Women. They never did what you thought they should.

He blinked in surprise when he saw the police car pull into the drive. He rubbed his suddenly sweaty hands over his jeans seat. He always got nervous when he saw the cops. Then he grinned. He'd forgotten. They didn't know he was here. He was invisible.

He grinned wider as the police went into her apartment alone, just like there was a dangerous person waiting in the dark rooms.

Out here, he wanted to yell. *Your dangerous person is out here!*

Got that, Stanley? I'm dangerous!

Leigh-Leigh, the kid, and the brother guy went in next. He waited with growing impatience and an ever deepening chill. After forever the police finally left, but the brother guy stayed.

He lay there in the sand with his cell phone in his hand and fumed. The brother guy was not part of the plan. Then he thought, *Why can't the brother guy be there when I call? I'll just scare him too!*

Feeling invincible in the dark, he dialed. Leigh-Leigh answered, and he told her everything he'd planned. He made his voice as low and mean as he could. He could hear that she was afraid, really afraid. He smiled. Power. It was his.

Then the brother guy snatched the phone and yelled at him.

He dropped his own phone on the sand in surprise. He grabbed it and punched off. He slithered backward off his dune and raced to the beach. He ran until he came to the house of the rich guy and his drunk wife, the one with all the windows. He ran into their backyard and hid behind their garage.

When he had the courage to look behind him, he sagged against the garage side when he saw the brother guy wasn't on his tail. No Stanley tonight.

As he tried to catch his breath from his race across the beach, he replayed the phone conversation in his mind. He smiled. Leigh-Leigh was scared, real scared. Her voice shook and everything. The shaking was almost as good as a scream.

Satisfied with his night's work, he sneaked from his hiding place, his mind full of the next step in his plan. He'd show her he meant business, he would. When she saw what was going to happen next, she'd run to him with the treasure as fast as her little legs could carry her.

Still grinning, he crept by the big house with all the windows. Movement in the big room with the TV caught his eye. He turned his head and watched the rich guy pop his wife right in the jaw. She went down fast, out cold, spilling her drink all over her husband and the floor. The rich guy stared at her for a minute, then walked from the room. He stared at her for a minute too. When he saw her chest was still moving up and down, he nodded. She'd be all right. He went on his way.

But he knew he'd never hit Leigh-Leigh like that. Never.

She was too nice.

Ten

TWO HOURS LATER, Leigh stared through the darkness at the ceiling of her bedroom. She was so tired both physically and emotionally that she was desperate for sleep. If she slept, she wouldn't think, at least not consciously. And she wanted not to think. She needed not to think.

But sleep eluded her.

I'll pray! That always calms me down. In fact, it calms me so much it sometimes puts me to sleep at night. Sorry, Lord, but it does.

But she couldn't marshal her thoughts enough to pray. Instead she saw vignettes, little movies unreeling through her mind.

She saw Clay staring at her across Ted's room, watching…watching.

She saw Clay as he told her she'd make a beautiful blonde.

She saw Clay mopping up the kitchen floor with an old beach towel, wringing it out time after time in the sink.

She saw Clay patiently washing the peanut butter/syrup mess off the kitchen counters, carefully stuffing all the miscellany back into the desk drawer and the end table drawer, replacing the phone on the small table by the stairs after the threatening call.

She saw Clay reaching his arms to hug her and

Billy, and tears burned her eyes. She heard him pray for her and for Billy. It was the height of irony that they were really a family clutching each other, though no one knew it but her.

It was more than she could deal with. *He* was more than she could deal with.

She started to weep. She tried to control herself, but the harder she tried, the more she wept. She rarely shed tears, hadn't wept for years, and here she was, crying twice in the same night.

Great, wracking sobs borne of past hurts and present fears rose in her throat. She rolled over to bury her face in her pillow so Billy couldn't hear her. He was unnerved enough as it was.

Billy, the source of her greatest joy and the focus of her greatest fear.

Oh, God, may it be Your arms that wrap around him through the night. Give him a peaceful sleep. Keep him safe, Lord. Keep him safe. And may I long only for Your arms about me, not another's.

Billy had been less than a year old the first time they'd been included in a group hug. He'd rolled off the sofa and banged his head, raising a huge, bruised lump over his left eye. Leigh had cried almost as hard as he had, convinced she was a terrible mother, certain he was irrevocably injured.

"Oh, baby, what have I done to you?" She cradled him against her and sobbed. "Mommy didn't mean to look away! It was only for a minute. I'm so sorry, baby!"

Will and Julia came to visit her that day. They found her and Billy sitting on the floor in tears. Will made certain that all that ailed Billy was a sore head, and Julia comforted Leigh with tales of her own mothering blunders. When everyone finally calmed down, Will and Julia gathered her and Billy into a four-person hug.

"Group hug," Will said. "It cures all ills."

Leigh had never before experienced spontaneous, undemanding affection like that. Oh, Julia and Will frequently gave her little loving kisses on the cheek, and Julia and Ted hugged her, but the sweetness of that huddle with two sets of arms enclosing her and her baby was overwhelming. Afterward she had relived it over and over in her imagination, certain she'd never experience anything so wonderful again.

Will and Julia, being who they were, there had been many

other group hugs through the years, but none had rivaled the sweetness of that first one. Until now.

She shivered as she recalled how right it had felt for the three of them—father, mother, son—to huddle together before God. She closed her eyes and remembered the warmth and security, the peace and contentment of that moment.

She took a deep breath and dried her tears on her pillowcase. Today's events were forcing her to reconsider some very serious presuppositions around which she'd built her life and Billy's. Had she been wrong all these years in keeping Billy's paternity a secret?

She'd always hidden behind Clay's lack of interest in her after "The Incident," but perhaps she had been unconsciously punishing Clay rather than protecting herself and his family. That was a hard thought and, if true, revealed an ugly side of herself.

She gave some time to the possibility that she harbored such a hidden motive and finally came to the conclusion that striking at Clay hadn't been a consideration at all. She hadn't been and still wasn't vindictive. Foolish definitely. Naïve certainly. Unforgiving on certain days. But vengeful? Never.

So, didn't Clay deserve to know his son? Didn't Billy deserve to know his father? Had she failed them both in keeping her secret? The thought made her feel literally sick to her stomach, and she curled into a ball, her arms wrapped about her middle.

But Clay hadn't cared! The rejection she'd felt when he didn't try to see her again was hard enough to deal with. How would she have stood him looking down that long nose of his and disclaiming her again? Her life had been filled with rejection: her mother who had loved her but left when she was ten, Johnny who could barely abide her presence, friends at school who kept her on the periphery of their lives, Clay who never came back.

No, ten years ago she could not have told Clay the truth of the situation. She could not have borne it emotionally.

And how could she have told Julia and Will? How could she have shattered their view of Clay, especially in light of their kindness to her?

Slowly she uncurled as she accepted that, right or wrong, the path she had chosen to follow was reasonable. She might not make the same choices today, but she wasn't the same person today. Besides, what was done was done. She couldn't undo it.

But what of the future? What if Clay found out at this late date that Billy was his? The longer he was here, the greater became the danger that somehow he would discover the truth.

She tried to imagine his reaction to such overwhelming news. Anger at her because she'd kept the secret? Anger that it had been revealed and now he had responsibilities? Anger that he'd been denied his son?

Or maybe disbelief? Of course she could prove paternity through DNA tests, but if she had to resort to such means, that meant an adversarial situation. Pitting herself against Clay was bound to damage her relationship with Julia and Ted, and her heart froze at the thought of losing the very people who had helped her survive, who had taught her what love was.

Another sudden thought brought sweat to her forehead and cramps back to her midsection. What if Clay tried to take Billy away from her somehow? Icy fear wrapped itself about her heart, but only for a moment. She quickly realized that wasn't a possibility. She was a capable and loving mother. No one could take Billy from her. At the most she would be forced to share Billy with Clay, and there was a chance that that would actually be good for Billy.

But what if Clay didn't care to become involved in the boy's life? He didn't know the child. He hadn't been there at his birth, hadn't changed his diapers, hadn't bound up his wounds, cheered at his ball games. He had no emotional ties to Billy. He might not want a father's responsibilities.

How that would hurt Billy! He wanted a father so badly. And, the most alarming thought of all, what would her son think of her and her choices if and when he learned the truth?

Leigh wiped her eyes again on a dry corner of her pillowcase and turned onto her back.

God, we have a history together, You and I. You've provided for me in the past when I was desperate, when I was a colossal failure. Based on that and Your promises, I know You'll provide for me now. But he scares me, Lord. I scare me. The possible revelation of the truth scares me. Help me remember the deeds You've done in the past on our behalf so that I won't fear what man—or one particular man—can do to me.

With great deliberation, Leigh turned her mind back to the first time God had intervened in her life. She needed to remind herself of the miracles she had seen so she could believe in the miracles yet to come. The first miracle had been Julia's persistent interest in her for no good reason the young Leigh could see.

"Have lunch with me, dear," Julia—Mrs. Wharton—had said one day as Leigh's supervisor at the Acme told her to close her register and take lunch. "I don't feel like eating alone."

Leigh had protested; she was certain she had, but somehow she ended up walking down the street with Mrs. Wharton chatting about the lovely weather. Lovely? It was ninety-five in the shade with a land breeze that was baking the town!

"Here we go, dear." Mrs. Wharton smiled as they entered the air-conditioned relief of Bitsi's. "Have a seat."

Leigh looked at the woman sitting across from her. Well, *looked* might be too strong a word. She peeked up from under her lashes as she sat with her head down and her hands clasped tightly in her lap.

Why had Mrs. Wharton asked her out for lunch? What did she want from her? Did she want to tell her that she was a tramp to have corrupted her fine Christian son, and this lunch was like her final meal, her last supper? It was just too suspicious that the woman had suddenly started being nice so soon after The Incident.

Leigh found that if she could think of the time with Clay as The Incident, no names mentioned, no emotions attached, she could survive the memory without dying every time it popped up—which it did with the regularity of thirst.

She'd waited for his call the day after graduation. And the next day and the next. Then she began to get a clammy feeling in the pit of her stomach. By the second week she'd known. He wasn't going to call. Ever. Whatever she had imagined he felt, it had been just that, imagination.

And she'd thought she knew all about the agony of rejection and loss.

Even now, more than a month after The Incident, she still couldn't believe how stupid she'd been. She'd actually thought he was going to tell her he loved her. How pathetic! She blushed when she recalled how she'd said she loved him. Like he cared. Just because she loved him from afar for the past three years didn't mean he shared that feeling. She should have known better. After all, she'd read countless stories and cried at countless movies about unrequited love.

Now he was at Annapolis, a midshipman standing straight and handsome in his new uniform. There was no chance for her now. Not that it should be a surprise. Things never worked out for Leigh Spenser. Never. Not once. The Incident was really just one more failure in a long line of them.

She was as stupid as her mother had been, giving it away for free. She comforted herself with the idea that at least she had the sense to be attracted to someone like Clay rather than someone like her father; though come to think about it, her father stayed around to marry her mother. But then her mother had been pregnant, and she, of course, wasn't.

Oh, God, please, I'm not! I know I'm late, but it's just because I'm upset. It has to be because I'm upset!

"What can I get you?" asked the waitress, a chirrupy, sun-tanned girl doubtless in Seaside for a fun summer, waitressing on the side. All Bitsi's summer staff were perky like this girl, who without trying, made Leigh feel pale, wan, and weary. Her name tag read Staci with an *i*. She tossed her sun-streaked hair and grinned.

Leigh's own hair was pulled back and clipped at her nape, but somehow, even though neat, it looked frumpy. At least it felt frumpy next to Beach Princess Staci who probably got to the beach every day while Leigh couldn't make it even once.

"Get whatever you want, Leigh," Mrs. Wharton said, all friendly.

"I'm not very hungry," Leigh muttered. All the food smells were making her nauseous.

"Maybe a cup of soup? Or a salad?" Mrs. Wharton smiled at her like her choice really mattered, and Leigh scowled back. She hated not being sure what the woman wanted. All her life her only protection had been knowing what was happening. She studied her father, studied her teachers, until she could read them and anticipate and avoid trouble. When she didn't understand motives, she got uncomfortable and surly.

"Whatever you get is fine with me," Leigh told the tabletop and hoped she'd be able to keep down whatever came.

"Two cups of chicken noodle soup and lots of crackers."

"Right," said Beach Princess Staci as she wrote diligently on her order pad. "Do you want iced tea, or would you like a soda?"

"Iced tea," said Mrs. Wharton.

"Coke," Leigh whispered.

"What?" said Beach Princess Staci.

"A Coke," Leigh said in a voice so loud that the child at the next table spun to look at her. She ignored both the child and the embarrassed flush that crept up her cheeks.

After looking at Leigh strangely, Beach Princess Staci disappeared, and Mrs. Wharton said, "They have wonderful soups here. You'll like the noodle soup, I know."

Leigh nodded, swallowing bile at the very thought of eating. She stared down at her Acme shirt and wished she hadn't agreed to come. She had no idea what to say to this polished woman. When your father was the town drunk and a thief, having polite conversation with well-heeled society ladies wasn't something you were used to.

"Leigh, where are you planning to go to school in the fall?"

Leigh looked up, startled. Why did Mrs. Wharton care? "Rowan University. I have a partial scholarship. I—I want to be a teacher. Elementary school." Somewhere besides Seaside. Anywhere but Seaside.

"That's wonderful. I have to tell you, I was afraid that you planned to work at Acme all your life. Not that there's anything wrong with that, but with a brain like yours, it would be a shame not to develop it more. God gave it to you to use."

Leigh blushed at the compliment. Since Mom died, not many people had said such nice things to her.

Beach Princess Staci arrived at the table next to where Leigh and Mrs. Wharton sat. She had baskets full of hamburgers and fries and one full of fried shrimp and fries. The aromas wafted across the aisle, and Leigh felt her stomach heave.

She grabbed her midsection and bolted to the back of the restaurant and the ladies' room. She just made it to a stall before she lost what little food sat in her stomach. She knelt, panting, trying to get a grip. She had to go out and face Mrs. Wharton after that inelegant exit. Somehow she knew that escaping out the back door wouldn't deter the woman.

She went to a sink and ran the cold water. She cupped her hands and brought the water to her mouth. She swirled it around, rinsing away the bitter taste. Then she looked at herself in the mirror and sagged against the wall.

She had always been poor, and her clothes had always been wrong; but she'd been neat and clean, her hair shiny, her cheeks rosy. Now she looked like death warmed over, so pale with great circles under her eyes. And she was so tired! She slept every minute she could, but she was always weary, just one step from falling asleep on the job. And she couldn't afford to lose either of her jobs.

She closed her eyes to blot out her image and stepped hesitantly out into the restaurant. As soon as she slid into her seat, she grabbed her brown pocketbook with the hole in the one corner where pens kept slipping out. She fished inside for the TUMS she now carried everywhere. She stuck three in her mouth and chewed.

"Have you been feeling bad for long?" Mrs. Wharton asked, just like she cared.

Just since your son. "It's a touch of a bug," Leigh said. "It'll pass." *Please, God, let it pass!*

Mrs. Wharton looked sympathetic, but she didn't comment as Beach Princess Staci skipped up and served them their lunch. Leigh looked at the bowl of soup sitting in front of her and felt her face turn three shades of green. How was she ever going to manage this? She picked up her spoon and forced herself to take a swallow of the broth. Unexpectedly it soothed her stomach. She took another.

Mrs. Wharton leaned forward, looking very intent. "I'm going to ask you a few very personal questions, Leigh. Understand that I have a reason. I'm not trying to be nosey or to embarrass you. Truly I'm not."

Leigh nodded. She just bet the woman had a reason. To protect her son. It had to be that. What other reason would there be for this lady to care about her one way or the other?

But somehow the idea of Clay telling his mother of all people what had happened between them was beyond credibility.

"Can you manage going to Rowan financially?"

Leigh stared at Mrs. Wharton, too stunned by the question to be shy.

"I know that's a highly personal question," Mrs. Wharton said, obviously recognizing Leigh's astonishment. "But can you?"

Leigh looked at the pretty woman with her carefully tinted blond hair and her yellow cotton sweater and yellow floral slacks, all saying very clearly, "Money!" and wondered again what was going on.

"I don't know if I can make it or not. That's why I'm working two jobs this summer." She rubbed a hand across her forehead to soothe the pain she got there every time she thought about the expenses of her education, to say nothing of such simple things as eating and buying gas for her new-to-her rattletrap, an eight-year-old red Civic. "But I'm going to try. It might take a long time before I finish, but I'll do it eventually."

She said the last with a lot more assurance than she felt. Being on her own was such a scary thing that if she allowed herself to think of all that could go wrong, she'd go home, bury her head under her pillow, and hide for the rest of her life. Just buying the Red Menace had practically given her an ulcer. What did she know about cars? She had tried to look cool and assured, but she'd known she had patsy written all over her. The car salesman had probably ripped her off, but she didn't want to know for sure. This way she could sniff at his probable lack of ethics and still keep her pride.

"Are you planning to live in the dorm or get an apartment?" Mrs. Wharton brought her paper napkin carefully to her lips, then put it back in her lap.

"I'll have to commute."

"All the way to Glassboro? That's a lot of driving."

"I don't have a choice."

"Is your car in good shape?"

She thought of the Red Menace parked beside the Acme and shrugged. "I don't really know."

"Do you have someone to look at the car for you? An uncle? A family friend? I know I wouldn't know if a car was in decent condition or not until it suddenly stopped running. Then I could figure it out—broken! broken!—but I wouldn't have the vaguest idea how to fix it. It's not one of my interests. When we buy a car, my main job is to pick the color." Mrs. Wharton smiled. "Dr. Wharton does all the rest."

Leigh smiled slightly. Another automotive patsy.

"Well, would you let Dr. Wharton check the car over for you?"

Leigh couldn't respond; she was so floored by the very idea. She sat there with her packet of Saltines half open and stared.

"I'm serious."

Leigh dropped her Saltines onto the table. "I've got to go," she said with a look at her watch. "Thank you for lunch, Mrs. Wharton."

"But, Leigh, you've only eaten part of your soup. Didn't you like it?"

"It was very good," Leigh assured her, even as she pressed a hand to her abdomen and swallowed repeatedly. She shouldn't have had that spoonful of noodles. "I just have to go." *Before I throw up all over the table and upset Beach Princess Staci with the smell.*

"Are you feeling ill again?" Mrs. Wharton was all concern.

"I'm fine. Thank you again." And Leigh fled.

She continued to see Mrs. Wharton every day at the Acme. Sometimes she went through Leigh's checkout line with nothing more than a head of lettuce or a quart of milk. Sometimes she had to wait behind women with overflowing carts when the manager kept saying, "Checkout One is for small orders. It's open."

"I'm fine," Mrs. Wharton would insist, then wait her turn, smile at Leigh, and talk about the weather, Ted's latest letter, or Clay's lack of contact with home since he'd left for school.

One night less than a week after the lunch at Bitsi's, Mrs. Wharton showed up at the ice cream stand with Dr. Wharton in tow.

"Hello, Mrs. Wharton, Dr. Wharton." Leigh realized she now accepted that she would see Mrs. Wharton frequently, and Leigh couldn't decide whether she was pleased or unnerved by this fact. She didn't quite trust the woman's niceness, but she made Clay seem real and not so far away. And Dr. Wharton was very pleasant, so unlike her father. He was a big man, like Clay. "What can I get for you? Vanilla and black raspberry?"

"You remember!" Mrs. Wharton was impressed, but then nice people usually were easy to impress.

"When I actually know the people I'm waiting on, I tend to remember."

Dr. Wharton took his black raspberry cone. "When can you come over and let me look at your car? Julia's been telling me you need it checked so you know if it's good enough for the commute to school in the fall." He lunged at his cone to catch a drip before it fell onto his knit shirt with the little polo player over his heart.

Leigh stared at him in disbelief.

· "I told you he'd help you." Mrs. Wharton looked at him proudly.

He glanced at Leigh, eyebrows raised in question, and she felt compelled to answer. Before she knew what had happened, she was committed to drive over Thursday after work at the Acme. She didn't have to be at the ice cream stand until seven. There ought to be just enough time between jobs to get the checkup and grab a hot dog at the stand next to hers—if she could keep it down. She thought she probably could. Food eaten in the evening tended to remain where she sent it. It was mornings and early afternoons when the rebellion took place.

She was very nervous when she drove into the Whartons' drive on Thursday, but when Ted came running out and gave her a hug, she began to relax. In no time, Ted and Dr. Wharton were peering under the Red Menace's hood and listening to all kinds of noises.

"Come on in," Mrs. Wharton invited when the men began to speak mechanicese.

Feeling awkward and unsure but not knowing how to say no, Leigh entered the prettiest kitchen she'd ever been in. Everything matched, everything sparkled, and the blue and green and white colors blended with the ocean she could just see beyond the dunes. The smells emanating from the stove reminded Leigh of how long it had been since she'd had a real meal. Her mouth began to water, but she swallowed resolutely. A hot dog would be fine when the time came.

"Do you have time to eat with us?" Mrs. Wharton asked. "Ted would be so happy to have your company."

Leigh glanced up to see if her hunger had been obvious and the invitation had been made out of pity. But no. Mrs. Wharton was busy at the counter with her back to Leigh. "Oh. Well—"

Mrs. Wharton turned around, a warm smile on her face. "Please say yes, especially if you like chocolate cake." And she stepped aside, revealing the prettiest chocolate cake Leigh'd ever seen.

It was a delicious dinner, the best Leigh had had since Mom died. She tried not to feel too guilty when she decided maybe it was even better than one of Mom's specials. Mrs. Wharton could really cook. And Leigh's stomach was barely complaining, thank goodness.

"Come on outside with me, Leigh," Dr. Wharton said when everyone was finished. "I want to give you the report on your car."

Leigh nodded and stood. Ted rose too.

"I want to talk to Leigh alone," Dr. Wharton said, looking at Ted.

Ted looked surprised but nodded and sat down. "I'll just have another piece of that great cake. It's another winner, Mom."

Leigh followed Dr. Wharton outside. Now she was going to get it, whatever it was. Now she'd find out what they wanted from her, or she'd get that lecture about corrupting Clay. Cloak it in kindness, and then it hurt even more. She squared her shoulders and looked at Dr. Wharton with hostility.

"I think your car's in pretty good shape, Leigh." He slid his hand along the front right fender. "I see from the sticker that you bought it from Wade Richter. He's a fair and honest man. We go to the same church."

Leigh nodded, too nervous at what was coming to be very relieved about the condition of the car.

"But," he said, "that's not my main concern."

Here it comes, she thought, rubbing her hand across the pain in her forehead.

"You know I'm a doctor, don't you?"

She looked at him in surprise and nodded.

"Do you know what kind?"

"A baby doctor, right?"

He nodded and looked at her with concern. "Is there a possibility that you're pregnant, do you think?"

"N-no," Leigh said. "I'm not pregnant! I can't be pregnant. Why would you think such a thing?"

"Mrs. Wharton has been concerned because of some things she's observed when she's been with you. Your frequently upset stomach, your fatigue, and the circles under your eyes, for example."

Leigh thought of the take-at-home test that sat on her bureau—the test she'd been too scared to use because the possibility of a positive reading was too terrifying to deal with.

"I can't be pregnant!" she repeated. "I can't! I can't!"

"Are you saying that you were never with a man?" Mrs. Wharton asked as she slid an arm around Leigh's waist. Leigh hadn't even heard her come outside.

Leigh looked at Clay's mother and began to cry. She cried until she became afraid she'd never stop. The whole time she sobbed, Mrs. Wharton held her and rocked her and murmured sweet mother things in her ear.

When she finally calmed down a bit, they took her inside and sat her down. Then they washed her face with cool water, gave her a drink, and showered her with kindness.

"I've a hard question for you," Dr. Wharton finally said. "If you are pregnant, can we expect any help from the father?"

Leigh shook her head. "I haven't heard from him since—" She couldn't say it.

The Whartons nodded their understanding. "Don't worry. We'll take care of you."

And to her amazement they had. They helped her find an apartment in Glassboro so she could go to Rowan without the terrible commute. The rent was very low, too low, and she always suspected they underwrote it. She knew they paid her tuition.

"We've saved for the boys' college expenses for years," Dr. Wharton said. "Now Clay's going to a school where we don't have to foot the bill. Let us use that money for you. We'd consider it a privilege, and you should look at it as another scholarship."

They had paid for Billy's prenatal care and delivery. They had bought her all the baby things she had known she could never afford—a frilly bassinet, a wonderful crib with beautiful sheets and blankets, a car seat, and a highchair. Every time they came to visit her in Glassboro, they brought a CARE package for her and Billy: small gifts, silly gifts, necessary items. Because Billy was their grandchild, she was able to still her conscience as she accepted gift after gift.

Most astounding of all, Will and Julia Wharton loved her. At first Leigh couldn't believe it, distrusting them, looking for ulterior motives, waiting for their repayment demand. But she finally realized there was nothing here but Christian love freely given. And for some reason, God had chosen her to be the recipient.

Billy was three years old when it finally all came together in her mind, and she realized Jesus could come into her life and make her like them. He'd died to be her sacrifice and to forgive her of all her wrongs—which were legion. The gift of new life was hers for the taking. And she believed.

Will and Julia rejoiced with her, helped her find a church where she would grow, and continued to love her.

It had taken her six years including summers, but she'd finally graduated *cum laude*. By working part time, she'd made enough to feed herself and Billy, pay a baby-sitter and the miniscule rent left after the Whartons' contribution. Every year for her birthday, the Whartons gave her her car insurance, and Dr. Wharton made sure she and Billy were covered with health insurance.

When she graduated, they told her about the fourth grade teacher's position that had just opened up in Seaside, asked her to come back and live in their apartment and let them continue as Billy's surrogate grandparents. She'd agreed with trepidation because her memories of Seaside were not pleasant, but she could not abide the thought of losing them. They'd made her return as painless as possible, though not even they could protect her from the cruel people of the world.

When she finally fell asleep, she was smiling at all the proof of God's goodness through the years and full of confidence that He would come through for her again.

Eleven

CLAY WANDERED INTO the kitchen about eight-thirty Saturday morning, surprised that he had slept so well after all the chaos of the night before. He glanced out the window at the garage and wondered how Leigh had passed the night.

He shook his head. It bothered him that she always had to deal with the fallout of being Johnny Spenser's daughter. She had done so much with her life: finishing college, teaching, and according to Greg Barnes—or Greg Barnes's daughter—doing a fine job of it. She was responsible, efficient, and capable.

But then she always had been. When he recalled that young girl he thought so lovely, he remembered a whole person, not just a pretty one. He remembered her dedication to her schoolwork, her shy friendliness, her kindness, her determination to be more than Johnny Spenser's daughter.

Of course he remembered her beauty too. What man wouldn't? She had been enough to make his mouth go dry every time he looked at her. And she was lovelier now than she had been then. Maturity had given depth to her face, honed the girlish roundness from cheek and jaw. Granted, he missed that waterfall of chestnut hair that intrigued him so, but her brisk, chin-length curls were equally charming. She had a brightness to her eyes that made them spark with life and emotion, especially when she was telling him where to get off or trying not to tell the young cop Pete to mind his own business.

He grinned to himself. He didn't think he'd ever seen anyone do the Frost Princess better than she'd done it last night with the young cop. And he'd deserved every icy breath. Clay could still see the avid curiosity with which Pete had weighed Leigh in some mental balance.

It just wasn't fair that she had to be subjected to insolence like that, but then no one said life was fair. But it still galled him and aroused an unexpected urge to be her knight-errant riding his destrier to her rescue and becoming her protector. Don Quixote de la Seaside.

Careful, Wharton. Dangerous territory. You were there once before and look what it did to you. And her. You're the last person who should ever consider rescuing her.

Trouble was, he saw no one else riding over the horizon to tilt at her windmills for her, to raise his emblem in her name.

It was funny how he still saw her as that innocent, pure girl in the white dress with the pink flowers and green vines embroidered around the hem. Why he did was a mystery to him. Billy was proof that she was anything but. Still, there was something about her, about the way she carried herself, the way she cared about his mother and brother, the way she obviously doted on Billy that moved him. She had always been without artifice, and he saw that same quality in her still.

No wonder he had rarely come home over the years.

He poured himself a cup of coffee from the carafe warming on the coffee machine. He took a swallow and choked. Vanilla! He should have known. The whole kitchen smelled of it, but he'd assumed his mother had been baking. Instead, she had been making corrupted coffee.

He'd always thought Mom a purist, what with her made-from-scratch baking frenzies and dinners to die for. That she, a wonderful and previously incorruptible woman, had fallen for flavored coffee was a sad sign of the subtlety of the moral decay in America.

He sighed and poured the mugful down the drain. He resisted by sheer strength of character the urge to dump the whole carafe. He went to the refrigerator. There sat a can of real coffee-flavored coffee. He pulled it out and made himself a pot. It tasted wonderful.

He was just finishing a bowl of Cheerios and some whole wheat toast with real butter when his mother came in the back door.

"Hi," she said with a smile, fresh air eddying about her. She wore jeans, a blue plaid flannel shirt and sweater, and a red fleece jacket. She looked more like an older sister than his mother. "I've been walking on the beach."

"I wondered where you were," he said, smiling at the roses blooming in her cheeks.

She headed for the vanilla coffee and poured a cup. "It's going to be lovely this afternoon, but it's still brisk right now." She shivered. "I've got to get warm."

The back door slammed open, and Billy exploded into the room. Obviously he'd escaped before Leigh got him to brush his hair. He was wearing the same clothes he'd had on last night, a true ten-year-old boy with all the disdain for cleanliness that typified the age.

"Hey, Clay! Hey, Terror!" He dropped to his knees and hugged the dog who wiggled with delight at the attention. "Hey, Grandma Jule, did you hear about our visitor last night?"

"Someone besides Clay?" Mom asked, laughing as Terror enthusiastically kissed Billy.

"A vandal!" Billy swiped an arm across his face to wipe off Terror's saliva and looked at her, waiting for her reaction.

Clay couldn't help grinning at the boy. Now that order had been more or less restored to the apartment and the sun was shining, he was once again enjoying the excitement of this new adventure. Quiet little Seaside didn't often offer firsthand mysteries, and his front row seat to this one obviously delighted Billy.

Mom didn't disappoint the boy. "What? A vandal?" Her face blanched, and she put out a hand to grab the counter as if she needed help to keep standing.

The back door opened again, and this time Leigh entered. She was wearing jeans and a shirt and sweater just like his mother, but she reminded him of no one's sister, older or younger, and certainly not his. Nor did he feel anything remotely brotherly when he looked at her.

"Billy, what have you been telling Julia?" Leigh asked, taking in Mom's white face and strained expression.

"Are you all right?" Mom demanded, coming to Leigh and taking her hands.

Leigh kissed Mom's cheek and smiled reassuringly. "We're fine. Truly."

"Yeah, *now* we're fine. But last night there was mess and water everywhere! You should have seen it. Toothpaste all over the sink. Dirt all over the floor. Books everywhere. The kitchen floor was a little lake!" Billy was enjoying the drama, playing it with an over-the-top disregard for the sensibilities of his audience.

"That's enough, Billy," Leigh said in a firm voice. "You're scaring Grandma Jule."

"It's all right, Mom." Clay pulled out a chair for her. "Greg Barnes was here last night and took care of everything."

Well, almost everything, he thought. He looked at Leigh, and she nodded. She had reported the threatening call. She pointed to Billy and shook her head. The boy knew nothing about it. Clay inclined his head and wondered at the ease of their wordless communication. He hadn't understood Emilie, the giver of Terror, even when she used audible words.

"How's Ted this morning?" Leigh asked, changing the topic to the one guaranteed to distract his mother. Mom shrugged as she took the seat Clay had pulled out for her. "He seems very tired to me, even after a full night's sleep."

"Did he manage to eat anything?"

"He ate a couple of soft-boiled eggs with some bread mixed in, complaining the whole time about how tasteless they were."

"The medicine makes things taste strange?" Clay asked.

Mom nodded. "Though I think it was more a case of not being able to put salt on the eggs. You know Ted. If he can't bury it in salt, it isn't worth eating." She smiled. "I think his mouth is a bit better this morning. The stuff David gave him is helping."

Leigh poured herself a cup of the vanilla coffee and added a spoonful of sugar. She took a sip and sighed. "Delicious. I just love this stuff."

"You can't be serious!" Clay shook his head. "It's like drinking a hot milkshake. Now this is real coffee." He picked up his carafe and poured himself another mug. "That stuff's for wimps."

"Well, now at least I know what you think of me." She smiled to take any sting out of the words.

Mom looked wistfully at the almost empty carafe of vanilla coffee, and Clay felt suddenly guilty about the cup he'd poured down the drain. She topped off her mug with the remaining coffee and rose to rinse the pot at the sink. "Ted and I had a lovely, lively discussion this morning about whether his bouts with thrush were worse than these sores. It's amazing what becomes interesting fodder for contemplation in certain circumstances."

"What's thrush?" Clay asked. "Besides a bird."

"A fungal disease that causes lesions in the mouth and throat," Billy answered from his spot on the floor. "And on the lips. Very painful." He glanced at Clay's surprised face. "I'm going to be a doctor when I grow up, just like Grandpa Will."

"You're going to deliver babies?" Clay asked. "That means you have to deal with lots of girls, both grown-up and newborn. I thought you didn't like women."

"Girls." Billy grimaced. "I don't like girls. And I said a *doctor* like Grandpa Will, not a *baby* doctor like him."

"Ah, a broad stroke assumption of his mantle, not a specific one."

Billy looked at him and frowned in confusion. "What's a fireplace got to do with anything?"

"Not much." Leigh smiled at her son. "I think I'll just go up and say hi to Ted. I'd take him a mug of vanilla coffee if there was any left. He happens to have good taste."

"It figures he'd like it," Clay muttered as Leigh went upstairs, Billy following.

He forced himself to look away from her retreating figure and found his mother watching him, her eyebrow cocked.

"What?" he said with a deplorable lack of good humor.

"She's wonderful, isn't she?" Mom spoke with obvious pride. "I'm so delighted with what she's become."

"Yeah, she's great." To change the tender topic, he leaped on the first thought that came to mind. "Mom, why's Ted failing so fast? I thought they'd made great strides in the treatment of AIDS."

She stared into her cup. "They have, but often there comes a time when a patient develops a resistance to all the available drugs. Then even the sophisticated medical cocktails can't hold the encroaching infections at bay. It's just a matter of time until some infection like pneumonia gets hold and can't be pried loose."

He reached across the table and took her hand. It was cold in spite of the fact that she'd had it wrapped around her cup. He didn't say anything because he didn't know what to say. He wasn't surprised when he saw tears running down her cheeks.

"Oh, Mom." His heart broke for her pain. As if it weren't bad enough that she'd lost his father, now she was going to lose Ted.

"I'm okay," she said. "I just can't help it every so often." The pain in her eyes was devastating.

Clay squeezed her hand and struggled to push his anger at Ted to the back of his mind lest she see it in his face. "I'll be here for as long as you need me, Mom."

"Indefinite compassionate leave? I didn't know the navy was that understanding."

He shook his head. "I resigned my commission."

She fell back in her chair, floored. "You've left the navy? I thought you loved military life."

He shrugged. "I guess I did at one time, but civilian life has been calling for a while."

Mom made a wry face. "You know, there was a time when I actually thought I knew you two boys." She gave a short, humorless laugh. "Just goes to show you how easily a mom can be fooled."

"I don't think a change of jobs is that big a deal, certainly not big enough for you to worry about."

"You're not planning on being one of those kids who moves back home and never leaves again, are you?" she asked, looking anxious. "I've got a kid upstairs, another over the garage, and a grandkid. I'll never have an empty nest!" She turned a woeful face to him.

He laughed. "Don't worry. I'm visiting. I'd never be mean enough to stay."

She smiled her love to him. "You know I'll enjoy you for as long as you choose to stay, don't you?"

He nodded, thinking how much he admired her for the grace with which she'd handled life's adversities: her widowhood, Ted's life choices and imminent death. He'd known about Ted's secret life years before his parents learned about it. While still in high school, Clay had assimilated the fact of his twin's gayness clue by clue, not even aware of what he was learning most of the time. When it finally all coalesced in his mind, telling his parents had seemed wrong, like tattling. Shocked and angry as he was at Ted, he still wanted to protect him, his twin, his other half. And he wanted to protect his parents from the pain they would undoubtedly suffer.

Ironically, when the truth did come out, they handled it better than he ever had.

Sipping his coffee, he leaned his elbows on the table. "How did you learn about Ted?" he asked gently.

His mother looked out the window, staring at the blue spring sky. "Show us your shoes."

Clay stared. "You're kidding."

Mom shook her head. "I was watching the Miss America parade on TV the year after he graduated from college and you from the Academy. Ted was living in Atlantic City and had a good job at one of the banks. You were stationed in Hawaii. Your father and I were so proud of you both." She sighed. "How often since then have I thought about pride being one of the seven deadly sins."

Anger at Ted struck Clay again. "Mom, being proud of your kids isn't wrong."

"Maybe. Maybe not." She held a hand out and waggled it back and forth to show her uncertainty. "But I've discovered that what I was really proud of was my outstanding job as a mother. I'd raised two of the finest boys I knew. Since you two turned out so wonderfully, I must have done a great job."

"You did."

She raised an eyebrow, questioning his conclusion.

"Mom, you're not responsible for your sons' choices."

She shrugged. "So everyone tells me. Too bad my heart doesn't always agree."

Feeling helpless in the face of her sorrow, Clay got up and began pacing the kitchen.

"Sit down," Mom ordered. "You'll drive me crazy if you keep that up."

Clay grunted and forced himself to stand still. He leaned casually against the counter. Terror raced into the kitchen, and Clay put his cereal bowl on the floor. The dog inhaled the remaining milk, his tail wagging the whole time.

"You know," Mom said, watching the dog with an abstracted expression. "I almost wish they'd find a brain chemistry cause or genetic cause for homosexuality if only to exonerate your father. I've grieved and still do for what people might assume about him based on standard psychological profiles of gays' families."

"Mom!" Clay stared at her. "Anyone who knew Dad knows he wasn't an absentee or a dictatorial father or any other perversion of the role."

She glanced up, a sudden impudent grin on her face. "Of course they're not too nice to mothers in those studies either."

"Mom!"

She waved her hand at him. "Take it easy, Clay. You've got to learn to see the humor in this situation, or you'll turn into a prune."

He looked at her in wonder. "You're amazing." He came to her and gave her a quick kiss on the cheek. He picked up his cereal dish from the floor and gathered his others from the table. He rinsed them and put them in the dishwasher. "So you were watching the Miss America parade?"

She went back to her story. "The contestants from all the states were being driven down the boardwalk in convertibles or on floats," she continued, "and for once the weather was wonderful. As usual the local gay community was there to enjoy the glitz and glamour."

Clay knew what was coming, and the thought of what it must have done to his parents made his stomach teem with acid. The little show-us-your-shoes ritual was a regular feature of the parade.

"When the girls went by the cluster of gays, the guys called out their traditional, 'Show us your shoes,' and the girls raised their feet from their cars to show their shoes. Some had a special pair of shoes that they waved at the guys, duplicates of what they were wearing. One even threw her extra shoes to them. I was halfway laughing at the ridiculousness of the whole thing when suddenly there was Ted in the middle of these men. In fact, he was the one who caught the shoe."

Mom looked into middle distance, recalling the evening. Her face was full of sorrow.

"I must have made a choking sound because your father looked up from his newspaper and asked what was wrong. All I could do was point at the TV. Miss New Jersey was passing the guys, her leg raised as she twirled her shoe for them to see. They were clapping and cheering for the hometown favorite, and suddenly there was Ted again, raising his captured shoe in salute."

Mom returned to the present. "We were so mad at him, Clay. We were. How could he do this to us? How could he ruin our Christian testimony like that? After all we'd done for him." She rose from the table and began pulling out baking ingredients. "Talk about pride! At that point, while we cared about Ted, we cared more about ourselves."

She measured flour and shortening and began to cut the shortening into the flour for a piecrust. "But that was long ago, Clay. We've made peace with the Lord about our responsibility, if any, for the situation."

"You don't have any responsibility!" Clay was vehement. "You were great parents, and don't let anyone ever tell you differently. You supported us, loved us, and trained us in Christian values. You didn't just take us to church and Sunday school; you lived those principles in front of us every day. You couldn't have been better examples."

Mom smiled her thanks as she began to roll the dough. "Maybe. But it doesn't matter now. It's the past. That's one thing we learned. The past can't be undone. If we were wrong, I'm terribly sorry, but I can't change it. But we also learned that the past doesn't have to control today. I'm not angry at Ted. I love him and have forgiven him for the hurt he's given us."

She turned to Clay and laid her floury hand gently on his cheek. "You need to do the same, son."

Clay made a muffled snort of sound that could have meant anything.

Mom smiled sadly. "I know you're mad at him for the sorrow he's brought us."

Clay thought that was an understatement if he'd ever heard one.

"Have you ever asked yourself if what you feel is misplaced anger?"

"What?" He stared at his mother.

"Maybe you're really mad at God for letting your twin be the way he is, for not 'fixing' him."

Clay felt poleaxed. "Come on, Mom," he managed. "Where'd you ever get that idea?"

She shrugged. "Who knows? The Holy Spirit?"

Clay watched her walk from the room, his mind in turmoil. She was right, at least about the forgiving Ted part. He had to do something. He couldn't let Ted die without making peace with him. He knew he'd wither and die himself if that happened.

But what did he do with this anger he'd been harboring all these years? How did he say Ted's choice was all right when it wasn't?

He wasn't really mad at God, was he?

Oh, God, help! What should I do?

What he did was take a long walk on the beach. The sun was bright and almost warm. He was glad for the sweatshirt he had on and equally glad for the sunglasses. Terror trotted beside him, leaving little paw prints in the sand. When a seagull dived toward them, Terror ran back toward the house as fast as he could go, memories of Mama undoubtedly driving him.

"My hero," Clay called after him.

"You were breaking the leash law, you know."

Clay glanced up and saw Clooney walking toward him, metal detector in hand. The two men shook hands.

"Glad to see you home." Clooney lifted his baseball cap and ran his arm across his forehead. His gray hair was drawn tightly back into a ponytail, and a gold hoop dangled from his left ear.

Clay wondered absently if Clooney had found the hoop with the detector.

Clooney slapped his hat back in place. "Remember when I couldn't tell you two apart?"

"We used to love to tease people who got confused. And that was almost everyone."

"Couldn't confuse you now," Clooney said sadly, staring out to the horizon.

"No," Clay agreed, staring toward infinity himself.

Clooney shrugged. "To each his own, I guess. Sort of sad it turned out this way for him though." He turned and looked up at the Wharton house. The deck outside Ted's room was just visible above the dunes. "I see him sitting out there in the lounge chair, all bundled up in blankets and stuff. He always waves."

Clay nodded. It was all he could do with the pressure in his chest at the picture of Ted waving to Clooney. Ted who used to follow the man around begging for a chance to try the detector; Ted who loved the tales Clooney told of World War II treasures he found, especially the live bomb about three feet long; Ted who saved all his money the summer he was twelve to buy a detector of his own and ended up buying Clay a football and cleats instead. Neither of them ever mentioned that a football in Clay's possession might as well be in Ted's too.

Clooney shook his head, his gray ponytail shimmying across his back. His dark eyes were confounded as he turned to Clay. "I just can't imagine liking boys instead of girls." With that, he swung his detector with its digital readouts out over the sand and walked off.

The high tide line was littered with broken shells—fan-shaped clam, bumpy oyster, ridged scallop, the occasional black mussel, and slim razor clam. Seaweed, air bladders still intact, and sea grasses whisked from the dunes by the tides lay in untidy clumps among the shells. The tide was low, so he walked on the hard sand, watching the foam-flocked waves tumble gently a few feet from him. His mind skittered before him like sandpipers before the waves.

He loved Ted. He was his twin, the other half of himself. They had started life as one, sharing egg and sperm, then splitting to become an identical pair. They had wrestled for room in their mother's womb and jockeyed for attention all their lives. They had supported each other, applauded each other, encouraged each other, competed with each other. How could he not love Ted?

And they had loved God together too, at least until Ted turned away from all they'd been taught. The indescribable twinship they shared was what made Ted's betrayal of their training and background so corrosive, so excruciating, and that betrayal fueled an anger that got in the way of the love.

He stood, feet apart, staring across the inlet to Atlantic City. His heart ached, and his head hurt as a great vise tightened, tightened, constricting, squeezing, killing. It was a great surprise to taste salt at the edge of his mouth and realize he was crying. Leigh's comment last night in Ted's room came back to him.

"Tears are falling as often as spring rain around here."

Too true, he thought as he brushed at the wetness on his face. Unfortunately too true.

Twelve

CLAY TOOK THE chair beside Ted's bed and smiled at his brother. He knew if he was to learn to love Ted again, that meant spending time with him.

During his walk on the beach, he'd promised himself and God that he'd sit with Ted at least twice a day. He'd have nice, quiet conversations with him and get to know him all over again. He'd find out how Ted thought, how he felt about dying, about God and Jesus. Clay would not lecture, preach, or reprimand in any manner. He'd listen and learn.

He smiled mentally as he found a firm example for his actions. He'd be Barnabas, the Son of Encouragement.

When Clay sat down, Ted just looked at him, saying nothing, giving away nothing. Clay's smile quickly became strained. Where should he start? What topics were safe? Did they have anything in common anymore?

"Beautiful view," Clay said, looking out the French doors beside the bed. Scenery ranked right up there with the weather when you were desperate.

Dutifully, Ted looked out the windows. "Yeah. That's why I don't want to move downstairs."

Clay nodded. "I was out walking earlier and bumped into Clooney."

Ted almost smiled but caught himself just in time. "Strange duck."

Clay nodded. "But nice. He feels bad about your illness."

"I guess that's better than feeling good."

Conversation ground to a halt as Clay tried to decide whether Ted was sending him a not-too-subtle message that said Get Lost. Both brothers looked out the windows again.

The white dunes with their winter-browned grasses waving in the ocean breeze reared up behind the house; snow fences threaded through the sand to help fight erosion. The dunes themselves were artificial in that they were the creation of the Army Corps of Engineers rather than the hand of God.

The whole New Jersey coast was one huge battleground between the sea and the humans determined to hold on to the prime oceanfront land. Hurricanes and winter storms battered the beaches, eating tons of sand, only to have Mother Nature's temporary victory reversed by the huge pumps and pipes that brought sand from offshore or the bay to the beaches. Never mind the millions of taxpayers' dollars pumped into the reclamation. Everyone wanted wide beaches, time in the surf and sun, and homes on the water. New Jersey wanted the tourist dollars.

Beyond the dunes the beach became flat, the pale, sugar-fine sand above the tide line soft and shifting underfoot. The beach washed by the tides was packed firmly, scrubbed of personality by the constant ebb and flow of the water. Today the waves were gentle in the early afternoon sun, and here and there people walked the beach enjoying the slight foretaste of summer's warmth.

One of the nicest things about the point where they lived was that it wasn't the touristy area of town. Full-time residents occupied most of the houses in the neighborhood. The boardwalk was a couple of miles away, a huge distance by tourist reckoning. Even in high summer, their beach wasn't crowded.

"Yep, there's nothing like the beach and the ocean." Clay smiled. That was a safe beginning. He pointed to the small image of a pony-tailed man with the metal detector working the sand a couple of blocks away. "You'd think he'd get tired of looking after all these years."

"Did he show you his new state-of-the-art digital detector?"

Clay shook his head.

"Quite the machine. He can set the depth of his search or the type of metal to search for." Ted smiled as they watched the man bend and dig a small hole in the sand with a child's red plastic beach spade. Clooney straightened and brushed sand off something in his hand. "Wonder what he just found."

Clay leaned forward. "Remember when our highest goal in life was to get a metal detector of our own and discover buried treasure?"

Ted nodded. "Why should he have all the fun and all the money? Quarters, Kennedy halves. Remember the day he found the silver dollar?"

"You almost had a detector."

"Yeah, but I got tired of saving. I bought you a football and cleats instead." He was quiet for a moment. "Bad choice, considering how well we both played football."

They grinned at each other, then overcome with uncertainties, they both turned back to watching Clooney. Safer, Clay thought.

"Remember the day he found that diamond ring?" Clay asked, his eyes firmly fixed on Clooney as the man dropped his newest treasure in the fanny pack about his waist.

Ted nodded. "Buried in the sand down by Eighteenth Street. He advertised in the *Seaside Gazette,* but no one ever claimed it."

"That's because it was part of a pirate's treasure. Everyone thought it belonged to some shoobie who cried all the way home, but we knew better." He grinned at Ted. "The rest is still waiting for us."

"Shoobie," Ted said. "I haven't heard that word in years."

"That's because no one takes the train to Seaside for the day with their lunch packed in a shoe box anymore. They all zip down the Atlantic City Expressway and the Garden State Parkway with their Igloos snuggly tucked in the backseat."

"So we should call them Iglooies?"

Again came that momentary connection blown away all too quickly by pride and the past. They turned back to Clooney.

"You want to find pirate's treasure," Ted said. "I'd rather find some World War II artifacts myself."

"Like the shell casings Clooney finds."

"Like that live World War II bomb he found when he was a kid."

Clay watched Clooney wave his detector back and forth. "With our luck all we'll find is money."

"Yeah, and not even halves and silver dollars either. Just quarters and dimes and pennies." Ted sighed. "Another dream bites the dust."

They sat quietly for a minute, actually comfortable with each other.

"Can I have some water?" Ted asked.

Clay held the cup with its bent straw out to his twin and watched as Ted sucked down half the cup.

"Thanks," Ted said, sinking back on the pillows. "I was just too lazy to get it for myself."

Scared more than he wanted to admit by Ted's willingness to be waited on, Clay said, "You've never been too lazy to get what you wanted in your whole life."

Ted smiled in recognition of that truth. "Sort of like you."

Clay nodded. "It's the twin thing. We can't avoid being alike."

"In some ways," Ted agreed.

"We're both handsome dudes." Clay looked at his brother's gaunt face.

Ted grunted. "Sure are. We've always had the girls and the boys panting after us."

Instantly, Clay felt uncomfortable. "Don't."

"Don't what?" Ted asked, all innocence.

"Please, let's just talk. Innocuous things. Noncontroversial things."

Ted looked at him, defiant now in reaction to Clay's discomfort. "How can we just talk? You refuse to acknowledge who and what I am."

Clay shook his head. What had happened to their ease? Why had Ted deliberately destroyed it? "I acknowledge what you are all right, but we'll never agree on the subject, so let's drop it." He looked directly at his brother. "I don't want to argue."

Ted ran his tongue over his dry lips. "You're an ostrich, Clay. You're in denial. You think that if we don't mention it, it'll go away."

Clay looked out the window again, watching Clooney dig another hole in the sand. He rubbed whatever he'd found between his fingers to brush away the grit. Whatever it was satisfied him, and he put it in his fanny pack.

At least someone was having a good day.

Clay resisted the urge to leave the bedroom. He was here, trying to be nice because he knew he had to come to some resolution with Ted. He couldn't live with himself otherwise. Since it seemed that all Ted wanted to do was bait him, he had no idea how their reconciliation was to occur. All at once he felt unutterably sad that the two of them, who had once been so close, could now barely speak civilly.

"You've been a sore trial to me all my life," Ted said suddenly.

"What?" Clay stiffened in shock. This was more than baiting. This was insult.

"The perfect brother. President of this and captain of that. Always saying the right thing. Always smiling and polite. Always making Mom and Dad proud. Always right!" His pale face flushed.

"Come on, Ted." Clay's heart was pounding at the venom in Ted's voice. What had he ever done to deserve this attack? "Surely I wasn't that bad."

Ted stared at him a long, unblinking minute. "Sometimes I've come close to hating you."

Clay jerked. He exerted every ounce of self-control at his command and said softly, "Isn't that a bit extreme?"

"See?" accused Ted, finger-pointing. "You can't even get mad!"

"Oh, I can get mad all right."

"I don't believe it. It's an emotion, and you don't feel emotions."

Clay thought of his confusion over Leigh, his concern for his mother, and his resentment toward Ted. "Little you know."

"I know it's about time we were honest with each other." Ted glared at Clay. "You hate me as much as I hate you."

Clay's heart pounded. It wasn't Ted's words themselves that hurt as much as it was the bitterness, the antipathy shimmering hot and red from them. "I don't hate you, and that's God's honest truth."

"I don't believe you."

Clay shrugged. "Your choice."

"Right. My choice." Ted glared. "I made my choices, and that's why you hate me."

"I resent you," Clay said carefully. "That's different from hate."

"How?"

"If you hate someone, you just say, 'Forget him.' When you

resent someone, you try to get along. At least I do."

"So you 'resent' me for who I am."

"I resent you for what you've done to the family. You went off to have your fun and games, and look at what your choices have done to Mom!"

Ted pointed a finger at him. "You're yelling."

"I am not," Clay yelled.

"You hate me."

"I do not!"

Ted grinned, obviously pleased with himself and the rise he'd gotten out of Clay. Clay took a deep breath in an effort to calm himself.

"I've admitted that I resent you and feel bitter toward you," Clay said, proud that his voice barely shook. "But I repeat: I. Don't. Hate. You."

"The Bible says resentment and bitterness are as wrong as hatred."

"Thanks for telling me something I didn't know."

Ted laughed at Clay's response. "The perfect son is sinning!" Ted crowed.

"The Perfect Son never sinned. I, being all too human, sin regularly."

"But acceptable sins," Ted said. "Not like me."

"Not like you is right!" Clay turned his angry, bitter eyes on his twin, lying there so smugly and seeming to feel no remorse for his wrongs. "You picked the worst of the worst!"

"Picked? Picked?" Ted pushed himself up on his pillow, his eyes alight with his own deep anger. "Do you think I had a choice in being gay?"

"You bet I do!"

"You think I didn't fall on my face before God and beg for this to be taken away? You think that I didn't plead with Him to be 'normal'? You think I didn't cry over verses like: 'In the same way the men also abandoned natural relations with women and were inflamed with lust for one another. Men committed indecent acts with other men, and received in themselves the due penalty for their perversion'? Or how about this one: 'Do not lie with a man as one lies with a woman; that is detestable.' See? I've thought about them so much I've memorized them."

Clay stared. "I thought you were always proud of being gay. You sure flaunted it enough."

Ted shrugged. "I learned to be proud. It was better than being ashamed. But first I went through torment because I knew what the Bible says and what Mom and Dad would say. And you," he added in a small voice.

Clay felt a faint flicker of hope. "You actually worried about what I thought?"

Ted looked uncomfortable. "Yes."

Clay shook his head, confused. "Then why did you allow it to happen if you knew what it was going to do to all of us?"

Ted sighed. "Do you know how selfish that sounds?"

"What?" Clay was lost.

"You talk like I did this to spite you!"

"That's not what I meant."

Ted hit the heel of his hand against his forehead. "You still believe being gay is a choice, don't you?"

We come to the crux of the matter, the crucial disagreement. "I sure do. 'Choose today whom you will serve.' I'll never believe God predisposes someone to perversion."

"No more than you're predisposed to pride!"

Clay blinked, then rallied. "My pride is not the issue here."

"No, it's not, but it brings up a good question, O Perfect One. Is being gay a worse sin that being proud? Huh? Is it? Is it? Isn't all sin offensive to God?"

"Of course! But at least I'm willing to admit that I need to work on my pride, that it is wrong. I know I can't let it run rampant. I work on controlling it."

Ted didn't respond, and Clay knew he had him.

"We have to fight sin." He flinched inwardly at how pompous that sounded even though it was true. "We have to be like Joseph and flee when the opportunity to sin arises."

Still Ted said nothing.

"Right?" Clay pressed. "Right?"

"You don't understand!" Anger and desperation laced Ted's voice.

"I understand enough!"

"Hah! You haven't got the least bit of understanding and certainly no sympathy. You're hard and unforgiving!"

Stung by the truth of the accusation, Clay put on the armor of self-defense and charged full speed. "Just who do you think you are to point the finger at me? You're the one that talks of hate, not me. You're the one—"

"Stop it! Stop it, you two!"

Clay blinked and turned. Leigh stood at the foot of the bed, literally shaking, her hands clasped and pressed against her heart. Her fine dark eyes were wide with tears and her face white.

When had she come in? He glanced at Ted and saw his twin was as startled to notice her as he was.

"Don't you two have the sense you were born with?" she hissed. Her eyes, distress and disapproval shining through the tears, moved from one brother to the other in accusation.

"What's wrong?" they asked, almost in unison.

"What's wrong? Aside from the fact that you're both idiots? You're yelling and screaming like shrews."

Clay looked at Leigh in amazement. How did she project so much censure without raising her voice? Must be all those years of disciplining fourth graders.

"We were not yelling. We're discussing." Ted frowned at her.

"Ha! Your voices are carrying downstairs."

Clay glanced out the bedroom door at the stairwell and realized that it served as a funnel to carry their voices. Some of their accusations replayed on his mental tape recorder, and he flinched.

"Your mother is down there crying in her cake batter as we speak," Leigh lectured. "You don't think she has enough heartache? She needs to hear her sons yelling their hatred of each other?"

"I never said—" Clay started automatically.

.She just stared, disdain dripping, and he shut his mouth. He also dropped his eyes before the righteous wrath in hers.

"So stop it!" Leigh's chin suddenly wobbled, and she pleaded, "For her sake, at least try to be civil. She loves you both so much."

"He—" both Clay and Ted began at the same time, each pointing to the other. It was an automatic response, honed through years of childhood and instantly reactivated under the pressure of the moment.

In the space of a heartbeat Leigh's countenance transformed from reasoned plea to fury. "Stop it, I said! Stop it!" She was so upset she was breathing fire. Her cheeks were flushed and her eyes wide with the force of her anger. She was beautiful.

"Let me tell you two idiots something." She jabbed her index finger at first one brother, then the other.

"Hey, love," Ted interrupted with a half smile, indulgent and a little bit condescending. "We were having a private conversation." His tone of voice, Clay noted, was much kinder and gentler than it had been with him.

"Not when the whole neighborhood can hear you yelling you weren't," Leigh shot back. "And don't you talk down to me, Ted Wharton."

Ted glanced at Clay and rolled his eyes, a move Leigh saw and that made her furious. Clay started to grin, but when Leigh turned her attention to him, he swallowed the smile fast.

"As I was saying—" she looked back at Ted as if daring him to interrupt again—"there are all kinds of reasons why a person becomes gay. I certainly don't know how to separate what's truth from what's mere theory. In actuality I imagine the reasons are as varied as the men involved."

Clay opened his mouth to comment, but when he received another stinging stare, he made believe he meant to cough all along.

Leigh swept on. "Whatever the reasons or excuses for the temptations and tendencies to be gay—" she drew herself up, and it was obvious she was about to make her main point—"the biblical standard outside of marriage is absolute. It's abstinence, plain and simple, whether you're gay or straight."

Ted frowned and swallowed, obviously unhappy with her comments.

Clay watched her with delight. He liked her reasoned argument, but mostly it delighted him that she was finally giving Ted what for. And Ted would listen to her. He liked her.

Go get him, Leigh.

"And in this room," she continued with a dark look first at Ted, then Clay, "I don't see anyone who's practiced abstinence any more than I see anyone who's lacking in an overabundance of pride!"

With that pronouncement, she turned on her heel and stalked from the room.

All Clay's momentary affability disappeared, and he felt his temper boil over. To be painted with the same brush as Ted, and by Leigh no less, was more than he could stomach. He strode from the room, the light of battle in his eyes. He caught up with her in the hall and grabbed her arm. He dragged her away from the steps to the far corner of the hallway and spun her to face him. He glared down at her with the same intimidating expression that brought the most rebellious sailor to heel.

She looked taken aback by his manhandling, but only momentarily. Her eyes slitted, and her frown became fierce. She was not in the least frightened by him towering over her in a rage. She fisted her hands on her hips and glared back.

"Don't you put me in the same category as Ted," he hissed, his face close to hers. "Or you for that matter."

She glowered back, contempt written clearly on her features. "Why not?" Her voice was a whisper, but it vibrated with emotion. "You took advantage of a lonely girl who wanted nothing more than for someone to love her. She was ripe for the picking, and you picked. Don't you ever talk to me about being lumped with anyone!"

"He's promiscuous." He pointed to Ted's room.

"Not for many years."

He didn't listen. He was too full of pride and his pharisaical honor. He narrowed his eyes at her. "And she was more than willing!"

Leigh flinched, paled, then rallied. "Of course she was willing! You were her hero. That you finally paid attention to her was a dream come true. Many nights she lay awake, fantasizing that you'd deign to talk to her. Then you took her home. You kissed her. You made love to her. And it wasn't just anyone loving her. It was *you.*" Her voice broke on the last word, and she scowled fiercely.

Just that quickly all his anger dissipated, and he stared at her impassioned face, trying to protect himself from the truth, the pain of her words.

"Do you know," Leigh continued, her gaze moving to the wall behind him, almost as if she couldn't stand looking at him any longer. "I was actually dumb enough to believe you cared. When you left, you started to say something and fumbled with the words." Her gaze slid back and skewered him. "Do you remember?"

Clay nodded. He remembered all too well. His conscience had been roaring in his head as he'd stood by that door, and he'd tried to say he was sorry for what he'd done. The words had refused to come, lodged as they were somewhere below his Adam's apple.

"When you kept saying, 'Leigh, I—' and clearing your throat, I was stupid and naïve enough to think you were trying to get up the nerve to say you loved me." She gave a bitter laugh.

He felt again after all these years her hand soft upon his lips and saw her sweet smile. *"It's all right if you can't say it tonight, Clay."* She raised her other hand and rested it against his heart. *"I love you too. Just hug me good night. You can say it later."*

"Leigh." As overcome by remorse now as he'd been then, he reached out a hand in apology.

She jerked back as if burned. "Don't touch me," she hissed. "Don't you dare."

Anger simmered in him once again. She'd been glad enough for his touch last night when she needed his comfort.

"It's not like I was your first," he said in a cold voice. "You were already pregnant when—" His voice died in his throat when he saw the look of fury and utter contempt she turned on him.

"At times like this I wish I swore so I could call you a few of the choice names you deserve," she hissed.

"You used to be such a sweet, quiet little girl," he hissed back. "How things have changed."

"And you used to be honorable!"

She spun on her heel and rushed down the stairs while he stood frozen to the spot. Talk about a shot to the heart!

He heard the back door slam and automatically looked out the window. She was running across the lawn to her apartment, head down, curls gleaming in the sun.

Suddenly she wiped her hand across her eyes, once, twice, again.

He'd done that to her, brought her to tears.

His heart broke.

Thirteen

*L*EIGH LEANED OVER her kitchen sink and threw great handfuls of cold water over her flaming face. While the liquid cooled her flushed cheeks, it did nothing to reduce the anger and shame that burned within where her heart felt boiled to bursting.

He thought her a tramp and a floozy! He thought she slept around!

Well, maybe he didn't think she did now, but he thought she did then. How could he think such things of her? She'd been Miss Prim and Proper, Miss Socially Inept. But even if she'd been Miss Popularity, how could he? How *could* he?

How could he not?

She sagged against the edge of the sink as realization struck with a devastating blow. She had decreed his opinion of her by manipulating the script of Billy's birth as surely as the playwright led the audience to his preordained conclusions. The only difference was that the playwright realized what he was doing. She, foolish woman that she was, saw only now what she had done, and it was years too late to rewrite the living script based on a warped combination of logic and half-truths.

When it came right down to it, since Clay didn't know Billy was his, what alternative did he have but to think there had been someone else? What were the words he had backhanded her with?

"It's not like I was your first. You were already pregnant when—"

She shivered as she remembered the accusation in his voice, the condemnation.

It doesn't matter what he thinks. I don't care. You know better, God. You know the truth. You understand.

But it did matter. It mattered a lot, probably too much, and she resented Clay for making her care so deeply about his opinion without his even trying, for making her feel this intense pain at his disgust. And she was furious at herself for being so needy, for wanting his approval, for wanting him to look at her as special— good special, not trampy special. Around him she became that young girl again, yearning for his attention, his acceptance.

But not his love. Not anymore. Never his love. She was beyond that at least.

But that didn't mean she wasn't still furious at his presumptions.

She cranked the spigot closed, taking out her frustration and angst on the innocent chrome faucet.

She took several deep breaths and moved away from the sink. It was almost time to leave for the Little League opening ceremonies. She had to compose herself before she saw Billy. She went to her room to fix her makeup and comb her hair. She studied herself in the mirror and sighed. Her eyes were still redder than they should be and slightly swollen. She poked at her puffy eyelids. Too bad she didn't have a cucumber. She'd read somewhere that slices placed on your eyes relieved swelling.

She heard Billy thunder up the steps. She grabbed her purse and sunglasses. She jammed the glasses on just before he zipped into her room. The kid was too quick by half about spotting tears.

"Mom! Mom!"

His excitement was a live thing, dissipating much of her melancholy and wrapping her in the pleasant anticipation of learning about the unknown delight. She was actually smiling as she turned to him.

He looked at her strangely, momentarily distracted. "Why are you wearing your sunglasses in the house?"

"I don't want to forget them."

He frowned at that, then shrugged. She watched the excitement grip him once again. "Guess what?"

"What, tiger?"

"You'll never guess!" And he stared at her, obviously awaiting her speculations.

"I'm not up to guessing today, sport. Just tell me, okay?"

"Clay's coming to Little League with us!" His eyes shot sparks of happiness.

Leigh blanched and grabbed the bureau for balance. "What?"

"Clay's coming with us!" He danced where he stood.

"How did that happen?" she asked, feeling like the words were being pulled from her like slow-running molasses from the bottle.

"I asked him."

Great. Raise a gregarious, friendly kid and what does he do? He talks to people, any people, even dangerous people, people like Clay. Her shoulders slumped.

"I don't know, Billy," she began, turning toward the bathroom and a double dose of extra strength Tylenol.

But he wasn't listening. He raced to his room and with much thumping and thudding, changed his clothes. He reappeared in his baseball pants, cleats, and shirt with Spenser and a big eleven written in purple on the back. The Purple People Eater was printed in purple letters across his chest with a logo of a purple parrot with a beak that would topple a real bird.

The name and the bird were the cause of much embarrassment for the whole team. They lent themselves so well to razzing calls of, "You guys are a bunch of birds," or "Here come the birdbrains," just to name a few of the less offensive offerings of their opponents. The only thing that kept the team from outright revolt was the fact that The Purple People Eater was actually a way cool surfing shop run by a pair of former surfing champions, or so they claimed. Leigh had her doubts, but the Little League officials weren't about to turn down a sponsorship. And the kids believed the claims.

Billy grabbed his mitt and ran for the stairs. "Come on, Mom. We don't want to be late. Coach Jeffers said we had to be there fifteen minutes before the opening ceremonies began."

"Now you tell me." She grabbed her navy blazer and tossed his jacket to him.

He grinned unrepentantly and caught his jacket.

"Listen, Billy." She followed him down the steps and out into the yard. "I'm sure Clay was just being nice when he said he'd like to come. He's got more important things to do than spend the day at the ballpark with a bunch of screaming kids and irate parents." She hoped, she prayed.

Billy looked at her like she was crazy. "Screaming kids? Irate parents? This is just Little League, Mom, not a class trip."

"You know what I mean. All noise and confusion. He doesn't want to come."

"Sure I do," a quiet voice said.

Leigh jerked to a stop and shut her eyes behind her dark lenses. *You are not embarrassed,* she told herself. *You are not.*

"In fact, I'll even drive."

Mr. Consideration in his jeans and crimson corduroy shirt. That he should be so pleasant, so unaffected by their hissing confrontation of mere minutes ago set a new fuse to the dynamite of her emotions. She felt her face turn red and her jaw clench.

"I'd rather drive myself," she spit out, hearing the lack of grace and not caring.

Clay shrugged, a deprecating grin tugging one corner of his mouth. "Just trying to be helpful."

She wanted to kick him in the shins with a pair of pointy cowboy boots, never mind that she didn't own any such footwear. She just figured they would hurt a lot.

"Come on, Mom." Billy grabbed her hand and began pulling her toward Clay's Grand Cherokee. "I never rode in one of these cars." He turned to Clay. "Black's such a cool color."

Knowing there was no way she could avoid riding with Clay without appearing the complete fool in front of both him and Billy, Leigh let herself be led to the oversized Jeep. Without a smile she allowed Clay to usher her into the passenger seat while Billy climbed in the back. Billy leaned over the seat, studying the dash, his eyes alight with that mad glow men of all ages got over automobiles. She stared straight ahead, as removed from the situation as she could make herself while still physically present.

Billy and Clay talked cars all the way to the ballpark at the other end of the island. Motor stuff and zero to sixty in nothing flat and four on the floor and four-wheel drive and 4.2 liter engines and on and on. They didn't even notice her miffed silence.

How she hated it when Clay looked good—the thoughtful chauffeur and interested male role model—while she looked bad—the unwed mother and temperamental female.

Then stop being temperamental.

She closed her eyes and leaned back against the headrest. There were times when the last thing she wanted to hear was holy logic. It felt safer to be angry, to hide behind spite. She also knew it was unwise and self-defeating. And wrong. The little tune based on Philippians 4:4 ran through her mind: *Rejoice in the Lord always and again I say rejoice.*

I get the message, Lord. She sighed. *I'll try.*

They had to park a block from the Little League field and walk, all the places provided at the ballpark itself long filled.

"The whole town's here," Clay said conversationally as he walked at her side.

She didn't answer, but she didn't scowl either. She felt that was progress.

He didn't seem to mind her silence. "Billy, I remember when Ted and I were in Little League. We played on the Potter Pontiac Indians. But we never had our names on the backs of our uniforms."

"I bet you didn't have to buy them either, did you?" Leigh asked with what she perceived as very little frost. More progress.

"Not unless we ruined them somehow. Ted was always ruining his sliding into base. He slid even when he didn't have to because he liked it. His pants and his thighs were always torn up. Not that he cared. Mom was always cleaning up one wound or another for him."

"Having a doctor for a dad must have come in handy, huh?" Billy looked at Clay wide-eyed.

"Having Dad for a dad always came in handy," Clay said.

They joined the ever-expanding stream of parents and kids making for the bleachers that surrounded the main field, and Leigh saw she had been right. Screaming kids and irate parents. Worse than any field trip due to sheer numbers.

As if she wanted to prove Leigh's point, the woman in front of her yelled, "Adrianna Murray, you get back here, or I'll whip you but good!"

"Gotta go join my team," yelled Adrianna over her shoulder as she ran the opposite direction from her loving parent.

"Brat." The woman looked around as if hoping for someone to commiserate with her about her disobedient child. She spotted

Leigh. Her frown changed to an embarrassed smile. "Ms. Spenser. How are you?"

Leigh smiled back warmly. Big-time progress. Of course it wasn't Clay she was smiling at, but still. "Mrs. Murray, it's good to see you. How long has it been? Since the Christmas class party?" She smiled at Adrianna's diminishing figure. "Quite the girl, isn't she?"

"Are you sure you don't want to adopt her?" Mrs. Murray asked hopefully.

"Five days a week are challenge enough."

Mrs. Murray nodded sadly. "It was just a thought. You control her better than anyone I know, certainly better than her father and me."

"Punishment for disobedience, Mrs. Murray. We talked about that before."

Mrs. Murray nodded. "I know. I just can't stand to see her cry." And with that comment she veered off and yahooed a friend.

Leigh felt Clay's eyes on her. She turned, a chip the size of a two-by-four back on her shoulder.

"She can't stand to see the girl cry?" he said.

"Adrianna manipulates them with tears whenever they try to exert any control over her, and they invariably give in to her."

He shook his head. "She's going to be some teenager."

"I know. Remember, Billy, you may never date her. I couldn't deal with her even if you could."

Billy looked at her aghast. "Mom, she's a girl!"

"That's who boys commonly date," Clay observed.

"If they're stupid enough to date."

Clay looked at Leigh and grinned, welcoming her to join him in the knowledge that a day would come when Billy would change his mind. She couldn't help but smile back. She wasn't certain when she'd dropped that chip she'd been wearing, but she didn't search for it. She felt so much lighter and freer without it.

A group of sixth grade boys on skateboards glided past. "Hey, Ms. Spenser," they said more or less in unison. "Billy." They eyed Clay with curiosity.

A group of giggling sixth grade girls jogged by, tailing the skateboarders. "Hi, Ms. Spenser," they said. "Having a good vacation?" They too eyed Clay with curiosity, and suddenly Leigh saw the handwriting on the wall.

Oh, Lord, please let them keep their mouths shut! Strike them dumb.

One of the girls leaned toward Leigh. "Who's the guy?" she asked in a stage whisper that carried for blocks. "Is he your boyfriend?"

Leigh made believe she didn't see Clay's broad grin as he waited with interest for her answer. "An old friend," she said with nails in her voice. "An old *family* friend."

She regretted the last as soon as she said it. This doing things *en famille* was just too hard. It felt too good. She made herself smile at the girls and turned in the opposite direction, not caring where she was going. Clay and Billy followed.

Billy spotted several other Purple People Eaters and took off, leaving her with Clay. She straightened her back and stuck out her chin. She could handle an afternoon in Clay's company no matter the embarrassing comments. She was no longer eighteen.

Act naturally.

"Wow! They've even got lights!" Clay shook his head as they approached the main field. "And two fields, both with bleachers. Times have sure changed."

They found two seats in the crowded bleachers, and Leigh made believe she didn't notice that they were the objects of much speculation. Between her students and their parents and Clay's life-time friends, they were greeted more times than a rich man at a fund-raiser, and she read avid curiosity in every set of eyes.

Still Leigh watched proudly as Billy and the Purple People Eaters marched onto the field with the other teams for the opening ceremonies. She couldn't help but grin when he took his hat off for the national anthem and, placing it over his heart, stood stiffly at attention. She knew he saw himself as Mr. Major Leaguer, as did every other kid out there.

After a mercifully short speech by the mayor and a pep talk by the local baseball commissioner, during which the boys and girls in uniform behaved remarkably well, the teams gathered in circles, giving each other high fives and fanny pats. Then each team ran around the diamond as they were announced, waving their hats to the stands. Parents cheered, calling the names of their various off-spring as they passed. Leigh yelled just as loudly as the rest.

"Hey, Billy!" Clay called as the Purple People Eaters ran past. He put his fingers in his mouth and gave an earsplitting whistle.

Billy's face lit up, and he jumped up and down, waving both hands over his head to them. One of his team members grabbed him in passing and pulled him back into the throng.

Clay turned to her and asked, "How does one ever get up the nerve to yell, 'Go, Purple People Eaters'?"

She answered easily. "One doesn't. We shorten it to Eaters."

"Go, Eaters?"

They grinned at each other at the absurdity.

Ceremonies over, Leigh and Clay climbed down, his hand on her elbow to steady her.

"Now what?" he asked when they stood on the ground.

"Field two in fifteen minutes."

Billy raced up to them, halting in a cloud of dust. Leigh noticed that most of the other Eaters had run off in a cluster to field two.

"I'm hungry," he announced to Clay.

"Me too," Clay said.

"Billy, you ate lunch already." Leigh shot her son a look that said no begging!

"What's a ball game without a hot dog and a Coke?" Clay began to look around. "Where's the concession stand?"

Billy led them toward the stand with a proud smile, which dimmed significantly when he saw the huge line snaking all the way down the center of the parking lot.

"You'll never get anything before the game," Clay said. "We'll fill you after, okay?"

With a disgusted twist to his face, Billy ran off to join the other Eaters.

Clay kept walking, falling into place at the end of the line. "Unlike Billy, I didn't get any lunch. I'm starving."

Leigh nodded. She was too. She had been too upset to eat earlier.

"Will we miss anything important if this takes a while?"

Leigh gave a wry smile. "Unfortunately not, at least from my point of view as the parent. My somewhat limited athlete doesn't usually play until the last two innings, and only then because the rules dictate that they have to play everybody at least two innings. Then he plays left field."

Clay frowned. "That bad?"

"Not bad exactly. Just not good. But at least he doesn't day-dream out there like some of the kids."

Eventually they reached the snack shack window and purchased three hot dogs and two large Cokes. They threaded their way carefully through the crowd, Leigh carrying the Cokes and Clay the hot dogs.

"It's hard to avoid painting someone's back with mustard in a crowd this thick," he said.

"I thought you were buying Billy's food after the game."

"I am." He glanced at her as she walked beside him and saw her eyeing the third hot dog. "That's for me."

"Ah," she said as a bat cracked loudly just over the fence to her right. "Big man, big appetite."

A cheer went up at the crack, then quickly turned to groans, then to shouts of, "Heads up! Foul ball!"

Leigh looked up to see a baseball speeding in an arc, its trajectory aimed right at her. A gurgling noise erupted from her throat as she knew with certainty she would be hit. She turned to run.

She'd taken one step when she plowed into an older man standing directly behind her. Her Cokes went flying, drenching the man. His eyes went wide as sticky brown liquid pocked his glasses and dissolved the hair spray that held the long strands that he combed with evident care from one side of his skull to the other.

Leigh didn't even apologize. She ducked, lifted her hands above her head, and braced for the wallop when the ball connected. She waited for her life to flash before her eyes.

Nothing happened.

A cheer went up, and she opened her eyes to see Clay's hand just above her, the baseball seated firmly in his outstretched palm. He grinned down at her as he held the ball aloft for everyone to see.

She began to breathe again. "Thank you, thank you, thank you."

He held the ball out to her. "My pleasure."

She shook her head at the proffered ball. "This isn't the Phillies. We can't keep it. We have to throw it back."

As he lobbed it over the fence to the umpire amid the wash of more cheers, Leigh turned to apologize to the man she had given the cold bath. She felt terrible, imagining how he had come to cheer some grandchild to victory and instead endured a frigid shower. Hopefully he had a strong heart.

He was gone. She looked over and around all the bodies between her and the street but couldn't see him. She even stood on the first step of the bleachers and scanned the whole area, but the man had disappeared.

She felt bad. She'd driven some poor, innocent man from the ballpark, and not only hadn't she been hurt, but she didn't even have significant damage done to her by the Cokes.

As she made her way back to the concession stand for more Cokes, she shook her head at the farce of it all. While she, ever the klutz, drenches some poor stranger, Clay, ever the hero, makes a miraculous catch, saving her from certain injury. He'd even had the presence of mind to transfer the three hot dogs to his left hand before bagging the ball.

She sighed. Life was never fair.

Fourteen

SATURDAY EVENING, Clay tossed the baseball back and forth with Billy and his buddy Mike in the driveway, trying to work off the jitters that made it impossible for him to be still. He had had quite a day. There was his disastrous attempt to spend time with Ted and his hissing bout with Leigh. He'd made her cry. He'd made his mother cry.

Clay sighed. Nothing like a mature Christian to bring light to the darkness. Or more appropriately, pour salt into open wounds. He thought he'd redeemed himself somewhat in Leigh's eyes with the Little League thing. He'd said yes to Billy mainly to impress her, and to his surprise he'd had a great time. It had been a real kick to cheer for the Eaters and Billy who not only made a good catch but actually made it to first base. And his own hero-making catch that kept Leigh from getting beaned hadn't hurt any.

He still got chills when he thought of that ball heading straight for her. It would have clobbered her if he hadn't gotten there first. His hand ought to stop stinging in a week or two tops.

"Yo, Mr. Wharton," called Mike as the ball sailed past Clay's head.

"Sorry," he called, loping down the drive to recover the ball. At least if it went into the street, it was no big deal down here on the cul-de-sac. He scooped up the ball and tossed it to Mike who made a big jump to catch it even though it was only shoulder high.

"You've been watching too many *Great Moments in Sports* films, Mike."

"Wait until you see me," Billy yelled. "Put it here!"

Billy's contortions made Mike's look like the clip on the editing room floor.

"Let me hit you some pop-ups," Clay suggested, trying not to laugh. These two might not be long on talent, but they certainly got into the spirit of things.

"Be careful of the windows," Billy said.

"Have you had some experience with windows?" Clay asked.

"Sure. On my computer," Billy answered, all innocence.

"Hah!" Mike pointed his finger at the window over the kitchen sink. "That one."

"Well, it wouldn't have been so bad if Grandma Jule hadn't been at the sink peeling potatoes."

Clay laughed as he popped one high. The boys clustered under it, both yelling, "Mine. It's mine. I called it!"

"It's Mike's," Clay called as the ball dropped. "But don't take your eye off it!"

Mike looked at Clay at the last minute. "What'd you say?"

The ball bounced harmlessly to the ground.

"My turn," shouted Billy. "But not quite so high."

Clay swung and the ball arced.

"The window," yelled Mike. "It's going to go through the window."

Billy reached for the ball and caught it in the webbing of his glove just as he lost his balance and fell in the hydrangea bush under the kitchen window.

Billy pulled himself out of the bush as Mike rushed over, and the boys examined it thoroughly for injuries.

"It's okay, I think," Mike said. "Man, hurting that would be worse than breaking the window. For some reason your grandmother loves this little tree."

"Bush, not tree. That's because Grandpa Will bought it for her the birthday before he died," Billy explained. "It's sentimental."

Clay looked at the leafless bush. Clusters of dried, pinkish beige flowers left over from last year still clung to it. He hadn't known the story of it being Dad's last gift. He sighed. What else didn't he know that he should? He'd definitely been away too long, though he had an idea or two that might rectify the problem. He still needed to think and pray more about his future plans before he told his mom anything. He didn't want to get her excited prematurely. He laughed to himself. He'd never thought he'd want to come back to Seaside to live.

"I think we'll go to the beach," he said to the boys, his many years in the military teaching him when it was time to seek a more suitable venue.

They tramped through the dunes to the empty beach. Even the ever present Clooney was missing. Time after time, Clay hit the ball as far as he could, and the boys chased the hits tirelessly. The longer they played, the more obvious it became that Billy wasn't really a bad player. He just needed practice. And someone to practice with.

"Mike," called Leigh from the path through the dunes, interrupting them in the middle of a play. All eyes turned to her while the ball Clay had just hit sailed down the beach and bounced to the jetty.

The three ballplayers waved to her as she stood there in her bathrobe and slippers. She waved back and called, "Mike, your mom called. They need you at home."

Mike waved at Leigh. "Thanks, Ms. Spenser." He walked to Clay. "That's my bat, Mr. Wharton."

Clay handed the Louisville Slugger over and looked off toward the ball. Mike looked in the same direction. "That's Billy's." He turned to leave, stopped, then looked at Clay. "It was very nice to meet you and thanks for playing with us."

He trotted across the dunes after Leigh. Clay turned to Billy. "Mom says you and Mike want to be rock stars."

Billy nodded. "I'm doing drums."

"Yeah, so I hear." Clay glanced again at Mike's receding figure. "I don't know about you, but Mike'll never make it."

Billy stiffened at this insult to his best friend. "Why not?"

"He's too nice and polite."

Billy frowned. "And I'm not?"

Clay grinned. "You do pretty well too. I think you're going to have to look elsewhere for quick riches."

Billy sighed, then brightened. "We can practice being impolite and not nice."

"Your mother'd love that."

"Well, I wouldn't be not nice to her. I mean, she's my mom."

"She's a good mom, isn't she?" Clay told himself he wasn't really using a child to probe Leigh's privacy. He was asking a simple question. Just like he asked every kid he'd known for twenty-four hours.

"She's the best. Wanna go build a sand castle?"

"That's it," said Clay with a snap of his fingers. "You can be an architect."

Billy rolled his eyes. "Doing kid stuff like building castles doesn't mean you'd be a good architect. Besides, I'm going to be a doctor when I grow up. The rock stuff's just for fun for now."

"Billy." It was Leigh again, back at the path through the dunes. Why was she wearing a bathrobe at six-thirty in the evening?

"What?" Billy yelled.

Clay tapped Billy on the shoulder. "Don't you think it'd be nicer to walk closer to her so you don't have to scream your whole conversation?"

"Oh." Obviously this was a new thought. He started toward his mother. "Aren't you coming too?"

"Uh, sure." Clay trailed behind, watching Leigh and wondering about the bathrobe. As he got closer, he saw that her hair was all fixed and her face carefully made-up.

Uh-oh. She's got a date and hasn't finished getting ready yet. I wonder who the jerk is?

"I've got Spaghetti-Os for you to microwave," Leigh said when Billy joined her at the edge of the yard. She smiled absently at Clay. "The popcorn to go with the video is on the counter. You can take everything over to Grandma Jule's. Ted's expecting you."

"Okay." Billy nodded. "In a little bit. Clay and me are going to build a sand castle right now."

She glanced at Clay who smiled sweetly back. "Don't bother Clay, Billy. He doesn't want to build castles."

That was the second time today she'd known what he didn't want to do, and both times she'd been wrong. His hackles rose. Suddenly he wanted to do nothing more than build castles.

"I'm not bothering him." Billy looked insulted at the very idea. "He wants to build a castle, don't you, Clay?"

"Sure do, Billy." He smiled warmly at the boy, then looked pointedly at Leigh.

"Well," she said, eyeing Clay skeptically, "just be careful, Billy."

Be careful, Billy? Clay stared at her. Now what did that mean? Did she think hanging around with him put Billy in danger, like he was going to hurt the kid or something?

"Yeah, Mom. I'll be careful." He sounded so put-upon that Clay almost smiled.

"I mean it, Billy." She bent and gave him a quick kiss on the cheek. "I'll see you later." She turned and went back to the house without saying another word to Clay.

Miffed at her attitude, Clay looked at Billy. "Why do you let them all call you Billy?"

The boy looked at him in surprise. "It's my name."

"It's a little kid's name," Clay said, trying to keep his frustration with Leigh from his voice. It wasn't the kid's fault that just when he thought he was doing okay with his mother, she got all cool again. "You're too big for Billy. You should be Bill."

"Bill." The boy tried it out for size.

"You don't call Mike Mikey, do you?"

"Only when we want to make him mad."

"Then don't let people call you Billy."

"My full name is William Clayton Spenser. I was named for Grandpa Will." Billy spun and pointed. "Hey, Clayton. Clay. Just like you."

It was decidedly jarring to hear his name belonging to another. "Yeah, I'm William Clayton Jr."

"Then I'm the third." Billy's eyes sparkled.

A deep green Acura drove into the driveway and saved Clay from a response. It was a good thing because he didn't know how he felt about this imp of a boy sharing such a personal thing as his name. It was a little too father-son. So the kid's mother was driving him crazier every time he saw her. So he hadn't felt so emotionally rattled in years. That was a long way from wanting some boy to adopt a III after *his* name.

"Hey, Dr. Traynor." Billy waved to the tall, handsome man climbing out of the car in the turnaround.

"Billy," he acknowledged.

"Bill," the boy called. "I'm Bill now."

"Sounds good to me. How are you, Bill?"

"Doctors always ask that," Billy said to Clay *sotto voce*. "It's a doctor thing. Your father always asked too." He smiled at the doctor. "I'm fine, thanks. You here to see Ted?"

Dr. Traynor, looking anything but professional in jeans, a long sleeve black T-shirt, and a tweed blazer, smiled and said, "Partly."

"And partly to see me, right?" said Billy, grinning.

"Absolutely."

"Yeah, right."

"Dr. Traynor." Clay stuck out his hand. "I'm Clay Wharton."

"Obviously," Dr. Traynor said. "I'm glad to meet you."

"David." The quiet voice from the back door brought a smile to David Traynor's face even before he turned.

"Julia." His voice was deep and warm, very warm.

Clay felt a chill as he watched his mother blush. The chill intensified as Dr. Traynor climbed the steps to the house, pausing to put an arm around her shoulders. She in turn rested her head momentarily on his shoulder.

"No one told you about him yet, did they?" asked Billy with a knowing look. "I mean, *that* way."

Clay didn't answer, just stared at the closed back door.

"He's nice," Billy said. "We all like him."

Like that made it all right for his mother to go out with another man, to rest her head on his shoulder, for crying out loud! Clay turned and barked, "Go get whatever we need to build a castle. There's not a lot of time left before dark."

Smiling with much too much understanding, Billy went into the garage.

"I'm going out for a while this evening," Julia had told him that morning. She'd stood at the foot of the stairs, a mug of that vile vanilla coffee in her hand, ready to go spend some time with Ted. "I thought about canceling, but since you're going to be here for a while, I decided not to."

"No, no, don't cancel," he had said as he pulled on his sweatshirt preparatory to going to the beach. "Go. Have fun."

"Yes." She smiled. "I will."

He'd pictured her meeting some of her women friends for a movie or dinner. He'd never in his wildest imagination thought of her going out on a date!

He was still stewing when his mother came outside with David Traynor. Traynor's hand was resting in the small of her back as he guided her to his car, and she was smiling at him over her shoulder. She looked happy and beautiful in gray slacks, a bright blue sweater, and a dark blazer.

"It's okay." Billy, arms full of beach paraphernalia, came and stood beside him. "He really is nice, and he's nice to her."

"He's not my father," Clay muttered, amazed at how betrayed he felt when Traynor's car backed out and drove away.

The boy reached over and patted his arm like a little old lady might. "It's hard not having a dad, isn't it?"

Clay felt a giant hand grab his heart and squeeze, and he laid his hand on Billy's shoulder. There was such sorrow and longing in that little voice. And such understanding. Clay had to clear his throat several times. He slid his hand gently up to Billy's head and tousled his hair. "Let me tell you, Bill. Any dad would be proud to have a son like you."

Billy glanced up at him, then sighed. "Maybe. Mom says I need to remember that God is my Father."

"That's true."

"Yeah, but God can't play catch with me like you did. And he can't help me with my Pinebox Derby car. And he can't go to the father-son dinner at Awana."

"I'm sorry that it's been so hard for you." Who was the louse, he raged silently, who left Leigh and Bill alone?

Billy shrugged. "I had Grandpa Will and Ted. Grandpa Will went to lots of stuff with me when I was little, as long as nobody had a baby and he had to go to the hospital. And Ted came to lots of my Little League games before he got so sick. He'd even bring Matt with him. Matt was a bit loud, always yelling for me." Billy grinned a sad, lopsided smile. "He was almost as loud as Mom. I was sad when he died. So was Uncle Ted."

"I bet Ted gave you lots of good tips about playing. He was a great pitcher. I don't know about Matt."

"Yeah. Uncle Ted was good, very good. For an uncle."

Clay stared out toward the water and tried to imagine what his life would have been like without his father, without his love and encouragement, his example of a godly man, his repetitious lectures on the issues of life that had made him and Ted roll their eyes. *What would I have become without all these things?* Even now, a grown man of twenty-nine, he missed his dad with an ache that never quite went away. Many times he started to reach for the phone to ask his father's advice about a problem only to be brought up short with the painful realization that there was no help from that source anymore.

He took a bucket and a pair of putty knives from Billy. "Yeah, not having a dad's hard."

"But at least you knew yours." Then as if embarrassed that he'd said too much, he started for the beach, swinging his bucket as he went. In his other hand he clutched a collection of sand shovels.

"Why these?" Clay held out the putty knives.

"For smoothing," Billy explained. "And for making sharp cuts."

They walked to the packed sand in silence.

"First a big pile," Billy said. "Just a big pile."

Clay got down on his knees and began to dig. It had been a long time since he'd built a sand castle or anything else in the sand for that matter. A flood of memories of him and Ted creating masterpieces filled his mind. One of their favorite projects had always been burying their father until only his face showed and sculpting a sand body for him with impossibly big muscles and hair like snakes and feet like a clown's.

He needed to remember these fun times when he saw Ted. It would defuse a lot of his own antagonism, and then maybe Ted wouldn't be so defensive.

Lord, do you think we can ever learn to love each other again?

LOVE YOUR ENEMIES.

He's not my enemy.

LOVE ONE ANOTHER. THEY WILL KNOW WE ARE CHRISTIANS BY OUR LOVE.

Yeah. I get the message.

HER TOO.

Yeah. Her too.

Billy dropped to his knees and began sculpting like mad. He took a bucket and climbed onto the jetty. He lowered the bucket into a trough between two rocks, filling it with swirling seawater.

"It's easier that way than taking my sneakers off and wading in."

Clay nodded. "Especially when the water's still so cold."

Spring Rain ✓ 149

The two worked companionably for several minutes. A castle began to take shape if one had a good imagination.

"Why don't you like Ted?" Billy asked as he plopped another bucket of water beside the castle.

"What?" Clay was shocked at the question. He glared at Billy who kept his attention on the sandpile. This kid was too smart for his own good, and he had no inhibitions about going where wise men feared to tread. "He's my brother. I love him."

"Yeah, I know that. But you don't like him." Billy looked up from his squat. "Why?"

Clay looked out over the water. How could he explain to a kid the resentment he felt over the pain his family had suffered because of Ted's gayness?

"Is it because he's gay?"

Clay grunted noncommittally.

"Are you embarrassed?"

Clay shook his head. "No, I'm not embarrassed. It's not that simple."

"It's because he hurt Grandma Jule and Grandpa Will, isn't it? It's because he made them cry."

Clay looked at Billy with respect. "You're a smart kid."

"Yeah. I am." Billy took his shovel and with a slashing move made a ragged wall straight. "You're his twin. Did you ever think gay?"

"Come on, Bill! Where do these questions come from?"

Billy looked up. "It's a good question. Did you?"

Clay used his putty knife to cut crenellations in the top of the wall and grinned in spite of himself. This kid was a keeper. "No, I never thought gay. I've liked girls my whole life."

Billy looked skeptical. "Even at ten?"

"Well, maybe not at ten. That's antigirl time. But even then, when I couldn't stand to be near them, I knew they were special."

Billy nodded. "Me too. I mean, I don't like them, you know? They're yucky. But they're very interesting in a strange sort of way."

"Very interesting," Clay agreed.

"Do you think my mom's interesting?"

Clay blinked. Now there was a question. "Of course. Anybody with a brain would think your mom's interesting."

With a satisfied look at their glorious castle, which they could now barely see through the fast falling dusk, they collected all their implements and walked slowly back across the dunes.

They had just come into the yard when movement caught Clay's attention. His eyes narrowed as he watched Leigh come out-side in a flowing red dress, a soft white sweater draped across her shoulders. She looked absolutely lovely, and apparently he wasn't the only one to think so. A tall, burly man with a set of shoulders that would have done Arnold Schwartzenegger proud followed her. He had his hand on her arm as he guided her to his car. Nervy.

"Who's that?"

Billy glanced up. "That's Eric."

Clay eyed Eric suspiciously. "So who's he?"

"He's a teacher at Mom's and my school." Billy took the putty knives from Clay and carefully placed them in a bucket. "He teaches fifth grade. He's real nice." He glanced at Clay innocently. "I think he wants to marry Mom."

Clay blinked. "You're kidding."

Billy shook his head. "He's not the first, you know."

"He's not?"

"Of course not." Billy put the bucket down and pulled a sneaker off. He turned it upside down and watched the sand pour out.

"Of course not," Clay agreed. He had to swallow to dislodge the lump in his throat. It came right back.

"I mean, she's very pretty, don't you think?" Billy turned his highly intelligent eyes to Clay.

"Very pretty," he mumbled. "Beautiful, in fact."

"Yeah," said Billy. "Beautiful."

They watched Eric's car disappear down the street and around the corner.

"You should have seen all the guys who came around when we were in college."

Clay's head snapped around, but the boy was bent over, tying his shoe. He must have imagined the verbal taunt he heard buried in that comment.

"Uncle Ted kept telling her not to trust any of them. They all had only one thing on their minds."

Clay stared at Billy's bent head, having no trouble imagining what Ted was imagining.

Billy looked up with a sudden smile. "They all wanted to kiss her!" And he rolled his eyes.

Clay frowned. He couldn't decide whether he was more upset about guys wanting to kiss Leigh or Bill's subtle suggestion that he knew they wanted a lot more than a kiss.

"Did—" Clay swallowed and hated himself, but he couldn't stop asking. "Did she kiss many of them?"

Billy giggled. "Uh-uh. I was always around. Or Uncle Ted. Or Grandma Jule or Grandpa Will." He looked proud and pleased and smug. "We all made sure of it."

Clay almost swallowed his tongue at the thought of that gentle conspiracy. "Don't you want your mother to marry?"

"Sure. Sometime." Billy looked at him. "Don't you?"

"Don't I what?"

"Want her to get married. I mean, she'd be awful lonely if she never married anyone. I'll leave home as soon as Mike and I get our band contract—I really think we can make it even if we're nice—so she'll need someone."

"Um."

Billy shrugged. "She could do worse than Mr. Wilde."

"Mr. Wilde?"

"Eric." Billy waved in the direction Leigh and Eric had disappeared. "I'm not supposed to call him Eric. I might forget and do it at school, and that would be bad."

"I can see that. Kids can't call their teachers by their first names. Disrespectful."

"Can you call a teacher Dad?"

Clay shuddered. "Has he actually asked her to marry him?"

"I don't know. She doesn't tell me everything, you know." He looked thoughtful. "Maybe I'll wake up some morning and have a dad." He raised those wide brown eyes, magnified by the glasses, to Clay. "Do you think she'd do that?"

"Your mother's too smart to do that." *She'd better be too smart, Lord. After all, it wouldn't be fair. To Bill.* He noticed his stomach was starting to ache just like it did that morning when he'd made her cry.

"Of course maybe she'll decide to marry Hank. I don't think I like him as much as Eric. He wheezes when he breathes. Asthma. What if they gave me a brother or sister with asthma?" He shook his head. "It'd be too hard. He or she'd keep us awake all night.

But asthma's probably better than moving. That's what Mr. Henderson says we'd need to do."

"Who's Hank? And Mr. Henderson?" Clay beat down the feelings of panic that kept kicking up a fuss beneath his breastbone.

"Hank's the head guy at the bank on Twentieth Street. I think Uncle Ted introduced them. Mr. Henderson—he's old. He's got gray hair!"

Clay could swear he felt his own hair turning gray as a result of this conversation.

"He owns all those pizza places on the boardwalk. He's rich. He drives a neat little black Miata. What do you think of old men driving little sports cars? Does it mean they're unstable? I'll tell you, though, I wouldn't mind owning a car like that. He took me for a ride once. It wasn't a long ride, but anything's better than nothing in a case like that. I think he wanted to get back to Mom."

Clay forced himself to unclench his teeth. "How did she meet this old guy?"

"He goes to our church, but he wants to retire to South Carolina. And then there's Pastor Paul. I almost forgot him. He's single too."

"What does she do? Go out with every single man she meets?" The edge to his voice took him aback, but Billy didn't seem to notice.

"Oh no. Only those who ask her. Of course, that's a lot. Like we said, she's pretty."

Clay saw the wayward silken curl that had wrapped around his finger when he held her as she cried. He saw the warm eyes and the sweet smile she had given him when he helped clean up the apartment. "Yeah," he managed. "She's pretty."

"Very pretty."

"Very pretty," he agreed. Inside and out. That cute, young girl who had entranced him eleven years ago was now a beautiful Christian woman with character and grit.

"Well." Billy turned back toward the beach. "What do you think?"

"We've got to keep her from making a mistake and marrying some bozo."

Billy looked at him in disgust, fists resting on his bony hips. "I mean about the castle. How long before it washes away? Who cares about Mom?"

"Yeah, who cares about Mom?" Clay muttered at midnight as he heard Eric's car pull in. Finally. He clicked off the TV and went to peer out the window. He bit back a sneer as Eric opened the car door for Leigh and took her hand to help her out. He kept hold of the hand all the way to the garage.

Clay stepped back from the window when he heard a little voice whisper, "You're spying."

Clay spun. "Bill! Get back to bed. Your mom will think I'm a lousy baby-sitter."

He shook his head. "Mom doesn't even *know* you're my baby-sitter. She thinks I'm asleep at Uncle Ted's. Besides, it's fun to greet Mom when she comes home." He giggled. "It's how I keep them from kissing her."

A key turned in the lock, and the front door swung open. Two sets of footsteps moved up the stairs.

"Hi, Mom," Billy called, running forward and peering down the stairwell. "I'm so glad you're home! I missed you."

Clay peeked over Bill's shoulder, thinking the boy's enthusiasm was only a bit over the top. It was wonderful to see the disappointment splashed across Eric's handsome mug as he saw the faces staring down at them.

Leigh raised an eyebrow at her son, obviously onto his game. She ignored Clay.

"And look who baby-sat me." Bill pointed to Clay who grinned in his most disarming manner. Bill threw his arms around Clay's waist.

"Don't go too overboard," Clay whispered through his smile.

Bill giggled.

Eric's disappointment changed to a definite scowl.

"Hi," Clay said to Eric, all candor and goodwill. "I'm Clay Wharton, an old friend of Leigh's." He gave a wide smile and extended his hand.

"Ted's twin," Eric said as he unenthusiastically shook Clay's hand.

"The same," Clay agreed. "Would you like a cup of coffee or a soda before you go? Bill and I have been snacking on popcorn off and on all evening while we watched a couple of movies with my brother. We brought all the leftovers home and would be glad to share with you. And you too, of course, Leigh."

"Of course," Leigh echoed.

Never mind that the coffee was left over from early evening, cooked to a fine bitterness, and the popcorn had been reduced to kernels at about nine. Clay's strategy was to smother him in friendliness, and he'd leave sooner.

"Thanks, but nothing for me." Eric turned and took Leigh by the shoulders. He was pulling her toward him—and she wasn't protesting!—when Bill tripped over the coffee table.

"My toe!" he cried. "I stubbed my toe!"

Leigh rushed to his side, bending down beside the distressed boy, leaving Eric with his arms holding air.

"Oh, honey," she said, all concern. "How that must hurt."

"It does, Mommy." Bill gave a quavering little sob. Clay had to admit that the kid was very good.

"Let me carry him to his bed," Clay offered, going down on his knees beside Leigh. "We can take care of him there."

"Would you, Clay?" Bill asked, gratitude oozing from every pore.

"Hang on, old buddy." He pulled Bill into his arms and stood. Leigh stood with him, her hand resting on his arm as she looked at Bill.

Clay looked at Eric. "Poor kid. Stubbing your toe hurts so much."

"Yeah," muttered Eric. "Poor kid."

Biting back a grin, Clay strode toward Bill's room, Leigh right behind him.

"Leigh!" Eric stood in the middle of the living room, deserted and exasperated.

"Can you let yourself out, please?" Leigh called from Bill's door. Clay was almost certain she was biting back a giggle. "I'm sorry, but I have to see to Billy."

Clay let Bill fall to the bed where he bounced a couple of times on the mattress, a huge, smug smile on his face.

It was all the three of them could do not to laugh until Eric was safely out the door.

Fifteen

HE STARED AT what was left of the sand castle. Over half of it was gone, and a little more went every time a wave hit. He'd seen Billy and the brother guy building it. They'd worked hard, and now the water was washing it away. Just disappearing like the sand dissolved or something. All that was going to be left was a bump in the sand. It gave him a weird feeling, like maybe he could disappear like that too.

Those waves were sneaky. They dribbled in with little bits of foam floating on them just like they didn't want to hurt nothing. But they were eating the castle alive. *Chomp. Chomp.* He laughed at the picture in his mind of a wave with a big open mouth. *Chomp. Chomp.* Now there was a good joke.

He wondered why the brother guy spent so much time playing with the kid. They'd played ball before they built that castle. He thought hard, but he didn't think anybody'd ever played with him like that. Anybody grown-up, he meant.

Maybe if someone had played with him, he would have been good at sports. Then he wouldn't have been the last one to get picked for all the teams all the time. He hated being last.

A wave rushed up the beach and washed right over his shoe. He jumped and swore as more of the castle collapsed. How he hated the ocean, just hated it! You couldn't trust it. It ate things, and if he wasn't careful, it'd eat him.

Muttering, he walked up the beach to the path that led to the Whartons' house. He skulked cautiously to the edge of the yard. He wasn't wearing all black tonight, so he had to be careful. He glanced up at the garage. It was dark except for that one light Leigh-Leigh always left on. She had gone out for the evening, and so had the mother. Out on dates. He grinned, imagining what they were doing on those dates. Not that he knew from experience, but he'd seen lots of movies.

He frowned. Why didn't girls like him? Maybe he wasn't some movie star or nothing, but then neither was anybody else. Then he smiled. Wait until he got the treasure. Then the girls would flock to him. He'd strut around in fancy clothes and drive a big fancy car, and the girls would be hanging all over him, falling out the windows of the car there were so many.

Enchanted by the picture of his social success, he glanced up to where the AIDS guy lived. The greenish flash of a TV lit the room. The kid and the brother guy were up there with the sick guy watching something. He grinned. He knew what guys watched when they were being guys. Too bad he wasn't invited to the party. But then when he was rich, he wouldn't invite them to his party either.

He decided to go get something to eat. His stomach had been growling for a long time. He wandered down the driveway and started walking toward the main part of town where the restaurants and stuff were. He hated not having a car, but he didn't have the money to buy one or a credit card to rent one. If he didn't get the treasure soon, he wouldn't even have enough money to eat.

Pizza. That's what he wanted. They had lousy pizza in the joint, the crust dry and hard. The cheese didn't even taste like cheese. Johnny said once that he thought it was artificial. How could there be artificial cheese? It was either cheese or it wasn't.

He sighed as he walked. Nothing was going to happen tonight. Leigh-Leigh wasn't home, and she'd probably be real late getting in, if she even came home before morning. She needed to be there to get the full effect of the next step in his plan. He grinned and scratched himself. He was sure going to show her. Maybe tomorrow night.

His feet were tired and sore when he finally reached town and the pizza place, but the pizza was real good, and the cheese was definitely real. It got all stringy and gooey, and he had to pull at it with his fingers. It was a good thing Ma wasn't here to crack him over the knuckles and scream, "Don't eat with your hands, you little moron! And chew with your mouth shut."

Of course she never kept her mouth shut, chewing or not. Yadda, yadda, yadda. The lady never shut up! That's one reason the old man whopped her so much.

He got back to the Whartons' about ten-thirty. It wasn't too long until the mother came home. She and that doctor went into the house. He was giggling behind his hand about their plans for the rest of the night when the doctor came back out. He got in his car and drove away. What was going on here? Wasn't he spending the night? Who dated and didn't spend the night? Were they too old for stuff like that or what?

It was after eleven when Billy and the brother guy crossed the yard to the apartment. What did Clooney say his name was? Oh yeah, Clay. Like modeling clay. What a dumb name. It wasn't too much longer until Leigh-Leigh and her "friend" drove up. He held her hand as they walked across the yard, and they didn't see the brother guy watching from one of the apartment windows.

He had watched Leigh-Leigh all day today himself. He'd even gone to the Little League opening ceremonies, taking the bus. The thing that he couldn't get over was how much everybody there seemed to like her. They smiled at her and waved to her and talked to her. Johnny thought she was a loser, but nobody else seemed to. It was very strange.

It had been exciting when that ball almost hit her. He was standing just behind her, and all he had to do was reach out and he'd touch her. He remembered the feeling of power it gave him to be so close, yet be invisible. She didn't know who he was, but he knew who she was. And he had power over her. Then the foul ball came, and she turned around to run. He saw her face real good, and she was scared. Real scared. It made him want to smile.

Then she ran into him! He still remembered the shock of the ice cold Coke washing over him. He shivered all over again. He just hoped that Coke washed out of clothes without staining. After all those years in orange jumpsuits, he didn't have that many nice clothes.

He waited in the dark, and it wasn't long until the apartment door opened and the "friend" came out. Going home already? Then she would keep the brother guy. Now that was interesting. But no. The door opened a little bit after the friend drove away, and Clay came out and went to the main house. Soon the apartment lights went out.

He frowned. What was with all these people? If the old man was out of town or off on a binge and Ma brought someone home, he stayed. If Ma was gone, the old man brought bodacious babes home and they stayed. The guys in the can always bragged about their women. It was the way life was.

But these people were different. A thought hit him. He bet anything they were in some weird religious cult, like them nuns in their black dresses, and no sex was part of the deal.

He muttered to himself as he shuffled off down the beach to the house with all the windows. Some people he just couldn't understand. He'd go look in on those he did.

Sixteen

SUNDAY AFTERNOON, Julia glanced out the tall living room windows. It was a bitter day outside, the sky pewter, the sea topped with frothing whitecaps, the wind chilly and insistent. It was a day for collars to be turned up and hands to be stuffed in pockets, a day when winter reminded everyone that it may be stepping aside for a while, but it, like General MacArthur, would return, and they'd better not forget that fact.

She turned and looked around the green-and-crimson living room with its accents of palest yellow and cream. Inside all was cozy and warm with everyone she loved here. Her heart swelled. *Thank You, dear Lord, for these occasional perfect moments. They make the others, the painful ones that come with living, bearable.*

Leigh and Billy sat on the sofa looking at a scrapbook of pictures taken when the twins were little. Every so often Billy's chortle would ring out as he pointed in disbelief at a photo.

"I hate to say this, Uncle Ted, but you guys were such dorks."

Ted, looking wan and weary after expending so much energy eating dinner with them, managed to appear offended. "What do you mean, dorks?"

Billy jumped up and assumed an *en garde* position, feet apart, one arm raised like it was holding a rapier.

"Ah," Ted said, nodding. "For your information,

everyone in our class wanted our *Star Wars* light swords."

"Sure. And you've got some oceanfront property in Arizona."

"Clay," Ted called. "Tell him."

Clay was standing by the bank of windows looking onto the dunes, talking with Pastor Paul Trevelyan who had come home with them after church for dinner. They were discussing the Phillies' chances for a decent season without any apparent hope. Clay had been acting as Paul's host for the afternoon, a role he had taken on himself without any encouragement from her. Truth be told, Paul came over so frequently, he didn't need a host. He was very much at home here.

Still she appreciated Clay's effort. He just didn't know how familiar Paul was with all of them. He didn't know that Paul had made Ted a special project, spending large amounts of time with him.

But it seemed to her that there was something strange about Clay's attention to Paul. It was as if he was trying to keep Paul from talking to Leigh, though why he would do that was beyond her ken. Three times she had seen Clay deliberately step in Paul's path when he had turned to say something to Leigh. Clay did it so pleasantly that Paul didn't seem to notice. Neither did Leigh. The upshot was that Paul never had any conversation with Leigh.

"You say we were dorks?" Clay stepped to the sofa, glanced at the photo Billy was deriding, and grinned. He slashed the air a few times with his imaginary light sword, parrying and thrusting right into Billy's stomach. Billy squeaked and fell back onto the sofa. "Can dorks defeat the vile Darth Vader?"

"We spent a lot of time keeping the universe safe for democracy," Ted said.

"Yeah, right." Billy looked at the picture again and shook his head. "You look dumb is all I can say."

"Just wait until you get old, and we laugh at your pictures." Ted lay in the leather recliner, feet raised to relieve his swollen ankles. Julia hated to see that retention of fluid, fearful of what it meant.

Her eyes skittered to David who had dragged a dining room chair beside Ted and was talking quietly with him when Billy wasn't interrupting them with picture commentary.

David.

She took a deep breath as she looked at him. Last night they had gone to dinner and then bowling. She couldn't remember the last time she had bowled, and it showed. He beat her soundly, and all she did when he told her the final score was 193 to 87 was giggle. She shook her head at the memory. She had actually giggled! She hadn't giggled since she couldn't remember when.

He felt her gaze and turned his head, giving her that slow warm smile of his.

She giggled.

His eyes lit at the sound, and she flushed. He held out a hand, and she walked to him. He took her hand in his, unself-conscious in front of the room full of people. She wished she could say the same. She could feel Clay's frown cut through the amiability of the room like a laser through the darkness. Still, she left her hand in David's warm grasp.

"That was a wonderful dinner, Julia." David squeezed her hand. "And the apple-caramel pie was out of this world."

She beamed with pleasure and swallowed back another giggle. Really, it was too much, the way this man made her feel like a teenager. She'd just begun wearing an estrogen patch this very week, for Pete's sake! And the flush coming on at this minute had nothing to do with David's proximity and everything to do with her age. She felt a drop of sweat at her hairline slide down her temple.

"Hey, Grandma Jule."

Julia turned to Billy, ignoring Clay's narrowed eyes as he studied the handclasp. She wanted to giggle again at his scandalized look. Poor boy.

"What's up, Billy?"

"Bill," he said. "My name's Bill."

"It is?" Julia made herself look surprised and confused. "You mean I've been calling you the wrong name all these years?"

Bill shook his head. "Clay says that *Billy's* for little kids. I'm too old for it now."

Julia looked at her son. "Clay says, eh?"

Leigh was also looking at Clay, Julia noted, and her look wasn't too friendly.

"Yeah," Bill said. "We had a guy talk last night about names and girls and not having dads. He said Bill was best."

"A guy talk?" Ted looked amused.

"About girls?" David raised an eyebrow.

And not having dads, Julia thought, and felt her heart catch.

Everyone turned to Clay who looked a bit rosy in the cheeks. He looked at Leigh's enigmatic expression and spread his hands. "Hey, Bill was just a suggestion."

She snorted.

Julia stepped into the breach with the practice of a mother who'd ended many an argument between her sons by diplomatically changing the subject. "So what did you want me for, Bill?"

"Oh," he said, called back to his original purpose. "I wanted to know if you have any more old pictures. These are so funny."

"First we're dorks, and now we're funny," Ted said. "That's my childhood you're laughing at, kiddo."

Bill held up a school picture of Ted wearing a plaid flannel shirt. His hair hung below his ears and touched his shoulders. His bangs were in his eyes. It looked like someone had tried to comb it before the photo, but the effect was still that he had just rolled out of bed. "You look like some homeless kid who lives in his father's car. Didn't you ever go to a barber?"

"They didn't. Nobody did." Julia studied the picture, then grinned at Ted. "You do look like a little ragamuffin whose mother shopped in the rag bin."

Ted put his hands out to the side. "See? What can a little kid do if his mother doesn't take care of him?"

"I think you look sort of cute," Leigh said, tongue firmly in cheek.

"That was when all the guys had long hair." Julia turned to David. "Remember?"

"Do I." He brushed his free hand over his close-cropped graying temple. "I had hair that fell below my shoulders."

"You?" Bill stared at the carefully groomed man in his Sunday slacks, button-down dress shirt, and loosened tie.

"I was a rebel, my boy," he said with pride. "I still don't know why my parents didn't disown me. I'll have you know that during my junior year in college I even thought momentarily about joining a commune, but I wanted to go to medical school more." He grinned. "Leslie thought I was wonderfully nonconformist. I lived in jeans and T-shirts, all with holes. You had to have holes to be a real antiestablishment figure."

"Did you go to Woodstock? Were you a Jesus people?" Bill asked in awe. "I saw all about them on a TV special."

"I did not go to Woodstock, and I wasn't a Jesus people, at least not in the strictest definition," David answered. "They were a California phenomenon, and I lived in New Jersey. But I sure looked like one, and I believed in Jesus like they did."

"How about Grandpa Will? Was he a hippie too?"

"Apparently not as much as David," Julia said, thinking how much she'd like to see a picture of the young David with his long hair and holey jeans. She just knew he'd be as handsome as all get-out. "What we need is that old box of pictures I keep stashed in the attic. You can see Grandpa Will's long hair and giant sideburns in some of those pictures. You know the box I mean, Clay?"

He nodded. "Come on, Bill. You can help me find it."

The two left the room together. Julia smiled after them. It was good to see Billy—Bill—with a male to emulate.

David tugged gently on her hand. "Sit. I'll get another chair from the dining room." She sat. David pulled a chair beside her, and she was a bit disappointed when he didn't take her hand again.

Several thuds and a groan or two announced the imminent arrival of the rest of the photos. Julia flinched as she thought of her walls and the sharp corners on the box. Bill shuffled into the room, lugging the large box. Clay followed, calling out navigational directions.

"Be careful of that coffee table. To the left, Bill. The left! That's right. Now straight ahead. Watch the edge of Ted's recliner. You're going to trip over it."

Bill hit the leg rest and howled, mostly for show, Julia was certain.

"My shin! My shin!"

"Is it as badly hurt as your toe was last night?" Leigh asked.

Bill stopped howling and grinned at his mother. "We sure got old Eric, didn't we?"

Leigh shook her head. "Billy, you've got to stop picking on my dates, you know." But there was no heat in her directive.

"It's Bill."

"Oh. Right." She frowned at Clay who didn't notice. Paul slid over and took a seat beside Leigh. Poor man, Julia thought. He must be bored silly with all our family pictures.

"I'm serious, Mom. I'm too big for Billy."

Once more Julia leaped into the breach. "Let's look for a picture of Grandpa Will, see who can find the funniest." As she talked, she reached up and opened the top button of her blouse. She fanned the material back and forth to try and create a breeze.

David patted her on the shoulder. "Don't worry. The patch will kick in sometime soon."

"Every night at one, three, and five I get awakened in a drenching sweat. I toss the covers off, fall back to sleep, then wake up freezing. It had better start soon."

Bill put the box down on the sofa between his mother and Paul and rooted through the hundreds of photos inside. Leigh grinned at them with him.

Julia crossed the room and grabbed a great handful from the box. She brought them back to Ted and David.

"Hey, Mom, remember this?" Ted held out a picture of himself and Clay standing on the bank of a stream. "That campground in Colonial Williamsburg."

Julia groaned. "I don't think I ever spent a hotter week in my life! Even the swimming pool was close to boiling."

"At least we learned never to go south in the summer," Ted said.

"Well, look at this, will you?" David held out a picture of a young Julia in a frothy pink evening gown, orchid at her shoulder, her hair parted in the middle, hanging long and straight and shiny. Her face was young and smiling and full of hope. "Quite a beauty."

Julia glanced at the photo, then at David, and blushed, quite a phenomenon considering how warm her face already was.

"But more beautiful now," he said softly as he reached across her to show Ted.

She didn't quite manage to swallow the giggle, and it came out as an undignified snort. "My senior prom. Just before everything formal went out of style."

Ted held out a series of photos. "Look at these old Little League pix."

David leaned over. "I bet Adam's in there."

"Here." Julia stood. "You sit here so you can see better."

She and David changed seats, and he smiled his thanks. Soon he and Ted were laughing at the earnest faces of Seaside's Little

Leaguers, Ted and Clay and David's son, Adam, among them. Julia looked at the next picture in her hand and stared, perplexed.

It was a picture of Billy, mussed hair, glasses, and impish grin, but at the same time it couldn't be him. The clothes were all wrong, the photo itself was too old to be Billy, and the three-by-six black-and-white picture bore scalloped edges like photos sometimes had back in the fifties.

With a trembling hand she turned the picture over. *Will Wharton, age 10,* was written on the back in her late mother-in-law's hand.

Will. Her Will.

She turned the picture over again and stared at the boy frozen in time. He had been small for his age, not getting his height until his last two years in high school and his weight in college. Not long before he died, he had talked to Billy about being small.

"I know it's not easy being the littlest guy in your class," Will had said to the woebegone Billy.

"Tell me about it," Billy said. "How do you survive as a little guy when all the bigger guys are picking on you all the time?"

"You learn to run real fast until you finally grow. Then you get back at those guys for all the years of agony."

"Will," Julia said, appalled at his advice.

"Yeah," the then seven-year-old Billy said, his eyes bright with vengeance. "I'll beat 'em to death."

Will grinned, first at Julia, then at Billy. "That wasn't quite what I had in mind," he said. "How about we plot strategy in a few years?"

Julia's eyes misted as she studied the photo. There would be no strategy sessions now. She ran a finger gently over the black-and-white face.

Then she looked across the room at the living Bill. It was like looking at a twin. She looked at her real-life twins, Ted and then Clay.

Will and Bill. Ted and Clay.

She smiled. How she loved all her men, so much alike, so very different.

She glanced back at the picture, marveling at Bill's resemblance to Will.

And she knew. Just like that, she knew.

Shivers slid up her arms, standing all the soft hairs on end, and a soft gurgling sound erupted from her throat as the picture fell from her suddenly lifeless fingers. She stood abruptly, hand pressed to her middle in an attempt to lessen the nausea that roiled through her. She had to get away. She had to be alone. She had to think.

Will and Bill! Clay!

"Mom?" Ted said. "Are you all right?"

"Julia?" David said.

She barely heard them. Without a word she left the living room, the house, the property, and did what she always did when troubled. She went to the beach and began walking.

The wind whipped her hair and tried to force itself down the raised collar and up the cuffed sleeves of her jacket, but she barely noticed. She just stuffed her hands into the pockets and walked toward the water, head down against the blast. Little patches of sea debris—clam shells, scallop shells, seaweed, sea grasses, all washed up and tumbled by the tide—littered the edge of the packed sand line. She passed them, then turned north to walk parallel to the water on the sand, packed hard by the tide.

"Hey, Julia!" It was the ever ebullient Clooney, metal detector in hand. Little spade holes pocked the beach where he had been.

Automatically she waved, trying without success to force a smile, but she didn't slow. The last thing she wanted to do was look at one of Clooney's latest finds, oohing and aahing over a brass shell casing or a Kennedy half dollar or a lovely ring, sand still clinging.

"There's a pair of oystercatchers down there," he called, pointing toward the north curve of the beach. "You'll love them."

She waved again and kept moving. Ordinarily she'd be delighted with the rare opportunity to see the black-and-white birds with their bright orange-red beaks, but not today. Her world had just undergone a paradigm shift of major proportions, and all ordinary things were reduced to ashes. Her mind reeled, grappling with the immensity of what she now knew was truth, and she was overwhelmed with a tumult of emotions.

First anger and despair. How could Clay behave so badly? How could he ignore his responsibilities all these years? Hadn't he learned anything they had tried to teach him about being a Christian man? And Leigh. Why had she kept Billy's paternity a secret? What did she hope to gain? Or did she mean to protect?

Then heart-stopping joy. Billy was her grandson. He was really hers! Grandma Jule wasn't just a courtesy title; he belonged to her and she to him.

And the overwhelming ache of failure. Sheer, unadulterated failure. She had once again fallen way short in her role as mother.

She stopped, buried her face in her hands, and cried from the depths of her soul, *God, oh, God! How do we unravel this without causing great pain?*

It wasn't God who slid his arm about her waist and pulled her to him, but David, surely sent by God to give her the comfort she craved, the support she needed.

"I'm here," he said. Just, "I'm here," and her eyes filled with tears. She turned into him and clung, her hands clutching his jacket. He wrapped his arms about her and rested his head against her hair. For a long moment neither said anything.

Then, "I saw the picture." His voice was gentle and quiet, just above her ear.

She nodded against him, glad she didn't have to explain. "They could be twins."

"Yeah, they could."

She took a long, uncertain breath and leaned back. When the wind slapped her face, she felt wet cold and realized with surprise that she was crying. She reached up to wipe her face dry.

"Let me." Still holding her with one arm, David dug into his pants' pocket and pulled out a handkerchief. He wiped the tears off the right side of her face, then the left. His sweet concern touched her heart.

"You have a wonderful bedside manner, Doctor," she murmured with a tremulous smile.

"I bet you say that to all the doctors." His hand slid down her arm to take a firm grip on her hand. "Come on. Let's walk."

It's funny, holding hands with David, thought the part of her brain still capable of analyzing in spite of the emotional chaos whirling within. *It's so different from Will, but it's so comforting, so wonderful. And I thank You, God, that he's here for me now. To go through this with no one…* She shuddered and thought of Leigh fighting all her battles for all those years alone. Julia's heart broke while her respect for Leigh soared.

She and David came to a jetty marching across the sand and into the water, a static boulder army waging unrelenting warfare with the enemy sea. They slogged through the thick, dry sand to the landward end of the great rocks and walked around them. And there on the other side at the edge of the sea, sitting motionless, was the pair of oystercatchers Clooney had mentioned. Their black feathers gleamed in the sun, and their great bright orange beaks looked too long and too heavy for them.

Julia's breath caught at their beauty. Life might have turned upside down, but even so there were wonder and hope and the glory of God's hand. The birds slowly spread their great wings and lifted off, their white wing and tail patches glowing. They banked to the left and flew out of sight around the bay side of the island.

She looked at David and saw the same wonder on his face. Impulsively she grabbed him around the middle and hugged. He was so kind, and he was here, a caring man who wasn't going to let her go through this crisis alone. Then, embarrassed by her audacity, she drew back quickly. He looked at her and smiled his slow smile. One hand lifted to her face and brushed some of her windblown curls back. Of course the wind grabbed them immediately and tossed them right back where they had been. David fingered one.

"Talk to me, Julia," he said as his fingers played with her hair. "Tell me what you're thinking, what you're feeling."

She closed her eyes a minute, wondering at the miracle of emotions that allowed a person to experience the sweetness of his concern and the pain of that picture at the same time.

"Clay has to be Billy's father." She swallowed. "It sounds so bald, thrown out like that, but that's the way it must be."

David nodded. "I agree. At least I agree that with such a strong resemblance between Will and Billy, there has to be a genetic connection. Is there any way that Leigh's family could be connected to Will's through some distant relative or something?"

Julia shook her head. "Mom Wharton was very much a genealogy buff. We have family trees tracing the Wharton family back to the midsixteenth century. There's no possibility of an old Spenser-Wharton connection." She sighed. "Any connection appears to be in my son's generation."

David nodded and squeezed her hand. "You have to eliminate all possibilities."

"How could he?" she demanded, all of a sudden overcome with anger at her son. "Tell me that, will you?"

David just looked at her.

"Not that," she said, waving away the obvious. "I understand how he could be attracted to Leigh, how they could be together. It breaks my heart because I know how young they would have been and how lost she was at that time. But I understand. I cannot understand though how he could just ignore her afterward." She felt the tears on her cheeks again and brushed impatiently at them. "I thought he had more character than that." She looked into David's solemn eyes. "I thought we'd done a better job than that." The last was the merest whisper. Even saying it tore her heart.

"Julia." David pulled her to him. "Don't. It's not your fault. Clay was grown, at least grown enough to make his own choice." He rested his cheek on the crown of her head. "You and Will did a wonderful job. You were wonderful parents. I know. I saw you both with those boys. I saw you with each other. And I saw a couple who loved each other, loved their boys, and loved and faithfully served God."

His affirmation felt so good, a soothing balm on her emotional wounds. "But we failed somewhere, David." She stepped back and looked at him. "We must have. First there was Ted. Now there's Clay."

He studied her a minute, then looked out to sea. "It's easy to feel like you failed as a parent even though rationally you know better."

She nodded. "That's it exactly."

He held out his hand and she took it. They walked quietly for a minute.

"I understand what you're saying because I've felt the same way myself." His voice was soft, like he was making a great confession.

Julia blinked. "About what? Your girls are wonderful. And Adam was a wonderful boy."

"But I let him drive when I shouldn't have into circumstances he wasn't ready for."

Julia stopped and turned to face him. "Do you mean that all these years you've blamed yourself for the accident that killed Adam and Leslie?"

David shrugged. "I bought him the car. I let him drive on roads he wasn't skilled enough to handle."

"And I suppose you set up the driver who was speeding and lane hopping and who clipped Adam's front bumper and sent him into the skid?"

"See? Rationally I know I didn't, but emotionally I keep thinking that if I'd prepared Adam better, it wouldn't have happened."

She rested a hand lightly on the front of his jacket. "Why do you think they call them accidents?"

He smiled sadly at her and nodded. "What it really comes down to," he said, "is that we do the best we can with the help of the Lord, but our kids' choices and their fates are ultimately theirs, not ours. And they are ultimately responsible to God, not to us, for those choices."

She shivered as a fierce gust raced down her collar. "But even when we know we're not really responsible, we still have to live with the consequences. Or in this case, Billy has to live with the consequences." She blinked against the too-ready tears. "Ten years without a dad because my son didn't own up to his responsibility. David, that breaks my heart."

David had no answer for her. He merely took her hand again, and they walked until they came to the next jetty.

"Come on." David climbed up on the rocks, pulling her after him. They passed the Keep off the Jetty sign and, jumping from rock to rock, made their way to the end of the breakwater. Seawater swirled on both sides of them, the algae that clung to the rocks rising and falling with the gentle ebb and flow of low tide. They stood side by side, hands clasped.

"I have a grandson," Julia said, staring at the horizon. She turned to David with a blinding smile. "I have a grandson."

He grinned down at her. "I don't know about this, Julia. Do I want to keep dating a grandmother?"

"Are grandmothers allowed to date?"

He put out an arm and drew her against his side. "This one better be."

She rested her head against his shoulder, and they stood silently, comfortably.

She spoke first. "You know, I keep thinking about Leigh. I think I understand why she never said anything to Will or me about Clay, but at the same time, I feel hurt that she couldn't trust us enough to tell us. Does that make sense?"

"I think so," David said after he thought about it for a minute. "Certainly she didn't want to hurt you."

Julia gave a bubble of laughter. "Oh, my. I wonder what she thought when Will and I first started showing such a strong interest in her. There she was, pregnant by Clay, and suddenly his parents were in her face almost every day. In fact, I made it a point to go through her line at the Acme literally every day. She must have been beside herself trying to figure out what was going on."

"Did you ever ask her about the baby's father?"

"When we first found out she was pregnant. She just said he wasn't an issue. We didn't push." She smiled wryly. "We didn't want to seem intrusive."

David nodded. "Unfortunately an uninvolved father is not an uncommon scenario. Of course you never questioned her comment."

"And Billy doesn't look like the twins. We had no reason to ever look so close to home when we wondered. We knew Ted was her special friend, but clearly only a friend. We never gave Clay a thought."

She paused, brow furrowed in thought. "But now that I think about it, I can see that through the years, Leigh had done everything she could to avoid Clay. It wasn't a big problem when she lived in Glassboro. It's got to have been more of a challenge since she moved here. When he did come home, she and Billy frequently went away for the weekend. If they remained at home, she stayed away from the house. And since Clay's been here these past couple of days, I now see how prickly and cautious the two of them are around each other."

"All signs of a history," David said.

"All signs."

A wave gurgled up to Julia's toe. David took her hand, and they climbed back down to the beach and began walking toward home.

"So now what do you do?" David asked.

"I don't know. I talk to them, I guess." Julia detoured around one of Clooney's holes. "But I need to think for a bit about what I'm going to say. And I need to pray."

David stopped, and she turned to face him.

"Have I told you how special I think you are?" he asked.

She smiled. "You're the special one. I came out here a wreck, but you've talked me through things, and I feel much more in control, at least for the moment. Thank you."

She turned away and began walking toward the house. He followed, but not before she had seen more than "special" in the way he looked at her.

Oh, Lord, considering everything, I don't think I can deal with the depth of affection I see in his eyes at this moment, but I don't want to be without his comfort. Does that make me terrible?

And feeling torn, she waited for him to catch up. They were walking through the dunes to the yard when a terrifying thought struck her.

"David, what will all this do to Billy?"

Seventeen

Sunday evening the phone rang, its shrill call filling the small apartment.

"Don't answer, Billy," his mom called from the kitchen. "I mean it."

"Mom! Why not?" The phone had been ringing off and on all day, and now it was night, and it was still ringing and driving him crazy. He couldn't stand to hear a phone ring and ring like that. Phones were meant to be answered. They made no sense otherwise. She made no sense.

They'd been having such fun just a few hours ago laughing at Uncle Ted and Clay in those silly pictures. Then Grandma Jule and Dr. Traynor disappeared all of a sudden, and Clay got all grumpy and started looking out the windows.

"It's okay if they're together. He's nice," Bill said, but Clay didn't listen.

Then Mom found a picture of Uncle Ted and Clay in their graduation robes with those stupid flat hats on their heads and got very quiet. Pastor Paul tried to move the box of pictures from between her and him, probably because he could tell Mom was upset about something, but Clay leaned over and dug into the box so he couldn't. Then Pastor Paul sighed and left. Clay walked him to the door. When he came back into the room, Mom shot him a dirty look.

When Bill found a picture of Clay by himself at graduation, his diploma in his hand and a goofy smile on his face, he hooted about how silly those graduation hats were. Clay came over to look, the start of a smile on his face. He studied the picture, looked at Mom, then lost his smile. She wouldn't look at him though and *boom!* Suddenly she grabbed Bill by the arm, and they were leaving.

"But I haven't finished the pictures!"

"Another time," Mom said.

"Good-bye, Uncle Ted," he yelled as Mom dragged him out the door, but Uncle Ted was too busy studying one of the pictures to even look up. "Good-bye, Clay," Bill yelled next, but Clay was too busy watching Mom.

Since then he'd been sentenced to hours of the phone ringing and ringing.

"Come on, Mom. Answer it! You're being ridiculous."

"No, Billy. We are not answering the phone." She clicked on the garbage disposal.

"Bill. It's Bill." He stared at the ringing instrument, then at the kitchen. Keeping his voice low even though the disposal ground on, he said, "What if it's an emergency? Huh? What if someone really needs to talk to us, like Grandma Jule needs help with Uncle Ted or something? I think I should answer just in case."

She didn't reply. He smirked to himself. That means she must agree. He grabbed the receiver.

"Hello. Spenser residence," he said, but more softly than he'd ever spoken into a phone before. She had ears like a rabbit, and it'd be just like her to hear even over the rumble of the disposal and the gush of the water.

"Is this Billy?"

"Bill. Yeah. Who's this?"

The man ignored his question. "Have you seen Terror lately?"

"What?"

"You know, kid. Your dog." The man sounded impatient.

"He's not my dog. He's Clay's." Why was the man calling about Terror? Was something wrong? Had this man found him wandering or something? But how would he have gotten out? Or if he was out, how would he have gotten off his chain?

Bill's hands got clammy as a scary thought hit him. Maybe

somebody sneaked up and unhooked the dog! He would run off if that happened. What if he got hit by a car? He was so little and fast a driver might not see him until it was too late. What if he was lying in the street somewhere bleeding and crying?

"Is something wrong with him?" He swallowed to get the wobble out of his voice. "Is he hurt?"

"Not yet, I don't think," the voice said, and Bill heard a wicked chuckle. "But you'd better check the jetty before the tide gets any higher."

Bill went cold all over. He dropped the phone and ran wildly down the steps, out the door, and across the yard. He charged through the dunes and across the beach. He didn't stop until he was climbing on the jetty.

"Terror! Terror!" He couldn't see the dog anywhere.

He tried to see to the end of the dark jetty stones as they marched into the sea, but he couldn't. It was very dark out here on the beach, the moon hidden by clouds. The only illumination was the dull, deep gray wash reflecting off the heavy clouds from the bright lights of Atlantic City in the distance. All he could make out about the jetty was the white foam of waves breaking around invisible rocks.

He stood absolutely still for a minute, listening. Was that a bark he heard over the rushing and breaking of the waves?

"Terror! Where are you, boy? Come here. Come to Bill." He slapped the side of his leg, then realized the dog could never hear the slap over the water's noise.

Then he heard it, weak and far away but definite. A bark. A terrified bark. From way out on the jetty.

"Come on, boy," he called again. "Come to Bill. You can do it. You can make it back here."

More barks, but they didn't move toward him like they would if the dog was coming. They stayed far off and eerie.

He's stuck out there!

The thought raced through Bill's mind as he climbed over the first black rocks. Somehow the little dog had caught a foot or something, and he couldn't get free. Bill's mouth dried as he realized that the pup could drown out there, wet and scared and alone, if he didn't save him.

"I'm coming, boy," Bill called. "I'm coming. I'll get you. Don't be afraid." As he talked, he began a cautious trek across the uneven assortment of great rocks. It was so easy to run and climb and jump on them in the daylight. He and Mike did it all the time. It was spooky at night when you could barely see where you were putting your foot. The last thing he needed was to step into a hole between rocks and get stuck too. He'd never be able to help Terror then.

He jumped across a large gap between two rocks and rushed to the next rock. The darkness hid what in daytime was a mere bump in the rock's surface, but now it reared up and ambushed him. He tripped over it going full speed and went down. He threw his hands out to protect himself as he pitched forward, and they hit space. He came to rest with his belly teetering on the edge of the rock and his chest, head, and arms tilted downward. His hands were actually dragging in cold seawater swirling at the bottom of the cleft between the rocks.

He lay gasping, his chest tight with fear. He felt like he might never breathe again. How had he missed bashing his head?

Terror barked. No, Bill decided. He squealed, fear lacing the sound.

I've got to help him! God, help me!

The water in the cleft gurgled higher, covering his arms to the elbows and slapping him gently in the face. Bill lifted his head and raised his hands. He reached out. His fingers touched the rock in front of him, and he pushed. He slid back on the rock where he half lay until he could leverage himself to his knees. He was wobbly when he stood, and his right knee hurt like blazes, but he was all right.

"I'm coming, Terror. I'm coming!"

He looked at the part of the jetty still stretched before him, waves creaming against its sides. It had never looked so long. Water swirled in and around the rocks, and each wave brought the water level a bit higher.

Each wave put Terror in greater danger.

Bill went around the cleft by climbing over the rocks beside it and made it over the next several rocks with no difficulties, but he came to an abrupt halt when he saw the chasm that lay ahead of him. The Grand Canyon.

At least it looked like the Grand Canyon right now. He and Mike always thought that the army guys who had built the jetty had forgotten to add one giant rock, and it made for a deep ditch between the rock where Bill stood and the rock on the far side. Water, a dark gleam in the heavy night, fell and rose as the waves ebbed and advanced. A piece of driftwood floated on the surface. He had to cross this chasm because the rocks beside it were too jagged to climb on in the daytime, let alone at night.

Bill knew he'd jumped this chasm many times when he and Mike played here, but it looked so wide in the dark. What if he misjudged? He could break a leg or something, and then both he and Terror would be the victims of high tide.

He looked down into the canyon and saw the black water heaving and the foam swirling. It scared him just looking down, but he knew the water wasn't really deep. It just looked that way. There were rocks under there, like the second layer. If he fell in, he wouldn't go under. He'd just go to his waist or something. And he'd break a leg or an arm. Or his neck.

You can do it. You can do it.

Terror's howl pierced the night, and Bill looked out to the end of the jetty. He could just make out a large wave rolling over the top of Terror's rock. The dog was a shadow, jerking and pulling, trying to get away from the water. Soon a wave would come and cover him. It would pull him right off the rock, sucking him back into the water. He'd be dashed against the rocks and killed if he wasn't drowned first.

"I'm coming, Terror! I'm coming!"

Swallowing his fear, Bill sat on his rock and lowered his feet into the hole. His feet disappeared into the swirling water.

You're taller than the hole is deep. You'll be okay. You're taller than the hole is deep. You'll be okay.

He took a deep breath and pushed off. For a minute he felt suspended in space. Then cold water grabbed at him. His sneakers hit the algae slick rock at the bottom of the ditch. He felt his feet slip.

"No!"

He flailed about, trying to save himself, but couldn't on the slippery, uneven surface. He knew a moment of pure panic as he fell.

His head didn't quite go under, at least not all the way, but the rest of him did as his fall and a wave surge coincided. The piece of driftwood bumped gently against his cheek. The frigid temperature of the sea took his breath, and he was panting as he stood. He climbed onto the far rock. The chill air whipped about him, making him shiver.

But he was almost there. He could hear Terror's constant whine now, and he could see patches of white fur.

"Hang on, buddy! I'm almost there."

He took a step and froze as he realized his feet were under water and what little visibility he had was gone. He slid one foot forward, searching for the edge of the rock. The water ebbed, and the rock showed again. He breathed a sigh of relief but knew that any minute the water wouldn't pull back so far.

The noise of the waves amazed him. They crashed so much more loudly at night than in the day. He hadn't realized that before. It was scary, spooky. Even so, he kept moving, stepping in and out of rising and falling water as he climbed up and down and over the great rocks.

"It's okay, Terror," he called again and again. "It's okay. I'm coming."

He glanced up and saw a huge wave, crest white with spume, about to break over Terror's rock. It would definitely wash him out to sea. Bill jumped the last crevice and grabbed just as the wave broke.

The wave caught him full in the face as he bent over the pup. He coughed and sputtered and tried to lift the very wet and frantic Terror, but he couldn't. The wave receded, pulling him down on his knees beside the terrified dog. His toes hooked over the edge of the rock toward land and held on. Water now covered the rock with no relief, lapping partway up his thighs as he knelt.

He felt rather than saw the rope about the animal's neck. At first he didn't realize what it was. He squinted at it through water-spotted glasses, puzzled. Then it hit him with all the force of the line drive that had clipped him in the nose last year. Someone had tied Terror to the rock!

Anger burned in Bill, hotter than he'd ever known in his life. Who would have done such a terrible, terrible thing? He grabbed the rope and pulled. It wouldn't budge. He pulled again harder. Nothing. It was wedged firmly in a crevice, and with all the water, he couldn't see where and how.

Moving quickly he put himself, still on his knees with his back to the sea, behind Terror. When the next wave broke, it struck him in the middle of the back, but his body protected the dog, at least a little bit. He began working his hands around the rope at Terror's neck. He found the knot quickly, and his cold fingers began to pick at it.

Come on, come on!

Whoever the guy was who had tied Terror up had used the slipknot that boaters use to tie up to a dock, loop inside loop inside loop. He'd tied it himself lots of times when he'd gone out on Uncle Ted's boat with him and Matt. He stood, gave a brisk tug, and the loops fell apart. The rope dropped away just as a wave struck him in the back of the knees. He felt himself stumble and grabbed Terror.

As the wave receded and pulled at him, he braced himself. When the sickening sensation was gone, he picked up the dog and held Terror against him like a mom did a burping baby. He was relieved and surprised that they were both still solidly on the rock.

Thanks, God. Just a little bit longer, okay?

He cradled Terror, cooing to him as the dog lay shivering against his chest, his wet little head pressed against Bill's neck.

"Just stay still, okay? We'll be back on land real soon."

He looked back the way he had come, and in that moment Bill knew fear like he'd never experienced before. The houses were so distant, their lights little pin pricks, like stars. The night was so dark, and the water swirled wildly over the rocks in front of him. He couldn't see where to step. He just couldn't see.

"The dog and the kid are together."

Clay pulled the phone from his ear and squinted at it. "What?"

"The dog and the kid are together. And they're okay, at least for the moment. Just a bit wet." An evil laugh floated down the line.

"Who is this?" Clay demanded, but there was now only a dial tone. It had to be the same man who called Leigh last night. How many crank callers could there be in one neighborhood? And he had threatened Bill.

"The dog and the kid are together."

"Hey, Mom." He leaned into the hallway and called up to Ted's room. "Is Terror up there with you guys?"

"No." Her voice floated down the stairwell. "Isn't he with you?"

Obviously not, Clay thought as he pondered the call. *"Just a bit wet."* His mouth drew together in a hard line as he understood that there was only one place they could be getting wet.

Clay grabbed the big flashlight his mother kept on the kitchen shelf. He threw open the back door and almost knocked Leigh to the ground. He grabbed for her, but she saved herself by jumping backward down the steps.

"Are you okay?" He was afraid she might have twisted an ankle or something.

She brushed his question aside with a wave of her hand. "Is Billy here?" Her voice was full of tension, and he could see her chin quiver.

Clay shook his head.

Leigh ran her hand through her hair. "He's gone. The phone was off the hook, making that bleating noise. I told him not to answer!"

Clay hated to speak, knowing he was going to upset her more. "I just got a strange phone call telling me he and Terror were together."

Leigh went still. "Was it the same man who called me last night?" She spoke in a whisper, like it was all she could manage.

"I don't know. I didn't hear his voice then. But this guy had a nasty laugh."

She shivered in spite of the heavy jacket she wore, wrapping her arms about herself. "Yeah. He did. What else did he say?"

Wishing he didn't have to tell her the rest of the message, but knowing he did, Clay said, "He said they were getting wet."

"Wet? Wet!" She turned toward the beach and started to run. "I'm going to kill him." She didn't clarify whether she meant Bill or the caller.

Without speaking they ran through the dunes, Clay shining the flashlight ahead of them. When they gained the beach, Clay fanned the light along the tide line. Nothing.

"Where is he?" Leigh asked, panic edging her voice. She stared out over the ocean. Clay could see her nightmare thoughts flash across her face.

"He's not floating off to China, Leigh."

"A lot you know," she spit at him. "A lot you care!"

Clay blinked. Where had that venom come from? To set her

mind at ease, he fanned the flashlight beam across the water. Nothing but undulating waves. Then, to his great disbelief, he caught quick sight of movement as the band of light glided over the closest jetty. He threw the beam back across the rocks.

The light reflected off the spume of the incoming waves, making the foam almost iridescent against the black of the water. The beam also revealed a small form far out at the end of the jetty, water churning at its feet.

Leigh moaned and swayed, her hand at her throat. As he automatically put out a hand to calm her, Clay's own heart felt squeezed of life as fear unfurled in his chest. But he never touched her. She moved too quickly.

"Billy! Billy!" Leigh ran onto the jetty.

"Leigh! Wait!" Clay raced after her and grabbed her arm. "You're going to trip and fall."

"Let go of me!" She turned on him, slapping at his arm. "I've got to get Billy!"

He tightened his grip. "*We've* got to get Bill," he corrected. "Now wait for me and the light, or I'll have to drag you back too."

She made a hissing noise and pulled free.

Clay shone the light in front of them, but even so it was tough going. The shadows dipped and swelled, making the terrain shift and twist. He grabbed for her hand to help her, though she was nimble in her walking shoes.

She shook her head. "I can keep my balance better if both hands are free."

He jumped across the cleft a third of the way out and turned to shine the light for her. He reached across, and this time she took his hand. She jumped lightly over, and they climbed on.

Water hissed and coiled all around them, washing into all the crevices, rising ever higher. In the gleam of the flashlight beam algae expanded and contracted with the swells like green hair. Fat strips of seaweed rose and receded, floating on the surface on their air bladders.

Clay turned the light to the end of the jetty. "We're coming, Bill!" he called as loudly as he could, hoping the boy could hear him over the clap and drum of the water.

"Careful, Clay," Leigh yelled all of a sudden, pulling on his hand. "There's a drop about here."

Clay pitched the light down to his feet, away from Bill and a soggy Terror. The drop was just in front of them, and water swayed and bucked through it like a fast moving stream through a narrow culvert.

He eyed the distance and judged he could jump it without much trouble. He thrust the flashlight into Leigh's hand. "Shine it for me so I can see where I'm jumping."

"Take it with you. I'll be okay without it." Somehow they both knew she wasn't going across this chasm.

He shook his head. "I think I'm going to need both hands."

Nodding, she trained the light onto the far rock just as the waves spilled up out of the ditch and over the surface of the rock where they stood and the rock where he was to jump. They were wet to their ankles.

"Hurry, Clay!" she pleaded, her eyes on the shadowy silhouette of her son.

As if he needed to be told! He stepped back two steps, ran, and leaped. He landed with a splash. He spared a moment to glance back at Leigh and saw her nod. He turned back to Bill and cautiously slid his feet as he moved, feeling for bumps, edges, any danger hidden by the black wash of waves.

"Come toward me, Bill," he called. "Can you do that?"

The water around Bill was now consistently knee-deep, and the swell of the waves reached above his thighs. Soon a big surge would lift him off his feet. The only good thing about the deeper water was that the waves weren't breaking against the boy anymore. They were breaking against Clay himself. They slapped against his legs, but they didn't worry him. He'd grown up around the sea, and though he had a great respect for it, especially when it was angry, he wasn't afraid of it.

"Reach, Bill. Come on! Reach toward me!" The boy seemed frozen to his spot, unable to move.

"I can't!" Bill's voice was full of tears, but he yelled loudly. Still full of spunk in spite of his precarious position. "If I let go of Terror, he'll jump. I need two hands to hold him."

Just a few more feet, a few more feet. If only he could see where he was stepping! Leigh's aim with the flashlight wasn't the greatest, which was probably good since all he'd get if she shined it downward was a shiny reflection off the water. Understandably she had it fastened on Bill. In its gleam where it streamed behind the boy, Clay could see the rumbling lather of a large wave bearing down on the jetty, breaking early and coming fast.

"Drop Terror and run!" Clay ordered, expecting instant obedience.

Bill, unlike the men under Clay's command in the navy, balked. "No way!"

Clay knew there had to be a break in the rocks between his position and Bill's. He just didn't know where it was.

Help me, God! No broken bones or sprained ankles, please!

He leaped, coming down on Bill's rock beside him and Terror an instant before the wave rolled through. He spun around, braced his feet, and held tight to the boy and the dog, making sure their faces were turned toward shore.

The wave slapped him in the back, causing him to sway, but not really endangering him. It passed over Bill at shoulder height, and it would have certainly lifted him off his perch. Clay felt weak with relief as he lifted the boy and dog into his arms.

"I knew you'd make it," Bill mumbled as he burrowed close. He shivered convulsively, and Clay thought of hypothermia and hurried.

Slip. Slide. Pray. Slip. Slide. Pray.

After forever they reached the chasm where Leigh waited, water foaming about her shins.

"Can you stand, Bill?" Clay asked.

Bill stopped shivering and said, "Of course I can stand."

"What are you going to do?" Leigh asked as Bill took his place beside Clay, Terror still clutched tightly to his chest.

In answer, Clay slid into the water-filled ditch, yelling as the frigid water hit his stomach and chest.

"Here, Bill." He held out his arms. Bill stooped and fell into them. Clay twisted and held him out to Leigh. She stuffed the flashlight into a pocket so that the beam shone wildly up into the air. She held out both hands, grabbed her son under the arms, and pulled. Between Clay's push and her pull, Bill, still clutching Terror, was soon standing beside his mother. They moved cautiously back to make room for Clay as he put his hands on the rock and lifted himself out of the water.

"The Grand Canyon," Bill said, teeth chattering.

"What?" Both Clay and Leigh looked at the boy.

He pointed at the chasm. "That's what Mike and I call it."

Clay nodded, and doing his best to ignore how miserable he felt with the wind slapping him, he put one hand on Bill's shoulder and grabbed Leigh's free hand. Leigh shone the light ahead of them, and with care they picked their way until they were beyond the water's reach.

"Put Terror down now, Bill," Clay said as the dry rocks lay before them.

"I think I'm frozen in position," Bill said as he slowly opened his arms. "I've been holding him so hard, I can hardly move."

Terror gave a yip, hopped down, and made a straight run for the beach, the dunes, and home.

"The least he could do is say thank you," Bill muttered as a great shiver shook him.

"Come on, guy." Clay reached for the boy and picked him up. "Let's get you home and warm."

Weary and cold, Bill didn't even protest being carried. He wrapped his legs around Clay's waist and his arms about Clay's neck, resting his head on Clay's shoulder.

Leigh walked slightly ahead of them, the light shining on the ground, as the three of them went home.

Eighteen

*H*E SHRANK BACK into the shadows as they walked past. The last thing he wanted was to get caught in their flashlight beam. Not when everything was going so good. And it was going good. It was. It was. It was.

After they passed, he walked onto the beach and down to the water's edge. He stared at the waves curling almost at his feet, but he was careful to keep out of their reach. No wave was eating him, no siree.

He sighed and tried to figure out how he felt. Emotions raged inside him, but they were so confusing! It bothered him that he got so mixed up, but it was nothing new. He often thought two different things about someone or something, and it was hard on a man. At least it was hard on him. It gave him a headache. Like thinking Johnny was his best friend, but Johnny was slime.

His plan had worked tonight. He was happy about that. He had shown Leigh-Leigh that he meant business. He wanted that treasure, and she'd better give it to him or else.

But his heart was still beating too hard from fear. At first he'd just been nervous. What if it didn't work? Then the kid came running down and out onto the jetty, and he'd been so excited. It was working just as he planned. He called Clay on his cell phone and waited.

He hadn't counted on the tide coming in so fast or being so mean. Not that he trusted the ocean to cooperate, but he hadn't expected it to try and eat the kid. He didn't want the kid to drown. He didn't even want the dog to drown. When he stole it from its chain in the backyard, the little pooch kissed him all over his face like he was its best friend or something. He grinned at the memory and touched his cheek where he'd been kissed.

He'd always wanted a little dog just like Terror when he was a kid, but he never asked because he knew they'd say no. They always said no. They never gave him anything he wanted, and they gave Stanley everything. All Stanley had to do was look at something and it was his. Stinkin' Stanley. It was probably good he didn't have a dog back then because Stanley would have killed it. But he liked little dogs a real lot, and he really liked this one.

So he didn't want to hurt the dog any more than he wanted to hurt the kid. They were just supposed to get wet and scare Leigh-Leigh so she'd give up the treasure real easy.

He shivered even though he was toasty in his black jacket and cap. It was inside he was cold. It was like he was almost a murderer. It was like he was almost as bad as Stanley! It was enough to make him puke.

But he wasn't like Stanley. He wasn't! He didn't *mean* for the kid to be in so much danger. Stanley always meant every nasty thing he did.

He'd tried to make it as easy for the kid and the pooch as he could. He'd tied the dog with a knot that was easy to undo, the knot his mother used to tie him up with when he was real little. He didn't know where she'd learned it.

Once, twice she wrapped the rope around his middle. Then she made him sit on the ground and wrapped it twice around both him and the tree by the garage. Then loop, loop, loop. Almost like magic the knot appeared.

"Stop your whining, you little creep. I'm tying you up for your own good. You'll wander off while I'm busy if I don't. Stanley'll let you loose when he comes home from school."

Then she'd go in the house with her latest boyfriend, and he'd wait terrified, certain Stanley would hang him. For some reason he never did. Stanley liked to use his hands, not the rope.

One day as he sat tied to the tree, he'd gotten hold of the end of the rope. She never tied his hands tight or anything. She wasn't that mean. He just reached his hand out and picked the end up. He was just playing with it when the knot started coming undone. Just like that. He pulled harder, and the next thing he knew, he was free. He crawled behind the garage and hid until dinnertime. Then he put the rope back in the garage. Nobody knew he could get free, and he never told. It was his secret, his way to beat Ma.

But he never forgot that knot. After all, he seen her tie it— loop, loop, loop—enough times. He used it for Billy because he was *not* like Stanley. He wasn't even like Johnny, the slime. He was a *nice* man.

He stared across the inlet at the lights of Atlantic City. They were so bright and beautiful. He wanted to go over there so much he could taste it. He couldn't wait to have the treasure.

Nineteen

*L*EIGH WALKED OUT of the apartment slowly. The sun was bright today, the wind brisk but warm. A perfect shore spring day. A perfect vacation Monday.

She stopped just outside her door and looked toward the beach. In the light of such a glorious day, it was hard to believe last night's horror actually happened. She shuddered as she thought of Billy out on that jetty in the dark with the tide advancing, and fear sank its talons into the soft tissue of her heart and drew new blood. She knew she'd have nightmares for years.

And it wasn't over. *He* was still out there, whoever he was, demanding the treasure.

Her eyes closed. *Oh, God, the fear is still here. You've got to help me deal with it. I'm terrified something will happen to Billy that I can't fix, that he'll be badly hurt or killed. He came so close last night. Help me to trust You! And please, help me figure out what the treasure is!*

She opened her eyes just as Clay opened the back door to put Terror on his chain.

Clay saw her, smiled, and waved as Terror barked a happy greeting. She nodded, solemn as she watched him. What would she have done without him last night? He had been wonderful, going after Billy without a second thought. With his greater height and strength he had moved over the jetty so quickly and easily. And he had handled Billy so well.

"You'll be okay in no time, pal," he'd said as they reached the apartment door. He gave the boy a hug and set him down. "A warm bath and some hot tea and under the covers with you. You'll be warm before you know it."

Billy nodded and started for the steps, though without his usual panache. He was so weary he could barely move. He stopped and turned. "Thanks, Clay. I may have saved Terror, but you saved me."

Leigh nodded. "You did." Her voice cracked with gratitude and emotional exhaustion. "How do we ever thank you?"

"You don't." He smiled and touched her cheek with a knuckle. "I'm just glad I'm here."

He'd shivered then as a gust of wind rushed across the yard. "I've got to go follow the same advice I gave Bill." But first he looked at her, concerned. "Will you be all right?"

It was the second night in a row he'd asked her that question. "I'll be fine. Now." She went up on her toes and gave him a quick kiss on the cheek. "Thanks again." And she rushed upstairs, amazed at her temerity.

Now in the bright light of a new day she shivered at the memory, at the memories.

She walked to the beginning of the path through the dunes and sank to the bench Julia had put there to sit on when you dumped sand from your shoes. Mama, majestic in her dismissal of the barking, tethered Terror, walked over and hopped up beside her, curling into a ball in the warm sun. Absently petting the huge cat, Leigh stared at the sliver of beach and sea visible through the dunes.

He's nice.

She tried to ignore that thought, but it kept percolating to the top of her brain no matter how hard she tried to squash it.

He's very nice.

Nice is what you say when you can't think of anything else to say. It means nothing. Blah, bland. Nothing.

Nice is when you're kind and concerned and helpful and considerate and put yourself in danger to help another.

Yeah, well, he just happened to be here for a change. She had to fight against the feel-good emotions. She had to. *So he helped. Big deal.*

He's helped several times, hasn't he? He's nice.

What was he supposed to do? Let his dog drown?

It wasn't his dog he wanted to save, and you know it. It was your son. His son, only he doesn't know it, does he, Leigh?

She saw Clay last night, Billy clasped in his arms as he carried the boy home. The image of Billy's head resting on Clay's shoulder while his skinny legs in their wet jeans wrapped about Clay's waist made her vision blur. They looked so right together, the father and son, that it scared her.

It's my call. It's my right to keep my secret.

Is it?

She slammed her eyes closed again, as if that would stop the mental debate. No such luck.

What's wrong with admitting he's nice?

What's wrong? Are you crazy? I haven't the emotional stamina to open that Pandora's box.

You're afraid.

You're darn tooting I am. He can't be nice! He can't!

And in a flash she realized why. If Clay were nice, genuinely nice, then she couldn't continue to blame him for The Incident. She couldn't make him out to be the villain of the piece. She couldn't keep the cloak of righteous indignation wrapped protectively about herself. She'd have to admit to equal responsibility, and not just intellectually. She'd have to admit it emotionally.

And she was liable. She had let him into her house that long-ago night. She'd never said a negative word. If she were to be totally truthful, she'd been more than a little encouraging. A separate but equal responsibility.

She pulled her legs up onto the bench, wrapping her hands around her shins. She rested her chin on her knees and sighed.

Okay, Lord, what are You telling me?

She stared down the path through the tunnel of dunes. Of the great expanse of sand and sea, she saw only a sliver, a slim beige band of beach, and a gently rocking ribbon of gray-green saltwater.

Epiphany.

A narrow view of Clay, huh?

That was it, she knew. She had been suffering from an acute case of tunnel vision, looking at Clay for years from a deliberately narrow perspective. He had taken advantage of her loneliness. He hadn't come back to her. Period. He was therefore unworthy. Wholly accountable. To blame.

While those basic facts were true—he had taken advantage; he hadn't come back—she had to admit her conclusions were not. There was a lot more to Clay, and well she knew it if she was willing to be honest. He *was* nice. That quality had attracted her to him way back then. It was one of the reasons she had had such a crush on him. He was also intelligent, kind, and handsome, a natural leader. And he cared deeply about things.

He had such difficulty dealing with Ted because he cared inordinately about both Ted and what was right. She understood that with a clarity that made her wonder why she hadn't seen it sooner. When he couldn't reconcile Ted and truth to his satisfaction, he was deeply torn. Since truth was invisible, he took out his frustration on the all-too-visible Ted.

He also cared deeply for Julia. Even though he didn't come home as much as his mother would have liked, and Leigh now suspected that was as much because of her as because of Ted, she knew he wrote, called, and e-mailed Julia regularly. He was a loving and concerned son.

And on top of it all, Clay was a godly man, a man of integrity. One sin, one fall from grace, no matter how major, didn't negate years and years of living for the Lord. Granted it put a big dent in things, but it didn't change the basic truth that Clay loved and followed Jesus with an intensity and devotion she had to admire.

She lowered her forehead to her knees and felt like weeping.

Clay was nice. Very nice. More than nice. And if she had the courage to be totally honest with herself, she still cared for him. Maybe she even loved him. No wonder Eric didn't interest her, or Hank or Mike Henderson or any of the others she had dated through the years.

She shook her head. No wonder she was scared.

Not that she feared they'd jump into bed again. They were both older, both in better control of themselves, both regretful about the other time, both committed to following Christian principles. It was for her heart she feared. He could break it today as badly, maybe worse than he had before.

Oh, Lord, what do I do now?

"Mom?"

Leigh started and looked up at Billy's hesitant voice. "Hey, guy. I thought you were still asleep."

"Are you all right?" He stood midway between her and the apartment door, frowning in worry. Terror was calling a happy greeting, but Billy ignored him. Mama, of course, ignored them all as she slept on.

"I'm fine, baby. Just thinking." She held out her hand to him.

He walked to her and let her take his hand. She delighted in the feel of his small palm in hers for the ten seconds he let her hold it. Then he smiled weakly as he looked toward the main house and began tugging. Clearly he was worried about someone seeing him holding hands with his mom. Leigh smiled to herself and released him.

He promptly folded his arms, putting his hands safely out of her reach. "Do you know we only have raisin bran?" It was an accusation, however mildly stated.

She nodded. "It's good for you."

His look of disdain made her smile. "I'll just go to Mike's and get some decent cereal." He didn't even pause his customary ten seconds before beginning to trot across the yard.

"No, Billy!"

He stopped and looked back over his shoulder. "Bill, Mom. It's Bill! And why not?"

"You're not going to Mike's this morning." She ignored his frown. "We're going out to Pop-pop's."

"What in the world are we going there for?"

Leigh couldn't say, "To try to find the treasure so that your life will be safe." She didn't want him to know about the threat. "Because."

Bill blinked. "What?"

Leigh got up off the bench and strode to the main house. "You heard me. We're going to Pop-pop's."

By this time Terror was jumping against the end of his rope with such desperation for Bill's attention that he was gagging himself. Bill knelt, still frowning, and absentmindedly rubbed the dog behind his ears. Terror leaned against him in ecstasy.

Leigh marched into the kitchen just as Clay and Julia were finishing breakfast. Bill, scowling fiercely, was right behind her, an unchained Terror on his heels.

"She won't let me go to Mike's."

"I'm sure she's got a good reason," Clay said peaceably.

"Yeah. Because."

"Ah," Julia said. "I used that one every so often myself."

"Thank you," Leigh said, feeling vindicated. She poured a cup of coffee and took a sip. Mmm. Hazelnut this morning.

Bill still looked mutinous but knew he was beaten, at least for the moment. "What good have you got to eat?" he demanded. "All we've got is raisin bran."

"Homemade raisin toast," Clay said. "Mom made the bread this morning for an early birthday present because she remembers it's Ted's and my favorite." He smiled at Julia who smiled thinly back.

Leigh looked at Julia closely as the older woman got up and poured herself another cup of coffee. She was wearing jeans and a yellow, long sleeved T-shirt and looked like sunshine. Still she didn't seem her usual cheerful self.

"More raisins," groused Bill. He wandered to the counter and picked up the sharp bread knife.

"Sure you don't plan to run me through with that?" Leigh asked with a wry smile.

Snorting, Bill sawed two thick slices of bread from the loaf and stuck them in the toaster.

Leigh made herself look at Clay. He smiled warmly, and she looked self-consciously away.

Act naturally!

But it was easier when he was the bad guy.

"Have a good night's sleep?" Julia said. It was obvious Clay had told her nothing about last night's adventure. Leigh didn't want to deal with it at the moment either.

Bill slathered butter on his toast and announced, "I'm going up to eat this with Uncle Ted. He'll let me go to Mike's."

"Too bad he's not in charge," Leigh said. "Pop-pop's. In ten minutes."

The buzzer sounded on the dryer, and Julia stood. "Be right back. I've got to get that dress out and on a hanger before it becomes a mass of wrinkles."

"A dress?" Leigh asked her, quirking her eyebrows. "For a stay-at-home Monday? Where is David taking you tonight?"

Julia didn't answer, but she turned a delightful pink. She left the room smiling.

Leigh looked at Clay. "Stop scowling."

"I'm not scowling."

Leigh snorted.

"I'm concerned," he defended. "Any son worthy of the name would be."

Leigh waved a hand at him in disgust. "David's a wonderful man, and he makes your mother happy."

"He's not Dad."

Leigh heard the hurt and loss under the words. "Of course he's not," she said softly. "Will's with the Lord." She reached out with her coffee-moistened spoon and tapped him on the back of his hand. "Just remember this when you're feeling wary and protective. Your mother's been lonely for three long years, Clay. She deserves some happiness."

He looked out the window, saying nothing but obviously struggling. She knew he knew she was right. She also knew he'd come around eventually. After all, he was nice.

"Why are you going to your father's?" he asked, still looking outside.

Leigh was quiet for a minute. Then, "There was a message on the answering machine when we came in last night."

Clay spun to her and studied her face. "What did it say?"

"That last night was to confirm the warning that he meant business. He wants the treasure."

"So you're going to go get it? Just like that? You're going to give it to him?"

She laughed a bit wildly. "I couldn't get it if I wanted to. I have no idea what it is, or if it actually exists!"

"No idea?"

"None." She raked her fingers through her hair. "None."

"So you're going on a treasure hunt that probably has no pot of gold at the end of the rainbow."

She nodded. "That about sums it up."

"I'll come with you."

If the truth were told, she knew that was why she had come

into the kitchen this morning. Going home always gave her the willies, and his solid presence would help dispel them. "Oh, you don't have to do that."

He just looked at her.

"You don't. We can manage."

"Do you really think I'd let you go out there all alone after what's happened? What if he came? What if something happened to you? Or Bill? No, I'm coming."

She nodded, relieved that he'd ignored her protest. "Thank you."

"Did you call the police about last night?"

She nodded. "I talked to Greg."

"And?"

"He says they'll look into it. They're going to come out and see if the rope is still wedged in the jetty. Bill wanted to go get it this morning, but I wouldn't let him. 'You don't want to disturb the scene of a crime,' I told him. He didn't like it, but I think he bought it."

"He ought to. You're right. It is the scene of a crime."

She smiled slightly. "I think they plan to talk to the prison officials where Johnny was to see if they had any thoughts about someone recently released or something."

"Sounds like a good step to me."

Bill sulked the whole drive to Johnny's, all ten minutes of it. At least he tried to. It was hard with Terror sitting in his lap and kissing him. Still he gave it the old college try.

"I still don't know why I couldn't do what I wanted to do," he complained as he climbed out of Clay's car. "After all, it's my vacation."

"Give it a rest, Bill." Clay looked directly into Bill's eyes. "Your mom doesn't need you grumpy all day. Not after the scare you gave her last night."

"Hey, that wasn't my fault. I didn't tie Terror out there."

"I know. But it was still hard on her, watching and not knowing if you'd get back safely and all."

Bill looked at Leigh out of the corner of his eye, and she tried to look as sad as she could, which wasn't easy with Clay defending her like that. This was the way it probably happened in two parent families, she thought, the dad speaking up for the mom and vice versa. She sighed with longing. It must be wonderful.

"Why don't you take Terror out back and play, Billy—Bill?" she suggested. "Just don't go onto the bird reserve. I want you close."

"Mom!" he squawked.

"Bill," she said in a steely voice.

Bill looked at her, then at Clay. He made a face and muttered, "Come on, Terror. There's at least five feet of yard we can romp in out there."

"Romp?" Clay said with a laugh as Bill raced off. "Whatever happened to *play?*"

Leigh just shook her head and turned to look at her family home. Her heart caught as she thought of all the sadness that had lived within those walls. Now nothing lived here but her own ghosts.

She studied the front door. It was a faded, uneven blue now, but one summer it had been beautiful. She'd painted it a rich Williamsburg blue with paint she bought with money saved from her new job at the Acme. Johnny had mocked her when he came home and saw what she had done.

"Who cares about a front door? Just so it closes and locks; that's all you need. That's nothing but a waste of money, girl. Now get me a beer."

"I just want our house to look pretty," she said, staring at the ground. "I thought I'd do the porch railings too."

Johnny hooted derisively. "Well, where are they?" he asked, looking up and down the deserted street.

"What? Who?"

"The magazine people who are taking our picture for *House Be-oo-tee-ful.*" And he laughed that mocking laugh that made her feel useless, worthless, and all the other *less* words in the dictionary. She'd never painted the railings.

She shook away the memory as she started up the steps. "I don't know how I survived."

"But the important thing is that you did, Leigh," Clay said as he started to follow her. "You're a woman of character."

She turned, surprised. "What did you say?"

"You're a woman of character?" He looked almost as astonished as she that he'd said it. "Well, it's true, you know."

"Hmm." She turned and crossed the porch. "Thank you." Especially when he knew how little character she'd had at one time.

He didn't respond as she pulled the old key from her jeans pocket and slid it into the lock. The blue door opened with a creak.

"Who owns this property now?" He looked at the sun-bleached shingles and the hanging downspouts.

"I do," she said. "Though I haven't the vaguest idea what I'll do with it. I sure don't want to live here."

"It's yours? Really? I half expected you to say that Johnny died *in testate,* and the property was now the pride of the state of New Jersey."

"He probably would have, but one of his cronies in jail was studying law with the idea of getting himself off on a technicality. He drew up wills for anyone who wanted one and was willing to pay him twenty-five bucks."

"Your father actually parted with twenty-five dollars for a will?"

Leigh grinned wryly. "Not him. Me. I paid it. I put it right in the hands of that jailhouse lawyer myself. So Johnny had a will. All his worldly goods he me endowed." She swung her hand in an arc. "This is the whole of it. Big deal."

"You can probably get a good price in spite of the house's condition. The land is the valuable thing."

"Out here in the middle of nowhere?"

Clay shrugged. "Some people like solitude. And birds," he added, obviously thinking of the reserve that abutted the property.

She shook her head, but she knew she'd think about selling more seriously. She'd always assumed that because she hated the place, everyone would. She saw now how foolish that was. No one else came to the house with a history in it. They came with a clean slate.

Maybe by leaving her the house, Johnny had actually done her a favor for once in his life. Maybe with the money from the sale she could buy her own house. Now there was a wonderful idea to ponder.

She pushed the faded blue door open and stepped inside. Immediately she halted. Time rolled back upon itself like a scroll rewinding. Memories poured over her, scalding, burning, searing. She must have made a sound because suddenly Clay's hands were on her shoulders.

"Hard?" he asked.

"It's always like this when I come here." She lifted a hand and rubbed the spot on her forehead over her left eye. "That's why I hardly ever come."

Her eyes swept the living room, shabby and ugly. Even before she'd gone to Will and Julia's, she'd recognized that the cheap, gaudy sofa and speckled rug were atrocious. Now that she'd lived with loveliness for so long, the sheer tastelessness of the room overwhelmed her.

Without being conscious of moving, she found herself leaning back against Clay. She knew she should straighten, but the house sapped her strength. She continued to lean.

"I feel diminished when I come here," she whispered. "Like everything I've gained has been a mirage, and this ugliness and misery are the only realities. I'm only fooling myself if I think I can be anyone but the foolish, inept girl who lived here."

His hands tightened, and she thought she felt a light brush of a kiss on her hair.

Johnny's chair, worn black Naugahyde with a button on the side that raised the foot piece and lowered the back, dominated the room as he'd dominated her life for so many years. Johnny sprawled there, beer in hand, watching ball game after ball game after ball game with time out for professional wrestling when he could find it. There might not have been money for necessities, but there was always money for his beer.

"Another can, girl!" he'd order, and she'd drop whatever she was doing and fetch it. After she made their dinner. After she did their laundry. After she cleaned up his mess. After she swept the living room so the sweeper marks all were parallel just as he liked. After she did the dishes. After…

In her lonely, bitter moments, she felt little more than an indentured servant. Once she rebelled when he called for another beer.

"Get your own, Johnny. I'm busy." And she was. She was doing her homework, writing a theme for Mrs. Bronson, her eighth grade English teacher. Johnny might not like her, but her teachers seemed to, and she ached to keep it that way. Someone somewhere had to like her.

"What did you say?" The disbelief in Johnny's voice reached from the living room into her little back room that was hardly more than a closet.

"I said I'm busy." But instead of anger and independence, she heard only fear and impotence in her wavering voice.

"You want Social Services to come get you, girl?" he roared. "You want to go into foster care? Or maybe live on the street? I don't have to keep you. You're only here because I got a good heart. I can throw you out anytime I want."

God! she cried silently in the depths of her soul. *Oh, God, if You're real, help me! I can't stand this!*

Just as she was about to get up from the card table she used as a desk and go get his beer, Johnny burst through her door. He'd beaten her so hard, she'd never challenged him again. She'd missed three days of school, and it had been a week before she could move without pain.

She stood in front of that black chair and felt all the old hatred well up, and it scared her. She shook her head. She couldn't—she wouldn't let the past imprison her again.

"I'm sorry it was so bad for you back then." Clay's voice was soft and sincere. "I wish I had been smart enough to understand."

She shook her head. "Don't blame yourself. I did everything I could to keep it a secret. It was too shaming."

"Johnny was certainly shameful, but you had nothing to be ashamed about. The girl I knew was wonderful, intelligent, kind. I'm the one who should be embarrassed because of my blindness."

She closed her eyes against the sting of tears and nodded. "When you're raised in a wonderful family like yours, I guess it's hard to imagine one as bent as mine."

"And when you're a selfish kid with only your own dreams and goals and needs occupying your mind, it's hard to look beyond yourself."

Sorrow edged his voice, and she knew he was talking about more than her growing up Johnny's daughter. "Don't, Clay. If there's one thing the Lord has taught me, it's that you can't go back. You can't undo the failures. You just offer them to Him in confession."

Her eyes fell on a crystal vase, the loveliest thing in the room. Its luster was much dimmed by dust and dirt, but it was still striking. Johnny had given it to Mom shortly before she died. It was one of the few gentle moments she remembered between the two of them.

Candace had looked at him with her heart in her eyes. "Oh, Johnny, it's beautiful!" She ran her fingers up and down the grooves in the sides and around and around the scalloped rim. She laughed and ran to the window, holding the vase to the light. Crystal rainbows were refracted and danced across the walls and ceiling.

"Look, Leigh, love," Candace said as the prisms of light swept the room. "It's my heart dancing with love for you and Johnny."

The young Leigh in jeans with holes and socks that no longer came white laughed and ran to her mother, her small hands eager to touch the vase. She reached Candace just as Johnny did. His big arms swept both of them in a hug. Even as a child, Leigh had known it was a mistake that she was inside that hug. Surely Johnny meant to embrace Candace only, and his long arms accidentally wrapped about her too.

Johnny dropped his arms without even looking at her, and she stepped quickly aside. He embraced Candace again, but Leigh had seen the look on her mother's face at the casual but definite rejection of their daughter. The sheen was off the gift, the balloon of pleasure popped.

Three days later, Mom was killed when she was broadsided by a kid who ran a stop sign, and Johnny never hugged his daughter again, even accidentally.

"Where should we start our search?" Clay asked, his breath stirring her hair.

Leigh blinked, abruptly returned to the present. She straightened away from Clay. "I have no idea. It's useless anyway. There's nothing here. I know it."

Clay released her shoulders and looked around. "We've got to at least appear to try," he said. "He might be watching."

Leigh shivered.

Twenty

*T*ED STUDIED THE photo in his hand as he lay back against the pillows. He'd grabbed it Sunday when David Traynor had looked at it, dropped it, then bolted after his mother who had taken off like a flare a minute earlier.

When Ted had picked it up, he had felt nothing but curiosity. The kick in the gut when he looked at that kid in glasses had taken his breath. He'd quickly stuck the picture in his pocket before Clay or Leigh noticed anything funny going on. He kept it to himself as, unutterably weary, he'd come upstairs.

Even two days later he still felt that initial shock of understanding, the frisson of how can this be? He ran a pale, too thin finger over the face of the young Will Wharton. The resemblance was uncanny. Even the goofy grin was Billy's.

How had his father never seen it? How had his mother missed it? They had watched Bill grow with all the interest and enthusiasm of true grandparents. But then his mother hadn't known his father when he was ten, and his father hadn't been looking for any likeness of himself in Leigh's child.

He lay the photo facedown beside him. He was supposed to be taking a nap. He opened his mouth gingerly to see how the sores were doing. He was able to open fairly wide before he felt the pull of the scabbing.

He'd be able to eat a piece of cake. David's medicine was working, at least in this one area.

Too bad it wasn't working overall. He could feel the continual lessening of energy, the weakening of muscles, the occasional lack of mental clarity that scared him more than anything else. How often had he pled with God to protect him from dementia?

He tried to be honest with David about every little diminishment, but he also tried to protect his mother. She was fragile, more so than Leigh, and his instinct was to shield her. She'd been hurt so badly when his father died. Personally he thought David's interest in her a good thing, and he was sort of proud that he precipitated their friendship.

Your mom lonely? Get sick so she can date the doctor. He grinned. Worked for him.

And now Clay was here for the duration. Funny how that both drained and energized him.

Oh, Lord, I shouldn't enjoy baiting him so much. I apologize, and I hope You noticed that I was good yesterday. It's just he's such a straight arrow that he asks for it. He does. But I won't ruin the birthday party tonight. I promise.

He was supposed to be sleeping so that he'd have enough stamina to enjoy tonight. After all, it would be his last birthday party ever and Clay's last as a twin.

Or were you still a twin even after your twin died? Interesting question. He was still Will Wharton's son even though his father was dead. Shouldn't that mean that Clay was his twin even after he was dead? He pondered this question for a few minutes, coming to no conclusion but suspecting that once a twin, always a twin regardless of circumstances.

Oh, Lord, I'm so tired. Bone weary. Wiped out. How will I ever make it through tonight?

Ted turned and looked out the French door to the beach and sea. How he loved the ocean with its constant motion, its beauty, its occasional ferocity. Its independence. Nobody told the sea what to do except, of course, God. It did as it pleased, and you'd better all beware.

Maybe he should ask Clay to help him get to the water this afternoon. It was sunny and warm. How many more sunny, warm days would he have? It was a cinch that he couldn't walk that far by himself. Maybe for a birthday present, Clay could carry him through the dunes to the sea while Leigh lugged a chair for him. He smiled. What a lovely thought.

If Clay were willing to help him.

Ted sighed. Back to the same old, same old. There had to be a way to resolve the antipathy between him and his twin. He knew Clay was trying. The twice daily visits were proof. They were also a terrible strain on him and, he suspected, on Clay. Neither knew what to say. At least they hadn't argued since Saturday.

Maybe if Clay had been distressed instead of angry all those years ago when he understood Ted's choices, the rift between them wouldn't have been so bad. Maybe if Clay had been willing to try to understand, they could have found a middle ground. But he had been furious, acting like he'd been betrayed.

"How can you be gay?" Clay had stormed. "How can you do this to me?"

"Do this to you? You think I'm doing this on purpose? That I planned to be different? To be anathema? You think I want to make you furious with me? Don't be so stupid, Clay."

"I think you're choosing to turn your back on everything we've been taught." Clay was adamant. "You know what the Bible says. Homosexuality is wrong."

"You're just afraid people will question your manhood." Ted threw the statement down with a tone that left no doubt that here was as much a challenge as any glove slapped across the face of a court dandy.

Clay was so mad he sputtered. "As if I'd ever stoop that low!"

"Ha!" Ted pointed his index finger. "You are afraid! You're afraid that because we're twins, you're going to be just like me."

"Never." Clay ground the word between clenched teeth. "If anything, being identical twins proves that you have a choice about lifestyle. If you are doomed to be gay genetically, shouldn't I be also? Same egg, same sperm. Well, I'm not. So you're not."

Ted sneered. "No proof."

"Logic. And no proof differently."

Ted ignored Clay's comments because he had no answer for them. "You're so goody-goody that you'd never stray from the straight and narrow even if you felt like it. You're Mr. Perfect. You'd never be like me. You'd die first."

Well, funny thing, he was the one who was going to die first, and all because he'd followed where his nature led him.

And Clay had followed where his nature led him too. That fact was amazing, overwhelming. Clay with feet of clay.

He looked at the picture again. Bill was Dad to a *T*, thanks to the immutability of genetics. He'd wondered once or twice if Clay could be Bill's father, but it had been such a mind-boggling thought that he'd dropped it almost immediately. He only considered the absurd idea because he'd seen Leigh look at Clay with that moony look girls got when they thought a guy was pretty terrific. But Clay went off to Annapolis and Leigh to Glassboro, and they never saw each other. Certainly, Leigh gave no indication at all that Clay was Bill's father.

But those momentary suspicions had been right all along. William Clayton Spenser might have been named after William Clayton Wharton Sr., like Leigh always said. But he was also named after Clay.

And old Clay had no idea.

Ted couldn't decide how he felt about Clay's ignorance. If Bill were his own son and no one ever told him, how would he feel? Of course if no one told him, he wouldn't feel anything. But how would he react if and when he did learn the truth? Anger? Disbelief? Regret? Fear? It was hard to imagine what he would feel in a situation he'd never face.

How would Clay react if and when he learned the truth? How would he feel toward Leigh? She had, after all, kept him from his son for years. Would he take to fathering at this late date? Would he help financially? Want visitation? And most perplexing of all, why hadn't he known? No matter how frustrated he got with Clay, he never doubted his brother's strong sense of morality. Clay would never sleep around. An accident, yes. Anyone can fall under the right circumstances. But lots of women? Never. So why hadn't he known Bill was his?

And how would Bill react to this unsettling news? Would he be happy to find out he had a father that his mother had kept secret? Would he forgive Leigh? Hate her? Hate Clay?

They were questions that made his brain spin.

Ted's eyes felt heavy, and he let them close, his hand still resting on the picture. His mind went empty. It was becoming harder and harder to hold thoughts together for long periods of time. The depression and fatigue were too strong. Just a few minutes rest. Then maybe the fever he could feel building would dissipate before becoming anything significant.

He smiled sadly at the idea of an insignificant fever at his stage of things. And he could just imagine what David would say when he found out that Ted had not told him about the sweats and following chills. It was the first time he'd withheld information. And the last. But he wasn't going to ruin tonight's party. It meant too much to Mom.

He blinked and turned to the clock, surprised to find he'd slept two hours. He wiped a film of sweat from his brow. The fever was settling in. Poor timing.

He reached for his water and took a long drink. Weary from the strain, he lay back. Another hour passed before he woke up again. This time he felt more rested, but he was shivering because his pajamas were wet from sweating. Now there was an interesting challenge for tonight: not to get red in the face or sweat when hot with fever.

He thought about Clay, the much-loved and greatly resented man he shared today with. Back to the same question: What should he do about him? He knew he had to decide soon. He knew there wasn't much more time, maybe a couple of weeks. Maybe a couple of months.

If he wanted to be mean, he could do nothing. Die without resolution. That would eat at Clay for the rest of his life.

Ted shook his head. No, that wasn't what he wanted. He wanted to die shriven, and he wanted Clay, the officious bigot, to live whole.

Why couldn't Clay treat this whole situation as Leigh did? She didn't approve, but she made her points so nicely.

"You don't understand, Leigh," Ted had told her on more than one occasion. "You just don't understand."

Leigh would then look so earnest and sincere he had to hold back a smile. "Yes, I do," she always said. "I understand."

He'd turn his bitterness on her. "You can't possibly."

She never flinched. She just looked at him and saw her best

friend since forever, the one who stood by her when no one else would pay any attention to her, the one who stood up for her when the other kids had mocked her. He was the one who had held her when she cried with loneliness and frustration, the one who had played father to Bill on so many occasions. He knew she suspected he was the one who had sent his mother to her, though he knew that wasn't true. That appeared to be a genuine God thing.

She fought a constant struggle to be true to both biblical orthodoxy and her love for him. He knew she *wanted* to say, "It's okay, Teddy. Be what you are. I approve. You know I'll always love you."

But she felt she couldn't, for both his sake and Christ's.

"Isn't temptation the same whether you're straight or gay?" she always asked. "Isn't longing longing and isn't love love?" She smiled sadly. "Believe me, I understand temptation, longing, and love."

Ted looked at her without blinking. If he agreed with her, and deep down he was afraid that he did, he knew and she knew that he would undercut his stance that he couldn't help himself. So he hurt her and hated himself for it.

"What do you know of love and longing, Leigh?" His even tone kept what could have eaten like acid from being more than a slight catch of her heart, but he knew it still hurt. "You've been alone for eleven whole years."

She gave him a crooked smile. "I've been alone for twenty-nine whole years minus one night. Does that mean I can't understand love? Or perhaps that I understand it all the more?"

"Mmm," he said. His eyes slid past her, sad that he made her sad. "So maybe you understand love."

"It's the love of God that's beyond my comprehension." She smiled and shook her head. "Where I've come from. What I've done. And even so He loves me and always will." She looked at him gravely. "You too, Ted."

"I know that," he said, his tone testy. "I'm not talking about God's love, and you know it. Though if He loved me, He'd have done things differently."

"You know we can't blame God for our choices and mistakes. And you know I'm right. Choosing not to yield to urges and hormones is very, very hard, but it's also what God wants. And when we fail, He wants us to agree with Him that we were wrong. I certainly agree with Him about me. And He wants us to change, Ted, where we're wrong. Like He told the woman taken in adultery, 'Go and sin no more.'"

And she would leave it there.

Clay, on the other hand, would go for the jugular every time.

"Sin is sin, Ted," he'd thunder. "Just think about that for a while. You need to repent."

Was it a male-female thing? Or a Clay personality disorder?

As he absently watched Clooney down on the beach dig more holes with his spade, he knew that was both too simplistic and too sarcastic an answer. It was more the case of a man who accepted biblical standards as absolutes unable to come to terms with one who flouted them.

But they had to come to terms. They had to.

The picture made a muted noise as his hand fell on it. He picked it up and studied his father's image again. He suddenly knew what he was going to do for Clay.

Twenty-one

"NICE PARTY," Bill said as he licked the last of the birthday cake off his fork. "Great cake, Grandma Jule. Love that caramel icing." He nodded to Clay and Ted. "Thanks, guys, for providing the occasion."

Clay laughed. The kid was such a character. "Glad to be of service."

"I really think you ought to be thanking me, Bill," Mom said from her seat at the head of the table. "All those two did was show up. I did all the work."

"Sort of like tonight?" Bill said.

Mom laughed. "Not quite. Tonight I had help." She blushed at David.

Clay felt Leigh's eyes on him and refrained from rolling his eyes. Instead he smiled weakly at her.

"But all *they* did was show up again, right?" Bill eyed Clay and Ted.

"Hey, that's the way it's supposed to be on your birthday," Clay said.

Bill shrugged. "If you say so. Now let's get to the next important part of the evening, the gifts."

"A man after my own heart," Ted said, smiling.

Clay looked at his brother seated across the table. He looked weary, but his eyes sparkled with life, and he had rosy cheeks. Tonight there was nothing about him of the somewhat bitter man Clay was familiar with, the one who lay in the bed by the French windows, studying the sea, watching Clooney find his little treasures.

I bet he'd like to go to the beach. Clay felt foolish that he hadn't realized that fact sooner. *Of course he would. He's always loved the ocean, the smell, the movement, the feel of the breeze from its surface. The deck is nice; the open French doors are nice; but they aren't the beach.*

He thought of how he'd feel if he were unable to walk at the water's edge or get sand in his shoes or feel the pull of the wind in his hair. *Maybe tomorrow I can take him there. I'll carry him because I know he could never walk it. And Leigh or Bill can lug a chair for him. Maybe Clooney can even find a treasure for him.*

Pleased with that thought, Clay rose and picked up a pair of cake dishes. "Mom, I'm about to reclaim my reputation and prove to a certain kid that I do more than just show up, even on my birthday. You take Ted and David and go into the living room and get settled. Bill can help me clean up."

"What?" Bill's face was a study in surprise.

"It's not your birthday today." Clay stacked more cake dishes in a neat pile. "You can work."

Wrinkling his face in disgust, Bill grabbed a glass in each hand and headed for the kitchen.

Leigh grinned at her son's retreating back. She collected a handful of dishes and followed Clay and Bill to the kitchen.

"How about, Bill, you clear, I rinse, and your mom loads?"

Leigh and Bill looked at each other, then at Clay and started to laugh. "Your military training is showing," Leigh said.

"Sorry," Clay said, not the least bit chagrined. "I'm so used to giving orders that I don't even think about it."

"At least you're pleasant about it," Bill said. "If someone has to order me around, it's nice if that someone isn't a grump."

"Are you thinking of any particular grump when you say that?" Leigh asked, eyes wide and innocent.

Bill grinned at his mother. "I wasn't, but as they say, if the shoe fits…."

"That shoe is much too big for your mom," Clay said as he turned the faucet on. "She's not a grump. She's a trooper." He caught Leigh's look of amused surprise. "Well, you are."

"Two compliments in one day," she said. "I'd better be careful, or the flattery will go to my head."

"And a lovely head it is," Clay said, pouring ice cubes and the dregs of iced tea down the drain.

Bill dropped a fistful of dirty flatware onto the counter. "She is pretty, isn't she?" He looked at his mother through narrowed eyes. "All the kids at school think she's pretty too. They all like her best. Yes sir. She's one in a million, a champ."

Leigh just shook her head, but Bill was on a roll. With great theatrical flourish, he continued.

"She never gets angry. She never gets impatient. She never yells at me. She never punishes me. She never orders me around. And she certainly is never a grump, not even Saturday morning when I wake her up to a closet full of kittens."

"Wow," said an unimpressed Leigh. "You must be pushing for a great Easter present."

"And I'm going to get hit by lightning for lying!" he flung over his shoulder as he disappeared into the dining room for more dirty dishes.

Laughing, Leigh and Clay worked quietly for a few minutes, the only noise the clink of glasses, the swoosh of water over a plate, the clatter of forks against knives.

"I thought of you this morning," Leigh said suddenly, looking up at Clay.

He blinked, absurdly pleased. "Yeah?"

She nodded. "During my devotions." She slid a pair of plates into slots in the dishwasher. "I was reading about Jacob and Esau."

"Ah." Clay handed her a large pot. "The biblical twins who couldn't stand each other. I wonder why they made you think of me?"

"I was at the part of the story where they reconcile after being separated for twenty years."

"And I'm Jacob, the returning evil brother who has tricked my twin out of his blessing and birthright?" Clay was surprised at how sour he sounded.

So, apparently, was Leigh. "Of course not."

"Oh." He handed her several large cooking spoons. "Of course not."

"Forget the returning brother/stay-at-home brother part of the story. You're Esau, the good brother who has been hurt by his twin's actions."

He stared at her in amazement. He was the good brother? *She* could say that?

"You see yourself as the one with the reason to be angry and hold a grudge because just as Jacob hurt Esau, Ted hurt you. Right?"

"I guess," he said slowly.

"You guess?" She raised an eyebrow at him.

He scowled. "I never thought of it that way before, okay?"

"I wonder if Esau got cranky when he talked about his brother?" she asked the air.

"All right. You're right." He was less than gentle with the pot he was rinsing. "I'm Esau mad at my brother Jacob."

She nodded, satisfied. "When the brothers finally met, Jacob had a huge chip on his shoulder, expecting trouble from Esau and planning how to counter it."

"Sort of like Ted always being defensive around me?"

She nodded again. "Now get this part that I'm going to say." She pointed a huge carving knife at him. "It's the important part."

Eyeing the knife hovering a few inches from his chest, Clay said, "I'm listening."

"It was Esau, the wronged brother, who rushed to embrace his twin." The knife bounced up and down with every word. "He threw his arms around Jacob and kissed him. *Then* the brothers wept and reconciled."

Clay turned to the sink and stared at the hot water streaming from the faucet. The pan filled and overflowed. "You're saying I've got my expectations backwards."

Leigh tucked the knife carefully into the dishwasher. "I am. You're waiting for him to apologize to you. Maybe you need to make the first move, to be the one to embrace him and apologize."

"But he's the one who's wrong."

"By biblical standards, yes, he's wrong. But, Clay—" she laid her hand on his arm and waited until she had his full attention—"by the same criteria so are you. And I'm not referring to our history."

He dropped his eyes from her intense gaze and stared at her hand resting on his arm. It was delicate in appearance but full of strength, like her, unafraid to call a spade a spade.

"Think about it," she said as Bill exploded into the kitchen. She lifted her hand and grabbed the dishcloth. She rinsed it in the flow of water and with a flourish began wiping down the counters.

"Aren't you done yet?" Bill asked as he came up beside the sink, impatience shimmering in the air about him.

"Almost," Clay said, looking absently for any dishes lurking in the shadows. "You go on in. Just don't let them start the gifts without me."

"Then you'd better hurry, or I'll open yours!" With that threat, Bill rushed out of the room.

Clay couldn't help the bark of laughter as he watched the boy disappear around the corner. "He's a great kid, Leigh."

She looked at the empty doorway with a soft smile. "Thanks. He's the joy of my life." She rinsed the dishcloth and hung it on the edge of the sink. She reached past Clay and turned the water off.

Clay decided to ask the question that had been burning in his gut for days. After all, if she could invade his privacy with her little lecture on Jacob and Esau, he could invade hers. "You've never heard from his father?"

Leigh looked out the window over the sink, avoiding his eyes. She shook her head. "No, not one word after The Incident."

"The Incident?"

She smiled self-consciously, still avoiding his eyes. "That's what I call it. It doesn't seem quite so terrible if I do." She shrugged. "I don't even know why I expected him to stand by me."

Clay looked at her in surprise. "Why not? Anyone with any character would take responsibility for his actions."

She suddenly turned to him, her eyes burning. "Did you know that even my failure of a father stood by my mother?"

Clay blinked as much at her intensity as at the news that unwed pregnancies were a generational problem for the Spensers. "If Johnny Spenser was more responsible than Bill's father, that doesn't say much for whoever he was, does it?"

"No, it doesn't." Her anger left as quickly as it had come, leaving her full of sorrow. "It doesn't say much for me either, that he could walk away without a backward glance." Her mouth curved wryly for a minute, then she sighed. "I get so scared for Bill sometimes. What if he follows the same pattern?"

"Don't devalue yourself like that." Clay grabbed her arm and gave her a little shake. "I don't want to hear you do that ever again. Do you hear me? And Bill will be all right. He's a good kid."

"So was his father." She pulled her arm from his grasp. "He was just young, too young."

"Don't make excuses for him, Leigh. Even if you didn't want to marry him, he should have at least assumed financial responsibility for the boy."

"If he knew." Her voice was so soft he scarcely heard her.

"You mean he doesn't know about Bill?"

"No, I don't think so." She spoke to the floor. "He wasn't interested, so why tell him?"

He lifted her chin and looked into her eyes. "The guy's still a louse to have left you like that."

She stepped back so that his hand fell to his side. "Many, many times I've thought so, especially in the early years."

"Of course you have. He should have checked."

"Yes, he should have."

Her face was so sad and forlorn that Clay's heart broke for her. Don Quixote de la Seaside was ready to ride again. He just didn't know whom to chase after.

She reached under the sink for the dishwasher soap and filled the two wells. She flipped them closed and shut the dishwasher door. She pushed the right buttons, and the machine began to hum.

"I don't know what I would have done without Julia and Will," she said, leaning against the counter. "God was so good to send them to me. They became my parents. And Ted became my brother."

Clay reached for her hand, holding it lightly in his, turning it palm up. He ran a finger gently over the lifelines. "And I missed the whole adventure, didn't I?"

Her smile was full of a sadness and longing that he didn't comprehend, though he wanted to. He realized with surprise that he wanted to understand everything about her.

She withdrew her hand from his grasp and said softly, "Yes, you missed the whole thing."

She walked quietly to the living room, and he followed, trying to figure out what it was about this woman that touched him so deeply. When she took a seat next to Mom on the sofa, he sat on the arm beside her. Ever so casually he put his arm along the back of the sofa. She had to know it was there, and it pleased him that she didn't lean forward but let it rest just beyond her shoulders.

"Now presents," Bill announced from his seat on the floor by Ted. He rose and went to the small tower of gifts that sat on the coffee table. "I'll play Santa Claus or whatever you call the giver of birthday gifts." Terror followed him and stood with wagging tail looking at the brightly wrapped packages.

"The Birthday Fairy," Mom said. "Cousin to the Tooth Fairy, but instead of money, you bring gifts."

"I don't think I'll tell anyone that, Grandma Jule." Bill shook a present at Terror who rose to his back legs to get a better look.

"That dog's like a kid," Clay said. "He thinks one's for him."

"Sorry, guy." Bill patted the dog. "This is for Ted, not you." Terror trailed happily as they took the present to Ted. They came back for another and took it to Clay. For the next few minutes everyone was busy oohing and aahing over the gifts, whether heavy sweat socks with blue stripes around the top for Clay and green stripes for Ted or wild pajamas for both of them with huge red hearts on a black watch plaid background.

"I'm supposed to wear these?" Clay asked Bill who had given them. "They'll keep me awake even with my eyes closed."

Bill laughed happily. "Birthdays are the best."

"I remember your birthday, Bill," Ted said. He was resting in the lounger just like yesterday, his feet raised. He now seemed a bit pale to Clay, almost gray, his rosy cheeks gone, but he was animated, wired. He barely broke verbal stride when he coughed a couple of times. "It was quite a night, let me tell you."

Clay saw David check Ted visually, saw David's small frown, but Ted looked happy and at ease. Whatever David was thinking, he kept it to himself.

"Tell me," Bill coaxed. "Come on; tell me." It was obviously a story he'd heard many times before, but it never grew old.

Leigh suddenly leaned forward. "Not tonight, Billy. Ted's tired."

"Bill," corrected Bill, Ted, and Clay in perfect unison.

She rolled her eyes, sighed, then settled back on the sofa.

"It was a bitter winter Friday night in the middle of January," Ted began in his best storyteller's voice. "The snow was coming down hard, and I'd just come to visit your mom for the weekend. She was quite chubby, if you know what I mean."

Bill nodded. "With me." He grinned over his shoulder at Leigh.

"We decided to go out for something to eat because she didn't feel like cooking."

"That's because I'd just worked a five-hour shift at the Acme, on my feet the whole time, and this after a morning of classes, and I had to work eight hours the next day," Leigh defended herself. "My ankles were balloons. And I think we should drop the story for tonight. Please."

Ted kept his eyes fixed on Bill. To avoid dealing with Leigh's request? Clay couldn't decide. All he knew was that he felt an unexpected tension fill the room. His mother suddenly sat up straight, no longer leaning comfortably back against David's shoulder. David was alert, his eyes moving from Mom to Bill and back. And Leigh was rigid.

"We came down the steps from the second floor apartment where you guys lived," Ted said. "We had to bend our heads into the wind, and snow was blowing down our collars. We were halfway up the walk to the parking lot when your mom looked at me and said, 'Not tonight. It's too snowy. By the time we're finished, it'll be really bad. Peanut butter and jelly would be better than this.' So we turned to go back to the apartment."

"And that's when it happened," said Bill, his imitation of Ted right on. "I was walking along—"

"Hey," Ted said. "Who's telling this?"

Bill giggled.

"Ted, please." Leigh held a hand out in plea.

"I was walking along," said Ted, eyes riveted to Bill, "kicking the snow, when I heard a terrible scream right behind me." Ted paused dramatically.

Bill picked up the story. "Slowly I turned, and there was your mother—my mother—flat on her back in the snow."

Ted nodded. Clay glanced at Leigh. She felt his gaze and looked up. "Ice under the snow. Knocked the wind right out of me, let me tell you." She tried to smile, but anxiety radiated from her.

"That's not all it did," said Bill, turning to her. It was obvious that he loved the drama of the tale and that he felt none of the apprehension that the various adults for some reason felt. "It made you go into labor!"

"I stuffed her in my car and drove to the hospital with her moaning and groaning the whole time," Ted said.

Mom looked at Leigh. "It's obvious *he's* never been in labor." She took Leigh's hands in hers and rubbed them. "It'll be all right," she said so softly that Clay almost missed it. "Today's as good a day as any."

Leigh looked at Mom in surprise, and Clay watched his mother lean over and kiss her cheek.

"When?" Leigh whispered.

"Sunday."

Leigh's shoulders slumped. "I'm sorry."

Mom shook her head, her eyes glittering with tears. "Don't worry. I love you. I always will, no matter what."

Through narrowed eyes Clay looked at his mother and Leigh. What was going on here? He put a hand on Leigh's shoulder to offer his encouragement though he had no idea why she needed it. He felt her shudder, but she reached up and patted him twice. She kept her eyes fixed on her lap.

Bill noticed none of the byplay and finished the story with a flourish. "And I was born twelve hours later!"

Ted grinned. "And a wee little one you were, Bill. Three and a half pounds."

"Mom." Bill turned to Leigh. "Were you scared for me?"

"Petrified," she said, forcing a smile. "Scared to death. You were so tiny!"

"Would anyone like another piece of cake?" Mom asked, standing so quickly she had to grab Leigh's shoulder for balance. "David? Ted? Clay?"

Ted kept his gaze fixed on Bill. "You were so little because you were two months premature."

"Yeah, I know. I was supposed to be born in the middle of March."

"The middle of March," Ted said slowly and clearly.

The room fell absolutely silent.

Bill mused over the fascinating fact of his due date.

Ted sat absolutely still, waiting.

Mom sank back into her seat, her face fixed on Leigh, while David looked with concern from Mom to Leigh to Clay.

And Leigh seemed to have stopped breathing.

Clay noticed all these things in a vague manner because the enormity of what he'd just heard drove every other thought from his mind.

The middle of March!

The room was suddenly devoid of oxygen, and his blood thrummed in his ears as he tried to breathe. A great groan tore from his soul as he dropped his head to his chest in distress and disbelief. Failure. Colossal, indefensible, unforgivable failure.

He was the louse.

He became aware through the great flood of misery pouring over his spirit that Leigh had taken his hand, wrapping her fingers around his.

"Are you all right?" she asked gently, her eyes full of concern. There might have been no one in the room but the two of them.

"What?" He looked at her blankly.

"Are you all right?" She traced her thumb from side to side across the back of his hand, offering comfort.

"I'm so sorry." It was all he could do to force the whisper out. His hand grasped hers tightly. "I'm so sorry." His voice broke.

"It was long ago," Leigh said. "You were young. We were young."

He stared at her in disbelief. "And that's an excuse?"

Again that sad smile. "No, but it's the best I can offer."

How could she be so nice? He reached a hand to rest on her cheek. "You're amazing."

Ted watched Leigh and Clay across the room. He had held his breath when he finally made the time frame of Bill's birth clear, uncertain what would happen. There were so many possibilities.

Would Clay miss the whole point? For all his intelligence he wasn't the smartest of men at times. Of course they'd all been incredibly obtuse about this issue, so he really couldn't dump on Clay for not getting with the program sooner.

Would he understand and get defensive? Ted's own experience with his brother proved that this response was one of Clay's more refined and long-lived reactions to situations he didn't like. If Clay took this route, they'd all just have to protect Leigh.

Or would he be okay with the truth, unpalatable and unbelievable though it was? Would he clasp Bill to his chest and proclaim, "My son"? Then would he look at Leigh and ask, "How much back child support do I owe?" The answer to that ought to keep Leigh in fine style for years to come. Or at least get Bill through college.

He knew he'd distressed Leigh and his mother by telling Bill's birth story. Both of them knew all too well the potential problems of opening this particular Pandora's box. But he'd hardened his heart and ignored their pleas for silence. He'd almost yielded when Leigh said, "Please" in that disbelieving, hurt voice. And then his mother had jumped to her feet with that question about more cake. It was only by looking straight at Bill and only Bill that he could keep going.

He was pleased that he'd had the fortitude to hold firm to his plan. It was basically a matter of his desire to help Clay being stronger than Ted's fear of hurting the women. And snide though his thoughts and comments about and to Clay often were, he knew he truly did want to help his brother. The man irritated him in so many ways, but he was his twin. Today was their birthday, their last birthday together. This gift of knowledge was his last gift to his twin.

"What's wrong with Grandma Jule?" Bill asked from beside him, Ted's new electronic game forgotten in his hand. "She's crying."

Ted glanced at his mother, deep in David's embrace. Thank God for David. He shrugged. "I guess birthdays make her weepy." Bill frowned. "She never cried at mine."

Ted shrugged again and turned his attention back to Clay and Leigh. Clay looked devastated, a reaction Ted hadn't foreseen, and he felt a clutch in his heart. Clay always seemed so secure, so sure of himself. That he could be so distraught shook Ted. His idea hadn't been to cause hurt but to promote healing, to give Clay the gift of knowledge, of a son. Clay'd never believe it, but he hadn't meant to wound him. He'd wanted to help. Ted shook his head. No, Clay'd never believe that.

Ted smiled softly at Leigh's earnest face as she continued to talk softly to Clay. Imagine the wronged woman offering succor to the villain in the piece. He knew he was seeing something unusual, a combination of Leigh being her usual sweet self and the power of God at work through her.

Satisfaction bloomed in his chest. He had done the right thing. He had. He'd accomplished his purpose. Clay knew. What he did with the knowledge was up to him. Now Ted could relax, lie back, and close his eyes.

As he let go of the fierce determination he'd gathered about him to see the revelation through, exhaustion overwhelmed him in a great, gray wave. The adrenaline drained away and left no physical reserves. He felt light-headed, faint. A coughing spell wracked him, his chest heaving, and he struggled to catch his breath. He began to shiver with fever.

He felt his mind go fuzzy, and he hadn't the strength to fight it. He needed to tell Matt about his success. Matt would be proud of him. He'd understand why he did it. He wanted to tell his father too. And he wanted to go to the beach with Clay and build sand castles.

Why doesn't he build castles with me anymore? I'm his twin. We always built castles together. And we buried Dad. In sand and for real. We buried Dad.

He wrapped his arms about himself trying to keep warm as shivers took him.

Twenty-two

JULIA TURNED AUTOMATICALLY to David when Ted's story was finished, and he wrapped her in the security of his arms. She felt as if her heart had been torn open, and she was almost surprised that she wasn't leaving bloodstains on his crisp shirt.

Why had Ted deliberately ruined their evening? Tonight had been so important to her. She'd planned every little detail with such care—the chicken cordon bleu, the twice baked potatoes, the brussels sprouts that Ted had loved from the time he was a boy. And the chocolate cake with caramel icing. She wanted them all to have a precious memory to pull out and relive in the dark days ahead.

Ted seemed to understand her plan without her even verbalizing it. He came to dinner wearing clothes instead of his pajamas and robe. He hadn't bothered with clothes for a couple of weeks. She'd been so pleased. And then he had told his story.

It wasn't like Ted to be so cruel. He was the son with the gift of mercy. He was the one who cared unflaggingly for Leigh and Bill, who helped her learn to live again after Will's death. But he had deliberately ignored Leigh's pleas and her own foolish cake comment.

"It'll be okay, Julia," David's deep voice whispered in her ear. "We worship a redeeming God. He'll bring good out of this seeming catastrophe if we give Him time."

She nodded and tried to make herself believe him, but at the moment the sentiment seemed only empty words. After a couple more comforting moments leaning on him, she made herself pull back. She had to stop acting like a weepy heroine from some sappy romance, throwing herself into his arms every time something upset her. She had managed on her own for the past three years. She must continue to do so. She rubbed at the tears on her face.

She looked at Clay and Leigh, intensely focused on each other, and felt near despair. What was going to happen to them, these people she loved so much?

"They're both good people, and they both love the Lord," David said quietly, as if he could read her mind. "Trust them. They'll sort it all out."

She closed her eyes. "I hope so. Oh, God, let it be so," she prayed.

She turned to look for Bill. He was playing with the handheld computer game David had given Ted, Terror seated beside him watching the blinking lights and quirking his head at the beeps and burps.

"I don't think he understands what's going on," David said, again reading her mind.

She nodded, agreeing. The tension and loosed secrets flying about the room seemed to have sailed right over the boy's precious head. "Thank goodness! He needs to be told, but not like this."

"Leigh will tell him." David's voice was steady and confident. "She's been a wise mom so far. She'll be one again."

Julia rubbed the back of her neck even as she wrapped an arm about her middle. She couldn't decide which hurt worse, her tense neck and shoulder muscles or her bubbling mud pot of a stomach. She needed her ibuprofen and her antacids! She was too old for all this emotional chaos.

"Let me." David stepped behind her and began kneading her tight shoulders. She sighed under his touch.

"Uncle Ted!"

She jumped at the panic in Bill's voice, her hand reaching automatically to David. She spun toward Ted.

"Uncle Ted! What's wrong?"

Ted lay in his chair, head back, eyes closed, face white. He looked like a doll flung aside by a little girl too busy to play with it anymore, limbs askew, totally slack. For a moment, Julia thought he was dead, and her heart stopped.

Then he shivered and began to hack painfully.

"Ted!" she cried, rushing to her son, David right behind her. She put her hand on his forehead. "He's burning up!"

"Bill," David said, his tone clipped and urgent. "Go to my car and get my bag."

Bill ran, looking back over his shoulder at his uncle with fear in his eyes.

"Let's get him to bed so I can check him." David turned to Clay. "Help him upstairs."

Clay, attention frozen on Ted like everyone else, dropped Leigh's hand and went to his brother. He slid his arm around Ted's shoulders and tried to help him stand, but Ted wasn't up to the task. Finally, Clay just lifted him like he might a child, an arm behind his back and an arm beneath his knees, and carried him. The sight of brother helping brother made Julia's own legs weak.

Bill ran back in with David's bag. Leigh took it and turned Bill toward the TV. "Watch for a while." She spoke softly, giving him a gentle shove. "We need to let Dr. Traynor be alone with Uncle Ted for a bit."

Bill did as he was told, but Julia knew he wasn't watching the flickering image. He kept glancing up the steps while the weatherman on the Weather Channel, who under normal circumstances rated an "Ugh!", kept reporting the varying climatic conditions around the country for the coming holiday weekend. They were on the third installment of the local weather before David reappeared. By this time, Julia was so taut with apprehension that she vibrated.

As David ran a weary hand across his face, Julia rushed to him. He slipped an arm across her shoulders.

"He'll be all right." He patted her shoulder. "I hear crackles in his right lung base, but I don't think it's too serious yet."

"Pneumonia," whispered Julia. Fear rolled over her in a great wave. Pneumonia was deadly for AIDS patients.

"I had some sample antibiotics in my case," David said. "I've given him a dose and left some. I'll leave a prescription for you to fill tomorrow. If he doesn't become short of breath and if he takes lots—and I mean lots—of fluids, he can stay home for the time being. If he gets worse, I'll have to send him to the hospital. I'll check with the home health nurse tomorrow and stop by if I can."

She looked at him. She knew her eyes were wide and full of panic, and she hated it. Most of the time she kept a tight clamp on her fear, but sometimes it was more than she could contain. It burst forth, swirling, seething, a great undulating serpent wrapping around her and squeezing rationality and faith from her.

Ted was dying, maybe this week! Since his eventual demise was old news and as inevitable as the rising of tomorrow's sun, why did it continue to have this power to devastate her?

"But for now he can stay home?" she asked, trying with limited success to keep her voice calm. "Because he'll be all right? You're not just saying that?" She wanted to grab David's lapels and make him swear, make him promise on every Bible they could gather, that Ted would be fine.

David rubbed weary eyes. "He should be all right in a couple of days."

"Should be? Just should be?" It wasn't good enough.

"Julia, that's the best I can do. If the medicine works and the fever breaks in the next couple of days, we'll survive this crisis. He'll have more time. You'll have more time."

"And if it doesn't?"

He didn't answer, and she didn't need him to. "Sometimes I can't stand the uncertainty." She pulled away from him. "I just can't stand it!" She turned and started for the stairs, her steps jerky and her breathing rapid. She had to see Ted for herself, see that he was still breathing, still living.

David caught her arm. "Don't go up now."

She pulled against him. "I've got to."

"He's resting, and Clay's with him. He'll let us know if there's any change."

"Clay." She said it with scorn. "What does he know about caring for Ted?"

"Julia, look at me." David waited until she turned her frantic gaze on him, then shook his head slowly and deliberately. "Don't go up. You'll upset him more than help him."

"I have to! I'm his mother." She pulled against him some

more, trying to wrench her arm from his grasp.

He placed himself between her and the stairs. "You're too distraught. He needs to rest."

Huge tears slid down her cheeks. "Get out of my way, David. That's my baby, and he needs me." *And I need him.*

He didn't move. Instead he said in a wry tone, "By how many minutes?"

"What?"

"You said he was your baby. How many minutes later than Clay was he born?"

David's question burst the bubble of Julia's near hysteria like a well-placed pinprick. In that instant her fear metamorphosed into anger. "Are you laughing at me?" she demanded, her voice quivering with fury.

"Hardly," he said evenly. "I'm trying to calm you down."

"Calm me down?" Her voice rose. "Calm me down? Why, you—"

David enfolded Julia in his arms, surprising her and pinning her arms against her sides.

"Let me go," she hissed, struggling. "Let me go."

He ignored her and held on as she pushed and shoved against him. "Shh, sweetheart," he whispered over and over again. "Relax. Just relax."

She continued to struggle halfheartedly for a few minutes, then sagged against him. Her arms snaked around his waist, and she went still, weeping softly, her fiery defiance tempered into slow-burning despair.

"David." Leigh's face was pale. "Why don't you take her outside for some fresh air? I'll go up and help Clay."

Julia looked at Leigh through her tears. She couldn't seem to grasp the meanings of Leigh's words, simple words, regular words. They sounded like an unknown tongue.

"Julia." Leigh laid her hand on Julia's arm. "You know I can care for Ted, right? And you know I'll call you if you're needed?"

Comprehension came and Julia nodded.

Leigh gave a soft half smile. "I'm going up now. You go for a walk with David."

"But—" Julia looked up the stairs, her face full of yearning. Then she nodded. "I need to calm down, and he needs to sleep."

"Good girl." David held out her jacket. When she made no move to put it on, he stuffed her arms into the sleeves and zipped it up. He grabbed his own jacket and the flashlight by the back door, then took her hand and led her through the dunes onto the beach.

She followed docilely. The waves mumbled a greeting, and the moon, low in the sky, laid a path of brilliance over the sea to their feet. They stood in silence as the water advanced and retreated. His hand tightly grasping hers felt like the only untainted thing in her world.

"David, I can't stand the pain." She gasped for air.

He pulled her against him and held her. She wrapped her arms around his waist and wept out more of her fear. He rocked her gently, running his hand soothingly over her hair.

"You'll be all right," he whispered. "You'll be all right."

"It hurts differently," she said against his damp jacket, her voice hoarse from her tears. "From Will's death, I mean. Then my chest ached, and my heart felt squeezed by a giant hand. The pain was so intense it was physical." She leaned back and placed her fist on her chest just left of center. "Right here. I felt the hurt with every breath. But this takes my breath away. Literally. Sometimes I think I can't breathe. My whole body is alive with pain. I can't think. I can't read. I can't pray. And he hasn't even died yet. What will the agony be then?"

He nodded. "I know." His voice was soft and full of its own aching.

She blinked at him as a thought struck her. "And you had to deal with both at the same time, didn't you? Leslie and Adam." She felt an awe, an amazement that he was still functioning, still willing to get involved with people, still willing to risk caring. "David, how did you do it?"

"One minute at a time." He brushed back a curl the brisk wind had blown across her mouth. "There's no other way. You just hang on to God by your fingernails and live another minute. I kept repeating over and over, 'I will never leave you nor forsake you. I will never leave you nor forsake you. I will never leave you nor forsake you.' I said it even when I felt so alone that I wasn't sure I believed it anymore."

Julia shivered. "Your children aren't supposed to die before you. It's against the rules. And your spouse is supposed to die of old age quietly in bed." She shivered again.

"Are you cold? Or is it emotions?"

She considered his question. "I don't know."

"Come on. I know where we can be warm and still watch the water and the waves and the moon."

He led her back toward the dunes, stopping beside one of the little cliffs where a winter storm had eaten away part of a dune and left a drop of five feet. He sat and pulled her down beside him.

"This will block the wind for you."

It was true. It was as if a little vacuum existed under the cliff, the wind whipping past without stopping to investigate the lee of sand. He put an arm around her and pulled her against his side. Still she shivered.

"The sand's cold."

"Come here." He took her hands and pulled her onto his lap. She sat sideways to him, her shoulder leaning against his chest. He wrapped his arms about her and pulled her closer. Her head rested against his shoulder.

She sighed, feeling comforted by his closeness, feeling his warmth gradually seep into her, as near to peace as it was possible to be these days. "You've been so good to me, David. I don't know what I'd do without you."

She could just make out the faintest of smiles on his face. "I don't intend that you have a chance to find out." His voice was soft but firm, full of promises and a future she didn't know how to deal with right now. Today was hard enough. She said nothing as her thumb fiddled with her wedding ring, but he didn't seem to expect a response.

They sat quietly for a while, watching the moon over the water, listening to the soft murmur of the waves breaking on the sand. If she angled her head right, she could see the water and the moon without the lights of Atlantic City to distract from them.

"'Though He slay me, yet will I trust Him.'" Her voice was soft. "I think that will be my verse."

He nodded. "That's what it comes down to many times—trust. Nothing more because there is nothing more."

"He looked so—" she hesitated, searching for the words she wanted—"so *not there*." Her hand went to her heart. "It terrified me. 'Not on their birthday, Lord,' I kept thinking. 'Not on their birthday!'" She gave a sad smile. "As if another day will be better. But I don't want Clay to have to carry that burden for the rest of his life. It will be bad enough that his twin is gone. To think that he died on their birthday would take so much of the pleasure of future celebrations away."

David's arms tightened about her, and he leaned over to kiss her cheek. "You're an amazing woman, Julia Wharton. And you're a lot stronger than you think."

She settled against him and stared at the moon.

Twenty-three

$\mathcal{L}$EIGH HURRIED UP the steps to Ted's room. Concerned as she was for both Ted and Julia, her heart was strangely light in both its definitions: light as in freed from a great burden, buoyant, weightless, the heavy chains of her secret unlocked from her soul; and light as in flooded with brilliance, the doors of her self-inflicted prison thrown open to the radiance of sunlight pouring over her spirit.

She wanted to laugh, to sing, to dance, but Ted's bedroom was hardly the place. Instead, she grabbed hold of her elation and pushed it firmly down to percolate just below the surface of her skin, to bubble through her veins. Later she'd have time and be in the right place to explode with her emancipation.

Clay now knew. She grinned. She had to admit to an all-too-human satisfaction at his despair. If he had brushed off his paternity, she knew she'd have spent the rest of her life struggling to forgive him. Any warmth she'd begun to feel toward him would have been frozen in the winter of his contempt. But it was obvious he ached to the marrow of his being, and that pleased her. Not that she delighted in his pain, for she didn't. Not at all. But she did rejoice that he took the situation so to heart.

Happy birthday to you, Bucko!

She stopped in the doorway for a minute and just

watched the brothers. Ted was in bed, and Clay was trying to get him out of his clothes. Ted was so limp that it was like undressing a doll except that you couldn't push and pull the limbs any way you wanted. Every few seconds, Ted would hiss, and Clay would close his eyes in frustration and try again.

Leigh bit back a grin. Julia was right to be concerned about Clay's nursing skills. She bet that if he took one of those tests for spiritual gifts, his mercy scores would be about zero. Administration, now, that would probably be off the charts.

Her shoulder resting against the jamb, she studied Clay. He was such a commanding presence with his height and strength. He had that same aura of competence that Will had had and that used to mark Ted before his decline. The Wharton men were all leaders, the kind of men people automatically followed, but Clay even more so. Bill showed the same presence, but then why wouldn't he? He was a Wharton man too.

As Julia often said about the boy, "He's going to lead somebody someplace. It's just a matter of who and where."

Clay must have felt her eyes on him because he looked up. She smiled and was delighted to see his mouth turn up in that half grin she had always loved. That he could smile at all considering the punch he'd taken in his metaphorical gut was a wondrous thing.

"What?" Ted mumbled, aware that he'd lost Clay's attention. He turned his head.

"Leigh. Help. He's killing me."

"Poor baby." Leigh laughed as she came into the room. She placed a hand on his forehead and felt the heat.

He batted at her weakly, making a noise like a growl. "Don't baby me. Rescue me."

"He's very grumpy," Clay said in a disapproving voice. "Very."

"So would you be if you felt like he did," Leigh said. "Now let's get these clothes off him."

In a matter of minutes, Ted was tucked under a sheet and blanket, too weary to even scowl any longer. He was slick with sweat as his fever ate at him, and he tried with feeble kicks to get the covers off.

"They have to stay on to keep you from getting a chill," Leigh said, laying a restraining arm on his leg.

He muttered something indecipherable though obviously uncomplimentary, but he stopped kicking.

Leigh looked at the chart posted on the wall. "What meds are you due, Ted?" With quick, practiced movements she collected the proper pills from their vials and bottles.

"Lift him up a bit, Clay," she ordered.

As Clay slid his arm under Ted and raised his shoulders, Leigh poured fresh water. She stuck the angled straw in the glass and handed the medical cocktail to Ted. He stared at the collection of pills for a minute.

"Why bother?" he whispered.

Leigh ignored the tremor those two words caused in the pit of her stomach. "Because you can't give up. It's against the rules. Whartons never give up."

"She's right," Clay said. "I'm sure it's written down somewhere in all that genealogy stuff Grandmom Wharton collected."

Ted snorted, but when Leigh raised the medicines to his mouth, he swallowed them. Gently Clay lowered him to the pillow.

"Hot," Ted whispered.

"Get a washcloth, Clay, and a bowl of cool water."

"Yes, sir," Clay said, amusement in his voice.

"Watch her," Ted managed, turning on his side and curling in on himself. "Dictator."

Laughing, Clay left the room.

Ted grabbed her hand as soon as he was gone. "Are you mad at me?"

She looked at his questioning face. "It was a rotten thing to do, both to me and to Clay."

He nodded. "But are you mad at me?"

"What if Bill had caught on? He's got to be told, but not like that."

"A risk worth taking." He coughed harshly, his face creased with pain.

Immediately, Leigh reached for the cough medicine. "Take more."

He swallowed obediently. "Love you both," he muttered as he closed his eyes.

She gently brushed his hair back from his forehead. "I know, and I've got to admit, I'm glad the secret's out. It's a relief."

He smiled blissfully. "Good."

"But how did you figure it out after all these years? How did your mother?"

"The picture," he said, nodding to the bureau.

Leigh looked on the cluttered top of the bureau, searching among all the medical paraphernalia for a picture. She spotted it where it had slid between a container of body lotion and a bottle of mouthwash.

She looked at the photo in amazement. "It's Billy, but it's not." She turned it over. "Will Wharton, age 10. I can't believe the resemblance!"

"It was in the box from the attic," Ted said with a shiver. His teeth knocked against each other as he tried to curl into an even tighter ball. "How come I'm freezing all of a sudden? How can I be cold and hot at the same time?"

Leigh dropped the picture back onto the counter and didn't bother to pick it up when it missed and fluttered to the floor. She went quickly to Ted. She climbed onto the bed behind him and wrapped her arms around him, pressing his back to her front. She felt his shudders and the slickness of his sweat and closed her eyes against the tears. How she hated his illness! She rested her forehead against the back of his neck and tried not to cry.

The click-click of toenails on wood announced the entrance of Terror who came zipping into the room with his usual energy. He bounded onto the bed, stopped dead when he saw Ted and Leigh. He stared at them for a heartbeat, then went unerringly to Ted. He licked his face, then settled down against his chest.

Ted sighed. "Wonderful."

Clay came in, a basin in his hands.

"Go away," Ted muttered. "I'm happy."

"I'd be happy like that too," Clay said. He put the basin on the bureau in a space he made by pushing a dozen medicine containers to the side. He dipped the washcloth into the cool water and wrung it out. He sat in the chair beside the bed, leaned over, and washed his brother's face, neck and chest, the latter in spite of Terror's complaints. Then he rinsed the cloth and did Ted's face again.

Leigh watched from behind Ted, her heart moved by the gentleness of Clay's movements. Maybe he had the gift of mercy after all.

Oh, Lord, help them!

"I checked on Bill," Clay said quietly as he sat back in the chair. "He's watching TV. David must have convinced him Ted was okay because he's lost that pinched look."

Leigh nodded, relieved. "How's your mother?"

"She's not there. Bill says she went out with David."

Leigh nodded. "Good. They must still be walking on the beach. David didn't want her to come up here because she was so upset."

"Sorry." Ted sounded resigned. "What I do best."

"Be quiet and rest," Leigh whispered softly in his ear.

The three kept a companionable silence for a while. Then Clay asked, his voice tight, "Does she love him?"

Leigh resettled her head more comfortably on one of Ted's pillows. She still lay spooned against him, offering her warmth, her comfort. She heard uncertainty and something like fear in Clay's voice. Her heart ached for him. "I don't know if she loves David. I think he loves her, but I don't think she knows how she feels yet. There's so much going on that it's difficult for her to sort it all out."

"She loves him," Ted said and began to cough. "Doesn't realize it yet," he managed between gasps.

"You might be right." Leigh rubbed her hand across his back, patting him gently to help ease the cough.

Silence settled on the room again. Then, cautiously, Clay spoke. "He seems very nice."

"He is." Leigh raised herself on one elbow to look across Ted. "I know it's hard for you to see your mother with someone besides your father, but try to think what's best for her."

"Nice man," Ted mumbled. "Nice for her." Terror gave a sleepy sigh of agreement.

"It's so strange," Clay said. "Things you never in a million years anticipate happen when you're away, and it takes a while to come to terms with them. You two are used to the idea of David. You've seen the whole thing develop." He sighed. "I'm trying."

Leigh smiled at him. "You're a good man, Clay Wharton."

He smiled uncertainly back and reached absently for the picture on the floor. He looked at it and blinked. He sat up straight and blinked again. He turned it over and read aloud, "Will Wharton, age 10." He turned the picture face front. "Unbelievable!"

Leigh smiled wryly at his reaction. "That's how they all figured it out."

"I brought this down from the attic?" he guessed. He studied the picture, his expression greedy. "I suppose this means he'll look like Dad when he grows up." He glanced at Leigh and said hastily, "That wouldn't be a bad thing. Dad was a good-looking man."

"That he was. And I think it would be wonderful if he looked like your father."

"Quiet." Ted sounded imperious even at a whisper. Terror whuffled agreement.

Leigh thought of Will Wharton bending over her little red Civic. She thought of him saying, *Is there a possibility that you're pregnant, do you think? Don't worry. We'll take care of you.* "But I'd rather he has your dad's character and compassion and godly heart."

Clay nodded. "He was an extraordinary man."

"Not many busy doctors would take on a pregnant eighteen-year-old just because his wife said God said they should."

"Is that how it happened? Mom said God told her?" Clay looked at Ted. "I thought it was you."

Ted managed a head shake.

"Tapped her on the shoulder in my line at the Acme," Leigh said.

"That doesn't sound like Mom."

Leigh shrugged. "Maybe that's why Will listened."

"Downstairs," Ted muttered. "Go. I need sleep!"

"Sorry," Leigh whispered. "We'll be quiet. We don't want to leave you." What she really didn't want all of a sudden was to be alone with Clay. She rested her head against the back of Ted's because in that position she couldn't see Clay.

She knew they had to talk because there were so many feelings and issues to sort through. Still, the thought of being that vulnerable and open after years of protecting herself was terrifying. What if he guessed how she felt about him, had always felt about him? All she foresaw was potential humiliation, and it petrified her.

"Go," Ted ordered. "Won't die while you're gone. Promise."

"Ted!" Leigh gave him the slightest bump, and he gave a little laugh that turned into a deep cough. When he stilled, she kissed his ear.

He batted a hand at her. "Go. I mean it. I'm okay now."

Clay got up and walked around the bed. He held out a hand to Leigh, and she didn't know what to do but take it. He helped her to her feet. He kept her hand as they left the room and made their way downstairs. She felt as awkward and shy as she had all those years ago, and she hated it. She took a deep breath and whispered, "I am a new creation in Christ."

"What?" Clay smiled down at her.

She shook her head. "Nothing." But she felt better as she held that truth close.

They looked in the family room and found Bill asleep on the sofa, the TV flickering, the volume so low it was a wonder he had heard anything.

"He didn't want to disturb Ted," Leigh whispered, proud of that kind of consideration from a boy his age.

"He's a wonderful kid," Clay said, and her heart swelled. She knew he meant it. After all, he had said it earlier this evening, before he knew Bill was his.

"Sometimes he reminds me of you so very much," she said, hoping it was a good thing to say.

Clay blinked and shook his head. "I still can't believe it."

Bill stirred, and they wandered to the kitchen before their talking woke him. They stood facing each other, each leaning one hip against the counter. Clay, still holding her hand, cleared his throat, but Leigh spoke first.

"Are you mad at me?"

"What?" He looked surprised at the question.

"You have a right to be mad at me, to be furious. I've kept you from your son."

He nodded. "Maybe there's some anger, but there's much more shame over how I behaved. I guess I wish you'd told me when you found out you were pregnant. Then I wouldn't feel like such an idiot now."

"If I'd told you, you'd have wanted to do the right thing and marry me for all the wrong reasons, and they'd have kicked you out of the Academy."

He shrugged, like it wasn't a big deal. "You're right. No married midshipmen. But there were other colleges."

She shook her head. "Not for you there weren't."

He didn't deny that truth, and she wondered if he really would have married her. Or if he even should have. He'd gone off on vacation, off to Annapolis, off to a life of his choosing while she'd been forced to live the life she'd been handed. A compulsory marriage would have been a disaster, a worse catastrophe than his ignoring her was.

But there could have been, should have been a middle ground.

As his thumb drew circles on the back of her hand and she felt his sincere regret and remorse, she felt herself falling under his spell all over again. Because in spite of everything in their past, today he was a wonderful man. Because in spite of everything, she was so very attracted to him.

He squeezed her hand and said in a voice rife with sorrow, "I didn't even check to see if you were all right."

Remember that, she told herself, steeling herself to ignore the aching tenderness in his voice. *Just because you're an idiot who's still in love with him doesn't mean he feels anything for you but regret.*

She lifted her chin. "At least you know now that I'm not all those terrible things you thought I was."

He flinched. "I should have known better."

"You should have."

"I mean, there was no evidence."

"None at all."

"I watched you. I know."

She frowned. "What do you mean, you watched me?"

He shrugged. "Just what I said. I watched you. I observed you. You fascinated me."

"You observed me." For some reason, that idea made her feel violated. "Sort of like I was a virus growing under a microscope?"

He waved away that picture. "No, no. More like you were a beautiful diamond glinting in the sunlight. All your mysterious facets intrigued me."

A diamond was definitely better than a virus, but still. "When?"

"Then. Now. Back in high school. On visits to Mom and Dad. Here at the house. Whenever I was around you, which I admit hasn't been much."

"Why?"

"Because you captivated me. You always have. You still do."

She blinked. She knew she'd just been paid a high compliment, but she couldn't allow herself to be impressed by it. She would remain aloof, independent. It was her only protection. "I mean why haven't you been around?"

"Recently because it was painful to see you, so very painful."

She brought him pain, not the soaring joy he could bring to her. She bled a bit at that hit. Well, what had she expected? Maybe she was fascinating, but so was a space alien or a two-headed goat. She was right to guard her heart.

"Back then I did drive past your house before I left for the Academy," he said. "Several times. You were never there."

"I was working two jobs."

He nodded. "I even got up the nerve to call when I came home at Christmas."

"By then I was already six months pregnant and living in Glassboro."

"But I didn't know that."

"You could have learned it with a couple of quick questions."

He sighed, regret evident. "I could have."

"Too bad I didn't matter enough to you to motivate you to ask the questions."

"You mattered." His voice was deep, intimate.

"I did?" She hoped she sounded skeptical rather than delighted.

He nodded. "You do."

She stared at their joined hands. When had he taken her other hand? How she wanted to believe him, to trust him, but she'd been down that path before. She didn't have the courage to open herself like that again. She pulled out her old mantra: If she'd truly mattered, he'd have come to her, for her. So she snorted and pulled her hands free.

"I only mattered hormonally, and then only for an evening." She turned and walked from the room before she started to cry. She told herself she had been right all these years. He *was* a louse.

She stopped at the family room door. "Come on, Bill. Time to go home." When he didn't move, she walked over and shook him. "Come on, bub. Up you go."

"I can carry him," Clay said from directly behind her.

"No. He'll walk."

She shook Bill until he staggered to his feet. She turned him toward the back door, holding on to him to show him the way. He sleepwalked as she directed.

How many times through the years have I left this house with my son? How come it never hurt quite like this before?

Clay stood by the kitchen door, waiting. "I'll walk you across."

She shook her head. "Why don't you just watch?" Her voice could have cut the glinting diamonds he had compared her to.

The door opened as she reached for the knob, and Julia and David walked in, windblown and much at ease with each other. Julia looked relaxed. The tension in the room hit them both immediately, and they looked from Leigh to Clay.

"Good night," Leigh said quickly. "Billy and I are just leaving."

"Bill," the boy muttered as he stumbled down the steps.

The two of them walked across the yard, Mama falling into step as they reached the door.

The two of us, she thought. She glanced at Mama and corrected herself. *The three of us. My family.*

"I didn't know," she heard Clay say in wonder and sorrow to his mother as he watched her. "I didn't know."

"And you didn't bother to find out, did you?" Julia asked, her voice more acerbic than Leigh had ever heard it. Julia's sigh drifted on the night air. "That's what hurts and disappoints me the most."

Give it to him, Julia. He deserves it. Make him bleed.

So why, she wondered as she climbed the steps to the apartment, *do I feel so miserable for him?*

Twenty-four

HE STARED ACROSS the lawn at the house for a few minutes, then turned and looked up at Leigh-Leigh's apartment. His insides were tossing with anger.

Just like the waves, he thought in an unusual flight of fancy. *My stomach feels just like the waves look.* He shivered. He hated the waves! He hated feeling this way.

But the waves weren't his problem right now. Frustration was.

They weren't taking him seriously.

He'd almost killed that stupid little dog and the kid, and they still weren't taking him seriously. They were throwing birthday parties and having fun!

When Leigh-Leigh and the brother and the kid went out to her house, he thought they'd get the treasure and bring it right to him. That was the way it was supposed to happen. That was the way it should have happened.

But no. They'd come home empty-handed. They'd even been smiling! They should have been shaking with fear, fear of him.

And she wouldn't answer her phone. How was he supposed to threaten her if she wouldn't answer her phone?

Somehow he had to make them pay attention! All he needed was an idea.

Once when he was a kid, his old man had come home drunk and passed out before he made it inside. He lay on his back in the yard. Somehow he threw up, and all the ugly, smelly stuff just lay there in his mouth, the part that didn't spill out and dribble down his cheek and into the grass. He started to make terrible choking sounds.

He had grabbed the old man's arm and tried to turn him over, tried to move him so the stuff would go out of his mouth and throat. He'd been shaking and so scared.

"Ma," he yelled as he pulled and pulled, but he was too weak to move the heavy weight. He ran inside. "Help!"

"Get out of my sight, you little weasel," his mother said as she kicked in his direction.

"Pa's sick!"

She snorted. "He sure is."

"He's choking! He's gonna die!"

She just stared at him. "Liar." She walked into the kitchen without a backward glance.

"Little liar," Stanley taunted him from the sofa where he was slouched watching TV.

"Stanley, you've got to help." He ran to his brother and grabbed his arm. "He's choking!"

Even today as he stood in the quiet backyard, he remembered his terror and the metallic taste of fear on his little boy's tongue. He hated the old man, but he didn't want him to choke to death in the front yard. It wasn't right somehow.

Stanley had sneered at him and hit him on the side of the head, knocking him to the floor. He saw stars and bit his tongue, and blood fell onto the rug. He'd get a beating for that, he knew. Tears fell too, but he couldn't tell if they were because he hurt or because no one paid any attention to him.

The old man was going to die because no one would listen to him. Just like when Stanley set the garage on fire, and no one believed him when he said it was burning until the fire engine came. They had a burned-out garage for five years before it finally fell down.

"Hey, sweetheart, honey bunch!" The voice was deep and loud and came from the front door. It was Ma's latest, Georgie. "I got me a drunken bum here who was drowning in his own vomit right there in the yard. Looks bad to the neighbors, baby."

Ma came running from the kitchen with a great big smile. "Georgie!"

So the old man wouldn't die. He guessed he felt relieved. He pushed himself back against the wall, hoping Georgie wouldn't notice him. Georgie always rapped him on the head with his knuckles, and it hurt lots.

Ma pushed open the door, and Georgie dragged the old man into the house. "Where?" he asked Ma.

"Who cares?" she said, looking with disgust at the limp figure with the awful slime down his front. He stank, and Stanley made mocking noises like he wanted to throw up too. Worm gagged for real, but he didn't let himself get sick. The blood on the rug was bad enough.

"How about we leave him here?" Georgie asked Ma.

Ma nodded, and Georgie dropped the old man. He hit the floor with a terrible thud, but he landed face down. Georgie stepped over the body and grabbed Ma. They started giggling and kissing. Then they ran upstairs.

"Go outside, Stanley, Ernie," she yelled. "Don't come back 'til I call you."

Nobody called to him now. He was alone, but he was going to be rich. It was just a matter of time and a good plan.

Twenty-five

CLAY SAT ON THE jetty facing toward land, watching Terror run down the beach at breakneck speed, apply the brakes, spin and run back with just as much energy and zest. He had rarely looked happier.

At least someone's happy, Clay thought as the dog grabbed a pile of browned and broken sea grasses in his teeth and tossed it in the air. As it rained down on him, he chased as many pieces as he could, nipping at them, snarling and barking to chase away the grave danger they represented to the canine population of Seaside.

Maybe there's a magic wand in one of those piles. Clay took a deep breath and exhaled slowly. Wouldn't it be great if life's problems could be dealt with that simply?

He'd been sitting here since before sunrise, thinking, praying. He'd gone back to the house a couple of times to refill his coffee mug and get something to munch. He nodded to his mother when she came to the kitchen, and she nodded back, but they didn't speak. Neither one seemed to have anything to say.

But he'd heard her all night, over and over.

"And you didn't bother to find out, did you? That's what hurts and disappoints me the most."

Rarely had either of his parents said he disappointed them. Her comments, deserved though they were, cut deeply.

It wasn't just that he'd disappointed her. It was that

she knew what Leigh had been through, and when she spoke, it was from knowledge. Her distress showed him quite clearly how much Leigh had suffered because of him.

He was on his third large mug of coffee as he watched Terror pick his way across the jetty to him. A brisk rub on the head and the dog was off again. Sighing, Clay turned back to the sea, and, forearms resting on his knees, stared blankly at the horizon.

God, I didn't know! I should have, but I didn't. How did I not know? How could I not know? Shouldn't you feel it somehow when you have a son? Shouldn't you be able to sense it somewhere deep in your heart or soul?

And shouldn't you know when you've irrevocably changed the life of a girl you loved, however adolescent and selfish that love was?

Obviously not.

Last night when he'd realized what Ted was telling him, he'd been devastated. She'd known that, and she'd held his hand. She'd comforted him. She'd tried to make him feel less guilty, less a failure.

She was amazing. She'd broken his heart and mended his spirit at the same time.

And then she'd withdrawn. She'd stuck her firm little chin in the air and become the stone princess again, pulling up the drawbridge and leaving Don Quixote standing alone on the other side of the moat.

And he hadn't the vaguest idea why.

The surprise was that her distancing herself hurt as much as Ted's bombshell of a story. The very last thing he wanted from her was detachment, separation. She'd shared her concern, her warmth. She'd looked into his eyes and offered absolution and understanding. He wasn't sure about a lot of things this morning, but he knew with certainty that he wanted to be the recipient of that grace again.

Maybe if he could figure out why she pulled back, he could figure out how to fix whatever was bothering her. As an officer and an engineer, he was by nature and training a problem solver, and he was good at it. He stared at the horizon and played back their conversations of last night again and again. Try as he would, he couldn't put a finger on any one thing that upset her. She'd just slowly pulled away.

"Why's everybody mad at you?"

Clay jumped, turned, and found Bill in jeans and a Phillies sweatshirt and cap standing behind him. "Hey, champ." He slid over and patted the empty place on his rock. "Up pretty early, aren't you?"

"Uh." Bill lowered himself beside Clay. He studied the sky intently. "It's going to be a nice day. No clouds."

"Just right for Easter vacation." Clay smiled at the boy. At his son.

Bill nodded and stared out to sea. After a moment's silence he took a deep breath. "Why are they all mad at you?"

"I take it you've seen Grandma Jule this morning?"

"Yeah. She's acting real quiet, like she's gone inside herself."

Clay looked at Bill, amazed at his perception. The kid didn't get that from him, that was for sure.

"She acted like this a lot when Ted got sick." Bill scratched his forehead. "I think it's how she works things through."

"So what makes you think she's mad at me?" Clay asked, interested in spite of himself.

"I asked. 'Who got you upset, Grandma Jule?' That's what I said."

If you want information...

"She wouldn't tell me. She's too nice." Bill glanced at Clay, a quirky little smile on his face. "So I asked again, 'Are you mad at me? At Mom? At Ted? At David? At Clay?' No, no, no, no, silence. I'm smart enough to take it from there."

Clay popped the bill of the boy's cap, knocking it down over his eyes. "Good detecting, champ."

Bill righted his hat. "Notice that I asked if it was you last. Grandma Jule was so happy to see you when you came that I figured she'd never be mad at you. But you're the man." His eyes narrowed. "Why?"

It was Clay's turn to study the horizon. "Because I did something a long time ago that was very wrong and stupid, and they all just found out. It's especially hard on Mom."

Bill thought about that. "It hurts when you learn bad things about people. I cried when I learned Uncle Ted was going to die. So did Mom."

"Well, I'm not going to die. I just did something I shouldn't have done."

"But we all do wrong and stupid things. That's what Jesus is for."

Clay half smiled and looped an arm about Bill's neck. He pulled him close and ran a gentle knuckle across his skull. "Thank you, Bill. That was very kind."

Bill shrugged. "Maybe, but it's true."

The pride that uncoiled in Clay's chest threatened to choke him. This child of his was marvelous. Leigh had done a wonderful job. And his parents. And Ted.

"And I missed the whole adventure."

"Yes, you missed the whole thing."

Well, not anymore.

Bill looked at him. "So Grandma Jule's mad at you because you hurt someone?"

Clay sighed. "Yeah."

"Who?"

Clay wished he could ignore those piercing eyes staring through the smudged glasses, but he couldn't. "Your mother."

Bill nodded. "I thought maybe."

"And Grandma Jule's not exactly mad." Clay rubbed the back of his neck. "She's more upset because I disappointed her." The thought that he had hurt his mother as surely as Ted had was painful indeed. Another proof of his failure with the people he loved most. "She thought I was a nice man, and she found out the truth. It disappointed her."

"Moms are good at that disappointed stuff, aren't they? My mom gets disappointed in me too."

"Hurts, doesn't it?"

"A lot."

The two stared companionably at a small, distant school of silver porpoises swimming north, their fins piercing the water as they arced and played. One leaped high, and they both laughed.

"Flipper," Bill said.

"Undoubtedly." Clay was afraid to move as he became aware of Bill leaning softly against him, the boy's bony shoulder pushing against his bicep. Or, interesting thought, maybe it was him leaning into Bill.

"Is Ted mad at you too?" Bill asked.

"Ted's always mad at me. He just has a real reason now."

"And Mom?"

Clay could feel Bill's eyes on him and turned to meet his gaze. "I have no idea what your mother feels. I really don't. But I doubt it's very kindly toward me at the moment."

Bill nodded, turning back to the view. "She'll come around. You just have to give her time. Look how she came around with Mama. Of course she didn't come around with the kittens."

Clay wanted to lean over and kiss the top of Bill's head. He'd never kissed his son, he suddenly realized with a jerk of his heart, and the kid was already ten years old. He settled for pulling off Bill's cap and rumpling the boy's already rumpled hair.

"Just in point of interest," Clay asked. "Did you comb your hair this morning?"

Bill looked at him as if he were crazy. "Of course not. It's vacation. I want to see how long I can go before Mom sees me and makes me comb it."

A shaft of memory stabbed Clay. "You know, your Uncle Ted and I used to have competitions to see which one of us could get by our mom longer without combing his hair."

"Who won?"

"Me. I'd put on a baseball cap just like you, and she couldn't see the mess. Ted said I was cheating, but I knew I was just smart."

"I've tried the baseball cap thing with Grandma Jule, but she always makes me take it off. Then Mom makes me go comb."

"Now who do you think Grandma Jule learned the baseball cap trick from in the first place?"

Bill kept his eyes toward the sea, but Clay saw the satisfaction there. And a small smile. The baseball cap story pleased him. Concern flicked. Why? It could only be because he liked sharing the trick with him and Ted. Or was it just with him? His heart kicked up a fast, erratic rhythm, making his post-jogging heart rate seem low. How much did the boy know?

Oh, dear God, how will we—I—ever tell him so he won't hate me?

Bill leaned more solidly against Clay even as he continued to look toward the horizon and the endless miles of ocean out there. His words, when they finally came, were so soft that Clay almost didn't hear them against the splash and gurgle of the water as it breathed against the jetty.

"Are you mad at me?"

Clay blinked. "At you? Never! Oh, Bill, never!"

"Really?"

"Really."

"You're sure?"

"I'm sure!"

Clay felt a tension leave the boy's body as Bill leaned even more heavily against him. "I was afraid you would be, you know. I can be a real problem sometimes. I don't mean to be. I just am." The last was a puzzled whisper.

"Bill." Clay's voice was husky, and he had to clear his throat before he could speak again. "Bill, look at me."

Slowly, Bill turned his head until their eyes met.

"You, son, are the one fine thing in this whole mess."

Bill blinked and looked away, but Clay had seen the tears. He'd also seen things more important than tears. He'd seen desperation and fear and knowledge and yearning.

Bill knew.

Clay's stomach pitched when he thought of the pure courage it had taken for Bill to approach him this morning. What if Clay still hadn't wanted him? The boy's desire for relationship was so strong that he had been willing to take the risk of rejection for the prize of belonging.

Oh, Lord, I love this kid. I really do.

In truth there was nothing Clay wanted more than to be this boy's father, to be worthy of his love, to share his name, to hear himself called Dad. Clay wrapped his arm about Bill's shoulders and pulled him close. He allowed himself the luxury of removing the baseball cap and kissing the boy's head. He allowed Bill the privacy of not noticing his sobs.

Ten years without a dad when Bill didn't know who he was, when he'd never spent time with him, when he never really expected to meet him except maybe some imaginary day in the nebulous future, made the rejection have an academic feel to it. Not that it hurt less than having a flesh and blood person say, "I don't want you." It just hurt differently. While intensely personal, it was also strangely impersonal, and for that reason he could build an image of a wonderful man—rich, intelligent, powerful— just waiting to hear from him, longing to meet him.

Now, poor kid, all he has is me.

"I never meant to hurt you," Clay said, his head resting on Bill's hair. "I never meant to hurt anyone."

Bill didn't say anything, but he didn't pull away.

"If I'd known, I swear to you on a stack of Bibles, I'd have been there." He thought about that statement as he heard it leave his mouth, and knew that from his perspective as a man, it was true. He also knew that he'd be there in the future. Just what form being there would take, he didn't know yet, but be there he would.

But as a boy, the seemingly good Christian young man with the selfish streak a mile wide, would he have been there in any way that counted? Who knew? What he had become was a pharisee of the pharisees just like St. Paul, only he'd killed a young woman's dreams instead of New Testament believers.

And Leigh, as kind and tenderhearted and intelligent as they come, recognized him for what he was. No wonder she pulled away from him. No wonder she couldn't trust him.

"It's okay," Bill said as he wrapped his arms around Clay's waist. "I know you didn't know."

"Bill, you are a wonderful kid."

"Yeah. Mom says I have my good times."

"I'm proud to be your father."

"I'm proud to have you."

They sat quietly for a few minutes, shoulder to shoulder, watching the restless waves. Then Clay asked, "How'd you know?"

"Everyone thinks I'm dumb, but I'm not."

Clay laughed. "Dumb is the last thing you are."

Bill nodded agreement. "Grandma Jule saw a picture, dropped it, and ran. Dr. Traynor saw the same picture, dropped it, and ran after her. Then Uncle Ted picked it up and stuffed it into his pocket when he thought no one was looking. You think I don't want to see that picture? You think I won't see it?"

"Sneaky little guy, aren't you?"

"If I have to be." He frowned. "I really look like Grandpa Will, don't I?"

"You really do."

"So he was a wimpy guy at ten too."

"But he grew out of it," Clay said. "You remember how big and handsome he was, don't you?"

"So are you," he said shyly. "Maybe I'll grow up to be like you."

Clay thought his heart would melt. He couldn't resist hugging his son. "I should be so lucky."

"Hey, Billy!" Mike's voice called from the dunes.

Bill pulled away from Clay and looked back at his friend and waved. "Mike! Guess what?" He jumped to his feet. "Wait until you hear!" He began running. "He's my dad!"

Just like that, Clay thought in amazement. Just like that he tells the whole world.

"What? Who?" Mike yelled, running toward them. Terror raced by his side.

"Him!" Bill pointed back to Clay who watched in bemusement.

"Him?" Mike was clearly surprised as he skidded to a stop. He frowned, staring from Bill to Clay and back. "How come? Is he going to marry your mom or something?"

"Nope. He's just my dad. Like your dad is yours."

Mike squinted at Clay. "Huh."

"Yeah," agreed Bill. He turned back to Clay. "Tell Mom I went to Mike's, okay?" The two boys started back through the dunes, Terror trailing along.

"Bill!" Clay called, climbing to his feet. "Wait."

The two skidded to a halt and waited for Clay, muttering to each other and giggling as they watched him. Clay decided he was glad he didn't know what they were saying. His ego had taken enough shots from the adults around this place. He didn't want to know what the kids were saying.

The three walked into the backyard as Clay said, "I don't think you should go to Mike's today."

Bill spun around and put his fists on his bony hips. "What's with this not letting me out of the yard? First Mom and now you. I'm not some little kid!"

Mama, who'd been washing herself in a puddle of sun by the hydrangea bush, froze with a leg in the air. Terror, standing a good three feet from Mama for his health's sake, frowned.

"Your mom'd just rather you stay around here," Clay said mildly, hoping he sounded parental but not overbearing. How did fathers do it? Of course most fathers started when the kid was too little to complain and grew into it. Starting with a half-grown genius of determination and imagination was going to be a great challenge.

Bill looked disgusted. "It's got to do with the break-in and Terror on the jetty, doesn't it?"

The kid was definitely not dumb.

"What's Mom think will happen?" His voice dripped sarcasm. "The guy's going to rush Mike's house and grab me or something?"

Clay didn't answer. He didn't know how.

Bill's mouth dropped open. "That *is* what you think." He looked at Mike. "They think the guy's going to kidnap me."

"What guy? And who'd want to kidnap you?" Mike asked as the Seaside police rolled quietly down the drive. This time Mike's mouth dropped open. "Cheez, it's the cops."

"Get your mother, Bill," Clay said quietly.

Bill took one look at the police car and raced up the stairs yelling, "Mom, the cops are here! The cops are here!"

He reappeared almost instantly, a slightly unkempt Leigh in tow. She might have been out of bed at this early hour of—he checked his watch—eight o'clock on a vacation morning, but she clearly wasn't ready to face the world. Clay swallowed a smile as he thought that she needed a baseball cap to hide her tousled hair. Curls haloed about her lovely face in wild disarray, making her eyes seem bigger than usual. Or maybe that was an illusion caused by the dark circles under them, dark circles to which he'd undoubtedly contributed much.

He smiled at her, and she nodded politely but coolly. She seemed relieved to focus her attention on Greg Barnes as he climbed out of the police car.

"What's up, Greg?" she asked. "Have you learned something about the man, the—" She stopped and looked at the boys.

"We know all about him, Mom. He wants to kidnap me."

Leigh frowned and looked at Clay.

He held up his hands in a not-guilty manner. "Not me."

"And you call him the perp, Mom," Bill supplied. "I keep telling you that you need to watch more TV."

Greg smiled at Bill and turned to Leigh. He looked tired after a night on duty, a turn that should have ended an hour ago if Clay computed his schedule right.

"We think the man who has been giving you trouble might be an ex-con named Ernie 'the Worm' Molino."

"The Worm?" Bill laughed, Mike joining him.

"The Worm," Greg confirmed. "He was a friend of your grandfather in jail, and he was paroled three weeks ago. No one has seen him since."

It made sense that he was an ex-con, a friend of Johnny Spenser, Clay thought. He had, after all, called her Leigh-Leigh, Johnny's pet name.

Greg slouched wearily against the side of his car. "He's a little guy who's sly and has got some street smarts, but he's not got much brainpower. "

"Is he a little guy like in short or a little guy like in not very important?" Bill asked.

Greg blinked at the astute question but answered easily. "Little like in not important, though come to think of it, I don't think he's too big physically either. Skinny guy about forty-five with a bald spot he combs his hair over by growing it long on one side and spraying it into place. Know what I mean? He's been a bookie, a bagman, a dealer, you name it, but he's always been small-time because he's not got the intelligence to be anything else. He's also been in and out of prison several times because he's always getting caught."

"And somehow he got the idea from my father that I have something valuable." Leigh shook her head. "He actually believed whatever story Johnny was telling."

"Like I said, not too swift."

"What's he want with me?" Bill asked. "I don't know anything about a treasure."

"Leverage," Greg said.

Bill nodded. "That's what I thought. If he's got me, he thinks Mom'll trade the treasure to get me back."

Greg nodded. "Or she'll give him the treasure immediately to prevent him from grabbing you in the first place."

Bill grinned at Leigh, impudence oozing from every pore. "I think I'd better stay on your good side for the next little bit, Mom." He looked at Clay. "Yours too. After all, you might be the one to find whatever it is."

"It isn't anything, Bill," Leigh said, clearly not overjoyed that her son had included Clay in the program.

Greg looked at Leigh. "The word from the pen is that Johnny talked about his treasure with enthusiasm for the past few months. Before that, no one heard anything from him but gripes."

Leigh blew a gust of air. "Now the gripes sound like Johnny."

Clay suddenly wished he had known Leigh's mother. Perhaps she was the secret behind her daughter escaping Johnny's influence. And the Holy Spirit, of course, making her more and more each day into the image of Christ.

"Have you thought about the idea that there might actually be something valuable, that your father might have been telling the truth?" Greg asked.

"An actual treasure?" Leigh laughed at the idea. She indicated Clay and Bill. "We went out to the house the other day and searched, just to keep him—Molino—happy with the idea that we were looking. We found nothing but dirt, spiders, and mildew."

Greg nodded. "Has Molino called again?"

"No, though I've got to admit I jump every time the phone rings. I keep expecting something to happen."

Before he realized what he was doing, Clay reached out and ran a soothing hand down Leigh's back. When she didn't flinch, he let his hand rest at her waist.

Greg pushed himself away from the car. "Before I went home and fell into bed, I wanted you to know what we've learned. There's an APB for Molino throughout the state. In the meantime, we'll do our best to keep an eye on you. Just be careful, okay? And, Bill, stay close to home."

Leigh took a couple of steps forward, and Clay's hand fell to his side.

"Thanks, Greg," she said, reaching to shake his hand.

Greg took her hand, smiled briefly, and climbed into his car. He wasn't even out of the drive before Bill turned to Leigh.

"I want to go to Mike's. Nobody's going to grab me over there. It's dumb to even think they might."

Leigh blinked. "Uh, I don't think so. You heard Mr. Barnes."

Bill opened his mouth to protest, but Clay beat him to the punch. He laid a very heavy hand on Bill's shoulder and squeezed. "Bill, I have an idea for a great Easter gift for your mother. If she says it's okay, will you come with me and see if you agree? Mike can come along too if he'd like. We'll stop at his house so he can ask his mom if it's okay."

Leigh didn't look delighted with the idea, but she didn't say no either. With Bill's rebellion momentarily quelled, the three males climbed into the Grand Cherokee, Bill pulling Terror into the backseat with him and Mike. Clay felt pleased with himself as he turned the key in the ignition. He'd averted a confrontation. Maybe this parenting wasn't so hard after all.

He waved to Leigh as they pulled away. She smiled weakly back. Obviously she was still hiding behind her stone princess persona. He'd figured out how to keep Bill safe for the time being. He'd figure out how to get back in her good graces.

He settled back in his seat, pleased with himself. Life had never been more complicated, but it had also never had more possibilities.

Twenty-six

CLAY WALKED INTO the kitchen later than usual on Good Friday morning, intent on getting a cup of coffee and some food. He was surprised to see Leigh there. She had been avoiding the house—and him—since Monday night, living in her stone tower across the yard.

It was amazing the emotional distance of one small yard.

"Am I glad to see you," he said, probably with more enthusiasm than was wise under the strained circumstances.

She gave him a frightened-doe-caught-in-the-headlights look and headed straight for the door.

Her flight at his mere presence in the same room angered him. "Running away, I presume."

She glanced over her shoulder, her face flushed. "Yes."

Her voice was low and strained, and he regretted his temper. "I'm sorry."

"Um." She grabbed for the doorknob.

"Leigh, don't leave. Please." She looked wonderful in shabby jeans and a long sleeved, red T-shirt with bleach stains all over one cuff. Her hair had been pulled back on the sides and held with some kind of little combs.

"I've got stuff to do," she said vaguely as she pulled the door open.

With one hand he grabbed her arm and pulled her back into the room while the other pushed the door closed. He slid his hand down her arm and laced his fingers through hers. "Have a cup of coffee with me. Please. I don't want to drink alone."

"Turning into a solitary drunk, are we?" She smiled a real smile, and when he squeezed her hand, she squeezed back.

"I miss you, sweetheart. I miss your company and your sweet spirit."

"I haven't gone anywhere. I'm right here."

He shook his head. "Not in the ways that count." He reached out and traced the line of her hair from temple to comb. He felt a fine tremble go through her at his touch. Encouraged, he said, "Have dinner with me tonight."

"I've had dinner with you several nights since you came home."

"Yeah, me and Mom and Bill, maybe David and Ted too. You know that's not what I mean."

She looked at him with sad eyes. "I don't know, Clay. It's probably not a good idea."

He pulled her close, wrapping their joined hands behind his own back. He slid his other arm about her waist, both to keep her from bolting and to enjoy her closeness. "What's wrong, Leigh? Tell me. I'm going crazy here trying to figure this out."

Carefully, carefully he disengaged their interlaced fingers and placed his hand on top of hers, still behind his back. He pressed her hand against him just above his hip. He waited a couple of seconds until he was confident she was comfortable with what amounted to her embrace. Then he released her hand and slid that arm about her, his fingers meeting at the small of her back. He took a step until they were mere inches apart. When her free hand came up and rested on his other hip, he felt hope soar.

He was totally unprepared for the tear that slid from the outer corner of her eye and bled down her cheek. "Leigh!" Without thinking he leaned down and kissed it away, tasting both her salt and her pain.

She made a strangled sound deep in her throat, and her head fell forward so that her forehead rested on his chest. He cupped the back of her head and rested his cheek lightly on her hair.

They stood like that, bodies touching only where her head lay on his chest, but he was conscious of a near-painful yearning to pull her to him and never let her go. He wanted the easy camaraderie that had been developing between them. He missed her laugh, her humor, her quick mind, her compassionate heart. He missed *her*.

"Leigh," he whispered, tilting her chin up. He kissed her, a gentle kiss that contained all the longings of his heart. At first she held herself apart, those careful inches between them maintained. Then with a soft cry, she melted against him, her arms tightening around his back. He held her close and tasted her tears.

Too soon she broke the kiss and pulled away. He caught only a glimpse of her anguished face as she pulled the door open and raced across the yard. He didn't try to stop her, stunned as he was by the depth of his response to her.

No wonder he had never gotten serious with Emilie or any other woman. For him it would always be Leigh and only Leigh. The question was, would she come around for him like she had with Mama, or was he one of the kittens? And was he having dinner with her tonight or not?

Lost in thought, he climbed the stairs to Ted's room. The sight of his brother brought him up painfully.

Ted lay on his back, arms resting beside him. His hospital bed was raised, and pillows were stacked behind him to ease the pressure on his lungs. His eyes were closed, the dark lashes resting on pale cheeks. An oxygen canula forced pure air into his nostrils in the effort to make his breathing easier. Even though he appeared to be sleeping, he coughed frequently, ragged, croupy coughs that made Clay's hair stand on end.

There was no question: When the home health nurse came, she'd call David and recommend Ted be in the hospital before the morning was out. The pneumonia had taken root, and home care wasn't sufficient to dig it out.

Oh, God! Don't let him die! Please don't let him die!

Mom sat slumped in the chair beside the bed, watching Ted breathe. Her own breath was timed to his as if by following the same rhythm she could guarantee that his would continue as steadily as hers. Clay knew she'd been here all night. She was still wearing her nightgown and robe, and her hair was in disarray from where she'd pushed her hands through it in despair.

"Mom." He walked to her, lowering himself to kneel beside her. He leaned over and kissed her cheek. "Why don't you take a break for a few minutes?"

She glanced at him and smiled wanly, reaching out and pushing his hair off his forehead. "I'm afraid to."

He nodded. Every time he left the room, he was afraid too, afraid Ted wouldn't be here when he came back.

"He's not going anywhere just yet." *Please, God, may that be true.* "Visit the bathroom. Take a shower. Go make some of your terrible coffee. Take a quick walk by the water. Whatever will help you most. I'll be here, and I promise to call you if there's any change. Besides, the home health nurse will be here soon."

Finally she let herself be persuaded, leaving the room with a backward glance at the bed and a dubious one at Clay.

He made shooing motions with his hands. "Go. We'll be okay."

Clay collapsed into the chair she'd just vacated and stared at Ted. He felt so helpless whenever he was in this room. He hated helpless!

He got up and studied the chart on the wall. Maybe they had forgotten some medication. If he could figure out which one it was, he could give it to Ted, and he'd be all right. Clay compared the chart with the various bottles and vials littering the bureau.

All dosages checked off and accounted for.

He sighed. It would have been too easy a resolution.

Maybe more of that vitamin and nutrient-laced drink they were always forcing down him. Clay went to the box stowed in the corner and pulled a can out. He popped the top and stuck in one of those bent straws. When Ted woke up, he could drink it.

"Sit down already," a barely audible voice said. "You're driving me nuts."

"Ted!" Clay rushed to the bedside. "Here. Drink this."

Ted just closed his eyes. His face spasmed.

"What?" Clay demanded. "What?"

"Chest hurts."

"I'll rub it with Vicks Vapor Rub," Clay said, suddenly aware that the room was redolent with its aroma. Mom. She'd always rubbed their chests with Vicks when they were kids. He began looking frantically for the little blue jar.

Ted coughed. It was a deep, fluid sound that scared Clay all over again. When the coughing jag passed, Ted lay exhausted.

Clay reached for the phone.

"Who?" Ted demanded.

"An ambulance. You need the hospital."

"No."

"Yes! Ted, you can hardly breathe."

"Home." His eyes were hard and mutinous. "Living will. My call."

Clay looked away from his brother, out the window to the beautiful spring day, sun warm and benevolent, breeze light and soothing. He'd walked the shore earlier, praying for Ted, praying for Leigh, praying for Bill, praying for his mother. Praying for himself.

"Call Pastor Paul," Ted said, his chest straining with the effort not only to breathe but to talk.

"What?"

"Pastor Paul. Ask him to pray for me."

"I'll be right back. I have to get a phone book." Clay started for the door.

"Over there." Ted managed to point to a list posted beside the medicine chart.

Clay found a list of emergency numbers, everything from the hospital to Pastor Paul. He dialed.

"Seaside Chapel. Pastor Paul Trevelyan speaking. How can I help you?"

"Paul, this is Clay Wharton."

"Ted." Paul said the one word, but Clay could hear him coming to attention as he spoke.

"He's got pneumonia."

"Yes. Julia called me."

"He's in pain and breathing distress. He asked me to call you and ask you to pray for him."

"Are you still at home?"

"He doesn't want to go to the hospital."

Paul sighed. "I never know whether to push him or not. If he goes, he'll probably have more time, but there's no guarantee. And he deserves the privilege of dying at home if that's what he wants. Okay. Can Ted hold the phone, or will you hold it for him?"

258 ~ *Gayle Roper*

"I can hold it for him."

"Okay, then. Put it by his ear."

Clay did as he was told, holding the phone beside Ted who lay with his eyes closed.

"Ted, this is Pastor Paul. I hear you're not doing very well today." Paul's electronic voice was audible in the quiet bedroom.

"Right," Ted mumbled. "Hurts."

"Ah, Father," Paul began, "I'm so sorry to hear Ted is hurting today. It hurts me that he's in pain, and I know it hurts You. Ease his discomfort, Lord. Touch him and relieve him. I ask You to glorify Yourself through Ted."

Clay stared at the phone. Glorify Yourself through Ted? Through a man who has rejected God's standards?

"Today's Good Friday, Father," Paul continued, "the day Your Son gave His life for us. What pain He suffered for our salvation. What love He demonstrated for a sinful people who've turned from You. What eternal joy is ours when we believe the truth of this sacrifice. We've all sinned, Father. Ted, me, Clay. But Jesus bore it all and more. Thank You, thank You.

"It's because of today's sacrifice made all those years ago that we have the courage to come to You and ask Your help for Ted. Touch his body, Lord. Ease his pain. Heal him if You will, we ask in Jesus' name. And touch his spirit. May he know Your peace and Your relief. And above all, may Jesus Christ be glorified."

The room was silent as the soothing words of Paul Trevelyan's prayer hung in the air. Ted lay with his eyes closed, but Clay noted his breathing, though still labored, didn't have the frantic quality it had had after the last coughing bout.

"Ted," Pastor Paul said, "you do as the nurse tells you. If she says hospital, you go."

Ted snorted.

"For your mom, Ted." Paul's voice was firm. "When it's inevitable, that's one thing. Stay home then. But today, well, who knows?"

"Thanks," Ted said. "I'll think about it."

"I'll pray for you all day. I had planned to stop by this afternoon, and I'll still do so."

"Thanks," Ted said again.

Clay lifted the phone. "If you're coming this afternoon, you'd better call first to see if he's here or at the hospital."

"I'll be praying for you too, Clay," Paul said. "I'm glad you're there."

Clay hung up the phone and sat staring at his twin. He absolutely hated seeing him so ill. He hated that he couldn't fix it. He hated that Ted hated him.

"Stop staring."

Clay jumped. "I thought you were asleep."

"With you boring into me with your X-ray vision?"

"You're breathing more easily."

Ted nodded. "Paul's got a great pipeline to the Lord."

"Why didn't you ask me to pray for you?" Clay was as startled that he'd asked the question as Ted was by the question, but Clay realized he was offended that Ted had ignored him. And hurt. Deeply hurt.

"You?"

"Yes, me." Clay's tone was impatient. "I pray, you know."

Ted fluttered his hands. "I know. But I didn't know if you'd pray for me."

Clay flinched. "I pray for you every day. Every single day. I always have ever since I can remember."

Ted looked stunned.

For some reason his reaction made Clay mad. "What? You think just because you make me mad I don't love you? I do, and watching you so sick is eating me up inside."

In answer, Ted shut his eyes.

Clay stared at the pale face before him. Here he was pouring out his heart, and Ted closed his eyes. Closed him out!

"Read to me." The request came in a reed thin voice.

After a moment of silence where he struggled with his own labored breathing, Clay said carefully, "Sure."

He pulled the Bible off the bedside table, knocking a small blue bottle onto the floor. The Vicks. He picked it up and put it back. Fat lot of good that would do at the level of illness they were contending with. What had he been thinking?

He flipped through the pages until he came to Habakkuk 3. He read as slowly and dramatically as he could the verses that he read to himself frequently, the verses that were to him the only possible solution to failure.

"Even though the fig trees have no blossoms, and there are no grapes on the vine; even though the olive crop fails, and the fields lie empty and barren; even though the flocks die in the fields, and the cattle barns are empty, yet I will rejoice in the LORD! I will be joyful in the God of my salvation. The Sovereign LORD is my strength! He will make me as surefooted as a deer and bring me safely over the mountains."

After a moment of silence, Ted said, "Again."

Then, "Again."

After the third reading, Ted remained silent, and so did Clay. He stared at the verses, seeing again the barrenness of his life, the failures that ate at him. Leigh and the hurt he'd given her. And he'd thought that pained him before! His son and the ten years he'd lost, they'd lost. His brother and the gulf that his own pharisaical pride had built between them.

"The Sovereign LORD is my strength! He will make me as sure-footed as a deer and bring me safely over the mountains."

He glanced at Ted, still lying with his eyes closed. *Safely over the mountains* undoubtedly meant something far different to him. But to Clay it meant that despite all the errors, all the conscious and unconscious mistakes, all the sin, God was still there for him and always would be. He would bring him safely to what? Not success. Men thought of that as the opposite of failure, but spiritually speaking, no, it wasn't the answer. Reconciliation.

Suddenly, as clearly as if she were beside him, he saw Leigh.

"Now get this," she was saying. "This is the important part. It was Esau, the wronged brother, who rushed to embrace his twin. He threw his arms around Jacob and kissed him. *Then* the brothers wept and reconciled."

Safely over the mountains meant forgiving and reconciling.

Suddenly the tears came, and Clay fell to his knees beside the bed.

"I'm sorry, Ted. I'm sorry." He grabbed his brother's hand and felt his jolt of surprise. "Forgive me! I've behaved so badly toward you." And he threw his arm across Ted's chest in the closest approximation he could give to an embrace, burying his head in the hollow of his brother's shoulder.

It was a minute before Clay realized that Ted was utterly still, totally unresponsive.

Oh, dear God, he doesn't want my confession! You might have, but he doesn't.

Embarrassed and full of sorrow, Clay pulled back. "I'm sorry," he began, only to freeze at the startled, no, make that appalled expression on Ted's face and the trancelike look in his unblinking eyes.

Oh, Lord, I killed him!

Then Ted blinked. "What did you just say?"

Clay went limp with relief. "I said I'm sorry."

"For what?"

"For not being a good brother to you. For being proud and self-righteous. For being a pharisee."

Ted looked wary. "Watch it. Your halo's slipping."

"It's fallen on the floor and deserves to be stomped underfoot." Clay came off his knees and slid back into the chair.

"But you still think I'm wrong."

Clay nodded. "I still think, based on Scripture, that you're wrong, but I *know* I've been wrong. You'll have to deal with your failures with the Lord. I can only deal with mine. And one of my many has been my attitude toward you. Forgive me?"

Ted stared at his feet, obviously at a loss. "I don't know what to say," he admitted after a few minutes. "I've been mad at your self-righteous attitude for so long."

Clay nodded, fighting to keep his disappointment from showing. He wanted Ted to respond like Jacob apparently did by weeping with joy and reconciling. "Take your time. I know this is a shock."

While Ted lay still, eyes closed, for what seemed an eternity, Clay fidgeted. Finally, Ted turned and looked at him.

"Clay?" he said through chattering teeth.

"Um?" Why was Ted cold? He'd been burning only a couple of minutes ago. He reached forward and touched Ted's forehead. Cool for the moment. The fever had dipped, and he was reacting to the great internal temperature change.

"Pray for me?"

Clay felt his spirit lift. Ted hadn't said, "I forgive you," but didn't this request mean the same thing? He reached for Ted's hand. It was cold and clammy. Suddenly he pictured Leigh lying behind Ted, hugging him. "I've got a better idea."

"There's something better than prayer?"

Clay grinned, the first relaxed smile he could remember giving his brother in years. "Can you sit up?"

"I am."

"I mean, can you lean forward?"

Ted frowned as Clay stood and began to climb onto the bed. "What are you doing?"

"Lean forward," Clay ordered. He slid behind his brother. "Now lean back."

Gingerly, Ted reclined against Clay. "What do you think you're doing?"

"Helping you get warm, I hope."

"Are you feeling all right?" Ted asked even as he relaxed against Clay. "I'm not used to all this concern coming from you, and it's making me nervous."

Clay reached around Ted and pulled the covers up. "Believe me, no one's more surprised than I am that I'm doing this, but I want to. Now we can pray."

"You know," Ted said, his voice drowsy, "I'm going to die of pneumonia, and you're going to die of heat stroke." He yawned. "Poor Mom."

He was asleep before Clay realized how uncomfortable he was. With Ted's pillows low behind his back, he had nothing to support his head.

Lord, I hope his nap isn't too long. I don't think my neck can stand it. And while he sleeps, I'd like to talk with You about him. And I'd like to ask a big favor. I know You can grant it if You choose. Can You restore Ted's health so that I can have time to be his brother, his twin again? Would You grant us time?

Clay started when he felt Ted move. He blinked and realized he'd fallen asleep himself, right in the middle of his prayer. He smiled slightly. No better way to fall asleep than talking to the Lord. He shifted a bit and groaned. His neck creaked and cracked, incredibly stiff from the strange angle his head had assumed while he was unaware.

"You really are there." Ted tried to look over his shoulder. "I was sure I was dreaming it."

Clay caught Ted's earlobe between his fingers and squeezed lightly.

"Hey!" Ted reached up and rubbed the offended flesh. "I believed in you without the pain."

"Just wanted to be sure." Clay pushed a pillow up behind his upper back. "Ah, wonderful. And how do you feel?"

Ted became still, and Clay could almost hear him assessing himself.

"You know, I think the fever's gone." There was wonder in Ted's voice.

Clay reached a hand to Ted's forehead. "You know, I think you're right. When I climbed in here, I thought you were going to roast me. Now you're certainly keeping me warmer than I like, but the oven seems to have been turned off."

Clay climbed out of the bed as Ted took a deep breath.

"I don't feel that tightness in my chest." He made himself cough. It was a hollow noise, totally devoid of the croupy sounds that had plagued him for the past three days.

The brothers grinned at each other. "It's gone," they said in unison.

When the home health nurse arrived an hour later, she took Ted's temperature three times, listened to his chest four times, and stared at him in amazement.

"It's unbelievable, Dr. Traynor," she reported over the phone, "but the pneumonia's gone. No crackles, no fever, no coughs. Clear chest and bright eyes. It's a miracle is what it is."

Twenty-seven

LEIGH, DRESSED IN her robe after a quick shower, stood in front of her closet and knew it was hopeless. No matter what she decided to wear, she would look terrible. How could it be otherwise? She felt terrible.

"What do you mean I have to stay with Ted?" Bill demanded from the doorway. "Where are you going?"

"Clay invited me out for dinner."

Bill frowned, and her heart checked. "Do you mind?" What should she do if Bill minded? If he got jealous?

He shook his head, and the frown slid away. "Why should I mind? The only problem is that he knows my toe-stubbing trick."

Leigh grinned and reached for the red dress, made a disagreeable face, and drew her hand back. Too bright. Too pretty. Tonight she had to dress in a low-key manner to prove that this dinner meant nothing to her. "He and I are just friends."

Bill looked a bit skeptical but didn't comment. "Why don't you wear that blue one?" He pointed to the closet.

"Which blue one?" she asked, studying the navy blue, the midnight blue, the teal blue, and the aqua outfits.

"The pretty one. You know."

Bill turned to leave, but Leigh called him back. "Bill, we need to talk."

"Now?"

"It's as good a time as any." She had rehearsed what she would say at least a million times. She shot a prayer heavenward. "It's about Clay."

She sat on the bed and patted the place beside her. "Sit here, champ."

He sat. "Champ. That's what Dad calls me."

"Bill, a long time ago, Clay and I—What did you say?"

"When? About what?"

"About champ."

"I said that's what Dad calls me."

She went hot all over and said in a furious voice, "He told you?" How could he do that? She was Bill's mother. It was her responsibility. What right did he have to butt in after all this time? He had no right, that's how much.

"Nope, he didn't tell me." Bill straightened his bony shoulders. "I figured it out myself."

"Oh." Her anger deflated like a popped balloon. "How?"

"The picture. I saw it. So I asked Dad."

Feeling uncomfortably left out, Leigh asked, "How long ago was this?"

"Tuesday morning."

"Three days ago?" Her voice spiraled up as the anger returned. Three days that Bill had known, and no one had seen fit to tell her.

Bill looked at her in surprise. "It's no big deal, Mom. It's not like you didn't know."

"Of course I know. That's not the point. The point is that I'm your mother."

"I don't think anyone doubts that."

"It was my job to tell you!"

"Ah." The lightbulb clicked on. "Dad and I hurt your feelings."

Dad and I. She shuddered. How odd it sounded from his lips. "Do you call him Dad?"

Bill looked uncomfortable. "Only in my mind and just now with you. I don't have the courage to say it to his face."

"I guess those things take time," Leigh said. "Don't rush where you don't feel at ease going."

"We didn't mean to hurt you," he repeated. "We just had a guy talk, and I asked him about it."

Another guy talk. Swell. The first one changed Billy's name. The second one confirmed his parentage. What would the third one do? Move Bill to some out-of-the-way naval base with Clay while she taught alone here in Seaside? Leigh was surprised and ashamed at how resentful she felt.

For years she had been the most important person in Bill's life. Having someone pull up beside her, maybe even surpass her in influence was frightening and galling.

This is not a race or a competition.

Oh yeah? It sure feels like one.

Only if you make it so.

She rubbed the spot above her eye where she felt the headache moving in, bag and baggage.

"How do you feel about having him as your father?" she asked in a carefully neutral voice.

He nodded and grinned. "Great. As I told Mike, I—"

"You told Mike?"

"Sure."

And he told his mother who told her neighbor who told her neighbor who told her neighbor. By the time she went back to school on Monday, the whole town would know. Great. Now she'd not only have to live down being Johnny Spenser's daughter but Clay Wharton's one-time—in more senses than one—paramour.

Life just didn't get any better.

"Don't get too attached to him, guy," she said quietly.

"Why not?"

"He's going to be leaving soon for wherever the navy sends him." Even saying it made her heart bleed a bit.

He was silent a minute, then bounced. "We'll just go visit him, wherever he is. Grandma Jule can come along."

She became suddenly interested in the condition of her nails. She couldn't let him see the pain that idea caused.

"Too bad he's not still in Hawaii. We could ride in one of those outrigger canoes."

"Yeah. Too bad," she managed. She closed her eyes and shot another prayer heavenward. "Bill, do you know what my biggest fear is?" *Aside from the fear that Clay will take you away from me.* "I'm afraid that you'll use our wrong behavior as an excuse for yours when you get older."

"Do you mean that you're afraid that because you had sex before marriage that I will too?"

She flinched. The bluntness of a precocious child. "Yes, that's it."

He waved his hand like that thought wasn't worth having. "Don't worry." He stood and walked to the door. "I'm never having sex, and I'm never getting married. Both would mean being friends with some girl." He shuddered. "Yuk!"

When he closed the door, she flopped back on the bed. She didn't know whether to laugh or cry. *Oh, Lord, I'm not doing very well here.*

She forced herself to get up and walk to the closet. She grabbed the midnight blue pants suit and threw it on the bed.

Bill knocked and at her "It's okay" poked his head in. He saw the midnight blue outfit on the bed. "That's not the one I meant, but it'll do. Are you going to feed me before you leave?"

"Would you rather eat with Grandma Jule?"

"Yeah! And Uncle Ted."

"Don't you bother Ted. You know how sick he is."

"Not anymore." Bill grinned broadly.

Leigh looked at him. "What do you mean, not anymore?" She'd spent the day inside grading papers. At least she had tried to do the schoolwork, but thoughts of Clay kept getting in the way. By forcing herself, she'd been able to concentrate hard enough and long enough to finish three book reports. Then she gave up and took a nap where Clay invaded her dreams. "What have I missed?"

"Pastor Paul prayed, and Clay prayed, and God answered. The pneumonia's gone."

"Oh." She sank onto the bed. "That's wonderful!"

"Yeah. It's a miracle."

Much of the guilt about going with Clay tonight evaporated at the news. Ted was doing better. *Thank You, Lord!* She wasn't leaving Julia in a potentially tragic situation while she went out and had a good time. Well, the good time part was problematical, but she would be leaving Julia alone. Now it was okay to do so.

She and Bill grinned at each other a moment before she said, "Why don't you scat and let me get dressed."

When Bill left, pulling the door shut behind him, she flopped back and stared at the ceiling. No more guilt over Ted, just high-level stress over Clay. For the hundredth time she knew she should have said no to dinner. She shouldn't have sent Bill over with the one word message yes. It should have been no.

But she wanted to have the time with Clay. Desperately. Granted he could rip her heart out with one easy comment, one casual move. He could even take her place in her son's heart, whether he meant to or not. He was, after all, that magic person: Dad.

But being with him was worth the risks.

Pathetic, Leigh. You're one sorry specimen.

That kiss this morning had shown her just how much she cared and how vulnerable she was. He had kissed her before and turned her to mush. He had done it again. But not tonight. No physical contact of any kind tonight. Not even his hand on her elbow to guide her. She could find her own way, stand on her own two feet. She had found great satisfaction in her accomplishments, and being an independent woman was one of the things she did best.

Clay would leave soon, and she'd be alone again anyway. They'd be alone again. Best not to dream or hope. Best not to trust. It'd save a lot of anguish in the long run.

Being firmly committed to a noninvolvement policy in the safety of her bedroom was one thing. Carrying out that policy with Clay at her side was a whole different thing. All he had to do was smile, and she became a blithering idiot. Their date, their first ever, would be the most wonderful/terrible night of her life.

The Good Friday service moved her deeply, especially the cross placed at the front of the sanctuary, not a lovely cross but a crude cross made of wood that would give you splinters if you touched it, that would break your heart if you hung from it. A circlet of entwined thorns of horrific length rested on the crossbeam.

When they left in thoughtful silence, she had tears in her eyes.

"Are you okay?" Clay asked softly.

"I'm always moved when I think of what Jesus did. I know who I was and who I still am, and—" Her voice caught.

He gave her shoulders a gentle squeeze. "Thank you for caring so much. I've known the Lord so long that sometimes I lose the wonder and the enormity of it all." He helped her into the car. "Do you want to go home instead of out to get something to eat?"

She smiled her appreciation of his question. "We have to eat. Let's just go somewhere quiet."

He drove off the island to a marvelous restaurant where people still wore dressy clothes, and the napkins were linen, and the service was impeccable. It was a night like no other. When she yielded to her heart, enchantment shimmered over them. The candles at the restaurant glowed romantically, his Cherokee was Cinderella's coach, and he was St. George, ready to slay all the dragons in her life.

When she remembered to think instead of feel, the restaurant's flatware was water spotted; the Cherokee was much too much car for one man, an unjustifiable extravagance, and he was a sailor who went AWOL when she needed him.

He told her about his afternoon with Ted, his contrition over his past attitude, and the miracle of the fever's breaking. She rejoiced with him, and when he held her hand across the table, she smiled into his eyes. He smiled right back, and she felt hope.

It was when they were walking to the car, his hand resting lightly on her waist, that a thought struck her. Ted was feeling better. Clay didn't need to stay close to home any longer. Soon he'd go away.

The stardust dissipated in an instant, and her edginess returned, making her delicious shrimp scampi sit leadenly in her stomach. They pulled into the drive, and the vise about her middle ratcheted itself a couple of turns tighter.

Clay took her hand as he helped her from the car and kept it as they walked to her door. When he stopped and faced her, she immediately began searching her bag for her key. It was the excuse she needed to pull her hand free since it was clearly a two-handed operation. Then she turned her back to him as she unlocked the door.

"Thanks, Clay," she said over her shoulder as she went inside. She turned to close the door quickly before he could make a move.

"Want to take a walk on the beach?" Clay asked.

"Now?" She wanted to walk anywhere anytime as long as she could do it with him. Dare she risk it?

"Of course now. It's only eleven, too early to call it an evening."

"I don't know, Clay." Moonlight, the soft soughing of the waves, and Clay. Bad combination. Wonderful combination. Tempting combination. "I–I'm not certain that's a good idea."

"Sure, it—"

Her phone rang, the sound loud and demanding.

"I've got to go," she said and shut the door in his face. She raced up the steps and grabbed the receiver. "Hello?"

"Hello, Leigh-Leigh. Missed me?"

Twenty-eight

BILL STOOD AT THE kitchen door of the main house and watched his mother and father get out of the Grand Cherokee. He waited for them to come to the house and get him. They hadn't let him go anywhere alone for days now because of that Ernie Molino guy. It bugged him, but it meant they cared. He liked the idea of the three of them—Mom, Clay, and him—sort of like the Three Musketeers, only they didn't have swords and horses. Or muskets.

He waited, but they didn't come for him. Instead they walked toward the apartment holding hands.

He watched them together, and something about the way they were together made his stomach flip-flop uncomfortably. Earlier today when Mom said she was having dinner with Clay, he'd made believe it didn't bother him. He'd even teased her about it. Later when he had time to think about it more, he wasn't so sure it was funny.

What if they decided they wanted each other but didn't want him? What if they decided he was in the way? After all, he was a mistake. He wasn't supposed to happen when he did. And he knew as well as anyone that he could be a trial, always asking questions, always looking for a better way to do things, always trying to be the boss.

Sure he was smart, and he didn't get in trouble at

272 ~ *Gayle Roper*

school. He could be helpful around the house if he thought of it. The trouble was that he didn't think of it very often. Mom had to keep reminding him when she had a job for him to do. It wasn't that he wanted to disobey her; he just had other things on his mind. But he could work on being more thoughtful. If he was as smart as they said he was, he should be able to do that.

Just so they liked him and wanted him. Just so they were happy with it being the three of them, not the two of them without him. The very thought of not being included made him feel queasy.

It was so confusing. On one hand he was glad Clay was his father. He liked Clay. He was cool. He was smart. He was *tall*. The two of them had had a good time taking care of Mom's Easter present, working together real well.

On the other hand he felt threatened somehow, and it had to do with Mom and Clay together. Of course he wanted them to like each other. It would make seeing Clay easier if Mom liked him. She wouldn't mind if he went to Clay's house if she liked him.

But what if they got lovey-dovey? Or what if Clay just up and left them again? Mom had said he'd be leaving sometime soon. What if that was the end of it all? What if when Clay left, he forgot all about him? All about Mom?

Bill wasn't sure which would be worse, Mom and Clay being lovey-dovey and forgetting him, or Clay forgetting both of them. Of course he could stand not having Clay around. After all, he wasn't used to having a father. But could his mom stand being rejected again? He'd heard her crying the other night, and while he didn't know exactly why, he knew it had something to do with Clay.

No wonder his stomach ached.

He blinked as Clay started up the back steps. He hadn't expected to see him this soon. He was sure he'd go in the apartment with Mom and forget all about him.

"Hey, champ," Clay said as he opened the door.

"Hey," Bill said, stepping back. That was another thing. Should you hug your dad or not? Or should he hug you? He'd seen Grandpa Will and Ted hug lots of times, but then they knew each other forever. The same with Mike and his dad. What should he and Clay do?

"Did you have a good evening?" Clay asked.

"Yeah, it was okay. I watched an old John Wayne movie with Grandma Jule. I think David better watch out. She really likes the Duke."

"I think David's safe," Clay said. "The Duke's dead."

Bill scuffed his foot on the floor while he tried to think of something else to say. His mind had never been so blank.

"What are you doing by yourself in the kitchen?" Clay asked. "Waiting up for us?"

Waiting up for Mom. Not *us.* "Getting something to eat."

"My mother didn't fill you up while you watched TV?" Clay whistled. "She's really losing her touch."

The door of the apartment flew open, and Mom ran out.

"Mom!" Bill called, instantly concerned.

"Leigh!" Clay called.

"Clay," she called. "Clay!" Not Bill. Clay. Wouldn't you know.

Clay and Bill both ran outside and met her. Clay grabbed her by both arms, automatically, unintentionally blocking Bill. "What's wrong?"

"What's the matter, Mom?" She reached out a hand and rested it on his head, lightly brushing at his hair, but she kept looking at Clay like he'd solve all her problems.

"Molino. On the phone." Her teeth were chattering. Nerves. Bill's nerves weren't too steady at the news either, but he made himself look strong for her.

Clay put his arm around her and hugged her. "It'll be okay, sweetheart. It'll be okay."

Sweetheart? Puh-lease! "It's okay, Mom." Bill grabbed her free hand and held it tightly.

Clay led her up the steps to the house, and Bill trailed along, still holding her hand. "Come on," Clay said. "We'll call Greg Barnes right away." He held the door for her, stepping back so she could go first.

How polite, Bill thought as he was forced to release her hand so she could go forward. Bill followed close behind Clay and was shocked when Clay let the door fall shut right in his face.

Standing outside staring in, Bill watched his father fuss over his mother. They weren't acting lovey-dovey in a kissy way, but he knew lovey-dovey when he saw it, no matter its form.

274 ～ Gayle Roper
274 ～ Gayle Roper

And I'm on the outside. His chest hurt in the region of his heart. *There's a screen between me and them, and I don't like it one bit.*

Even when Mom saw him staring in and held out her hand to him, even when Clay reached out and ruffled his hair as he walked to her, he felt like the screen was still there.

Twenty-nine

WORM STOOD ON the beach and looked over at Atlantic City. He smiled, which was no easy thing with the pounding head he had. Too much booze and grass. Too little sleep.

But it was worth every painful moment. He had been king of the hill for three whole days, staying at the Trump Taj Mahal, winning and losing, then winning and losing again. When he had the treasure, that high living would be his regular life.

He hadn't planned on going to AC, but one night standing on the beach with the squirrelly ocean licking at his shoes, he knew he just had to go. The Whartons weren't going anywhere, and he deserved a bit of fun after all those years in jail.

Hitchhiking there had been easy. So had acquiring a stake. Little old ladies and their purses were meant for sharp guys like him. AC was full of little old ladies, and a lot of them liked to walk to automatic teller machines. Follow them for a couple of blocks after they left, and when no one was near, grab and run.

He didn't get caught because he had a disguise—a blond wig and mustache. He always ran around a corner fast, pulled it off, and stuffed it in his pants. Even Johnny would be impressed if he knew, but he didn't think you knew things like this in hell. Wasn't that part of the whole idea?

Most of the ladies he robbed didn't have much money, but one lady had one thousand dollars in crisp fifties in her purse. He wasn't sure where it came from because those ATM machines wouldn't give you that much, but he wasn't complaining. In fact, he felt like he ought to run back and kiss her, but she was lying in the middle of the sidewalk sobbing when he turned his corner, so he guessed he wouldn't.

With twelve hundred dollars total he took on the casinos. He loved the one-armed bandits. With those guys you could play all night and still have money left over. One night he won a jackpot, and tokens poured out until they overflowed the tray and spilled on the floor. A lady who wasn't exactly young or pretty was so excited for him that she gave him a hug. She stayed with him in his room at the Taj Mahal where they slept all day and partied all night.

He only had two hundred left now, and he was back in Seaside to get the rest. Sugar was waiting for him back in AC. She'd promised. He grinned. When he was rich, really rich, he'd trade her in for a better model, but she'd do for now. She only called him stupid once, and that was when he tried to pour some champagne into her mouth straight from the bottle, and she was laughing as it splashed all over her face.

"Ernie! Don't!" She laughed so hard she almost choked. "You're being stupid! We don't want to waste the stuff, now do we?"

"Making you laugh ain't no waste, Sugar."

Saying stupid like that was okay. It was even fun.

Look, Ma. I got me a girl, and I'm having fun!

A wave with more punch than its predecessors broke over his feet, wrecking his daydream, and wetting him clear to his ankles. He shrieked as salt water sloshed in his shoes. He turned and ran until he was in the dry sand where the rising tide couldn't get him. Stinkin' ocean, trying to eat him. He couldn't wait to leave here! At least in AC you had the boardwalk to protect you.

He squished through the dunes to the Wharton house to see if Leigh-Leigh was home yet. With every step his head threatened to explode, but he knew you couldn't drink when you were doing business. Booze made you sloppy, Johnny said.

He lay down on a dune, thinking about how much he missed Johnny. Slime, but a wonderful friend. Johnny would have liked

Sugar. He squinted and thought about that for a minute. Yeah, it was probably a good thing Johnny was dead.

Worm lay on his back and looked at the stars. Why did they stay up there? Were they there when the sun was out? Were they really hot like people said, or was that just another story like the one about that big snake thing that lived in that lake someplace far away?

Who cared? He fell asleep. The sound of that giant Jeep woke him up.

He rolled onto his stomach and watched Leigh-Leigh and the brother, Modeling Clay, get out of the car. He liked that car. It was big, but he wondered why anyone called that thing a Jeep. He'd seen enough war movies to know what a Jeep looked like. He guessed you could probably paint one a different color than puke army green, but how did they pump it up like that? When he had the treasure, he was getting a Cadillac. That was a classy car.

He pulled his phone from his pocket and dialed. Leigh-Leigh was saying good night to Modeling Clay. It looked to him like Modeling Clay didn't want to leave, and she wanted him to.

Hey, Modeling Clay, I know what you're going through. The story of my life until Sugar.

Yeah, it was good Johnny was dead.

Leigh-Leigh's phone rang, and she shut the door in Modeling Clay's face to run and answer it. Worm grinned.

"Hello?" Leigh-Leigh said, real pleasantlike. What was she doing answering the phone so nice in the middle of the night? Didn't Johnny teach her nothing?

"Hello, Leigh-Leigh. Missed me?"

There was a gasp that warmed his heart. Keep her scared and she'd cooperate.

"Mr. Molino," she said. Worm almost dropped the phone. "Leave me alone, please."

How did she know who he was? He was invisible, like those Special Forces guys who sliced everybody's throats. Maybe he ought to slice her throat.

"Mr. Molino, are you still there?" She sounded mad.

"I don't know who you're talking about," he said, trying to sound mean. He sounded more scared, like he did when Stanley grabbed him. He looked all around to see if someone was watching him. Somebody had to be, or they wouldn't know who he was.

Suddenly the dunes were spooky. They were full of places where people could hide. It dawned on him how stupid he'd been. If he could hide here, so could other people. Were there cops behind that dune? Or maybe Modeling Clay himself?

He forced himself to turn back to the yard. Modeling Clay was going in the kitchen door. But the cops could still be out here with him. His skin started jumping.

"I want that treasure," he said. "Sunday and no later, or you'll be sorry."

"There is no treasure, and if you touch my son again, I'll wring your neck myself."

"I never touched your kid!" Did she think he was that kind of man that he'd lay a hand on a kid? "Sunday!" And he hung up.

Now he had to get off the beach before the shadows grabbed him.

Thirty

SATURDAY AFTERNOON, Ted stepped onto the back porch and inhaled deeply. He held the breath as long as he could in his clear lungs, then exhaled slowly and with great pleasure. The briny air smelled delicious, wonderful, intoxicating. He had never expected to smell it again when that pneumonia had taken hold. He'd really thought it was the beginning of the very end.

But miracle of miracles, he was feeling better. Not only were all David's "crackles" gone and his mind more alert, but he was also going to the beach. He couldn't stop smiling. He also couldn't stop shivering.

"Are you cold?" Bill asked in disbelief, eyeing Ted's down jacket.

Ted stared at the boy in his Phillies sweatshirt. "Aren't you?"

Bill blinked. "It's warm today. It's sixty-five degrees!"

"I don't have any body fat left." Ted smiled as Leigh draped a blanket over his shoulders. "No insulation."

"Get Ted that lounge chair from the garage, will you, Bill?" Leigh had a second blanket draped over her shoulder.

Ted pointed to it. "That for me too?"

She smiled. "If you need it."

Ted moved slowly as he went down the steps and

crossed the yard. When he reached his mother's bench by the path through the dunes, he sat. He was breathing heavily but without distress.

"I can't believe I'm out of breath that fast!"

"You haven't done anything physically taxing for several weeks, and you were one sick puppy just a day ago." Leigh patted him encouragingly on the shoulder.

"Hey, don't leave without me." Clay took the back steps in one leap and joined them at the bench, Terror trotting behind.

A loud crash brought heads around to stare at the garage and Bill.

"Stupid chair," he muttered as he picked it up from the floor. "Bumped into the door jamb."

"All by itself?" Leigh asked, grinning.

Bill stuck his nose in the air. "Well, I certainly didn't tell it to knock itself silly."

Laughing, Leigh walked to him. "Here. You take the blanket. I'll take the chaise."

"No, let me." Clay started forward.

"Always trying to impress the ladies." Ted grinned, rose, and took a step. To his distress, his legs had all the strength of cooked spaghetti. "Forget the chair, Clay. I think you'd better take me."

Clay grabbed Ted's arm, and they moved slowly through the dunes. Leigh followed with the chaise, and Bill danced beside them, Terror grabbing at the end of the blanket as it trailed in the sand.

"Here, boy." Bill grabbed the dog and set him on a trailing length of blanket. "Sit. Stay."

Terror looked at Bill, head cocked uncertainly, but he sat.

"He doesn't quite trust you," Ted said.

"Sure, he does. Don't you, boy?" Bill pulled the blanket slowly. When it began to move, taking him with it, Terror immediately stood.

"Don't jump off," Bill ordered. "Sit." Bill waited until the dog did so. Then he began pulling the blanket slowly again. Terror looked uncertain, but he remained still. When he realized he was moving but safe, he looked up at his audience with a broad canine grin.

"He'll never want to walk again," Clay said.

With great fanfare, Leigh set up the chaise, and Ted sank gratefully into it. He lay back, eyes closed, and gave a deep sigh. How wonderful to feel the sun on his face and the ocean breeze in his hair, to listen to the low music of the softly purling sea and the gentle slap of the waves breaking against the jetty.

When he opened his eyes after a few minutes of sensory delight, he saw that Clay, Leigh, and Bill were walking down the beach away from him.

Abandoning me already? He opened his mouth to call the trio back when he realized that he normally would have fallen asleep after the exertion of walking to the beach. But he wasn't tired. He was filled with energy and enthusiasm and excitement.

It was a miracle, a real straight-from-God miracle, how much better he felt today, even better than yesterday when he was declared free of the pneumonia. His blood sang through his veins, and his spirits soared higher than the squawking gulls.

He watched as Clay reached for Leigh's hand, and she turned to him with a smile. Ted smiled too. Good old Clay seemed to be doing pretty well for himself.

Good old Clay? Ted frowned. Where had that come from? A large dollop of his euphoria dissipated, replaced by a general unease. How did he feel about Clay since the big confession scene? Certainly he loved and appreciated his twin, but what about all that resentment he'd felt toward Clay for so long? What was he to do with it if Clay was no longer a jerk?

"Hey, Ted. How're you doing, man?"

Ted turned and found Clooney and his metal detector standing beside him. Today a piece of red yarn tied the man's ponytail, and he wore a large diamond stud in his ear.

Ted stared, fascinated. "Did you find that earring in the sand, or did you have to buy it?"

"You think I'd spend money for something like this when I can get it for free?" Clooney fingered the shining jewel. "I found this about three years ago."

"So the detecting business is going well, I see."

"It's sure more fun than driving the garbage truck."

"Still doing that, huh? I always thought you'd get yourself to community college and go into computers or something."

Clooney shrugged. "Too much work. This way I have a regular

income and lots of free time to do what I really like."

"Found any more bombs recently?"

"Found a gold Rolex last week."

Ted blinked. "The genuine article?"

Clooney held out his arm for Ted to examine the slim gold watch that peeked out from beneath a ratty sweatshirt cuff.

"Why would anyone wear a Rolex to the beach?"

Clooney grinned. "I've wondered that about most of the stuff I find. I mean, this little diamond cost a pretty penny." He fingered his earring. "I went to the local jewelers and had it appraised." He shrugged. "People are nuts. Careless. It's that simple."

Ted laughed. "Let's see your detector."

Clooney handed the state-of-the-art instrument over. Ted ran his hand lovingly over the enameled metal and studied the digital readouts.

"Go ahead and play with it," Clooney said, squatting beside Ted.

"I won't mess up something for you?"

"Nah. It's easy to reset."

Ted pushed pads and varied settings for several minutes, humming softly. "This thing does everything but dig the hole for you."

"Why don't you try it out?" Clooney stood. "See what you can find."

"You mean it?" Ted's heart beat fast.

Clooney shrugged. "Sure. Maybe there's another Rolex just waiting for you."

"Or the other diamond stud." Ted climbed off the chaise. He felt like a kid on Christmas morning. He grinned. "What's the best depth to find the really good stuff?"

Clooney thought a minute. "Anything that's here has been here at least since last fall, so it's pretty deep." He suggested a depth, and Ted programmed it into the machine. He pushed the setting for coins.

"Close to the sand but don't touch it," Clooney instructed. "Swing it slowly back and forth."

Ted followed Clooney's directions. Almost immediately a red light began blinking in the corner. It disappeared before Ted could react to it. He moved the detector back until the light appeared again. Clooney handed him the little red spade.

Ted knelt in the soft sand and began to dig. He pulled a string of seaweed from the hole and beneath it lay a small, clear plastic change purse. Ted lifted it free and poured $3.57 into his palm. He looked at Clooney and laughed.

"I feel like I've found Captain Kidd's treasure."

He put the money back in the purse and stuffed it in his pocket. He began waving the detector again. In the next fifteen minutes, he acquired three quarters, four dimes, and two nickels, raising his total to $4.82.

"I'm rich!" With a huge grin he reprogrammed the machine for gold. "Now I'm going to find something really valuable. I can just feel it."

Clooney shook his head. "I've created a monster," he muttered. "Next thing I know you'll be over at the casinos. 'I'm going to win this hand. I can feel it.'"

It took much longer to get any response from the detector on this setting, but Ted's enthusiasm didn't dim. He hadn't had so much fun in ages.

Suddenly the light blinked. Clooney handed over the spade and held the machine. Ted dug until he bumped into a sand-encrusted lump. He pulled it out and held it in his palm for Clooney to see.

"Nasty looking mess," Ted said.

Clooney poked at it with a finger. Particles of sand fell away, revealing a glint of gold. "Rinse it in the surf."

Ted nodded and walked to the water's edge. He bent and swished his closed hand in the chill water. He stepped back just as a little wave broke over his foot. He opened his hand. Most of the sand had been washed away, and resting in his palm was a deeply inscribed gold cross.

"The nice thing about gold," said Clooney as he peered over Ted's shoulder, "is that the seawater doesn't corrode it like it does silver."

Ted reached down and swished his hand in the water some more. When he checked his booty this time, the cross was clear of sand. It sat in his hand, gleaming in the sun. "It must be two inches high and over an inch wide." There was awe in his voice. "It's beautiful."

Clooney made a disgusted noise in his throat. "How'd I work this beach so often and miss that?"

Ted held it out to him, knowing he'd scream if Clooney actually took it from him.

"Nah." Clooney shook his head. "Finders keepers and all that stuff."

"You're sure?" Ted tried to be nonchalant about keeping his treasure, but he was certain he failed.

"Yeah, I'm sure. By the way, I thought you were supposed to be really sick."

"I am. I'm dying."

"Yeah, right. You're skinny as a skeleton, but otherwise I hope I look as good as you when I die." With a wave, Clooney turned away, swinging his detector back and forth across the sand.

Thoughtfully, Ted stared after Clooney. Slowly he began to take inventory. He wasn't tired, an absolute wonder after months of constant fatigue. His legs felt strong, certainly stronger than when he'd walked out here just—he glanced at his watch—a half hour ago. Holding the detector and swinging it back and forth hadn't tired his arms. In fact, they felt strong, capable of lifting something much heavier.

Clasping the cross in his hand, he made his way back to his chaise and sat. He glanced down the beach and saw Clay and Leigh and Bill walking slowly back. Clay was no longer holding Leigh's hand. In fact, Bill walked between them.

His eyes lingered on his brother. Once again he thought about Clay's apology yesterday. And not for the first time he thought about the conflicting emotions that apology evoked.

He was very pleased that Clay no longer hated him. No, wait. He caught himself. Clay had never hated him. Ted had liked to accuse him of that emotion because then he had reason to be angry at his twin. If Mr. Good Guy Clay hated him, then he was free to disagree with anything Clay said or thought. And he had a legitimate argument to hide behind when he felt God getting too close.

My brother hates me! I'm sorry, God, but I can't have anything to do with the standards of a man who hates me. And I don't want to be accountable to his God.

But that thinking was based on a sham, and Ted was now

forced to acknowledge it. Clay admitted he'd been harsh and unforgiving. He admitted he'd disagreed with his twin's life choices and hated what he saw as Ted's sin, but he'd never hated Ted. And Ted could no longer pretend to believe he had.

So what should he do now? Ted thought in something close to panic. If he couldn't hide behind Clay's nastiness, if it could no longer be his excuse to God, what was he to do? There was certainly a joy in the reconciliation, but there was a great empty hole in his emotions where all his resentment toward Clay used to live.

He stared blindly at the gold cross in his hand until slowly his vision cleared. He looked at the cross, really looked at it. It was beautiful, plated, according to the fine print on the back, in fourteen-karat gold. But it hadn't been beautiful before he'd washed the crud off it.

Oh, Lord, I'm having a terrible time here. He ran his finger over the golden cross beam. *I'm losing my way, and I'm not sure I'm ready to wholly embrace Yours. It's pride, I know, but I'm not yet willing to admit I was wrong, at least in every area. I admit to being wrong in my pride and my nastiness to Clay. I admit to being wrong back when I was promiscuous. But how can I turn my back on Matt?*

Ted clutched the cross and stared out at the horizon. His heart was pounding in his chest, and it was not for health-related reasons.

I'm as crusted with sin as this cross was crusted with sand. How easily I washed it clean, and now it's beautiful. But me—I don't know.

I'LL WASH YOU CLEAN AND MAKE YOU BEAUTIFUL.

Ted shut his eyes against the sudden flood of tears. *I know, but I don't deserve it.*

SO WHO DOES?

Ted heard Bill yell, and he turned to watch the boy scramble after Terror onto the jetty. Clay took advantage of the boy's absence and took Leigh's hand again.

He studied Clay and Leigh. They'd messed up big time, but God had forgiven them whether they deserved it or not. He forgave them because they admitted their guilt and asked for forgiveness.

Can I make the choice to turn my back on everything I've been defending all these years? Can I agree with God that He's right and I've been wrong? And that's probably not turning my back on Matt because he agreed with God too.

Ted looked at the cross again. The symbol of his faith. The place of death made beautiful by some jeweler. How astonishing that it had been left where he would find it the very day after all his puny arguments against God were removed, the very day he felt a chasm yawning in his soul, the very hour he knew he had to choose.

But if I choose to agree with Your standards and admit my guilt, Father, do I have to tell Clay? Do I have to tell Mom? Or Leigh? Can this be between You and me? I know it's pride, but I can only do so much at one time.

Clutching the cross in his hand, he turned back to the horizon. *Okay, Lord. I admit that I was wrong. Does that make You happy? I knew what Your Word said, but I knew better. I knew I was hiding behind Clay's disgust. I knew I was hurting You.*

"Hey, Uncle Ted, are you awake?"

Forgive me, Lord, for all my sins.

"You'll never guess what I found," Bill called as he raced closer. He held out a great cluster of seaweed. "I'm going to smush all the air bladders. Want to help?"

"You'll never guess what I found," Ted countered and held out his cross.

Thirty-one

*J*ULIA AND DAVID entered the kitchen Saturday night, slipping their jackets off and hanging them on the pegs by the door.

"You were right, David." Julia smiled at him. "Getting out like that was wonderful. I hadn't realized how much I needed it."

He draped his arm over her shoulders and squeezed. "You had a tough few days, my dear."

There was no denying that. When Ted lay so still and wan, victim of that raging interior fire, so susceptible to the pneumonia, she could hardly function. She feared that Easter weekend, the season of Life Eternal, would be for her a season of death.

Suddenly a burst of laughter came from the living room. Julia went to the doorway and peered in, David right behind her. What she saw filled her with joy, for there sat Ted in the recliner, face alight as he watched *Princess Bride* with Bill, Clay, and Leigh. Bill was seated between the latter two, sprawled on his back with his head in Leigh's lap and his feet in Clay's, his popcorn dish resting on his chest.

As Julia watched from the doorway, Clay got up to get himself some more popcorn from the huge bowl on the coffee table. When he took his seat, he went to a new one beside Leigh.

He reached down and ruffled Bill's hair. "Slide over,

champ. It's my turn to enjoy your mother."

Bill grumbled but moved. So did Leigh. As Clay sat, she straightened, sitting primly upright. He caught her hand and pulled her gently to him.

"Relax," he whispered. And she did, gradually settling against his shoulder, her hand still clasped in his.

"The future should prove interesting where those two are concerned," David muttered.

Julia nodded. "They went out to dinner last evening after church. I've never seen Leigh so nervous."

But it was Ted who filled Julia's vision and caused her to lift psalms of praise heavenward. Not only were his lungs clear and his fever gone, but he also had energy. He was still pale, underweight, and sometimes unsteady on his pins, but his eyes were alight with inner life. He looked happy for the first time in a long time.

And that was Clay's doing.

"Did I tell you that Clay took Ted to the beach?" she asked David.

He smiled. "Several times. Why don't you tell me again."

She grinned at him. "You're a nice man, David Traynor."

"Does that mean you're not going to tell the story again?" He raised his eyebrows hopefully.

"A good story is meant to be repeated."

"And here I thought you were a nice lady."

"Where'd you ever get that idea?" She walked toward the kitchen, and he followed. "Clay half walked, half carried Ted through the dunes because he's still weak, Leigh carried an aluminum chaise, and Bill danced in circles."

"Why didn't you go with them?"

Julia thought about that for a moment. "Because it was their moment, Ted's and Clay's. They didn't need their mother."

"They had plenty of others. Why not you too?"

"But Leigh is theirs in a way I'm not. And so is Bill."

He took her hand in his. "I think I know what you mean, though I'm not sure I agree."

"I watched from the deck outside Ted's room. That way I could cry all I wanted."

David ran a finger under her eye. "And I bet you cried a lot."

"Buckets." She sighed. "It was wonderful! And he looks so good."

David glanced toward the living room and nodded. "For the moment."

She poked him. "I know you don't want me to have unrealistic expectations, but I won't let your doctor caution ruin this time for me. Whether we find that it's just a brief respite or a total cure, God's given us a miracle this Easter."

He nodded. "You're absolutely right. Now didn't you promise me a piece of pie to cap our gourmet night on the town at Pete's Pizza?"

She gathered mugs and cream while the coffee brewed. She pulled out the pecan pie she'd made that afternoon. David came to peer over her shoulder as she cut.

"Hanging around you is making me get fat," he said in obvious untruth.

"Then I'll just cut a little piece." She grinned to herself, knowing there was no chance he'd accept that.

"Big," he ordered, just as she'd known he would.

Suddenly the quartet watching the movie spoke as one. *"My name is Inigo Montoya. You killed my father. Prepare to die!"*

"Prepare to die," David finished with them, grabbing her at the waist. His threat, whispered softly in her ear, stirred her hair and made goose bumps appear on her arms.

She looked over her shoulder at him and his wicked grin, so close she could barely focus. "Is this big enough?" she managed to whisper around the constriction in her throat. Her knife rested on the pie.

"What?" He blinked and looked down at the pie. "Fine." She watched as his gaze moved from the pie to her eyes to her mouth. "Julia." It was a mere breath of sound.

And she was in his arms being well and thoroughly kissed, her eyes, her nose, her cheeks, her mouth.

At first she froze. She hadn't been kissed like *this* by anyone but Will in more than thirty-six years. She hadn't been kissed like this by anyone at all for over three years.

"Relax," he whispered against her lips.

Right.

"And put that knife down."

David's kiss was strange, wonderful, awkward, and exciting all at the same time. And it was tingly. Parts of her that she thought had died with Will surged to life. Surprised at herself and with a feeling of great daring, she wrapped her arms around his neck and proceeded to kiss him as enthusiastically and ardently as he was kissing her.

Right there in her kitchen with all the kids just steps away in the living room and the lights on for anyone driving by to see!

David pulled back first and took a step away, his hands sliding down her arms to grasp her wrists. She knew his sensitive doctor's fingers could feel her pulse slamming, but she didn't care. She knew his pulse rate was as out of control as hers. She'd felt his heart pound as he held her against him.

He just stared at her for a minute, his heart in his eyes. She stared back.

"I think I'll just get the coffee and sit at the table now." His voice wasn't quite steady. "You sit over there." He pointed across the table as, carafe in hand, he sank into a seat. "On the other side. Where it's safe."

She nodded dumbly. "Pie," she managed and turned to the counter. She was certain her face was as flushed as her heart was overwhelmed. She gripped the edge of the Formica to hold herself erect while she waited for her blood to stop surging and her knees to stop shaking.

She muffled a giggle. She was dangerous! He had to sit across the table where it was safe, where he couldn't reach her. She studied his reflection in the window as he carefully poured them coffee. He liked vanilla flavoring just like she did, unlike someone else she could mention. In fact, if she could believe David, he liked everything about her.

Well, he wasn't too bad himself.

With a trembling hand she picked up the knife and cut a really big slice for him. She moved to the microwave and nuked it for a bit.

"Ice cream?" Her voice barely shook.

"One scoop."

When she felt like she could face him again with a modicum of equanimity, she took a deep breath, turned, and put the pie in front of him. She cut a sliver for herself to keep him company as he ate.

"One sugar, no cream," he said. "Right?"

At her bemused nod, he put a teaspoon of sugar in her cup and stirred. He pushed it across the table to her.

"You know," he said thoughtfully, studying his Seaside by the Beautiful Sea mug as the cream swirled into his coffee, "I have a hard time remembering what Leslie looked like unless I actually look at a photograph."

Julia blinked, surprised at his topic of conversation. Here she was, her heart rate not quite returned to normal, and he was talking about his deceased wife. How disappointing. She must not be that dangerous after all.

He lifted his cup and took a tentative sip, testing its temperature. "If my daughter, Mandy, didn't look so much like her mother, I'd not remember at all."

Julia nodded. She wasn't sure she wanted to talk about Leslie right now or even Mandy. He'd just kissed her, for Pete's sake, and it had been a kiss with a capital *K*. This wasn't the time to talk about Leslie. Or was it?

"I definitely don't remember her voice," he said. "It used to sadden me terribly."

"But not now?" Julia asked, knowing she had trouble recalling Will's voice. Not some of the things he'd said. She remembered many of those, especially the things that were for her ears alone. It was the timbre of his voice, the tone, the actual sound that was gone.

David shook his head. "It doesn't bother me anymore." He looked directly at her. "Time moves on. Life moves on. Even love moves on."

She nodded as she dropped her eyes to the tabletop, unable to deal with the intensity in his eyes and the truth of his words. For he was right. Love did move on, should move on. She knew it. So why did she feel so guilty? So scared? So thrilled? So confused?

When she didn't respond, David switched the conversation to his new grandson, Mandy's second. Julia managed to keep focused on the conversation by sheer willpower. She ate her pie as if the kiss hadn't happened. She had just put the coffee down after pouring him a refill when he reached for her right hand. He held it lightly in his, staring at it, running his thumb back and forth across her palm. Then he began slowly rotating her wedding band.

He looked up at her, his eyes very serious. "I think it's time you took this off."

As she stared at him openmouthed, he released her hand, took a quick swallow of coffee, then stood. "And I think it's time I took myself off."

She watched him leave and felt the emptiness left by his going. She automatically cleaned the kitchen, aware she was moving in slow motion, stopping again and again to relive that kiss. That wonderful, glorious, guilt-inducing kiss. She felt sixteen years old.

When she finally finished her cleanup, she stopped to check on the living room gang and was surprised to find them watching John Wayne as McClintock trying to win back Maureen O'Hara as his wife Katherine. What had happened to *The Princess Bride?* Had that much time really passed while she daydreamed? Standing in the doorway, Julia watched the wonderful fight in the mud, smiling in spite of herself as the glorious O'Hara slid down the hill into the muck.

But she didn't feel like joining the family. She wanted to be alone, needed to be alone, so she climbed the stairs and got ready for bed. She washed her face, creaming it carefully to keep the wrinkles at bay—futile hope that was—and brushed her teeth. She did not floss; she hated to floss. Her antifloss stance was one of her small rebellions, and so far she hadn't suffered anything terrible like gingivitis as a result. Those successful mutinies were the ones she appreciated.

She settled against her pillows and read for an hour, the novel keeping her mind occupied.

Then she turned off the light.

At 3 A.M. she finally gave up and turned the light back on. The bed was a mass of twisted sheets and blankets, mute testimony to her restlessness. She sat up and shook everything straight, plumping the pillows behind her.

Oh, Lord! Will or David?

She didn't know how to articulate her teeming thoughts beyond that one plea. She stared at her wedding band, twisting it much as David had done. She felt his fingers turn it, saw his eyes as he looked at her, felt his kiss.

She climbed out of bed and went to her jewelry box. She opened the top drawer. Will's wedding band lay there, and she lifted it out, feeling it cool against her skin. It was gold, worn, with *WCW & JTW Ps. 34:3* inscribed inside. William Clayton Wharton and Julia Therese Windsor. *O magnify the LORD with me, and let us exalt his name together.* The same verse was engraved inside her band, the same initials, only in reversed order.

She had met Will in their freshman English class at Ursinus College in Collegeville, Pennsylvania, when they had been assigned seats next to each other. Wharton, Windsor.

"Have you got a pen or pencil I can borrow?" he'd whispered when everyone was finally seated that first day.

She'd looked at him, frowning slightly, to see what type of student forgot a writing implement the first day of classes, only to find him grinning at her. She had fallen for the tall, skinny, premed student from New Jersey immediately and had loved him with her whole heart from that moment on.

But now Will was gone, and there was David.

Oh, Lord!

She laid Will's ring on the dresser and slid her own wedding band to her first knuckle. She knew she wouldn't be able to pull it off without the aid of soap. She was a bit heavier than she had been that day in June thirty-six years ago. Will had put it on her finger after the best man—what was his name?—had retrieved it from under the pulpit chair where it had rolled when he had tried to pass it to Will.

Somehow the necessity of soap—or maybe hand cream—to ease the removal of the ring made the decision to take it off seem more irreversible, more absolute. It wasn't a matter of just pulling it off; it was rather a definite choice, the putting away of Will and the putting on of David, or at least the possibility of David.

She squirted hand cream on her right palm and began working it around her third finger. She took hold of the ring and pulled. It caught momentarily on the knuckle and then slid free.

She stood with the ring in her hand. It was the first time since Will had given her a preengagement ring the Christmas of her junior year that her hands were free of a ring from him.

Oh, Lord! I don't know if I can do this! I don't know if I should do it. Help me, Lord! Help me to know.

It's just a ring, she told herself, not quite believing her own thoughts. *It's just a ring. I'm not married anymore. I haven't been married for more than three long years.*

Right. So why do I feel like an adulteress, standing here in my own bedroom with a high-necked, long-sleeved nightgown on and the only men on the premises my sons?

She laid her ring on the dresser beside Will's, noticing as she did so that her hand was shaking. She rubbed the hand cream until it was absorbed. Then she picked up the pair of rings and began nervously fiddling with them, sliding hers through his, laying them in her palm, sticking them both on her thumb. She pulled them off, panicking a moment as Will's caught on the knuckle. Relief flooded her when it popped off. She slid hers crossways into but not through Will's. They made a three-dimensional circle, a golden sphere with four ribs.

Her eyes narrowed as she studied the rings, and she began to smile. She opened her jewelry box again and pulled out a gold chain with a pearl hanging from it, a gift from Will when the twins were born.

"I wish it could be diamonds," he had told her as he sat by her bed. "But medical students buy the loves of their lives pearls. Well, one pearl and not a very good one at that. At least this medical student does." And he'd kissed her and told her how much he loved her and how proud he was of her and his new family.

She held the chain up to the circle of rings, the pearl hanging inside the golden sphere.

For the first time in hours she felt her shoulders relax. She didn't need to put Will away forever, hidden in a jewelry box, feeling guilty about denying thirty-three wonderful years. Their rings could be joined to symbolize the wonder that had been their marriage, and the pearl that represented their sons could hang in its center.

Thank You, Lord. Thank You. On Monday I'll go to the jeweler's and get him to make the necklace. She smiled. *And, Lord, maybe someday soon I can give it to Leigh when she marries our Clay.*

She laid the rings on the bureau beside the chain and pearl and climbed back in bed. The light was barely out before she fell into a deep if much too short sleep.

David was waiting for her in the church narthex the next morning, Easter Sunday. Oh, he might be talking quietly with the

Robinsons, but he was waiting for her. She knew it because she had been waiting to see him.

He seemed to sense when she entered because he immediately looked up from Lisa Robinson. His eyes met hers, and he smiled. Maybe it was the dimple that appeared in his left cheek. Maybe it was the way his dark eyes crinkled when he smiled. Maybe it was the love she saw there. Whatever the reason, the smile warmed her and made her heart beat faster.

He turned to Lisa and Ron and excused himself. He made unerringly for her.

This is ridiculous, she thought. *I'm fifty-seven. I shouldn't have to tell myself something outlandish like, "Be still my heart."*

But she did. Without a second thought she left Clay and Ted, Leigh and Bill and met David halfway. She smiled up at him as he stood close to her, purposely invading her personal space. He lifted a hand and ran a gentle finger under her eye.

"It looks like you didn't sleep well last night."

She smiled. "You should see the circles without makeup." She studied his face. "You look a little sleep deprived too."

"I spent the night worrying and praying," he confessed. "I don't usually have the nerve to be as forthright as I was last evening."

She nodded. "But you were right. I needed to make choices."

He looked at her, his heart in his eyes. "And did you?" He reached for her right hand.

She watched him as he studied her unadorned finger, his thumb rubbing back and forth over the indentation left from the ring. When he finally looked up, he had that wonderful smile.

"Come on, sweetheart," he said. "The service is about to begin." He took her hand and held it as he led her into the sanctuary.

Thirty-two

*L*EIGH WATCHED JULIA walk off with David and smiled to herself. That romance was clearly speeding down the freeway of life with both participants sitting in the same car and delighted to be driving in the same direction. It must be nice, knowing where you stood—or where you were going, if she held to the same allusion.

She couldn't help but glance at Clay, and she swallowed a smile at his frown in the direction of the door Julia and David had vanished through.

Almost as soon as they disappeared, they reappeared, hands firmly clasped.

"Come on," Julia said, holding out her free hand to Ted. Her cheeks were rosy, her faint blush the only evidence that she had almost forgotten her family in the joy of being with David. Ted took her outstretched hand, and they all trailed after her, Ted, Bill, Leigh, and a grumpy Clay bringing up the rear. As they slid into a pew, Leigh was aware of the interest they provoked. Julia and David holding hands. Ted well enough to attend the service. She and Bill and Clay. Her mouth twisted wryly.

Lord, I hope they can concentrate on the miracle we've come to commemorate!

The sanctuary was crowded with worshipers, the regulars and the *CE* attenders, those who showed on

Christmas and Easter. They listened attentively as Pastor Paul proclaimed, "He is not here. He is risen as He said!"

The crown of thorns was gone from the rugged cross this morning, and it was draped in royal purple. Easter lilies filled the room, their trumpets silently shouting, "Resurrection!" and their fragrance rising in a sweetly scented offering to the Creator.

Leigh's heart leaped in thanks. She could only imagine the bubbling joy within Julia, her spirit bulwarked in resurrection faith and her body bracketed by the man she had fallen in love with and the son who was well enough to come to church today.

As she sang "Up from the Grave He Arose," Leigh thought of the two who bracketed her, the child with whom she shared her hymnal and her life and the man who owned her heart.

Oh, Lord, lead us, Clay, Bill, and me. Teach us. Show us Your will.

When they took their seats and Clay's shoulder pressed against hers, she allowed herself to lean into him ever so slightly. She felt him turn to her and smile, and she glanced up with a smile of her own. When she turned back to Pastor Paul, she noticed Bill was leaning forward, looking at her and Clay through narrowed eyes. She patted his knee, and he slouched back in the pew. She took his hand, and he looked scandalized as only a kid can when his mother does something beyond the pale. She grinned at him and after a quick squeeze, released him. He gave a sigh of relief, and she turned her attention to worship.

When they gathered outside church after the service in the bright spring sunshine, Clay said, "We have a slight detour before we go home."

"We do?" Ted said.

"We do. How are you doing? Are you feeling okay?"

Ted brushed Clay's questions aside with a wave of his hand. "I'm fine."

"Where are we going?" David asked, standing behind Julia, his hand firmly on her shoulder. He was so close to her that Leigh doubted sunlight could slide between them. "We'll meet you there."

It was obvious to anyone watching him that Clay was about to put his foot in his mouth and say something stupid like, "Mom came with us; she'll leave with us." Leigh was much relieved when Bill shouted the answer to David's question before Clay had time to embarrass himself.

"Pop-pop's house! We're going to Pop-pop's house."

"What?" Leigh stared at her son.

"It's your Easter present," Bill said. Pride gleamed in his eyes as he looked at her. "Wait 'til you see. We—"

"Bill," Clay said in warning. He gave Bill the quiet signal, finger held over his mouth.

Bill looked at Clay and giggled conspiratorially, though he was clearly bursting to talk. Gone were the narrowed eyes and the suspicious looks. With a broad grin that showed every one of his back molars, he ushered Leigh to the Cherokee and seated her in the front passenger side. He and Ted climbed in the back.

Leigh turned and looked at her son. "What's going on here?"

Bill wanted to tell so badly he appeared to be in pain, but he kept his secret. "I can't tell. You have to see."

She turned to Clay. "When you two disappeared these past few days, you've been taking him to my house, haven't you? Treasure hunting?"

"Yes to the first and no to the second."

She waited but he said no more. "That's it? That's all you're going to say?"

He nodded, his attention riveted on the largely empty roads. You'd have thought he was fighting great hordes of summer tourists, so intense was his concentration.

"You know you're driving me crazy, both of you!" She flounced back against her seat, making a great show of her frustration. Bill laughed.

"You two apparently don't know one of life's basic rules," Ted offered. "Never tease a lady on Easter. This is very good advice. The lady will not like it—"

"And teasing isn't nice," Clay finished with him. The brothers laughed.

Bill and Leigh just stared.

"A corruption of one of our favorite children's books," Clay explained. "*Never Tease a Weasel.* Mom read it to us on the average of twice a week for years, hoping we'd get the lesson."

"Obviously you didn't," Leigh said, but she was laughing.

"Close your eyes, Mom," Bill instructed as they turned onto the street where the Spenser house sat in solitary splendor.

Leigh squeezed her eyes tight and put her hands over her

closed lids for good measure. The car slowed, then stopped. Expectancy filled the air.

"Now," Bill yelled. "Look!"

Leigh looked, blinked, then blinked again. She knew her mouth was hanging open. She climbed out of the car in a daze.

The once ragtag, falling-down house actually looked attractive. Not beautiful, that was asking too much, but pretty. In fact, it looked prettier than she'd ever seen it.

The downspouts and gutters were firmly back in place. The weeds were gone from the walk and the garden. The lawn, still more sand than grass, was raked and groomed. In the garden a quartet of small azaleas, alive with fat pink buds, nestled among the newly opened daffodils. The enormous forsythia was bursting with golden blooms, filling the yard with sunshine. The old aluminum lounge chair had disappeared, and the window frames had been sanded and repainted. The front door was a beautiful Williamsburg blue. It was the door that made her eyes fill.

"Bill," she said around the huge lump in her throat. "You did this?"

He nodded proudly. "Me and Clay. Happy Easter, Mom. Now you can sell it."

"Oh, Bill, thank you!" She grabbed the boy and hugged him so hard he made gagging noises.

She let him go and turned to Clay. "Thank you so much." How stilted and awkward she sounded. What she really wanted to do was grab him hard too, and not just with gratitude, but aware of her audience she stuck out her hand. "I can't tell you how much this means to me."

"I don't get a hug too?" He looked forlorn, a little boy who had just been told the bakery was all out of the sweets he'd come to purchase with his own cash.

Feeling slightly self-conscious under Ted's sardonic eye, Leigh wrapped her arms around Clay and squeezed lightly.

"You can do better than that," he whispered in her ear as his arms tightened about her.

"Oh, Leigh, how wonderful it looks," Julia exclaimed, climbing out of David's car and saving Leigh from the enticing danger of hugging Clay harder.

"Doesn't it?" Leigh turned to Julia in relief. Or was it disappointment? "Bill and Clay did it. It's my Easter gift."

"Just don't look at the windows on the sides or back," Clay said. "We'll get to them at a later date."

Everyone walked around the house, laughing at the many unfinished shutters and peeling window frames still needing work. At the back of the house they pointed to the kingfisher sitting on the phone lines that ran parallel to the old railroad bed. They oohed and aahed as a blue heron lifted gracefully from the marsh and flew off toward the bay.

David and Julia trailed the rest, with the group yet separate, holding hands and smiling at each other. Whenever the pack stopped moving, they stopped too, slightly behind, leaning into each other.

"You'd think they can't stand up alone," Clay muttered in Leigh's ear.

"Isn't it great?" she whispered back and patted his hand as his face darkened. She had noticed that Julia no longer wore her wedding ring, but she wasn't going to be the one to call that fact to Clay's attention.

She went to the huge forsythia and broke off a great armful of the floral sunshine. "I need enough for Julia, for me, and for my classroom." She sighed. "I don't want to go back to school."

Bill made a face. "Who does?"

"I don't mean to break up a good time, but we need to hurry or dinner will be ruined," Julia said.

Everyone climbed back in the cars and went home to an Easter dinner of ham, scalloped potatoes, broccoli casserole, pineapple bake, and fresh rolls. Dessert was Julia's wonderful apple caramel pie or pecan pie. Afterward, Ted went up for a nap, Bill went home to change into play clothes, Julia and David went into the living room, and Clay and Leigh began the cleanup. When Leigh returned to the dining room for another load of dirty dishes, she found Clay skulking near the living room doorway.

"Hey, sailor, I thought you were supposed to be helping me with the cleanup."

"What's going on with them?" he demanded with a fierce scowl, staring after his mother and David.

She looked at him. "Grumpy for Easter Sunday afternoon, aren't we?"

"I am not grumpy," he grumped. "I'm concerned. And I don't need your editorial comments. What I need are answers."

"Then ask them your questions." She nodded toward Julia and David.

"I'm asking you." His tone was testy.

"Extra sensitive to advice today too, I see."

He glared and she smiled sweetly. "Did you ever think that it's not your business?" she asked.

He glowered at her. "Not my business? She's my mother and—" He stopped himself and went back to skulking.

"And?" she prompted. She knew exactly what he was worried about, but she wanted him to say it aloud so she could rebut.

He scratched his head, clearly unhappy. "Here we all go off to church this morning, you, me, Bill, Mom, even Ted for the first time in who knows how long."

Leigh saw the brief flash of joy when he spoke of Ted. She wondered if it was for the reconciliation he and Ted were enjoying or for Ted's improved health. She decided it was for both.

"There we all are," he continued, the grimness returning, "and what does *she* do?"

"She being your mother?"

"Who else? *She* goes off with David without giving us so much as a backward glance."

"She came back for us."

He harrumphed. "We were clearly an afterthought."

Leigh couldn't resist. The man was just asking for it. She turned her saccharine smile full on him. "Poor boy. How did you ever manage to get through those few seconds without her? You must have suffered terribly from separation anxiety."

He looked down his nose at her. "Sarcasm is a nasty habit."

She stuck her index finger in his chest, twisting that lethal nail and taking a piece of his flesh, just like she'd done that first night they'd talked. "So's interfering in your mother's private life."

"A lot you know." He grabbed her hand to protect himself from losing another divot of prized skin and threaded their fingers together. "Your mom died before you were old enough to accept life's responsibilities. I'm the eldest son. It's my duty, my responsibility to protect Mom."

"Very commendable, but I see no grave dangers lurking about."

"I do. I mean, did you see the way she acted while we were out at your place?"

Out at her place. She felt her heart soften when she thought of what he had done for her. She barely noticed that he had laced the fingers of her second hand with his.

"He's a nice man, Clay. I know you haven't known him long, but take my word for it, okay?"

Clay grabbed her arm and pulled her toward the door to the living room. "Just look at them."

"I will not! That's spying."

"Just look, will you?"

It was easier to look than to fight, so she did. She saw Julia and David standing face to face, arms entwined.

"They're staring at each other," he muttered in Leigh's ear.

She backed up, elbowing him in the side and trying to pull him away. "Personally I think it's sweet."

He glowered.

"I thought we'd never be alone," David said softly, but the eavesdroppers heard him.

"I love you," Julia said softly. "I do."

Clay stiffened, and Leigh turned her head so he wouldn't see her smile.

David ran a palm over Julia's hair. His hand settled on the back of her neck, and he pulled her against him. "I love you too, sweetheart." And he kissed her. She wrapped her arms around his neck and kissed him right back.

Clay turned red and made a gurgling sound deep in his throat. Leigh grabbed his arm with the idea of pulling him into the kitchen. "That's what you get for being a voyeur," she hissed.

"That's my mother—my *mother!*—in there kissing like a teenager."

"I say three cheers for your mother." When pulling didn't move him, she got behind him and pushed. She felt like Sisyphus or whoever it was who pushed the rock up the mountain in the old myth. "You are one big man," she panted, but she kept pushing right through the kitchen and out the back door. He blinked at the brilliant sunshine.

"You're a danger to yourself and others," she muttered as she stopped in the middle of the yard. She folded her arms and fixed him with the stern look that worked so well with fourth graders. He seemed unimpressed. "Let your mother alone, Clay."

"I was doing fine with the idea that they liked each other, even that they went on dates." He shuddered. "My mother on dates. What's the world coming to? But now, sheesh. What if he wants to marry her?"

"What if he does?"

"I don't want a stepfather." He glared at her, but she saw in his eyes the hurt beneath the anger.

"Did you ever stop to think that maybe she wants a husband?" she asked gently. "That maybe she wants to love and be loved?"

Clay swayed back on his heels like he'd taken a hit. "But I love her, and my brother loves her."

Leigh rolled her eyes, and he flushed as he heard the foolishness of his comment.

"Of course you and Ted love her," Leigh said. "So do I. But you know as well as I do that there's a huge difference between the love we offer and the love and comfort David will give her."

He dropped his head onto his chest, his eyes closed. Leigh looked at him, this wonderful man who loved his mother and cherished his father's memory. She reached out a hand and laid it on his arm.

"Clay, the next few months are going to be absolutely terrible for her. If David can help her through them, you should be thanking God for him."

"I know." Clay looked at her with sad eyes. "I'd never have predicted how wrenching it is to see them together."

"You're struggling because it feels like she's turning her back on your father." She patted him gently. "Right?"

He nodded, embarrassed. "I want her memories of Dad to be enough. Selfish of me, isn't it?"

She nodded. "It is. But, Clay, memories won't keep her warm at night as she lies alone in her big bed." She grew impassioned, her fingers tightening their hold on his arm. "They won't give her strength when she's afraid of the future. They won't help her when she's tired of struggling against life all by herself or when she yearns for someone to take her in his arms and make her feel special. They won't help when she needs someone to be there for her when Ted dies, and when she wants someone to hold her when she cries and love her even when her eyes are red and puffy and—"

Leigh broke off and made a choked sound. She was horrified to realize that she wasn't talking about Julia anymore. She was talking about herself. It was her own heart she was laying bare, her own soul-deep yearnings she was revealing. She spun away and hurried toward the beach, mortified.

"Leigh!" Clay came after her. "Wait."

She ignored him, running faster. She had to get away before she said any more, before he realized how truly pathetic and needy she was, needy for him.

She burst out of the dunes and onto the beach just as he grabbed her wrist. She tried to wrench free but he held her fast.

"Let go of me," she begged, her voice low and unsteady.

"No." He pulled her toward him, reeling her in like some weak, insignificant fish. Did fish have enough brainpower to despair when they were caught? She hoped not. It hurt too much.

"Look at me, Leigh."

She refused, giving him her back.

He turned her toward him and wrapped his arms about her, pulling her against him. "Don't cry. I can't stand to see you sad." His voice was thick with emotion.

She stood woodenly in his embrace. "I'm not crying."

He put his hand under her chin and forced her face up to his. She squeezed her eyes shut so she didn't have to look at his beautiful face. Tears slid from beneath her lids and rolled to the corners of her mouth. She flicked her tongue out to catch them.

"Oh, Leigh." He wiped at the tears. She flinched at his gentle touch and tried to jerk free. He wouldn't let her.

"That was your heart laid bare, wasn't it?" His voice was soft and tender.

"Of course not." Her fingers became busy fiddling with his shirt placket and buttons, smoothing the already smooth fabric, adjusting his collar. "I was talking about your mother."

He nodded. "Okay. If you say so."

"I do." She sniffed, then burst out, "I was doing so well! Then you showed up, and it got so complicated and confusing."

"How did it get confusing?"

"The past. The present. Oh, just everything."

"I thought you said you'd forgiven me."

"I did. I do. I don't know!"

"If you truly forgave me, then you can't hold all those years against me. They're gone forever, sent away to be remembered no more." His voice was the epitome of sanity and reason, his doctrine irrefutable.

Her eyes snapped up, and she glared at him. "Don't you dare tell me what I can and can't do. You haven't the right. I can hold those years against you if I want."

She saw an answering flare in his eyes. "So I'm not allowed to be upset about Mom, but you're allowed to be upset about me forever?"

She didn't answer him. She couldn't. He'd skewered her through the heart. She simply stared stonily at his middle button while tears continued to run down her cheeks. All she wanted was to put her head on his shoulder. All she wanted was to love him and have him love her for real and forever. All she wanted was what Julia and David had apparently found.

For just a moment a shaft of jealously shot through her. Julia had found two wonderful men to love her, and Leigh couldn't even trust the one she wanted, the one who was thoughtful enough to fix up her derelict house, the one whose arms felt so right, the one who had left her to struggle alone for eleven long years. It wasn't fair!

Before these thoughts were even fully formed, shame washed over her in great waves.

Oh, God, I'm such a terrible person! Forgive me.

"Leigh, say something. Talk to me. I want to help, but you've got to tell me what's wrong."

He was back to being nice! She was dying here, and he was hastening her demise with his niceness. She rested her forehead on his chest, letting her shoulders slump.

Oh, God, I'm so scared!

"Talk to me, woman," Clay said softly, one hand running up and down her back, so soothing, so sweet.

She sniffed and raised her face to his. "Now just see what you've done."

He blinked his bewilderment.

She gasped for breath. "You made me cry, and my nose is all stopped up, and I can't breathe."

"And that's my fault?"

"Well, it certainly isn't mine."

He began to smile.

"And just what's so funny?"

"You." And he leaned over and kissed her.

She gasped again from surprise, pleasure, and lack of oxygen. He kissed her a second time.

Without conscious thought she leaned into him like she always did when he kissed her. He was a danger to the environment, she thought distractedly, the way he caused instant meltdown.

She pushed against him when she was out of breath. He released her immediately and took a step back. "It's all right, Leigh. It was only a kiss."

Only a kiss? "I couldn't breathe," she explained. Only a kiss? It was her life flashing in front of her, like she was drowning, going down for the third time—which metaphorically speaking she probably was.

He searched through his pockets and pulled out a square of material that he passed to her. She blew her nose. Such a sweet ladylike sound. He ran a knuckle across her cheek, and she felt her eyes slide shut. She lowered her head so he couldn't see. She turned to go home.

"Walk with me, Leigh," he asked, catching her arm. "Please. We have so much more to talk about."

She knew the truth of what he said. She'd been so cautious around him for days, careful to keep any conversation surface, and the issues that throbbed in the air between them hadn't lessened in the interim. If anything, they'd intensified.

In silence she turned and walked across the sand to the waterline. He followed. They turned and began walking toward the bay. Somehow he had gotten hold of her hand again, his grip sure, steady, delightful.

"This week has been the most bewildering week of my life," he finally said. "My conflicting feelings about Ted, my confusion over Mom and David, my discovering who Bill is." He stopped and looked at her. "But you have been the cause of more emotional chaos than I've ever experienced in my life."

She smiled sadly as she studied the horizon. There was a perverse satisfaction in knowing that this week had been as hard for him as it had for her. It served him right. She sighed. It served her right.

"Love, please look at me." There was desperation in his voice.

Her eyes flew to his. He had called her *love,* and he didn't even seem to realize he'd said it. That was a good sign, wasn't it?

"If I felt terrible when I thought all I did was steal your virginity, imagine how I feel now?" He brought a hand up and twirled one of her curls around his finger. He studied the curl intently for a minute. Then his eyes fixed on hers. "How can I ask you to trust me, to love me after what I did to you?"

He wanted her to love him, to trust him? She knew she loved him, and she wanted desperately to trust him. "Clay, you scare me."

He stared in appalled disbelief.

"Not that I think that you'd ever willfully hurt me," she hastened to say. "Never. I know that. But I gave you my heart once, and you rejected it. No, you didn't even bother to reject it. You ignored it."

He began to speak, but she put a hand on his mouth. "I forgive you for that. I do. I can say that before God and mean it. Having you around has confused me in many ways, but I know I've given up any desire to get even or to make you suffer. We were young. We were stupid. We were wrong. But it's over, long over. I've gone on. You've gone on." She searched his face. "But I don't think I could stand that pain again, which is why you scare me, especially since my love is so much deeper now than it ever was then."

His eyes brightened, and he grabbed her by the shoulders. "Are you saying you love me?"

With a sinking heart she realized she had revealed much more than she had ever intended. And she understood in that moment that it wasn't Clay she feared after all. It was herself: her emotions, her ability to deal with loss, even her confidence that God was big enough to get her through the coming destruction of all her dreams.

God, forgive me! I believe; help my unbelief!

She wrenched herself free from Clay's hold and turned to run. Tears filled her eyes and blinded her. She took two steps and stumbled right into one of Clooney's spade holes. She felt her ankle give and went down with a muffled scream.

Thirty-three

CLAY'S HEART TUMBLED right along with Leigh. He fell to his knees beside her. "Are you all right, sweetheart?"

Her face was too pale, and she held her ankle. "Just twisted it, I think."

"You'd better not put any weight on it until you get it checked. I'll carry you home." He reached for her.

She waved him away. "I'm not hurt that badly. I'm sure I can walk. Just help me get up."

"Why don't I call David, and he can check you before you move? I'm sure he's still up at the house."

"Don't you dare embarrass me like that!" She held out her hands. "Come on. Pull."

Foolish, strong-minded woman. Unhappy, he grasped both her wrists and pulled. She tried to rise but gasped in pain as she put weight on her foot. She sank back onto the sand.

"Let me see." He pushed her hands aside and ran his fingers lightly over the injured area. He couldn't feel anything that indicated a break, but that didn't mean there wasn't one.

"It just crunched," she said. "I heard it. It didn't break."

Crunch, eh? Not a good sign. "That'll teach you to try and run away from me," he said and felt pleased when she smiled slightly at his poor attempt at humor.

"I can't have a break. It's too cumbersome at school."

Together they stared at the ankle, already swelling.

"Stupid spade holes of Clooney's." Clay needed some way to release the fear he'd felt when she went down and the distress that she was hurt. The spade holes were a safe target. "I've got to have a talk with him."

"Like it's his fault I didn't look where I was going."

Knowing full well whose fault that was, Clay rose quickly in an effort to distract her. "Come on. Let's get you up to the house and get some ice on that."

Suddenly a short, slight man was on his knees beside them. Clay blinked. Where had he materialized from? He wore glasses and had a bald spot he was having trouble keeping covered with the hair he combed from ear to ear, largely because the wind was having a wonderful time scattering the long strands in spite of the gallons of hair spray he'd undoubtedly used.

"Is she all right?" he asked Clay. He turned a concerned face to Leigh. "Are you all right? I saw you fall, and then I saw you couldn't get up. I was afraid you were hurt bad."

Leigh smiled at the man. "I'm fine. I think it's only a sprain."

The man looked relieved.

"I just live up there." She pointed to the house. "And Clay will get me home."

The man looked at Clay and nodded. "He looks strong enough to do the job."

Clay took one of Leigh's arms, and the man took the other. They lifted her to her feet, careful not to bump the injured foot. She stood with her weight on the uninjured leg, wobbling slightly.

"You're sure you're okay?" the man asked.

Leigh nodded. "Thanks for your concern. It was very nice of you to care."

The man flushed bright red.

"I am going to carry you home," Clay announced, giving Leigh a stern look. "And no sass, lady."

"No sass," she agreed.

He kissed her cheek, then lifted her with one arm around her back and the other beneath her knees. She rested her head against him, and Clay was touched by the trust inherent in that move.

Maybe she had more faith in him than she realized. *Oh, Lord, please let that be so.* He strode toward the path through the dunes.

"Hope you feel better soon," the man called after them.

Leigh waved acknowledgment and laid her head back on Clay's chest.

"Does it hurt much?" he asked as he rested his cheek against her hair.

"Feels sort of good," she said dreamily. Then she stiffened as she heard herself. "I mean it throbs some, but I'll live."

He smiled to himself and kissed the top of her head. "You'd better. We're not finished with our talking yet."

She sighed. "I was afraid of that." She cuddled closer, wrapping an arm about his waist. "I should have known. You haven't won yet." Her voice was laden with sorrow.

"What?" He stopped midstride and stared down at her. Surely she didn't think he was the kind of man who was only happy when he had total control. Well, he was, sort of, but he'd been working on it. And he certainly knew better than to expect to dominate her. If there was one thing he'd learned since his return, it was that Leigh had a mind of her own.

She grinned up at him, pointing her index finger like a smoking gun. "Gotcha."

He didn't know about Leigh, but he was smiling broadly when they reached the backyard. If she could tease him that blatantly, things between them were definitely looking up, to say nothing of the fact that her ankle couldn't be hurting too badly.

"Just what do you think you're doing with her?" an ice-cold voice demanded.

Clay felt Leigh's jolt of surprise as he spun toward the sound.

Bill stood just outside the door to the apartment, his hands in fists on his hips, his jaw clenched. "I think you'd better put her down. Now."

Clay looked at the fierce emotion on Bill's face and slowly lowered Leigh to the ground. He kept his arm about her waist to help support her. She leaned heavily against him, an arm clutching him for balance. She held her injured foot off the ground.

"Get away from her," Bill ordered. "Stand over there." He pointed halfway across the yard.

Clay felt Leigh tighten her grip on him. He didn't move.

"I said get away from her." Bill took a step toward them, his angry eyes fixed on Clay.

Clay looked at his son with a combination of pride and amusement, though he was careful not to let the amusement show. The lion cub protecting his pack.

"Don't worry, Bill." His voice serious and respectful. "She's not hurt badly."

Bill looked his mother up and down. "She doesn't look hurt at all to me."

"Sprained ankle," Clay said, and Leigh held out the offending leg. "She stepped in one of Clooney's spade holes."

"Yeah. Right," Bill said, absolutely unconvinced. "I want you to leave her alone and go back to where you came from." His eyes shot sparks. "You've hurt her enough already. I won't let you hurt her again."

"I assure you, Bill, that I have no intentions of hurting your mom."

Bill just stared, lips compressed, jaw set.

"In fact, all my intentions are honorable." He found himself hugging Leigh, pulling her even closer.

"What if I say I don't want you to have any intentions toward her? We've done fine for all these years without you. We don't need you, and we don't want you. Just leave us alone!" Each word was clipped and vibrated with emotion.

For the first time, Leigh stirred. She straightened away from Clay and said, "Billy, watch yourself." The finger she had just shot Clay with was pointed at Bill, but there was no humor lurking in her eyes this time. "Clay hasn't done anything wrong. I did sprain my ankle, and he carried me home because I can't walk. I think you owe him an apology."

"Bill! It's Bill," he yelled. "And don't you tell me to apologize! I won't do it! I won't. He's just going to dump us all over again, and you'll cry and cry."

Leigh started. "What?"

"You think I don't hear you crying at night? I hear. And I know the tears are his fault." He looked at Clay with utter disgust.

Clay blinked. She cried over him at night? He wasn't the only one who suffered sleepless sorrow? He beamed down at her.

She popped him gently in the stomach. "Don't go getting a big head. It's only been this week. Before that I was over you completely."

"Um. If you say so."

"Mom, get a grip! He's going to bolt again. We can't trust him."

Clay studied his son, telling himself that he shouldn't be hurt by Bill's continuing tirade, but he was. This was the boy who had bragged about him to Mike, the boy who had worked beside him all week at the old Spenser place, the boy who had laughed with him. Where had this spitting defender of single moms come from? And how had he become the enemy?

"You keep letting him hold you like that, Mom, and *boom!* Tears again." Bill pointed a bony finger at Clay. "Let her alone!"

Slowly, Clay lowered his arm from Leigh's waist and stepped away. She yipped softly when her injured ankle took some of her weight as she tried to keep her balance. Clay grabbed her elbow and helped her as she sank to Julia's bench.

"Mom! You are hurt." Bill rushed over to her.

"I'll go get some ice," Clay said. "Put that foot up." He lifted her leg as she turned sideways on the bench.

"Get your hands off her," Bill said, his voice low and mean. *"I'll* take care of her. *I'll* get her ice."

"Billy—Bill—that's enough of that." Leigh's voice was clipped. "Clay's just being kind. I appreciate his help. I'm glad he was there to help me when I fell and that I didn't have to walk back on a sore ankle. I'm glad he carried me."

Bill looked at her incredulously. "You actually *want* him to touch you?"

Inadvertently, Bill had asked a loaded question. Clay waited, frozen, for her answer. Slowly she lifted her head to him.

"I want him to," she whispered.

Clay saw everything in her eyes: her love, her fear, her hesitant trust.

"You're crazy!" Bill ran past her toward the beach. "I hope you break your other ankle, and when you do, don't ask me to help after he's gone!"

"Billy! Come back here," Leigh called.

He ignored her and kept running. She tried to rise, to chase him, but she staggered as her weight hit her bad ankle.

"Sit," Clay ordered as he grabbed her and pushed her down. "I'll go after him."

He jogged through the dunes and returned almost immediately. "He's running down the beach. I'll chase him if you want me to."

She thought for a minute. "Maybe we should let him run off his mad before we try to talk to him." She ran a hand through her hair. "I wish there were some absolutes in this parenting business."

He looked over his shoulder toward the beach, as uncertain as she. "I don't ever want to come between you and Bill."

She smiled and held out her hand. "You haven't come between us. Nothing could. He's just afraid that you might."

"Leigh." He moved to her and grasped her hand tightly in his.

"Of course, you will change the balance of power, won't you?"

He bent to kiss her. "I guess I will."

"Ice," she reminded. "Then we'll talk."

"You'll wait for me here?" He hated letting her out of his sight with things still unsettled between them.

She looked ruefully at her ankle. "I'm not going anywhere."

Clay hurried into the kitchen and dumped what ice was left in the icemaker into a sealable plastic bag. He grabbed a dishtowel to wrap it in and rushed back to Leigh.

She half sat, half lay on the bench, the sun dancing on her shining hair. She was looking through the dunes to the sea with a worried expression until she heard the door slam behind him. Then she turned to him, and a slow smile slid over her face. Very deliberately she winked. "Hey, sailor."

His breath checked in his throat and his heart skipped a beat.

Oh, Lord, I want to spend the rest of my life rushing back to her. And Bill. Help us figure out how to make it all work.

When he reached her, he stood looking down at her lovely face, savoring it, wondering how he could have been fool enough to wait all these years to come back to her, why he had been fool enough to let her get away to begin with.

"I'm getting a kink in my neck," she finally said, matching him stare for stare. "You forget how tall you are, especially when I'm sitting."

"Oh." He dropped to the bench beside her and pulled her close so her back rested against his side.

"The ice?" she whispered.

"Oh. Right." He held out the sweating bag. She took it and wrapped it in the towel. She reached forward and placed it on her ankle. Then she leaned back against him again. He liked the feel of her against him, but with her legs stretched out in front of her, all he saw was the back of her head.

"We can do better than this." He took her by the waist and lifted her onto his lap. Immediately she snuggled close, tucking her head beneath his chin.

"What should we do about Bill?" he asked.

She shrugged. "Give him time to cool down and then talk with him."

"I thought he liked me."

"He does. He idolizes you. You're all he talks about. In fact, it's been driving me crazy, all this praise."

"Yeah? Jealous, are you?" he asked, amazed at the surge of pleasure that washed through him at the news that Bill liked him.

"I'm not jealous, but he is, I think. Jealous and threatened and fearful of change, sort of the way you feel about your mother and David."

He pulled back and looked down at her, aghast. "I do not feel that way."

"Ha!" She raised her eyebrow in challenge. "Like father, like son."

Like father, like son? What an extraordinary thought, even if it weren't so. He shook his head, denying her opinion of him.

She nodded in answer. "Absolutely."

He groaned. If he was going to be totally honest with himself, she was probably right. "How embarrassing."

"Only if you continue." She patted him comfortingly on the chest. "But I know you'll set the right example for Billy."

"Bill," he mumbled automatically as he wrestled with the idea of setting examples. What kind of an example was a failure like him?

"You'll do fine," she said with more assurance than he felt.

"Reading my mind, are you?" An interesting and strangely intimate thought. He lifted the hand resting in her lap and kissed her knuckles.

She looked away and didn't answer. Apparently she felt the unspoken closeness too, and it unnerved her.

"I won't leave you, you know."

She turned and looked at him for a long moment. "I want to believe that with all my heart. So does Bill."

"But there's a history."

She nodded.

"And that's why I scare you."

She nodded again. "You left the last time I loved you."

He didn't deny it or try to justify himself. "I love you, Leigh. I don't know; maybe I've loved you all these years. I've certainly never found anyone other than you who's interested me in the least."

"Not even the woman who gave you Terror?"

"Definitely not Emilie."

They sat quietly for a moment.

"You love me," he finally said. "I know you do."

She didn't deny it. Instead she dropped a small kiss on his jaw.

He took a deep breath and asked the question of questions. "Do you think you can learn to trust me?"

"There's nothing I want more in the world."

He felt himself relax.

"And, like I said, there's nothing that scares me more."

Tension roared back. "I'm not eighteen anymore, love." He placed their clasped hands over his heart. "I'm a man. I know what I'm asking of you when I ask for your trust, and before God, I will be worthy of it."

She looked into his eyes, studying, searching for he didn't know what.

He looked steadily back. *Oh, God, help me look reliable and trustworthy!*

She gave a small nod and settled back against him, tucking her head under his chin. He frowned. Did that nod mean she was willing to take the risk of trusting him? Or did it mean she had been right all along, and he wasn't worthy? Uncertainty gnawed at his gut.

But she was still cuddling. Surely that was a good sign.

When he could stand his doubts no more, he blurted, "Marry me, Leigh. Please."

She froze. She didn't even seem to breathe. "Marry you?" she whispered.

"Yes. On this Easter day that means Life, say you'll be my life."

Still motionless, she sat in his lap like a beautiful stone princess. Her head was turned from him, staring at her lap. Because he couldn't see her eyes, he had no way to gauge the reason for her hesitation.

"Are you sure that's what you want?" she finally asked, still looking at her lap. "You're not asking because you feel you have to because of Billy?"

"I'm asking because I love you. I want to be with you for the rest of my life." He held her away so he could turn her to look at him. She kept her eyes downcast, and he had to put his hand beneath her chin and gently force her head up until their eyes met. "Leigh, my one and only love, please marry me."

"Oh, Clay." Her voice broke, and she searched his eyes. Her own eyes swam with tears.

"What are you looking for?" he asked. "What do you want to see?" A thought struck him. "Or what are you afraid to see?"

She placed her hand against his cheek. A smile slowly spread across her face. "I was afraid I would see responsibility, a girding of the loins to do the right thing. You know—I wasn't there for her before, so I'll be there now. I don't dislike her, so it won't be too bad to marry her." She rested her other hand against his heart. "I couldn't have stood that."

Tension eased from Clay's shoulders as he said, "You didn't see that, did you?"

She shook her head.

"What do you see?"

"I see the way David looks at Julia."

"What?" He stared at her, nonplussed. "That wasn't quite the response I expected."

Her eyes turned dreamy. "I wanted you to look at me that way, you know. Like I was special. Like I held your heart. Because you certainly hold mine."

He took her hand. "My heart sits right there, Leigh." He lightly touched her palm. "It's yours to hold forever."

Slowly, gently she closed her fingers. "I'm not letting you go this time."

"And I'm not leaving." He gave her a quick, light kiss. "Marry me, love."

She wrapped her arms around his neck and squeezed.

He squeezed back. "Is that to be understood as a yes?" *Please, God.*

"Yes," she said, leaning back so he could see her radiant face. "Oh yes!"

After he finished kissing her thoroughly and she rested quietly against his chest once more, he said, "What do you think Bill will say?"

She sat up and lifted the ice pack. She slid off his lap, turned, and let her feet fall to the ground. "Why don't we go ask him?" She pushed herself upright and wobbled a bit.

He jumped up and grabbed her. "You shouldn't be walking around on that ankle. Why don't I go find Bill and bring him back here?"

She nodded. "He's been alone too long as it is. I'm getting nervous now that I'm thinking again."

"I interfered with your thought processes?" It made him feel good.

"Big time, bub. Big time."

They grinned at each other, and he wanted to smother her with kisses. Instead he tore his eyes from her and looked toward the beach. "He's okay. We haven't seen any small men in glasses with hair combed from one ear over to the other."

He turned back to her and watched as she went pale. "Yes, we have," she said.

He looked at her, confused. Then the color drained from his face too. "The man on the beach."

She nodded. "And Billy's on the beach."

Thirty-four

*B*ILL COULDN'T remember ever being so angry! How could Mom be so stupid? How could she stand there and look at Clay with that dumb moony look? She was just asking for him to hurt her again when he left. And he always left.

Not that he blamed Clay for wanting to spend all his time with her while he was here. Guys always liked spending time with her, and it made him sort of proud that they liked her that much. She was so pretty and nice.

The problem, as far as Bill was concerned, was that if Clay spent all his time with her, he wouldn't have time for him. What was the good of getting a dad if he never spent time with you? *He* wanted all Clay's time before he left, but *she* was getting it.

He snarled at a passing seagull that screamed raucously back.

It had been so great to have a dad for a while. Playing ball, painting the front door at Pop-pop's house, just talking. Even now he felt a heaviness in his chest at the thought of not having Clay around. It felt like the weight he'd been carrying at the thought of Uncle Ted dying. Well, it would be like Clay died. He'd go away, and they wouldn't see him again for ten long years.

Bill blinked. He'd be twenty when Clay came to town next time. He'd be a man. He'd be in college. He wouldn't need a father then. He frowned. Yeah, he would. He remembered how Clay missed his father, and he was twenty-nine! It seemed that if your dad wasn't there, you always missed him, no matter how old you got.

Did girls miss their dads too, or was that a guy thing? He wasn't sure since he'd never asked. Mom didn't miss Pop-pop much, he didn't think, but Pop-pop wasn't a good example of a father anyway. He'd have to ask one of the girls at school. He shuddered. He could do it. He was strong. One question wouldn't contaminate him, at least not too much.

He came to the jetty where he and Clay had sat and talked. His eyes burned, and he swallowed tears at the thought of that special time.

"Go ahead and cry," Mom always said. "It's okay. Boys can cry."

But he knew they couldn't, especially out in public. What if someone saw you, for Pete's sake. You'd never live it down.

He climbed out on the first few rocks, and he knew he desperately wanted a dad for always. He wanted to sit on the jetty some more and talk. He wanted to go camping or throw a Frisbee or build more sand castles. He wanted to bury his father in the sand so only his face showed, like Clay and Uncle Ted used to do to Grandpa Will.

He stopped for a minute as a new thought hit him. Did Clay surf? His heart beat fast at the idea of his very own dad teaching him to surf. Not that the waves in Seaside were the greatest, but they'd be just right for learning. He knew it. He and Clay could pick out his board together and find the best wax. He could get one of those ankle things that hooked you to your board so it didn't float away when you fell. Then when he got good, they could go on a vacation somewhere where there were huge waves. Hawaii maybe, or Australia. He'd seen guys on TV surfing in Australia. Mom could sit on the beach and read while he and Clay had fun.

Don't be dumb, kid. He's not staying. Or if he is, they'll forget all about you. They won't want some dumb kid around, getting in their lovey-dovey way.

He started to run again, his nerves jumping under his skin.

He couldn't explain what he felt when his mom and Clay were together. There was a special connection or something between them, and it left him out. He saw it when Mom rushed to Clay

after that Molino man called. He saw it while they were watching
TV last night, and Clay made him move so he could sit by Mom.
He saw it in the way he carried her just now.

They thought he was mad because Clay carried Mom. That
wasn't it. People carried injured people all the time, and there was
no fizz. But Clay and Mom had fizz big time, romantic fizz, and it
didn't include him.

He was going to be just like an orphan. He could see it coming as clear as clear. They'd get closer and closer and closer, and
there he'd be, outside on the other side of the screen. At least until
Clay left. Then Mom'd let him back in in a hurry. Then she'd need
him again.

If only he didn't know Clay was his father. If only Clay hadn't
come back to Seaside. Things had been fine before. Mom had
depended on him then. He was the one who made her laugh. He
was the one who scared off the unwanted boyfriends. He was the
one who was her company, and he had been all his life.

She didn't need Clay. All she needed was *him*.

He was finally forced to stop running because of the stitch in
his side, poking at him like a spear or something. He bent over,
hands on his knees, as he pulled in great gasps of air. His lungs
ached so much he knew he was going to die.

But that wouldn't be all bad. He'd just go to heaven and wait
for Uncle Ted. It was a cinch he couldn't go back home, not after
that performance in the backyard. Mom was going to kill him for
talking to her and Clay that way. Clay probably wanted to strip
some skin off too. He sighed. Not that he blamed her. He'd been
obnoxious.

He gave a half smile. Maybe he'd make a rock star after all.

When his lungs stopped aching and the pain in his side eased,
he kicked sand up in the air as high as he could and watched it
fan out and fall, sort of like dry rain. When kicking sand got boring, he started walking back the way he'd come. He realized he
wasn't going to be lucky enough to die. He was going to have to
go home and face Mom and Clay.

But what would he say? He couldn't apologize to Clay. He just
couldn't. Clay was butting in with Mom, and he was just going to
leave them again. Bill knew it. How could he say he was sorry
when Clay was the bad guy, not him?

He came to the jetty and looked out where Terror had been tied. He still had to swallow hard when he thought of that night. He'd never look at the incoming tide in exactly the same way again. He watched it for a minute, surging even now over the outer rocks.

Well, so what if Clay saved his life then. Big deal. What else could he do? Let him drown in front of Mom? Besides it was his dog Clay was after. Bill just happened to be there too.

His conscience dredged up Clay's voice yelling, "Drop Terror and run!" just as the really big wave rolled in.

Okay, so maybe Clay saved him on purpose, but that still didn't excuse him from butting into his and Mom's lives.

He sat down on the jetty and stared at the roof of Grandma Jule's house, just visible over the dunes. What in the world was he going to do? How was he going to save Mom? And how was he going to get Clay to be his dad and nothing more?

"Having a bad time of it today, son?"

Bill looked up into the face of a man with glasses that were almost as dirty as his own. The guy had a bald spot covered by long, long hairs combed from one ear to the other. Bill made a promise to himself right that very second that if he ever went bald, he'd never comb his hair like that. What was it about old guys that they thought they were disguising the problem with a haircut like that? And why did they think it looked good? Grandpa Will hadn't been that dumb, and neither was Dr. Traynor.

"I got a wonderful surprise for you over there," the man said. "Come see it. I promise it will cheer you up fast."

Bill stared at the man. Like he was stupid enough to fall for a line like that. "Thanks, but no."

The man looked very annoyed. He reached out a hand to take Bill's arm. "Come on. It'll only take a moment."

The man's hand on his arm made Bill's skin crawl. He took several steps back as his computer brain kicked in recalling Mr. Barnes's words: *"Little like in not important, though come to think of it, I don't think he's too big physically either. Wears glasses. Skinny guy about forty-five with a bald spot he combs his hair over by growing it long on one side and spraying it in place."*

Bill sighed. This guy was all he needed to make the day perfect. "Go away, Mr. Molino. You can't kidnap me."

Thirty-five

MR. *MOLINO?* He froze and stared at the kid. *How could he know?* "What are you calling me Mr. Molino for? I don't know who that is."

"Yeah, right." Bill looked disgusted. He turned toward the dunes and took the first step toward home.

Worm took a step too and grabbed the kid's shirt.

"Let go!" Bill said, swiping at Worm's hand.

The kid was more angry than scared. Worm wanted him scared.

Really scared.

He tightened his grip on the shirt and leaned his face into the kid's. He wished he knew how to laugh that crazy laugh of Stanley's. It was enough to scare the starch out of anyone.

Stanley used to do terrible things to him because he couldn't run fast enough to escape. Stanley'd get something to torture him with—the hedge clippers, Ma's scissors, her nail file. When he saw Stanley coming and tried to run, Stanley always caught him by tackling him and landing on top of him, crazy laughing the whole time. While he was busy trying to get his breath back, Stanley'd cut his hair or clip his clothes or see how far he could push the file under his fingernails before they bled.

I'm going to be rich, Stanley. I'm going to be rich. And all you are is dead.

"Who says I can't kidnap you?" Worm grinned evilly and pulled a gun from beneath his shirt. The kid's eyes widened, and this time Worm saw fear. He didn't even want to think about what his parole officer would say if he saw the piece. But what he didn't know…

A thought struck him. What if Leigh-Leigh was really hurt with a broken leg or something and had to go to the hospital? Then he couldn't get the treasure today.

He had to get it. Sugar was waiting.

With a feeling of great anticipation, he put the muzzle at Bill's throat.

Thirty-six

LEIGH TURNED TOWARD the beach, panic written clearly on her face.

"Now don't jump to conclusions, love," Clay said. "What can Molino do to Bill on a public beach?"

"An empty public beach." She raised frantic eyes to him. "No one was there when we left except that man."

The back door to the house slammed, and they both jumped.

"Hey, Leigh." Ted, still pale but with some zip to his step, walked toward them with the phone in his hand. He wore his down jacket again, all puffy and warm. "For you." He held it to her.

She turned a frightened face to Clay.

"It may not be him," Clay said, but he remembered other phone calls too.

She grabbed the phone. "Hello?"

Clay couldn't hear the words, but he grabbed her as she swayed.

"But you know I can't walk," she said and grimaced at the reply. "Give me a few minutes to get it." With slumped shoulders she clicked the phone closed.

"What did he say?" Clay demanded.

"We were right. He has Billy." She looked toward the beach. "I'm to come alone with the treasure. No cops, no brothers, or he'll hurt Billy. If I cooperate, I can trade the treasure for Billy."

"What treasure?" Ted asked. "What do you mean, trade it for Bill?"

Leigh looked at Clay. "'Just Leigh-Leigh and the treasure.' That's what he said. I have fifteen minutes."

Clay grunted, glanced at his watch, and hurried along the path through the dunes. He crouched and looked cautiously up and down the beach. When he looked left, he stiffened. He hurried back to Leigh and Ted.

"He's talking with Bill. I can't tell from this distance whether he's holding him against his will or not."

"What treasure?" Ted asked in a voice several decibels louder than normal. "What do you mean, holding him against his will?"

Clay explained the situation quickly and succinctly.

"But there is no treasure." Leigh said as he finished. She swallowed against tears of desperation. "I don't have anything to give him." She looked at Clay. "Maybe I can get him to step in one of Clooney's spade holes."

He loved her and her strong heart at that moment more than he'd ever thought possible. He leaned over and kissed her.

Ted thought for a moment, then grinned. "So you need a treasure?"

"Ted, this isn't funny," Leigh protested.

"Wait right here. I have just the thing." He hurried into the house.

Leigh turned to Clay. Her hands shook and tears filled her eyes.

He pulled her into a hug. "Hang on, love. We'll get him back."

She clung to him. "How? Oh, Clay, I couldn't stand it if something happened to him."

"Don't worry. We'll think of something. One thing's for sure—we can't go rushing out there without a plan. We'd put Bill at risk."

"Oh, God," she prayed and couldn't continue. She shuddered.

He tightened his arms about her and picked up where she'd faltered. "Lord, help us come up with a plan. Keep Bill safe. Please, Father. Keep him safe. Help us rescue him from this awful man."

"Please," Leigh whispered. She stood still for a moment, resting against him. Then she hopped back a step, stuck out that stubborn chin, and straightened her shoulders. He watched as she beat the panic back. He was filled with pride and an overwhelming need to protect her and rescue his son.

She turned toward the house, watching for Ted, but she leaned back against Clay. He rested his hands on her shoulders to balance her. It seemed forever before Ted came rushing out, but it was only a few minutes. He carried a small silver coffer about the size of a chest used to hold sterling flatware.

"Grandmom Wharton's treasure box." Clay reached to touch its gleaming surface, richly carved with intricate bouquets of roses, irises, and lilies of the valley.

"Oh, it's beautiful," Leigh gasped. "I've never seen anything like it."

"Sterling silver should look like a treasure, shouldn't it?" Ted asked.

"It was Grandmom and Grandpop's wedding gift from some rich guy they knew," Clay explained.

"He must have liked them a lot to give them something this wonderful." Leigh stared in awe. She traced the petals of a rose and the curve of a ribbon that bound a bouquet.

Ted looked at Clay, eyes gleaming. "Remember how we used to scheme to see what Grandmom had locked in it?"

He nodded. "We never succeeded. Is anything in it now?"

Ted shook his head. "Mom's been using it as a jewelry box, but I dumped all her things out." He traced a lily of the valley with an index finger, just as Clay had done. He held it out to Leigh. "Take it."

"I can't take that. It's a family heirloom," Leigh protested. "What will Julia say?"

"She'd say take it." Clay laid a hand against Leigh's cheek. "Bill's family, her grandson, and incredibly more important than this treasure or any treasure."

Leigh grabbed first Clay, then Ted, and kissed them both on the cheek. "Thank you, thank you! I love you guys."

She took the chest carefully from Ted and almost dropped it as its weight threw her fragile balance awry. "It's heavy."

"Very," said Ted as he took it back.

He and Clay looked at each other for several seconds and nodded. "Buster Cassidy," they said in unison.

"Who's Buster Cassidy?"

"Some bully who used to pick on us until we fixed his wagon," Ted said.

"We'll take Molino the same way," Clay said. "Ted will go with you to the beach, Leigh. The chest is too heavy for you to carry in your injured condition."

"I can manage," she said, even as she knew she couldn't. "I have to. He said I did."

Clay leaned over and kissed her forehead. "No, you can't, love. Even if you were 100 percent physically, for the plan to work, you need Ted. Trust me on this."

"Okay," she said slowly. "I can't manage by myself." She looked from him to Ted and back. "And while Ted and I go to the beach, you will be doing what?"

He explained the plan carefully.

"Poor Buster Cassidy," she said and dialed 911.

Thirty-seven

BILL COULDN'T BELIEVE that there was a gun, a very scary gun, touching him. Actually touching him! And Mr. Molino's shaking hands were even scarier than the gun. He'd probably pull the trigger just with the shakes.

God, please don't let him shoot me! Bill shuddered. The thought of some doctor cutting a hole in him to get out the bullet that had already made a hole in him made him feel nauseous.

"Can you move that away from my throat? It's just a suggestion, but what if someone came along? They'd call the cops if they saw a gun." He did his best to sound like he was trying to be a big help instead of the scared to death kid he really was.

Mr. Molino looked at him in surprise. "Not a bad idea, kid." He lowered the gun so it was aimed at his spinal cord, definitely out of casual view and more important to Bill, out of his range of vision. "Now we're just two guys sitting on the jetty, watching the tide come in." Mr. Molino looked at the oncoming water and shivered.

"Yeah. Two guys." Bill stared at the path through the dunes. Where was Mom? Weren't fifteen minutes up yet? It seemed like forever that he and Molino had been waiting here on the jetty. Mr. Molino began entertaining him with visions of what he would do with the treasure when he got it and horror stories of what his brother Stanley had done to him when he was a kid. One good thing—Bill didn't feel so bad about being an only child anymore.

A surging wave crashed noisily against the jetty, and some drops of spume reached them, making Mr. Molino jump.

"I hate the ocean," he yelled. "I can't wait to get away from here!"

"Don't worry. High tide won't cover us for a while yet," Bill said. "We should have plenty of time to get away."

Mr. Molino looked startled. Then he brought his face close to Bill's. "That's not funny, kid. You think I'm so stupid that I don't know high tide don't come this far?"

"Most days it doesn't," Bill agreed. "It probably won't today. At least I don't think it will. We'll just hope not, huh?"

They fell silent as Mr. Molino kept throwing glances over his shoulder like he expected the tide to come flooding in like an avalanche rushing down a mountain or something. Bill shook his head, unable to imagine being that afraid of the water.

"There comes your mother!" Mr. Molino climbed to his feet. "Get up, kid."

Bill rose and watched with a sinking heart as his mother and Uncle Ted walked through the dunes. Mom was supposed to come alone! Instead Mom limped beside Uncle Ted, hanging onto his arm for support. They walked very slowly.

"I said just Leigh-Leigh," Mr. Molino growled. "I told her." He grabbed Bill and squeezed his arm until it hurt. Bill bit his lip and promised he wouldn't embarrass himself by crying.

"She's hurt," Bill said, rushing to his mother's defense. "Remember? She can't walk alone." Why was Ted here? Where was Clay? He knew Clay wouldn't let them face Mr. Molino alone.

Bill's heart jumped with excitement now instead of fear. His father had a plan. He knew it. His father was going to save the day. Mom and Uncle Ted were just a diversion.

"Why are you smiling, kid?" Mr. Molino poked the gun against Bill's side.

"I'm not smiling," Bill said quickly. "Just a gas pain."

Uncle Ted was carrying something, but Bill couldn't tell what it was. A phony treasure probably. It had to be phony. Bill knew there wasn't a real one.

Mr. Molino grabbed Bill by the arm and pushed him off the jetty onto the sand. "We'll just wait here." He flicked the gun against Bill's side. "Don't be dumb and try something that could get you hurt."

Bill shuddered and looked away. So where was Clay? Bill felt suddenly uncertain. Maybe Clay was sitting in the kitchen eating a piece of Grandma Jule's caramel apple pie, so mad at Bill for his big mouth that he wouldn't come help. Bill couldn't blame him. He'd been awful.

No. Clay would come. He had to. He wouldn't be Clay if he didn't.

"We've brought you the treasure," Mom called. Her voice barely shook.

Ted held what he was carrying high over his head. Bill frowned. It looked like Grandma Jule's silver jewelry box. She'd showed it to him one time when he asked if she had any heirlooms. They were doing reports for school on heritage, and Bill had decided to borrow the Whartons' heritage since his own was so tacky. The silver box was the center of his report.

"It's made of silver so thick that the carved flowers stick up several inches," he wrote. "It is one of the prettiest things I have ever seen. I'm proud that it belongs to my Grandma and Grandpa. Maybe someday it will belong to me. I will take good care of it."

He'd gotten an A. He suspected the teacher had talked to his mother about his adopting the Whartons, but Mom had never said anything to him about it. He thought that was because she wished she were a Wharton too.

Suddenly it occurred to him that he hadn't been lying when he wrote about the Whartons. He *was* a Wharton. They were his heritage as much as the Spensers were. The wonder of that realization made him forget Ernie Molino for a full minute.

Because of Clay, he was a Wharton. He could even change his name if he wanted. He could be William Clayton Wharton III.

"Billy, are you all right?" Mom looked scared to death from worrying about him.

Bill pulled his attention to the problem at hand and nodded.

"Answer her out loud, kid. Tell her you're fine—for now. Just don't mention the gun."

"I'm fine—for now," he repeated.

Mom and Uncle Ted halted about twenty feet away. Uncle Ted put the chest down on the sand.

"Here's your treasure," Leigh called. "Now let him go." She held out a hand. "Come on, Billy."

Ernie Molino grabbed Bill by the shoulder. "Oh no. I'm not that stupid. I let him go, you grab the treasure, and I'm stuck with nothing. Uh-uh. You bring it all the way to me."

Uncle Ted picked up the chest, and he and Mom started walking. Bill watched Mom with concern. She was limping pretty badly.

"Not you," Mr. Molino hollered, pointing at Uncle Ted. "Just her."

"I can't carry it with my bad ankle," Leigh called. "It's too heavy."

"Yeah, baby, heavy," Ernie Molino muttered under his breath.

Bill was surprised the man wasn't drooling at the sight of his "treasure." If he had his hands free, he'd probably be rubbing them together in anticipation.

"Okay," Mr. Molino called. "You can both come."

Slowly and carefully, Uncle Ted and Mom walked toward the jetty.

Mr. Molino held Bill with one hand, the gun in his other hand resting between Bill's shoulder blades, out of sight of Mom and Uncle Ted. Bill found it hard to remember to be scared of the gun. It was too TV, too movies to be real. Besides, no one with any smarts would shoot someone with two witnesses present. Then again, there was some debate over Mr. Molino's intelligence. Anyone who believed Pop-pop's line about a treasure was suspect, at least as far as Bill was concerned. Still he stood quietly, thinking it better to cooperate than take a risk.

Mom and Uncle Ted stopped about ten feet from Mr. Molino and Bill.

"You." Mr. Molino gestured to Mom. "Bring it the last few steps by yourself. I don't want your boyfriend near me."

Bill blinked. He thought Uncle Ted was Clay. The man was not only dumb, he was blind. Couldn't he see the hollow cheeks, the pale face? Granted the down jacket made Ted look fatter, but still, Clay radiated health, and Ted certainly didn't. It must be a matter of seeing what you expected to see.

Mom took the chest from Uncle Ted and began limping toward them. Her eyes went to Bill. "Are you all right?"

He nodded, then watched with interest as her eyes slid past him, past Mr. Molino. She brought them back to him almost immediately, but suddenly Bill knew where Clay was.

"Now put it down, Leigh-Leigh, and back up."

Mom did as she was told.

"Now both of you back up." Mr. Molino waved the gun, and Mom and Uncle Ted backed up.

"Now let him go," Mom said.

Mr. Molino ignored her. "Grab it, kid," he ordered, his eyes glued to the treasure.

"The chest?"

Mr. Molino pulled the gun front and center and held it at Bill's Adam's apple. "Don't get fresh with me. Get it!"

"Don't hurt him!" Mom pled. Bill thought for a minute she might collapse. "He's only a boy!"

Bill leaned carefully away from the gun and reached for the chest. He almost dropped it. He'd forgotten how heavy it was.

"Don't try any tricks," Mr. Molino snarled.

"I'm not," Bill protested. "It's just real heavy. Lots of silver."

Mr. Molino grabbed Bill by the neck of his T-shirt. The gun rested against his jaw. "Okay," he shouted at Mom and Uncle Ted. "The kid and me are getting out of here."

"No!" Mom looked ready to faint. "You said you'd let him go if I gave you the treasure. "

"Oops." Mr. Molino smiled. "I lied."

Bill felt real bad as Mom started to cry. "Mom's real honest," he explained. "She thought you'd be honest too."

"Her mistake." He jerked on Bill's shirt, dragging him backwards. All the time he kept his eyes on Mom and Uncle Ted.

Mom's eyes darted beyond Bill for just an instant. It was a mistake on her part, because this time Mr. Molino saw her. It was enough to warn him. He pulled Bill against him and glanced over his shoulder. He let out a shriek of anger when he saw Clay mere feet from him. He spun ninety degrees, his back to the ocean. He looked from Clay to Ted and back.

"You're sick in bed!" He looked from brother to brother, confused. "One of you."

"I guess not." Clay took a step closer.

"I'll kill the kid if you come any nearer! I mean it!"

Bill looked out of the corner of his eyes and saw Clay freeze. He didn't know how Clay felt, but he felt real disappointed. The attack from the rear had come so close to success.

"You don't want to kill the boy," Clay said. "He's ten years old. You want a ten-year-old on your conscience?" And he took a step closer.

Mr. Molino backed up a step, dragging Bill onto the jetty with him. "So maybe I won't kill the boy. Maybe I'll kill you." He waved his gun at Clay.

"And have all these witnesses to murder? You might be a thief, Molino, but you're not a murderer." Another step. "At least you haven't been. You don't want to start now, do you?" Another step. "Think where they'll put you if you murder someone."

Bill thought for a minute that his hearing was playing tricks on him, but no, he did hear police sirens coming their way.

Mr. Molino heard them at the same time. "I said no police!" he shrieked at Mom. He leveled the gun at her.

Clay took two steps, big ones, up onto the jetty. Mr. Molino backed farther onto the jetty, moving away from the threat. A wave crashed and he flinched, the gun wavering.

"Don't kill my mom," Bill begged. "I haven't got any other family. I'll be an orphan!" He tried to squeeze out a tear or two.

"Shut up, kid. Who cares?" He backed away from Clay some more, dragging Bill.

"But you were Pop-pop's friend. Think how upset he'd be if you hurt me."

"Like I care. He was slime, and he's dead anyway. He'll never know."

"Bill." Clay called to him in a firm, unruffled voice.

"Shut up! Leave the kid alone," Mr. Molino yelled as the sirens wound down and doors could be heard slamming and voices calling out on the street.

"You're only a step or two from the Grand Canyon," Clay said.

Bill frowned for a moment. "That's in Arizona." Then he smiled and nodded ever so slightly.

Mr. Molino yelled to Clay, "Stay away from me! And keep the cops away. The kid and I need to get out of here."

"Want to have a game of toss after this is over?" Clay asked, staring intently at the silver chest.

Toss, not catch. Bill looked down at the chest and back at Clay. "Really?"

"Really." Clay was very firm.

Bill shrugged casually. "Sure." And he tossed the silver chest into the churning sea.

"No!" Mr. Molino screamed as he watched the chest sail off to port side. It hit the water just as a surging wave broke. It disappeared into the foam and sank immediately. "No!"

The breaking wave sent water creaming over the rock on which Bill and Mr. Molino stood. "No!" he screamed again. In his terror he clutched even more tightly at Bill's shirt.

At the same moment Bill threw the chest, Clay rushed Mr. Molino, grabbing for Bill who tried to wrench himself free.

"No!" Mr. Molino yelled at Clay. He aimed at Clay's chest even as he took a big step backward, right to the very edge of the rock. As he teetered and flailed, he pulled the trigger. The shot went wild as he fell into the hole in the jetty where the boulder was missing. Since the tide was almost high, the hole was full of cold brine, and Mr. Molino fell screaming and sunk below the surface.

As Mr. Molino fell, Clay pulled Bill from his grasp.

"Dad!" Bill threw himself into Clay's arms. "Dad!"

Thirty-eight

*I*T WAS EARLY EASTER evening by the time things quieted down. With a sigh, Leigh settled herself on the couch in her apartment. At her side was her tote bag of work, papers to correct before going back to school tomorrow. Criminals may come and go, but marking papers went on forever. She placed an ice pack once again on her ankle, grabbed a red marker, and reached for the bag.

Bill was over at the Whartons, being plied with cake and sympathy by Julia who was appalled when she heard what had happened.

"What would I have done if I had lost you too?" she had cried, hugging Bill so tight he gurgled, "I'm turning blue here, Grandma Jule."

She looked at her sons with disapproval. "Next time, don't put the child at risk."

"Next time?" Clay made the mistake of defending himself. "Mom, I don't think there'll be a next time."

"Don't get cute with me, Clay Wharton." Julia stared him down while Leigh tried not to laugh. Bill enjoyed the scene with unabashed glee. "You know exactly what I mean."

Clay frowned. "Mom, I'm a bit past the yelling-at age."

"Not in my book," she said with a sniff. "Never in my book. Once a mom, always a mom."

Clay looked at David who stood off to the side, a wise man staying out of the family squabble. "David, she's all yours. Take her off my hands, will you? If I'm going to settle here in Seaside, I don't want to have to watch my back for a mom attack."

Julia's face lit with delight. "You're settling here?" She rushed to him and hugged him. "Oh, Clay, I'm so glad."

He leaned over and kissed her soft cheek. When he straightened, he looked at Leigh, then at Bill. "My family's here."

Leigh closed her eyes as she lay on the couch, the wonder of that pronouncement still almost beyond her comprehension.

"Here, love." Clay stood beside her with a glass of sweetened tea.

"Sit with me," she said and moved over. He lowered himself, finding barely enough room on the edge of the cushions. He lifted her and sat her in his lap.

"This position is not conducive to correcting papers." She leaned against his chest.

He tilted her chin and kissed her. "I promise not to interfere."

They sat quietly for several minutes, just enjoying each other's presence. And, if Leigh were honest, Bill's absence.

"How's the ankle?" Clay finally asked.

"If I don't move it, it's only a dull throb."

"Are you sure you should go to school tomorrow? Chasing fourth graders doesn't make for quick healing."

"The school district gets upset if you take the day after a holiday off. You actually need a doctor's excuse."

"David'll give you one."

She looked at the bag of papers. "It's tempting," she admitted. She bent and pulled a stack of papers free. As she did, a FedEx envelope slid to the floor.

"I forgot all about that," she said as Clay retrieved it and handed it to her. She stared at it.

"What's wrong?" Clay looked at the envelope and saw the return address. "Your father?"

"Something about him. It was here when we got home from school on Friday a week ago. I stuck it in the tote bag and forgot it." She grinned at him. "A few things got in the way of my concentration this week."

He leaned over and kissed her. "I wonder what?"

"I love you," she whispered.

He kissed her again. "I love you too. More than you'll ever know."

She sighed as she leaned against him. "I still can't believe you're here, right here in my apartment with your arms around me and me in your lap. I'm afraid I'll blink and find it's all a dream."

"Shall we live right here in Seaside?" he asked.

She sat up and stared at him. "I heard you tell your mom you wanted to settle here, but how can you? The navy."

"I resigned my commission before I came home. I'm a civilian, an unemployed civilian."

"Really?" She frowned at him. And he hadn't bothered to tell her? "Here I thought I'd caught me a sailor boy."

"Want to throw me over now?"

She narrowed her eyes and looked thoughtful. Of course he was used to making all his decisions as an individual, not as part of a couple. And they hadn't been a couple when he resigned. Still he should have told her.

He wrapped his arms tightly about her. "Don't you dare throw me over, lady. I couldn't stand it."

Forget the anger, girl. He didn't mean to upset you. It's not worth ruining a golden moment. Besides, there was a lifetime ahead in which to talk about the necessity of sharing important information.

"Then I won't," she said, returning his hug. "Though I do recommend you get un-unemployed sometime soon. Bill's bound to notice you hanging around the house all day and have a few things to say."

"Isn't that the truth." Clay grinned. "What a kid."

"I've always blamed all his bad behavior on you, though now that you're going to be here all the time, it won't be so easy." She sighed.

"Do you mind staying in Seaside?" Clay asked quite seriously.

"You mean because of my father?"

He nodded.

She shook her head. "Most of the time most of the people are wonderful. Johnny's old news to them."

He nodded. "Good. I was hoping to open my own business, a computer engineering company, and I thought I'd rent an office downtown."

"That sounds wonderful, Clay." She smiled at him. "Of course I think you can do anything you set your mind to, you know. I always have."

He looked genuinely humbled by her confidence in him. "Leigh," he breathed and kissed her again.

She rested against him, and her hands began to fidget with the FedEx envelope.

"Go on," he said. "Open it. Get it over with."

She took hold of the tab and pulled. She peered into the envelope and found a business letter addressed to her father. There was also a note written on lined paper.

> Dear Miss Spenser,
>
> Your father gave me this letter to hold for him. He said that if anything happened to him, I was to make sure you got it. I been sick for a while and I just got around to sending it. I know it's important.
>
> Murray Lawton
>
> P.S. I was your father's lawyer in here. I been taking classes by correspondence, and I know everything a lawyer does. Too bad I can't practice on the outside. But I'll be here for a few more years and like helping the guys in here.

With a queasy feeling in the pit of her stomach, she studied the letter addressed to Johnny. The return address indicated the letter was from some lawyers. She blinked. "Look. It's been opened already." She checked the postmark. "He got it several months ago."

She slid her fingers into the envelope and pulled out a sheet of heavy stationery with the logo of Barnes, Chrichton, and Zelinski, Attorneys at Law embossed in red and navy at the top of the sheet.

> Mr. Spenser:
>
> We write to ask the address of your daughter, Leigh Wilson Spenser. We seek her in regards to the estate of her great-aunt Harriet Plummer Wilson. Please contact us at your earliest convenience as to where we might reach her.
>
> Sincerely,
> Alton Zelinski, Esq.

"Who's Harriet Plummer Wilson?" Clay asked.

Leigh shook her head. "I don't know, but my mother's maiden name was Wilson. That's why it's my middle name."

"Maybe I'm marrying an heiress," Clay said with a smile and a roll of his imaginary mustache.

"You should be so lucky," she retorted.

"I couldn't be any luckier than I am," he said with a look that made her want to cry.

Three days later, Leigh and Clay sat in the office of Alton Zelinski, Esquire, drinking cups of tea that he had made for them himself. Leigh found all the social pleasantries very nice, but her nerves were stretched with curiosity.

Finally, Mr. Zelinski leaned back in his chair and looked at her. "I understand that you never knew any of your mother's family."

"That's correct," Leigh said. "When she married my father, they basically disinherited her."

"So you never met your Great-Aunt Harriet?"

"I didn't even know I had such a relative."

Mr. Zelinski smiled. "I liked Harriet. She was a lady who never bothered to stifle her opinions, but she was from an era when the men in the family laid down the rules and the women went along whether they agreed or not. When your grandfather, her brother, dictated that your mother be cut off, Harriet protested loudly but to no avail."

"I remember my mother as a sad woman," Leigh said. "My father wasn't a very nice man, and she should have had the comfort of her family."

"Don't blame Harriet," Mr. Zelinski said. "Many a time she sat in my office and cried over Candace."

Leigh waved her hand. "I can't blame a woman I never knew."

"She was ninety-eight when she died, her mind still sharp as a tack." Mr. Zelinski looked at her with the air of one about to spring a big surprise. "She made you her sole heir, Miss Spenser."

"What?" Leigh looked in disbelief at Clay who grinned back.

"I *am* marrying an heiress."

"To some extent, you are," Mr. Zelinski agreed.

"What? Surely you aren't serious," Leigh said.

"Did you know that Harriet sent you money every month?" the lawyer asked.

"What?" It seemed to be the word coming out of her mouth most this afternoon. She shook her head.

"As long as your mother lived, the monthly checks for one thousand dollars went to her from Harriet's trust fund."

"Trust fund?" Leigh didn't even know anyone with a trust fund.

"Your mother's family is quite wealthy, Miss Spenser. That's one reason why your mother's marriage was such a tragedy to them."

"A bigger tragedy to my mother," Leigh said, thinking of the wounded look her mother wore so much of the time.

Mr. Zelinski nodded. "Candace was Harriet's favorite niece, and the rift in the family caused by your mother's ill-advised marriage hurt Harriet deeply. She had never married, and Candace was like her daughter. Years ago, Harriet came to our firm and asked us to set up a way for her to get money to Candace each month because she doubted your father could support you."

Leigh nodded at the truth of that statement.

"When your mother died, Harriet came to us and asked that the amount be diminished to five hundred dollars a month. She said she didn't want to support Johnny Spenser, just you, but the money should go through him because you were so little."

"I never saw any of that money."

"I never thought you would," Mr. Zelinski said. "I tried to change Harriet's mind, to get her to find another avenue of getting funds to you if she wanted to do that. But she was stubborn. Then you turned eighteen, and Johnny went to jail. We began making out the checks to you instead of your father and sending them to the bank in Seaside as always. The money continued to accumulate and has been doing so for the last eleven years."

"But no one told me," Leigh said, thinking of all those years of poverty and struggle in Glassboro.

"We realize that now, though telling you wasn't our responsibility," Mr. Zelinski said hurriedly. "It was your father's or your aunt's."

"So you're telling us," Clay said, "that Leigh has eleven years worth of checks deposited in an account with her name on it."

The lawyer nodded. "Five hundred dollars each month."

"That's sixty-six thousand dollars plus interest," Clay computed.

Mr. Zelinski nodded.

Leigh was floored. "Sixty-six thousand dollars? I have sixty-six thousand dollars?"

Mr. Zelinski smiled at her amazement. "And there's more."

She felt dazed. "More?"

"Property."

"Property?"

"I understand that your home stands in the middle of an undeveloped tract of land."

Leigh nodded.

"Well, Harriet deeded the house to Candace when she married. Your grandfather almost had apoplexy, but she owned the house, a gift from her parents on her twenty-first birthday because she loved the shore marshes and shore birds so much. But she loved Candace more."

Leigh clasped Clay's hand. "I wish I had known her," she whispered.

Mr. Zelinski smiled. "You would have liked her, and she would have loved you."

She blinked back the tears that threatened. "I knew the house was mine. I have a copy of my father's will."

"More than the house is yours, Miss Spenser. You own the whole street that your home is on, both sides of it."

"What?" That word again.

"It was part of Harriet's gift from her parents. She did not pass that land on to your mother because she feared what your father would do with it. But she has left it all to you. Given property values at the shore, Miss Spenser, you are now a woman of considerable substance."

Epilogue

Four Years Later

LEIGH LAY BACK on the couch. She didn't have any choice. Clay wouldn't let her do anything else, and two-year-old Candy kept saying, "Down, Mommy. Lie down," as she pointed with her index finger. Just like she was Terror. It was all Leigh could do not to go, "Arf, arf."

She supposed she should consider it a victory that she'd gotten out of the bedroom. She'd pleaded, begged, scrounged up a few strategic tears, and it had finally worked. Clay, who was taking time off from WCE, Wharton Computer Engineering, carried her downstairs, muttering the whole time about pregnant women and their unreasonable demands. She wrapped her arms around his neck and leaned against his chest, ignoring his grumps with the same skill she ignored the rampaging going on in her belly.

"Thank you, sweetheart," she said and kissed his jaw. "I love you."

He'd just grunted and put her on the couch. "It's only because today's our anniversary. Now stay put."

She reached out an arm and gathered Candy close. "How's Mommy's girl?"

Candy grinned, her dark curls and dark eyes dancing. She was definitely her father's child. She pointed to Leigh's tummy. "Baby."

"Baby is right. And he's going to come visit us any minute. Give me a kiss, lovey."

Candy complied, then kissed Leigh's tummy. "Kiss baby."

"Here, love." Clay handed Leigh a glass of sweetened tea. He eyed her huge belly. "I'd ask you to move over and make room for me to sit with you, but I don't think you can."

"Sure I can," she said as she lifted her head and shoulders. "You sit here, and I'll just rest against you."

"Sounds good to me." Clay sat, and she leaned against him. He rubbed a hand gently over her aching back.

She loved his tender treatment. It made her feel beautiful even in this extreme situation when she was anything but. She knew she looked like an elephant. Her ankles were the size and shape of watermelons, and she had to go to the bathroom every five minutes. The pregnancy had been a difficult one, the last two weeks spent mostly on her back, and she knew she looked as exhausted and bored as she felt.

"I feel so grungy," she said. "I haven't had a shower in three days!"

Clay ran his hand over her hair. "Cleanliness may be next to godliness," he said, "but the baby is more important at the moment." He placed his hand gently over her tummy and was kicked for his efforts.

"Hmm." She rubbed her aching side. "It seems Theodore is making a statement of some kind."

Candy laid her head on Leigh. "My baby."

"Hey, Candy Cane," Bill said as he entered the room, drumsticks in hand. To his great disgust, at fourteen he looked much as he had at ten, just a tad taller. The only thing that kept him from despair was the memory of Grandpa Will's height and the constant sight of his father's. "You've got to share the baby with me," he said as he stuffed the drumsticks in his back pocket.

"Bill!" The little girl shrieked in delight and threw herself at her big brother. He lifted her over his head and gave her a raspberry on her tummy. She giggled and demanded, "Again."

"Anybody home?" came a call from the kitchen.

"Grandma Jule," yelled Candy. "Come here."

Clay smiled at his cherub of a daughter. "Little dictator," he said proudly. "Just like her mother."

Leigh gave him the evil eye as she held out her empty glass to him. He took it with a wink and set it on the end table next to the silver chest with the glorious flowers. There was a large dent in one side of the chest where it had struck one of the great jetty rocks when Bill threw it away from Ernie Molino. Neither Clay nor Leigh wanted the imperfection pounded out. It was a constant reminder of God's grace during that season of miracles—the reconciliation of the brothers, the acknowledgment of Bill's paternity, and the declaration of their love. Leigh had only to look at it, and her eyes misted. Clay had only to look at it and he remembered going into the cold, cold water at low tide to retrieve it.

Julia and David walked into the living room of the house that had once been Julia's home. They were holding hands.

"Clay," Julia had said when she and David married a month after the Molino fiasco, "if you and Leigh want this house, it's yours. David and I want a house that's ours, not mine or his. This would have been yours someday anyway. I'm just offering it a bit early."

Now Julia and David lived three blocks away. Julia smiled and bent to smother Candy in kisses. "How's Grandma's sweetheart?"

"Did you bring cake?" Candy asked.

"She's got you pegged," David said, laughing. He bent to Candy. "How does angel food sound, my little angel?"

"Wif strawberries and whip cream?"

At David's nod, she ran for the kitchen to see for herself. "We gots angel food, Daddy," she cried as she raced back to the living room. David bent and captured her as she raced by. He lifted her, and she wrapped her little arms around his neck. "I love you, Grampa David," she said. "Thank you for the angel food."

Leigh could see him melt.

"How are you feeling, Leigh?" Julia asked.

"Fat." Leigh smiled at her mother-in-law. The baby would be good for Julia. Another Ted. She knew Julia still had times of deep grieving over Ted, and it was soon to be the fourth anniversary of his death. They had had Ted in relatively good health for three months after the Good Friday miracle. He and Clay reestablished their friendship during that time, and he had been able to stand as Clay's best man when Clay and Leigh married in June at the close of the school year.

"You know," he said to Clay one night at dinner just before the wedding, "if you can admit to me that you were wrong, I guess I can admit the same thing. Out loud, I mean. I admitted it to God back at Easter. I know what God asked of me, and I know what I did in defiance of Him. I was wrong." He smiled crookedly. "What with the examples of Dad, Matt, and you, how can I possibly hold on to my excuses?"

Then his decline had been swift and inevitable. When they returned from their honeymoon, he was barely alive.

"You should have called us," Clay told his mother and David.

"I wouldn't let them," Ted whispered. "But I hung on to tell you two that I love you."

Two days later he slipped into a coma. Two days after that, he was gone.

From her position on the sofa, Leigh looked at Candy and Bill, felt Baby Ted kicking about inside. She couldn't begin to imagine the never ending pain of losing a child. If Baby Ted could help assuage Julia's pain in any way, it was worth the discomfort and uncertainty of the past few months.

"Let's eat in here," Clay suggested. "Then Leigh won't be left out." He moved to get up.

"Stay," Leigh said, putting a hand on his chest. "Stay with me."

As Bill and David set up TV trays and Julia took Candy to the kitchen to "help" unpack the meal she'd brought with her, Clay looked at his wife. The love in his eyes brought tears to Leigh's.

"I'll stay with you, love," he whispered as he dropped a kiss on her forehead. "I'll stay with you always and forever."

Dear Reader,

Over the last thirty years as I've spoken to women's groups all across the country, I have often talked with women touched in some way by AIDS.

"My husband has AIDS," one told me tearfully, "and I can't tell anyone I know. Even though he contracted it by transfusion, he—we—would be ostracized in our community and our church if people knew. We've carried this information alone since he first learned he was HIV positive. I'm talking to you because I'll never see you again, and I just have to talk to someone."

In contrast was the pastor's wife who said, "My brother is dying of AIDS back on the East Coast. Our little congregation has been so supportive. It's like he's our church project. They pray for him and my family all the time, and they've flown me back to spend time with him twice already. They're gathering funds for a third trip next month."

One of my junior girls' novels, *The Secret of the Poison Pen*, was based on the true experience of friends who took in a foster baby with HIV. Someone in the congregation wrote anonymous notes saying, "Get that kid out of our church!" Our friends persevered, the nursery workers learned universal care procedures, and that baby is now a bright and charming ten-year-old girl who still hasn't contracted AIDS, and most important, has trusted Christ as her Savior.

There is no denying that AIDS is a terrible condition, all the more scary because it is contagious. However as believers we have a higher calling than avoiding illness and those who might infect us (though they shouldn't with proper care taken). We have a call to bind up the wounds of the world, to offer Christ to the lost, to urge repentance on the fallen. I find it terribly sad that committed health-care professionals and social workers often do a better job at the first responsibility than the church of Christ. And the church is the only organization to offer the spiritual relief of the latter two. If we fail here, eternity feels the impact.

Surely not all of us will be called to foster HIV babies or to care for AIDS patients, but all of us can have a godly mind-set that allows us to hurt for the victims, their pain, their spiritual needs. We must remember that any life cut short is a thing of sorrow. A life cut short while still at enmity with God is truly tragic.

Gayle Roper

The publisher and author would love to hear your comments about this book. *Please contact us at:* www.multnomah.net/springrain

A Gayle Roper Fan-Feast!

The Document

The search for her late mother's roots—and her own heritage—takes Deni Keene to Lancaster County, Pennsylvania. In light of a closed Amish society, is her quest destined for failure?

ISBN 1-57673-295-9

The Decision

When a car bomb explosion kills Rose Martin's cancer patient, she escapes into the arms of Jake, a man struggling with his past and his Amish heritage. Can the living find God's forgiveness for themselves—and justice for the dead?

ISBN 1-57673-406-4

The Key

Against the fascinating backdrop of Amish culture, a woman is unwittingly drawn into a web of intrigue that puts her life—not to mention her heart—in real danger.

ISBN 1-57673-223-1

Let's Talk fiction

A Free "Behind the Scenes" look at your favorite Fiction Authors!

Let's Talk Fiction is a free, four-color mini-magazine, created to give readers a "behind the scenes" look at Multnomah Publishers' favorite fiction authors. *Let's Talk Fiction* allows our authors to share a bit about themselves and gives readers an inside peek into their latest releases. *Let's Talk Fiction* is free and is distributed in the fall, spring, and summer seasons. It features our fiction titles released during these seasons and is filled with interactive contests, author contact information, and fun! Take a moment to review *Let's Talk Fiction* on-line at www.christian-fiction.com and tell us what you think. Or let us know if you would like a hard copy in the mail. We'd love to hear from you!

www.christian-fiction.com

How far would you go to fulfill a last request?

Patty Metzer

Lights of the Veil

Faith and purpose collide in the exotic setting of this powerful love story. Through mysterious circumstances, Erica Tanner meets her late sister's only child, Betul. Within hours, they are kidnapped and taken to India, where an unexpected friendship with the handsome Prince Ajari complicates Erica's escape—especially when she learns he is Betul's uncle. As friends attempt a rescue, Erica fights to fulfill her sister's final request—Betul must not become lost in Sajah Ajari's Hindu heritage. Can the light of Christ overcome the differences holding Erica and Sajah captive? Breathtakingly paced, *Lights of the Veil* moves with grand adventure toward the ultimate triumph of God's truth.

ISBN 1-57673-627-X

The Guardian

Marcus O'Malley is a U.S. Marshal charged
with protecting witnesses in high profile
cases. He must protect a family who saw a
judge murdered, knowing that the assassin
who was hired to kill them before they
can testify is one of the best in the world.

ISBN 1-57673-642-3

Danger in the Shadows

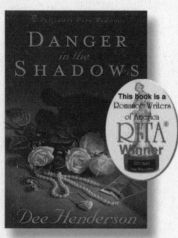

Sara's terrified. She's falling in love with
former pro football player Adam Black—
and it could cost her her life. She's
hiding from the man who kidnapped her
years ago, a man who's still trying to find
her and finish her off. Soon Sara and
Adam are caught in a web that brings
Sara face-to-face with terror—and with
the knowledge that only God can save her.

ISBN 1-57673-577-X

The Negotiator

FBI agent Dave Richman never
intended to fall in love. But when
Kate O'Malley becomes the target
of an airline bomber, Dave is about
to discover that loving a hostage
negotiator is one thing, but keeping
her safe is another matter entirely.

ISBN 1-57673-819-1

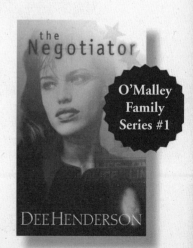